The
KING

TIFFANY REISZ

The KING

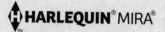
HARLEQUIN® MIRA®

Recycling programs
for this product may
not exist in your area.

ISBN-13: 978-0-7783-1583-4

The King

Copyright © 2014 by Tiffany Reisz

Printed in U.S.A.

First printing: December 2014
10 9 8 7 6 5 4 3 2 1

www.Harlequin.com

Dedicated to all the girls with short hair and
all the boys with long hair. You are fearfully and wonderfully made.

All men dream, but not equally. Those who dream by night, in the dusty recesses of their minds, wake in the day to find that it was vanity: but the dreamers of the day are dangerous men, for they may act on their dreams with open eyes, to make them possible.

—Lawrence of Arabia

1

KINGSLEY EDGE WAS PLAYING GOD TONIGHT. HE hoped the real God, if He did exist, wouldn't mind.

He'd told his driver to let him out a few blocks before his destination. Warm air, a late-April rain and a little English magic had sent a soft white fog twisting and flicking its tail down winding streets, and Kingsley wanted to enjoy it. He wore a long coat and carried a leather weekender bag over his shoulder. It was late, and although the city was still awake, it kept its voice down. The only sounds around him came from the soles of his shoes echoing against the wet and shining pavement and the distant murmur of city traffic.

When he arrived at the door he knocked without hesitation. After a pause, it opened.

They stared at each other a full five seconds before one of them spoke. Kingsley took it upon himself to break the silence.

"I'm the last person you were expecting to see again, *oui*?" Kingsley asked.

He expected the shock and he expected the silence, but he didn't expect what happened next.

He didn't expect Grace Easton to step onto the porch in her soft gray robe and bare feet and wrap him in her arms.

"If I'd known this is how the Welsh say 'hello,' I would have visited sooner," Kingsley said. Grace pulled back from the embrace and smiled at him, her bright turquoise eyes gleaming.

"You're always welcome here." Grace's words were tender, her accent light and musical. She took his arm and ushered him into the house. "Always."

Always…a lovely word. He never used to believe in words like *always*, like *forever*, like *everything*. Now at forty-eight he'd lived long enough he could see both ends of his life. *Always*. There might be something to it after all.

"Zachary's asleep," Grace said in a whisper as she took his coat, hung it up, and guided him into a cozy living room. "He gets up at five every morning, so he goes to bed at a reasonable hour. I prefer the unreasonable hours myself."

"You're the night owl?"

"It works for us," she said with a smile. "I can get work done after Zachary and Fionn fall asleep. Would you like tea? I can put the kettle on. Or something stronger?"

"I brought my own something stronger," he said.

He unzipped his weekender bag and offered her a bottle of wine. She examined the label.

"Rosanella Syrah," she said. "Never had it before."

"It's from my son's winery. Best Syrah I've ever tasted."

"Not that you're biased or anything," she said with a wink. She went to fetch wineglasses and a corkscrew from the kitchen, and Kingsley looked around. Zachary and Grace Easton lived in a small two-story brick house that made up one of many in a row of neat but narrow accommodations. It was an older neighborhood, a bit shabby but safe and clean from what he could see. Inside the house was the picture of quiet domesticity. Intelligent educated people lived here. And one very special baby.

"Am I interrupting anything?" Kingsley asked when Grace returned with the wineglasses. He took the corkscrew from her and opened the bottle. Grace had a low fire glowing in the fireplace and a table lamp on. Gentle light. Kingsley felt instantly at ease here.

"Nothing that can't wait," she said, and Kingsley saw stacks of papers on the pale green sofa. He took a seat in the armchair opposite her and crossed one leg over his knee. She curled up into a ball, her knees to her chest, her bare feet sticking out from the bottom of the robe. Her long red hair was knotted at the nape of her neck in a loose and elegant bun. In the soft light of the room she radiated a delicate beauty. A vision, freckles and all. How had he not noticed before how lovely she was? Of course, the one and only occasion they'd been in each other's company, he'd been preoccupied, to say the least.

"You're grading papers?" Kingsley asked.

"No, I'm still on maternity leave," she said. Next to her on the table sat a baby monitor. "These are proofs of my book. Nothing exciting. Only poetry." She held up a printed title page that read *Rooftop Novenas*.

"You're writing again?" Kingsley asked. He remembered from her file she'd had a few poems published in her early twenties.

"I am," she said, smiling shyly. "I don't know what it is… As soon as I was pregnant with Fionn I had so much creative energy. Couldn't stop writing. Zachary'd thought I'd lost my mind. He's an editor, though, not a writer. He thinks all writers are a bit mad."

"I might have to agree with him," Kingsley said. "You have my congratulations on the book."

She shuffled her pages, capped her pen. "Thank you, Kingsley. But I don't believe you crossed an ocean simply to talk about my poetry."

"Even if it was inspired by a mutual friend of ours?" Kingsley said.

"Even so," she admitted without shame. Good. Kingsley might have despised her if she'd had any regrets, any shame for what had happened. Instead, she'd come with an open heart to their world, an open mind, and had returned home carrying a blessing inside her. "It's back to school in a few months, and I'm trying not to think about having to leave Fionn."

"He taught at our high school after he graduated. Did you know that?"

She held her glass steady on the coffee table between them as Kingsley poured the wine.

"He told me he used to teach. Said he liked it. I didn't expect that from him."

Kingsley picked up a framed photograph that sat on the coffee table between them—a black-and-white picture of a newborn infant boy sleeping on a white pillow.

"That's one thing you can say for him," Kingsley said, turning the photograph toward Grace. "He's full of surprises."

She blushed beautifully and laughed quietly, and Kingsley couldn't help but join in her laugh.

"Is he why you're here? Are you checking on Fionn for him?"

"No," Kingsley said. "Although he'll never forgive me if I don't look in on him while I'm here." Kingsley ached to see the boy, but he had learned the hard way to never disturb a sleeping baby.

"I'm only asking why you're here out of curiosity. You never need a reason to visit us. I assume everyone is well?" Grace asked. "Juliette? Your daughter? Nora?"

"Juliette and Céleste are perfect as usual," he said. "But Nora, she lost her mother recently. A month ago, I believe."

"I had no idea. Zachary never said a word about it."

"She didn't tell anyone until afterward. She disappeared on us for two weeks."

"Nora." Grace sighed and shook her head. "Well, if she behaved like a normal person, she wouldn't be Nora, would she?"

"No. No, she wouldn't be." Kingsley laughed to himself. "But she and her mother…they had a difficult relationship."

"Because of him?"

"Her mother hated him. I don't use the word *hate* lightly," Kingsley said. "I think it was a peace offering to her mother for Nora to go alone. And she couldn't tell him. Nora ran away to her mother's once before, and he hunted her down like the hound of hell."

"I didn't know that. But I can imagine he's…*persistent* where she's concerned?"

"That is one way to put it." Kingsley took a sip of his wine. "She and her mother, they had unfinished business."

"That's the worst-case scenario then, isn't it? If you're close to your parents, you have no regrets when they pass away. If you have no relationship, you have no grief. If you want to be close, but you can't be…"

"She took it very hard," Kingsley said, knowing Nora well enough to say that in good faith.

"I'll call her tomorrow," Grace said. "Maybe she should come stay with us a few days. She loves being around Fionn. And she and Zachary fight so much, she'll forget all her sorrows, I promise."

Kingsley wanted to laugh. Only Grace Easton would call the woman who had slept—more than once—with her husband, offer her condolences on the loss of her mother and then invite her to stay in her home with Grace, her husband and their infant son who was fathered by Nora's lover.

Did Grace have any idea what an extraordinarily odd woman she was?

Then again, what room did Kingsley have to talk?

"Apart from that, we're all well. He's well," Kingsley said, saving Grace the embarrassment of asking about him.

"Good," Grace said with a smile. "I never know… He's the easiest man in the world to talk to…and the most difficult man to read. Rather amazes me that Nora's been with him over twenty years and is as sane as she is. Zachary was my professor when we fell in love, and I thought I'd go insane trying to keep that secret from my friends, my family, the school. To be with a priest for twenty years…"

"No one is more amazed than I that they've lasted. The sanity part is up for debate, but you can't question the love. Not anymore. And he hasn't made it easy for her, and she… Well, I don't have to tell you anything about Nora, do I?"

Grace grinned broadly.

"No," she said. "No, you don't." She took a drink of the Syrah, and her eyes widened in delight.

"Your son is quite the vintner. This is marvelous."

"I told you so," Kingsley said, taking a sip of his own wine. The Syrah was good, an excellent vintage, strong and potent. As much as Kingsley loved the taste, he found it hard to drink sometimes. The knot of pride in his throat made it difficult to swallow.

"Zachary was very impressed with Nico when they met. He's what? Twenty-five and he owns and runs his own vineyard?"

"I think about how I was at twenty-five, what I was doing with my life, and I can't believe he came from me."

"I can believe it," Grace said, giving him a luminescent smile.

"I won't keep you up all night showing you pictures of my children," Kingsley said. He had pictures of both Nico and Céleste with him, and he was seconds away from pulling them out. "I'm only here for a few hours before I catch my next flight. But I did come for a reason."

"Should I be concerned?" Grace asked.

"Non, pas du tout," Kingsley said with a wave of his hand. "Forgive me. French wine brings out my French."

"I speak some," she said. "You haven't lost me yet."

"Bon," he said and paused for another drink. "I have something to tell you. A story. And I can't tell you why I'm telling you the story until after the story."

"I see…" she said, although Kingsley knew she didn't. "May I ask what the story concerns?"

Kingsley reached into the inner breast pocket of his jacket. From it he pulled a crisp white envelope thick with documents sealed with wax. The wax was imprinted with what appeared to be a number eight inside a circle. Kingsley placed it on the table between his glass of wine and Grace's.

"The story is about that," Kingsley said, nodding toward the envelope. "And I can tell you the long version which is the true version or I can tell you a shorter, sweeter version. I'm happy to tell you either. But you decide."

"The long version, of course," she said. "Tell me everything I should know even if you don't think I want to hear it."

*"Everything…*dangerous word." Kingsley sat back in the chair, and Grace leaned forward. She looked at him with a child's eagerness. "But if you insist. The more you know about us, the better it will be if…"

He didn't finish the sentence, didn't have to, because he saw the understanding in Grace's eyes. She knew the end of the sentence he hadn't spoken, and her nod saved him the pain of saying the words that no one yet had dared to utter aloud.

If Fionn takes after his father...

"The story starts twenty years ago," Kingsley said, conjuring the memories he had tried to bury. But he'd buried them alive and alive they remained. "And it takes place in Manhattan. And although you don't know yet why I'm telling you this, Grace, I promise you, you won't regret hearing me out."

"I don't regret anything," she said.

Kingsley straightened the photograph of her infant son. No, none of them regretted anything. Not even Kingsley.

"It was raining," Kingsley began. "And it was March. I had everything then—money, power and all the women and men in my bed anyone could possibly want. And to say I was in a bad mood would be the understatement of the century. I was twenty-eight years old and didn't expect to see thirty. In fact, I hoped I wouldn't see thirty."

"What happened?"

Kingsley took a breath, took a drink and took a moment to pull his words to together. A pity Nora wasn't here. Storytelling was her gift, not his. But only he could tell this story and thus he began.

"Søren happened."

2

"WHAT'S YOUR POISON?" THE BARTENDER ASKED, AND Kingsley answered, "Blonds."

The bartender, Duke, half laughed, half scoffed as he pointed to the stage.

"Two bleach-blonde bottles of poison right there."

Kingsley eyed the two girls—Holly and Ivy—who now hung naked from their knees, which they'd wrapped around twin poles. Men sat belly up to the stage watching in silence, making eye contact with no one but the dancers. Dollar bills fluttered between their waving fingers.

"Not what I'm in the mood for tonight." Kingsley looked away from the stage.

"What?" Duke asked. "How can you not be in the mood for that? Are they too hot? Too sexy?"

Kingsley reached behind the bar and grabbed a bottle of bourbon.

"Too female."

"Don't look at me," Duke said, raising both his hands.

"I promise, I'm not." And he wasn't. Someone else had caught his eye. But where had he gone?

"It's too quiet tonight," Kingsley said to Duke. Usually on a Friday night at the Möbius, the place would be standing room only. Half the usual crowd was in attendance tonight. "What's going on?"

"You came in the back way?" Duke asked as he uncorked Kingsley's bourbon for him.

"Of course."

"Some church is outside holding up signs."

"Signs?"

"Yeah, you know. Protest signs. Sex Trade Fuels AIDS. Fornicators will burn. She's somebody's daughter."

"Are you serious?"

"Go look for yourself."

Kingsley took his bottle of bourbon to the front door of the club and took a long drink but not long enough for the sight that greeted him. Duke hadn't been exaggerating. A dozen people walked up and down the sidewalk carrying various white signs held aloft proclaiming the evils of strip clubs.

"Told you so," Duke said from behind Kingsley. "Can we call the cops on them or something? Shoot them?"

"We don't have to get rid of them," Kingsley said. "God will."

"He will?" Duke asked. "You sure about that?"

The sky broke open and rain began to fall. The protestors lasted about five seconds under the bite of the late-winter rain before running for cover.

"See?" Kingsley said to Duke. He looked up at the sky, "*Dieu, merci.*"

"God must be a tits and ass man."

"If He wasn't," Kingsley said, "He wouldn't have invented them."

He shut the door and glanced around the club again.

A psychiatrist—if Kingsley would let one near him—would have had a field day with his prodigious talent for finding the blond in every room he entered. If someone blindfolded him right now, he could, with picture-perfect recall, point out every last blond man in a fifty-yard radius. Five of them sat at various stations of the Möbius strip club—two at the bar (one real blond, the other a punk who'd bleached his hair), one working as a bouncer, one disappearing into the bathroom with a suspicious bulge in his trousers and a young one at table thirteen back in the corner. Kingsley had noticed the young blond when he'd first entered the Möbius half an hour ago. He'd been watching him, studying him, getting a read on him. Kingsley approached him.

The blond at table thirteen sat alone. He didn't look at any of the girls, but only at his hands, his drink, his table.

Kingsley sat down across from him and placed the bourbon on the table between them. The amber liquid licked at the sides of the bottle. The blond glanced first at the bourbon, as if wondering where it came from and how it got there, before his eyes settled on to Kingsley's.

"I'm going to ask you a question, and it's important you answer it correctly." Kingsley did his best to temper his French accent without disposing of it entirely. The accent got him attention when he wanted it but in such a noisy room, he needed to speak as clearly as possible. "Luckily for you, I will tell you the correct answer before I ask the question. And that answer is twenty-one."

"Twenty-one?" The blond spoke in some sort of accent of his own—American, obviously, but this young man was far from home. "What's the question?"

"How old are you?"

The blond's eyes widened. In the dim light, Kingsley couldn't make out the boy's eye color. Steel-gray, he hoped, although tonight he wouldn't be picky.

"Twenty-one," he repeated. "I'm definitely twenty-one."

"Blackjack," Kingsley said, smiling. The blond boy might be twenty-one. In two years he might be twenty-one.

"Do you work here?" the blond asked.

"I wouldn't call it work."

"I can go. I should go." The blond started to stand, but Kingsley tapped the table.

"Sit," he ordered. The blond sat. A promising sign that he could and would take orders. "Tell me something—no right or wrong answer this time."

"Sure. What?"

"Why are you here?"

He shrugged, as if the question were obvious.

"You know. Tits. Asses. Naked girls."

"You weren't looking at the girls. Not even the one who took your drink order. Which I found interesting, as she was mostly naked."

Kingsley took another sip of his bourbon straight from the bottle. It burned his throat all the way to his stomach. The woody aftertaste stained the inside of his mouth.

"Sir, I don't know what your problem is with me being here, but I can—"

"Do your parents know?"

"Know what? That I'm here?"

"That you're gay."

The blond tried to stand up again, but Kingsley kicked his leg under the table, and the boy landed hard back in his chair.

"You can go when I say you can go," Kingsley said. "Now, any other man in here would argue with me if I said he was gay. But you try to leave. I can only assume you won't argue with me because it's true."

The blond sat in silence and didn't meet Kingsley's eyes. A beautiful boy, Kingsley would have noticed him even if he weren't blond. A strong jaw, strong nose, angular face, high enough cheekbones to give him an air of sophistication and yet, he had wary eyes, watching eyes, eyes that never rested for long, as if he were forever looking over his shoulder. His hair was the pale variety of blond, the Nordic variety. Kingsley's favorite. He wore clothes designed to blend in with a crowd—faded jeans, white shirt, black jacket. But he'd failed in his attempt. Kingsley had noticed him at once.

"No, they don't know," the boy said. "I'm in town with my dad on a business trip. He's out with clients tonight. I'm... I walked around Greenwich Village last night. I met this guy outside a club. He told me some rumors about this place."

"Believe them," Kingsley said.

"You don't know what rumors I heard."

"Doesn't matter." Kingsley took another sip of the bourbon. "All of them are true."

"So the guy who owns this place—"

"What about him?"

"They say he's in with the mafia?"

"It's a strip club." Kingsley rolled his eyes. "Every club in town cleans money for the mob whether they want to or not. It's all cash here. It's part of the deal. What else have you heard?"

"That the owner of the club—"

"Yes?"

"He used to kill people for a living."

"Also true. But if it makes you feel any better, I did it for the government. Never recreationally."

The boy's eyes widened hugely.

"You own this place?"

"Haven't you ever gotten bored and bought a strip club?"

"No…"

"In my defense," Kingsley said, "it was on sale."

The boy narrowed his eyes at Kingsley. "You really own this place?"

"I do. Why don't you believe me?"

"You have to be rich to own a club. No offense, but you don't look rich."

Kingsley glanced down at his clothes. He, too, had dressed to blend in tonight—black pants, black shoes, gray shirt and black leather jacket. Nothing out of the ordinary. No one dressed up to go hunting.

"Rich people don't look rich. When you have enough money, you don't have to impress anyone."

"And you seem kind of young."

"I'm twenty-eight. I should seem ancient to you. Twenty-eight was ancient to me when I was nineteen."

"I'm twenty-one, remember," the blond said. "And you aren't ancient."

"What am I?" Kingsley raised his chin and gazed down at the boy.

"You're the most… I mean, you're…"

"Spit it out. Use your words."

"Gorgeous."

Kingsley raised an eyebrow. He didn't mind the flattery or the adulation, but he'd wanted the boy the second he'd walked into the club. Time to move things along.

"What else have you heard?"

The boy glanced around. He dropped his voice.

"I heard that there's another room—"

"It's more than one room."

The boy sat back. He ran a nervous hand through his hair. Kingsley envied his fingers.

"So it's true? You all do kink here? And…other stuff?"

"You know why this club is called the Möbius?" Kingsley asked.

"No. Weird name."

"A Möbius strip is an optical illusion. It looks like it has two sides, but it has only one."

Kingsley picked the napkin off the table. Embossed on the white paper was a small ribbon, oval-shaped. His patrons likely thought it was an elegant rendition of a vagina. The image conveniently worked on two levels.

"I don't understand," the blond said.

"Do you want to understand?"

"It's why I'm here."

"Then follow me. I'll be your tour guide through hell."

Kingsley grabbed the bottle off the table, and the boy followed him to a quiet corner of the club. To the right of the bar was a door bearing an employees only sign. Kingsley pushed through. The blond hesitated, but Kingsley grasped him by the wrist and pulled him.

"I told you I own this place. Do you think you're going to get into trouble?" Kingsley asked.

"Yeah," the blond said.

"If you're with me, you're already in trouble."

They walked down a short hall to another door. Kingsley paused to pull out his keys.

"I should go," the blond said. "I—"

Without even looking at him, Kingsley shoved the boy back against the wall and held him there with one hand.

He found the key but didn't put it in the lock. Instead, he dangled it in front of the boy's face. In the brighter light of the hallway Kingsley could see the blond had light brown eyes. Not the steel-gray color he'd hoped for, but still he would do.

"This key opens a door to a hidden part of this club," Kingsley said. "The part of the club you came to see. Doors are symbols, you know. Thresholds to cross, choices to be made. It's not often that a real door stands between you and a different life. Don't waste this chance. You go back that way, and you stay in your old world. You open that door, and you enter a new one."

The boy eyed the silver key dangling from Kingsley's middle finger.

"If you were me…" the blond said.

"I was you," Kingsley said.

"What did you choose?"

Kingsley didn't answer at first. There had been no door for him, no key.

"I ran through the door. And I never looked back."

Sweat beaded on the boy's smooth young forehead. Kingsley held him still and hard against the wall and under his hand he could feel the boy's heart battering against his chest.

The boy reached up and grabbed the key. With fumbling fingers, he shoved it in the lock, turned the knob and pushed through the door. This time, Kingsley followed him.

Behind the door, the world changed color. Out front, the lights were black. Here they were blue. Out in the club, a pantomime of sex played out on and around the stage. Girls gave lap dances, feigned interest and faked smiles. Here, behind the door, men groped in the dark, coupled frantically, secretly. Nothing was feigned. No one *pretended* to fuck back here. They fucked.

"Jesus," the boy whispered as they passed a man bent over a chair, another man behind him, inside him, fucking him without shame or restraint.

"If you're looking for Jesus, you won't find him down here," Kingsley said, stepping in front of the blond to guide him through the hall.

"Is this a bathhouse?" the boy asked.

"You see anyone taking a bath?"

The boy laughed. "No."

"It's not a brothel, either. No one's paying for sex here. I'm not a pimp."

"What is it then?"

"Sanctuary," Kingsley said. "Most of these men are married. Children. Jobs. They come to the club because no one cares if a man goes to a strip club full of naked women. They walk in the front door first. But it's the back door they're here for."

Kingsley laughed, but the boy didn't. The other blond would have gotten his joke.

"Are you married?" the boy asked.

"Do I look married to you?"

"Do you have kids?"

"Not that I'm aware of."

"Then why—"

Kingsley grabbed the boy and shoved him against the wall again.

"You talk too much," Kingsley said.

The blond swallowed visibly. He licked his lips, and Kingsley's groin tightened.

"Then shut me up," the blond whispered.

The boy wanted to be kissed, and Kingsley wanted to kiss him. The boy's lips trembled, his whole body trembled. But kissing him would make it all personal. Tonight he wanted anonymity.

"Why are you scared?" Kingsley asked.

"I don't... We just met."

"It doesn't matter. Nothing matters. Nothing but this."

Without warning the boy, Kingsley turned him and pushed him, chest first, against the wall. Kingsley pressed his chest into the boy's back, slid his hand down his stomach and opened his pants.

"We're in the hall," the blond whispered, and there it was—the fear in his voice. Fear, intoxicating, erotic fear.

"I own the hall. I'll do whatever I want in it."

Kingsley wrapped his fingers around the boy's erection and stroked him.

"You like that?" Kingsley asked, stroking again. "You're hard, so you must like it."

"Yeah," he breathed. His voice sounded pained. "I like it."

"What do you like? Say it?"

"Your hand on me, on my cock."

"What do you want? Tell me what you want."

"I want it all," the boy said. "I leave tomorrow. This is my only chance."

"Only chance? You're a beautiful child, young, new..." Kingsley kissed the back of the boy's neck. The kiss turned to a bite. "You'll have other chances."

The blond shook his head. "You don't know what it's like where I live."

"Where do you live?"

"Texas."

Kingsley laughed softly but felt the first stirrings of sympathy. He crushed it under his heel like a bug.

"You want it all?" Kingsley asked.

"Yes." The blond laid his hand on top of Kingsley's, as if he needed contact with the man who touched him so intimately. "Give me something to take home with me. I can live on the memories."

"I'll give you more than memories."

Kingsley bit hard into the boy's neck. He cried out in pain even as his hard cock twitched in Kingsley's hand.

He didn't give the boy a chance to straighten his clothes before Kingsley grabbed him by the wrist and dragged him down the hallway. When he'd bought the Möbius, he'd also bought the suite of unused offices behind it. Easy enough to convert them into bedrooms. Dozens of trysts happened each day in this hallway. Kingsley charged nothing but rent and the cost of the key. And a generous tip for the poor woman who washed the sheets every day.

The uninitiated might have trouble finding their way around the back halls. The only illumination came from the lamps in the rooms that spilled pale blue light from under the doors and onto the dull gray carpet. Soft and pained sounds escaped the rooms they passed. The men within had trained themselves to keep their desires quiet, and even when giving rein to them, nothing more than a few desperate grunts and the squeak of bedsprings could be heard in the hallway.

"Where are we going?"

"Hell. Or my room. Same thing."

Kingsley led him down a second hall toward his private room.

"What are you going to do to me?" the boy asked as they neared the final door.

"Beat you and fuck you," Kingsley said. "Do you have a problem with that? If so, I'd speak up now."

The boy's steps faltered. Kingsley grabbed him once more and pushed him back against the wall.

"Problem?" Kingsley asked. He kissed the boy's neck, pulled down his collar and bit his chest.

"Will I like it?" The blond slid his hands under Kingsley's shirt, seeking skin-to-skin contact.

"It's not fun for me if you don't like it, too," Kingsley said, grabbing the boy's wandering hands and pinning them behind his back. "I want you to look at your bruises in the mirror tomorrow and come all over yourself from the sight of them. I want you to see each welt and remember the moment I gave it to you. I want you to try to have normal sex with someone and lay there like a corpse because he's not hurting you and you need pain to feel alive. I want to ruin you tonight so that every other night feels like a waste of your life. Is that what you want, too?"

The blond boy pushed his hips against Kingsley's and rasped two words.

"*Ruin me.*"

3

KINGSLEY OPENED THE DOOR TO HIS ROOM, TOOK the boy by the collar of his jacket and pushed him inside.

The boy stood in the center of the bedroom. Bedroom, yes. Nothing but a room with a bed. Kingsley hadn't even bothered with a chair. Why waste the floor space? The bed itself was black—black sheets, metal frame. Light from the barred and grated window cast squares of weak yellow squares across the sheets and the floor.

"Can I ask you a weird question?" the blond said as he turned to Kingsley.

"Ask."

"I can't figure your accent out. Where are you from?"

Kingsley smiled.

"Not Texas."

He grabbed the boy by the throat and forced him to the floor. He slapped him once, hard. Hard enough that the blond gasped, not hard enough to leave a mark.

"Fight back if you want," Kingsley said as he stripped the boy of his jacket and threw it aside. "You'll lose. But you can try."

The boy was already struggling against him as Kingsley pulled his shirt up, exposing the bare flesh of his back.

Kingsley grasped the bamboo cane he kept under the bed.
"I'm going to cane you."

"Will it hurt?"

"Fuck, yes, it will."

The boy shuddered, but he didn't say no, so Kingsley took that as a yes.

Once, twice, five times he struck the boy's back, harder each time. The blond didn't cry out but only released soft grunts of pain. A passing car beamed a momentary spotlight into the room, and Kingsley could see the furious red welts already raised on the boy's otherwise pale and spotless flesh.

"Beg for mercy if you want me to stop," Kingsley said, digging his hand into the boy's blond hair at the base of his skull and forcing his face against the bare wood floor.

"Don't stop." The blond boy's voice was flush with desire and desperation.

Kingsley stripped him completely naked before striking him again with the cane—across the front of his thighs, across the back, all over him from his shoulders to his knees and back up again. Meanwhile the boy made no protest, begged no mercy and never once asked him to stop. The boy lay in the fetal position on the floor. Kingsley stood up, put a shod foot on his shoulder and pushed him on to his ravaged back. He flinched and arched as his brutalized skin met the floor.

"Touch yourself," Kingsley ordered. "I want to watch."

The blond took his erection in his hand and stroked upward.

"Keep going." Kingsley watched as the blond rubbed himself with his right hand. He knew it was agony, every movement he made would scrape the raw wounds on his back. And yet for all the agony, the blond was hard. Fluid dripped from the tip on to his lower stomach. Kingsley longed to lick it off. "It hurts, doesn't it? Your whole body?"

"It hurts," he breathed.

"Good." Kingsley walked to the bed and pulled a tube of lubricant out from under the pillow. Better to do this on the hard, unforgiving floor than the bed. He slept in a bed, was at his most vulnerable in a bed. He didn't want to be vulnerable tonight.

Kingsley knelt between the boy's legs, nudging his thighs wider. He pushed his fingers into the welts on the boy's legs. When the boy's groans reached a crescendo, Kingsley brought his mouth down on to his cock and sucked him deep. Pleasure and pain, pleasure and pain. He would couple them together tonight for this boy, and never again would he feel one without the other, desire one without the other. The boy would either hate him or thank him for this later—Kingsley didn't care which. But he knew one thing for certain; this beautiful blond teenager would never forget him.

As he sucked him, Kingsley wet his fingertips with the lubricant and pushed them into the blond's anus. The blond grunted but said nothing more. Kingsley poked and probed inside him, until the boy's grunts of discomfort turned to gasps of pleasure. Kingsley opened him up while licking and massaging every inch of him.

"I'm coming," the boy said between heavy breaths.

"Come, then." Kingsley put his mouth down deep over him and tasted the salt on his tongue. He wanted to swallow but didn't want to give the boy any ideas that this encounter meant more that it did. He spat it on the floor, pushed the boy on to his stomach, stroked himself to his full hardness and, without mercy, entered the boy.

The boy cried out, his hands scratching against the hardwood floor.

"Take it," Kingsley said. "Take it all. Don't fight it."

"I won't." The boy shook his head. "I want it."

Kingsley pushed in again. The boy was tight as a fist around him, and it took all of his hard-won self-control to keep from spilling into him right now. He'd only been with women lately. He'd almost forgotten how good it felt to fuck a young man, especially one so rare and lovely as this long-limbed youth with the perfect pale blond hair and the heart both afraid and fearless.

Closing his eyes, Kingsley rose up and bore down. The boy gasped beneath him.

"Please," he said.

"Please what?" Kingsley asked.

"Please, let me touch you."

Kingsley unbuttoned his shirt while still deep inside the boy. He pulled out, let the boy roll on to his back. He grabbed the boy's hands, pressing them to his chest.

"You have scars," he said, running his hands over Kingsley's bare torso.

"I am nothing but scars."

The blond pushed his palms against Kingsley's stomach and traced the muscles there.

"Your body's amazing," the boy said as he pushed Kingsley's shirt off his shoulders and down his arms. "I can't stop…"

His hands roamed all over Kingsley's exposed skin—his shoulders, his biceps, his scarred chest and taut stomach. But when the blond tried to touch his hair, Kingsley seized both wrists and slammed them into the floor.

Kingsley thrust deep and kept thrusting. Enough niceties. He should never have let the boy touch him like that. But it had been so long since he'd fucked someone without tying them up first, he'd forgotten what it felt like to be touched during sex.

Pressure built inside Kingsley's stomach and hips. He pushed repeatedly into the boy who raised his knees to his chest to take even more of him. Fucking turned into mindless rutting as Kingsley slammed into him with quick hard thrusts. No matter how much he gave, the boy only begged for more. When Kingsley couldn't hold off a second longer, he pulled out, shoved the boy on to his stomach and came all over his red-welted back.

Finally the room was still, and Kingsley was still and the blond boy on the floor was still. Kingsley wiped the semen off the blond's abraded skin.

Underneath him the boy shivered and shuddered. The salt into the wounds must have hurt more than anything else had.

"You did well," Kingsley said, and heard another voice saying those same words to him once.

Kingsley stood up, cleaned himself off and straightened his clothes. As if every movement caused him agony, the boy slowly sat up. He looked down at his body, at his welts, before looking up at Kingsley again. His lips were parted, his eyes wide. He crossed his arms over his stomach and pulled his legs to his chest.

"There's a shower through that door." Kingsley picked up the boy's shirt and gave it to him. "You can get cleaned up. You can stay here tonight if you want. Those welts will turn into bruises. Keep your clothes on until they're gone."

"Are you leaving?"

"Yes."

"Can't you stay? For a little while? We don't... We can talk."

"I don't want to talk," Kingsley said.

The boy scrambled to his feet and pulled his jeans on. He sat on the bed and spent longer than necessary buttoning his shirt. Kingsley finished pulling himself together. He'd shower back at the town house. Nothing worth bothering with right now. All he wanted to do was drink himself into a stupor and sleep until he woke up dead. As usual.

"You're young," Kingsley said. "You'll heal fast." He wasn't speaking about the welts.

He gave the boy one more smile before turning his back and heading to the door.

"My name's Justin," the blond called out after him.

Kingsley turned around and looked at him. A square of light from the window lay across the boy's face like a white mask.

"I've only been with a guy once. It wasn't like this. I didn't even come. If my parents knew I was gay, they'd kick me out. I just... I wanted you to know those three things."

"Anything else?" Kingsley asked, keeping his face composed, his voice devoid of emotion.

"You're beautiful," Justin said. "I feel stupid for saying that to another guy, but I can't find another word. And what you did to me was everything I've always wanted. So...thank you."

"You're thanking me?"

"They teach us manners in Texas."

Kingsley could taste the boy on his lips. Walk away. He knew he should walk away.

He pulled out his wallet and, from it, took a slim silver card with black ink.

"My name is Kingsley Edge. Not entirely, but it's what I answer to. I'm French. That's the accent you hear. And if your family kicks you out—and you're right, they might—come back to this city and find me. I can help you. I'm not saying I will help you. But I can if I'm in the mood."

Justin took the card and held it in his fist.

"Why did you pick me tonight? Only gay guy in the club?"

"There were three if I counted correctly."

"Then why me?"

"You're blond," Kingsley answered truthfully. Justin gave a little laugh.

"You must really love blonds, then."

"No." Kingsley smiled tiredly. "I hate them."

Without another word or a kiss goodbye, Kingsley left the room, left the hall, left the club and walked into the rainy streets of Manhattan. He should have called for his driver to come for him and take him home. But after so much sadism, a little masochism would do him good. The rain had turned the night near freezing, and Kingsley dug his hands deep into his jacket pockets burrowing for warmth. He walked fast, lengthening his strides as the late-winter rain soaked him to the skin. After two miles he arrived home to his town house. He paused outside and looked up. After six months living here, he still couldn't believe he owned a Manhattan palace. Three stories—four if one counted the pool in the basement— black-and-white facade, wrought-iron balconies, a glass con- servatory on the roof and luxurious bedroom after bedroom after bedroom...

Any one of his bedrooms would do him right now. He wanted to be warm and naked and drunk this very second. He ran up the stairs, opened the door and shut it behind him. He didn't lock it. He never locked the door. Someone was al- ways in the house, always coming or going. And people only locked their doors to keep the barbarians at the gate. He was the barbarian. Why would he keep himself out?

As soon as he entered the house, he pulled off his jacket and tossed it on the floor. Someone would take care of it. Someone always did. He heard music coming from within the house. Blaise, he guessed. She'd taken to staying here most nights, even the nights he didn't fuck her. She seemed the sort to like piano music—or at least to pretend she liked it.

He trudged up the steps but paused before he reached the first landing. The music...it didn't sound as if it came from a stereo or a radio. No, it sounded close, and live. Alive.

"Fuck." Kingsley stormed back down the stairs. He had one

rule in his house and one rule only. No one touches the grand piano in the music room. No one. It was to be looked at and never touched, never played, never even acknowledged. Whoever dared touch his piano would be thrown into the street and forbidden from ever crossing the threshold of his house again. The person who defied Kingsley's one law would curse the day he'd ever learned to play the fucking piano.

Kingsley threw open the door to the music room.

He stopped.

He stared.

He did not breathe.

It couldn't be…

But it was.

The room was dark, but Kingsley could see who played his grand piano. And even if he couldn't see, he would still know it was him. Only one man he'd ever known could play so skillfully without sheet music, without even seeing the keys. A sliver of streetlight penetrated the room and cast a circle of light around the pianist's hair.

His blond hair.

Søren.

Frozen in place, Kingsley could do nothing but stand and listen and watch and wait and wonder. Why? How?

The music—Beethoven, Kingsley believed it was—set the room afire, and the sound moved like smoke over the floor, up the walls and across the ceiling. Kingsley breathed it in like incense.

The piece ended. The final note rose like a burning ember before falling to the floor and fading into ash.

Shock had stolen Kingsley's courage, but now it returned to him. He couldn't get to the man fast enough. He rushed forward as the pianist closed the fallboard and stood. Over ten years had passed since Kingsley had seen him, had looked on him with his own eyes. Kingsley had almost given up hope he would ever see him again. They'd caused each other too much pain, and someone had paid the highest price for their secrets. But that was all in the past. It would be better now between them. No hiding. No lies. Kingsley would give him his heart and his body and his soul, and this time he'd ask for nothing in return.

But as the pianist rose, Kingsley noticed something different about him. He looked the same, only older now. How long since they'd last stood face-to-face, eye-to-eye? He would be twenty-nine years old, wouldn't he? God, they were grown men now. When had that happened? If it was possible, he was even more handsome than Kingsley remembered, and taller, too. How was it possible he was taller? His clothes, however, were far more severe. He wore all black.

All black but for one spot of white.

A square of white.

A square of white at his throat.

The pianist smiled at him, a smile of amusement with only the barest hint of apology. And not the least bit of shame.

Fuck.

Kingsley stared, incredulous. He took a small step back.

No...not that. Anything but that. Whatever hope had been in Kingsley's heart a second earlier shattered and died like the last stray note of a symphony.

The old love, the old desire coursed through his veins and into his heart, and there was no stopping it.

He met the blond pianist's eyes—the priest's eyes—and released the breath he'd forgotten he'd been holding.

"Mon Dieu..."

My God.

4

FOR A SILENT ETERNITY THEY ONLY LOOKED AT EACH other.

Finally Kingsley raised his hand.

"Wait here," he said and turned around. He turned back around again. *"S'il vous plaît."*

Søren said nothing. Even if Søren wanted to speak, Kingsley left before he could say a word.

Kingsley strode from the music room and shut the door behind him.

As soon as he stood alone in the hallway, Kingsley pushed a hand into his stomach. A wave of dizziness passed over him. He fought it off, ran upstairs to his bedroom and changed from his rain-soaked clothes into dry ones. He grabbed soap, a towel. He scrubbed at his face, rinsed the taste of Justin out of his mouth, toweled the rain from his hair and slicked his hands through it. In less than five minutes he looked like himself again—shoulder-length dark hair, dark eyes, olive skin inherited from his father. Did he look like he did ten years ago? Was he more handsome? Less? Did it matter to Søren anymore what he looked like?

"Søren…" He breathed the name like a prayer. How long had it been since he'd said that name out loud? What was he doing here? Last year Kingsley had been dying in a hospital in France, dying of infection from a gunshot wound. He remembered nothing of those days after his surgery but for the few minutes Søren had visited. He'd been too ill, barely conscious. He'd only heard Søren's voice speaking to a doctor, demanding they treat him, heal him, save him. Kingsley thought it only a dream at the time, but when he awoke to find he'd been left a gift—access to a Swiss bank account with more than thirty million dollars in it—he knew it had been real.

That should have been it. That should have been the last time they'd seen each other. Kingsley knew that bank account had been blood money—Søren's way of saying he was sorry for what had happened between them. The second Kingsley spent the first cent he'd accepted that apology. They were even now. No unfinished business.

So why was Søren here?

Kingsley took a steadying breath, but it did nothing to quell his light-headedness. He was almost giddy with shock. He laughed for no reason. As much as wanted to, he couldn't leave Søren alone in the music room all night waiting for him. He had to go back, talk to him, look him in the eyes again and find out what he wanted. And he would. He could do this. Some of the most dangerous men in the world pissed themselves at the mere mention of Kingsley's name. People feared him. They should fear him. He feared no one.

He took one more breath and readied himself to leave the bathroom and go to Søren. But then he stepped back, kicked the seat of the toilet open and vomited so hard his eyes watered.

Once he was certain he'd fully emptied his stomach of all its contents, he sat on the cold tile floor and breathed through his nose. He laughed.

Here he was, eleven years later, and Søren could still do this to him without saying a word. God damn him.

Slowly he stood and washed his mouth out again. He could run. He had money. He could leave. Go out the back door, fly away and run forever.

But no, Kingsley had to face him. He could face him. His pride demanded it of him. And if Søren had found him here, he could find him anywhere.

Outside the music room Kingsley willed his hands to stop shaking, willed his heart to slow its frenetic racing.

He threw open the door with a flourish and stepped inside.

At first he didn't see Søren. He'd expected to find him waiting on the divan or on one of the chairs. Or perhaps even standing by the window or sitting at the piano. He hadn't expected to find Søren bent underneath the top board of the piano. He'd turned on a lamp now, and warm light filled the room.

"What are you doing?" Kingsley asked as he came to the piano and peeked under the open lid. He spoke with a steady voice.

"Your bass notes are flat." Søren hit a key and turned a pin inside the piano. "You shouldn't have the piano near the window. The temperature fluctuates too much."

"I'll have it moved."

"When was the last time you had it tuned?" Søren asked.

"Never."

"I can tell." Søren hit another key, turned another pin. Kingsley watched Søren's hands as he worked. Large, strong and flawless hands. His clothes had changed, he'd grown taller, more handsome, and now he was a priest. But his hands hadn't changed. They were the same hands Kingsley remembered.

Søren stood up straight and lowered the lid of the grand piano back down.

"The action is stiff. Has it not been played very often?"

"You were the first. No one's allowed to play it."

"No one? Then I apologize for playing it."

"Don't apologize. When I say no one is allowed to play it, I meant…no one but you."

Søren glanced up and met Kingsley's eyes. It took all of Kingsley's resolve, fortitude and the alcohol left in his bloodstream not to break eye contact. Søren always had this way of looking at him that made Kingsley want to confess everything to him. Even back when they were teenage boys in school together, he'd had that power. But Kingsley kept silent, kept his secrets. They weren't boys anymore.

"I'll call someone," Kingsley finally said. "I'll have it tuned."

"Call a music store. They'll be able to recommend a good tuner."

Kingsley and Søren studied each other over the top of the piano.

"Do you want to keep talking about the piano, or should we have a real conversation?" Søren asked.

Kingsley gave him a halfhearted smile and sat down on the piano bench. The adrenaline had subsided, but the disorientation remained. If he awoke to find himself in bed and all this was a dream, he wouldn't be surprised.

"So…parish priest? Dominican? Franciscan?" he asked, the old words coming back to him like a language he used to be fluent in but hadn't spoken in years.

"Jesuit," Søren said, taking a seat on the white-and-black-striped sofa across from the piano bench.

Kingsley rubbed his forehead and laughed.

"A Jesuit. I was afraid of that. I knew they wanted you in their ranks."

"I wasn't recruited. It was my choice."

"So it's real? The collar? The vows? All of it?"

He clasped his hands in front of him between his knees.

"It is the most real thing I've ever done."

Kingsley raised his hands in surrender and confusion.

"When? Why?" He gave up on his English and fell back into his French. *Quand? Pourquoi?*

"I know you'll find this hard to believe, but I've wanted to be a priest since I was fourteen," Søren answered in his perfect French. It felt good to speak his first language again, to hear it again, even if every word Søren said stabbed his heart like a sword. "I converted at fourteen, so I could become a Jesuit. It was all I ever wanted."

"You never told me."

"Of course not. When I met you..."

"What?"

Søren didn't answer at first. Weighing his words? Or simply torturing Kingsley with silence? Kingsley remembered those long pauses before Søren would speak, as if he had to examine every word like a diamond under a jeweler's lope before allowing it to be displayed. Kingsley could live and die and be born again waiting for Søren to answer one little question.

"When I met you," Søren said again, "it was the first time I questioned my calling."

Kingsley let those words hang in the air between them before tucking them inside his heart and locking them away.

"Did you think I would try to talk you out of it?" Kingsley asked once he could speak again.

"Would you have tried to talk me out of it?"

"Yes," Kingsley said entirely without shame. "I'll try to talk you out of it now."

"You're a little late. I'm ordained. You know religious orders are sacraments. They can't be revoked. Once a priest..."

"Always a priest," Kingsley finished the famous dictum.

He wasn't Catholic, but he'd gone to a Catholic school long enough to learn all he needed to know about the Jesuits. "But a Jesuit? Really? There are other sorts of priests. You had to join an order that takes a vow of poverty?"

"Poverty? That's your problem with the Jesuits? Not the celibacy?"

"We'll get to that. Let's start with the poverty."

Søren leaned back on the sofa and rested his chin on his hand.

"It's good to see you again," Søren said. "You look better than the last time I saw you."

"The last time you saw me I was dying in a Paris hospital."

"Glad you got over that."

"You're not the only one, *mon ami*. I should thank you—"

Søren raised his hand to stop him.

"Don't. Please, don't thank me." Søren glanced away into the corner of the room. "After all that happened, after all I put you through, terrifying a doctor on your behalf was the least I could do."

He gave Kingsley a tight smile.

"You did more than terrify a doctor. I shouldn't tell you this, but my...employer at the time had decided to burn me."

"Burn?"

"Remove me from existence. Letting me die in the hospital was a nice, clean way to get rid of me and everything I know. The doctors, they'd been encouraged to let me die peacefully. I would have, if you hadn't shown up and given the counter order."

"I'm good at giving orders." Søren gave him the slightest of smiles.

"How did you find me? At the hospital, I mean."

"You listed me as your next of kin when you joined the Foreign Legion."

"That's right," Kingsley said. "I had no one else."

"You had our school as my contact information. A nurse called St. Ignatius, and St. Ignatius called me."

"How did you find me today?"

"You don't exactly fly under the radar, Kingsley."

Kingsley shrugged, tried and failed to laugh.

"It's not fair, you know. I couldn't open my eyes that day in the hospital. You saw me last year. I haven't seen you in... too long."

"I was in Rome, in India. I'm not sure I want to know where you've been."

"You don't."

"What are you doing with yourself these days?"

Kingsley shrugged, sighed, raised his hands. "I own a strip club. Don't judge me. It's very lucrative."

"I judge not," Søren said. "Anything else? Job? Girlfriend? Wife? Boyfriend?"

"No job. I'm retired. No wife. But Blaise is around here somewhere. She's the girlfriend. Sort of. And you?"

"No girlfriend," Søren said. "And no wife, either."

"You bastard," he said, shaking his head. "A fucking Jesuit priest."

"Actually, a nonfucking Jesuit priest. They haven't rescinded the vows of celibacy yet."

"How inconsiderate of them."

Kingsley tried to smile at Søren, but he couldn't. Not yet.

"Celibacy." Kingsley pronounced the word like a curse. It was a curse. "I thought you were a sadist. When did you become a masochist?"

"Is that a rhetorical question or are you looking for the exact date of my ordination? I'm a priest. Once you're firmly convinced that God exists, it's not that great a leap to ask him for a job."

Kingsley stood up and walked to the window. Outside, Manhattan had awoken and stirred to life. He had CEOs and Nobel Prize winners and heiresses as his neighbors here on Riverside Drive. They were the men and women who owned the city. And yet the only person in the entire borough who meant anything to him sat on his sofa in the music room and didn't have a cent to his name. Søren once had a cent to his name. A few billion cents to his name. And he'd given every last one of them to Kingsley.

"Why are you here?" Kingsley finally asked the question of the night.

"You might regret asking that."

"I do already. I'm guessing this is more than a friendly reunion? And I'm guessing you aren't here to pick things up where we left off?"

"Would you really want to?"

"Yes." Kingsley answered without hesitation. It didn't seem to be the answer Søren expected.

"Kingsley..." Søren stood and joined him by the window. Dawn had come to Manhattan. If dawn knew what she was doing, she'd take the next bus back out of town.

"Don't say my name like that, like I'm a child who said something foolish. I'm allowed to want you. Still. Always."

"I thought you would hate me."

"I did. I do hate you. But I don't... How can I truly hate the one person who knows me?" Kingsley studied Søren out of the corner of his eye and ached to touch Søren's face, his lips. Not even the collar could stem the tide of Kingsley's desire. Not even all the pain and the years between them.

"Do you remember that night we were in the hermitage and—"

"I remember all our nights," Kingsley whispered.

Søren closed his eyes as if Kingsley's words hurt him. Kingsley hoped they had.

"It was a night we talked about others. We were wondering if there were others like us out there somewhere."

"I remember," Kingsley said. And as soon as Søren conjured the memory, Kingsley was a teenager again. He stretched out on the cot on his back, naked, the sheets pulled to his stomach. Søren lay next to him. Kingsley could feel the heat of Søren's skin against his. No matter how many times they touched, it always surprised him how warm Søren was. He expected his skin to be cold, as cold as his heart. Kingsley's thighs burned. Søren had whipped him with a leather belt, then they'd made love on the cot. He knew it was teenage romantic foolishness to consider the sort of sex they had "making love," but he needed to believe that's what it had been—to both of them. He needed to think it had been more than mere fucking.

"Do you remember what you said to me?" Søren asked. "You said you would find all of our kind and lay them at my feet."

"And you said you didn't need hundreds. But…" Kingsley raised both hands as if he could conjure the memory between his palms and look into it like a crystal ball. "One girl."

"'A girl would be nice,' I said."

Kingsley laughed. "We were trapped in an all-boys' school. 'A girl would be nice' might have been a radical underestimation of how much we wanted to fuck a girl for a change."

"I didn't want you to think you weren't enough for me. You know I'm—"

"I know," Kingsley said.

Kingsley knew Søren wasn't like him. For Kingsley, sex was sex, and he had it when he wanted with whomever he wanted. Male or female or anything in between was simply a question of strategy. Søren had told him once he considered himself straight, that Kingsley was the sole exception to the rule. "That girl we dreamed of—I wanted black hair and green eyes. But you wanted green hair and black eyes? I assume you mean the irises would be black, not that you planned on punching her in the face."

"I'm not that much of a sadist." Søren smiled, and the world turned to morning from the force of that smile. Had Kingsley ever seen him smile like that? "And this girl of ours, she would be wilder than both of us together."

"We dreamed beautiful dreams, didn't we? But a girl like that? Impossible dream."

Kingsley had once dreamed he and Søren would spend their lives together. They'd travel the world, see it all, wake up together, sleep together and fuck on every continent.

"Nothing is impossible," Søren said.

"What do you mean?"

Søren turned his eyes from the sun and gazed directly at Kingsley.

"Kingsley," Søren began and paused. Whatever words would come next, Kingsley felt certain his world would never be the same again once they were spoken.

"What is it?"

"I found her."

5

KINGSLEY COULDN'T SPEAK AT FIRST. WHAT WAS
there to say to that? What do you say to an otherwise reasonable person who suddenly looks at you and says he saw a
unicorn on the side of the road or met Saint Peter while out
for a walk?

"You found her. You're certain?"

"I have never been more certain of anything in my life. And
that includes my call to the priesthood. It's her. Black hair and
green eyes. Green hair and black eyes."

"That's not possible."

"Her eyes change color in the light. Green to black and
back again. When I first saw her, she had streaked green dye
through her black hair. She's violent and foul-mouthed, and
she told me I was an idiot. Not only did she say that to me, it
was the first thing she said to me."

"Wild, is she?"

"I'd go so far as to use the word *feral*."

"Feral. A wild cat, then. With claws?"

"Sharp ones. Sharp mind, too. Very intelligent. Cunning.
Quick and clever. Almost fearless."

"My type of girl. Where did you meet her?"

"I was sent to pastor at a small parish in a town called Wakefield in Connecticut. She's in my congregation. I recognized her the second I saw her. You would have, too."

"What's she like?"

"Dangerous. She doesn't even know how dangerous."

"How dangerous?"

"She…" Søren stopped and laughed. "She made me make her a promise."

"*Made* you? No one makes *you* do anything."

"She did. I needed her to agree to something, and instead of being cowed like every other person I've ever attempted to terrorize before, she refused to accept my terms. Unless…"

"Unless what?"

"I promised to break my vows with her."

"Is that so? Which vows? Poverty? Obedience? Will she make you buy expensive things and tell the pope to go fuck himself?"

"She wants us to be lovers."

"Are you?"

"Not yet."

"Not yet?" Kingsley repeated. "So you plan to?"

"She made me promise I would."

"So, why haven't you?" Kingsley asked. He tried to keep his voice light, airy, amused. But he'd never had a more serious conversation in his life. If this girl was real, if she was the one he and Søren had dreamed of, and Søren had found her, that meant something. What it meant, he didn't know. But something. Something that terrified him and aroused him all at once.

"Because," Søren said, "I'm a priest. And she's a virgin."

"A dangerous virgin? I didn't think such a being could exist."

"You'll believe it when you meet her. But that's not all you should know about her."

"What else?"

"She's fifteen."

Kingsley inhaled sharply.

"Fifteen. Are you insane? Do you know what they do with priests who—"

"Which is why I haven't done it. As much as I'd like to."

"Beautiful, is she?"

"Kingsley, you have no idea…"

Kingsley heard pure aching need in Søren's voice. He hadn't heard desire like that since the last night they'd spent together.

I own you…you are mine…your body is mine, your heart is mine, your soul is mine… Søren had whispered that in Kingsley's ear as they'd fucked on the cold hard floor by the small hermit-age fireplace. *You want me?* Kingsley had asked, taking every inch of Søren into him. *So much,* Søren had said. *You have no idea how much.*

"I should meet our little princess," Kingsley said.

"Not a princess, a queen."

"Take me to her, then." Kingsley didn't actually want to meet her. He felt sick again at the thought of it. This was a dare. *You saw a unicorn? Prove it, then. You say you're Christ back from the dead? Show me the wounds.*

"I can't," Søren said.

"Why not?"

"She's in police custody."

Kingsley laughed.

"Now I know why you're here. Your Virgin Queen has gotten herself into trouble. You expect me to help her?"

"I'm asking you to. Begging you to if I must."

"Even when you're begging, it sounds like an order."

"Would you rather I ordered you to help her?" Søren asked, stepping away from the window. "I can still play the game."

"It was never a game to me."

Søren turned and faced him, his eyes cold and steely.

"No. It was never a game to me, either."

Kingsley sat down on the black-and-white sofa. He crossed his ankle over his knee and leaned his head back against the fabric. He rubbed his temples with his fingertips. God, what a night.

"Do I want to know what she's in police custody for?"

"She stole five cars. Her father apparently owns something called a chop shop."

"They steal cars, chop them up and sell the parts. Good money in it."

"He made her steal for him. The police caught her in the act. Her father ran for it."

"I hope they catch him and give him the chair."

"Death is too good for him. But he's not my concern now. She is. She's facing serious time in juvenile detention or worse. I can't let that happen. I found her a week ago. I can't lose her already."

Kingsley looked up at him through narrowed eyes.

"You..." Kingsley said. "You're in love with her."

Søren didn't deny it. Kingsley respected him for that. Honesty was its own special brand of sadism.

"I am."

"Well, then," Kingsley said, laying his head back again. "Maybe all hope is not lost."

He expected Søren to laugh at that, but when he looked up he saw the steel in Søren's eyes.

"We have to help her," Søren said. "Please."

"Please? You've learned manners in the past eleven years."

"Will you help her? Will you help me?"

Help the girl. How? Easy. He had a few judges who owed him favors. He regularly fucked the wife of an important district attorney. He could make some phone calls. He couldn't get the charges dropped. His contacts needed to cover their asses. But he could get her community service, probation with some luck. Nothing serious.

"What's her name?"

"Eleanor Louise Schreiber."

"Schreiber? German name."

"It is."

The corner of Kingsley's mouth quirked in to a half smile.

"That explains the Beethoven. I suppose you don't play Ravel anymore."

Søren had played Ravel for him the day they met and many days after. Ravel, the greatest of all French composers. And now his heart turned to Beethoven—the greatest of all the Germans.

"I would play Ravel for you," Søren said, his voice stiff and formal. "If that's what it took."

Kingsley's eyes flew open.

"I'm not going to make you fuck me just so I'll help your Virgin Queen. That's her game, not mine."

"Is there a price for your assistance?"

"You gave me a fortune. I'm richer than God, and you think you owe me something?"

"Don't I?"

"A favor," Kingsley said. "One favor."

"Anything. Name it."

Kingsley stood up, walked across the room and stood only inches from Søren.

"All I ask of you," Kingsley began, "all I beg of you…don't leave me again. Please. Eleven years. I thought I'd never see you again."

Søren grasped Kingsley by the back of the neck and pulled him into an embrace—not an embrace of lovers but, instead, of lost brothers, soldiers from enemy armies reunited at the end of a long, devastating war that no one had won.

"I thought I would die without ever seeing you again," Kingsley said, and his eyes burned with tears. "Every day I thought that."

"Thought or hoped?"

"Feared," Kingsley said, clutching Søren's forearms. "My greatest fear."

Kingsley closed his eyes, and if he kept his eyes closed he wouldn't have to see that white collar around Søren's neck. If he kept his eyes closed he could pretend it was eleven years ago and they were alone in the hermitage together. Søren would beat him and take him to bed, and after he'd finished, Kingsley would throw his arm over Søren's stomach, rest his head on Søren's chest and fall asleep. When he woke up Søren would still be there. Søren would always be there.

"I promise you this," Søren whispered, "I will never turn my back on you. I will never leave you. I will never forsake you. As long as it's in my power, I will be your friend, and I will be here for you whenever you need me."

"You paid for this house. It's your home even more than mine. Make it your home."

"I will if that's what you want."

"More than anything." He opened his eyes and looked up at Søren. "No one loves me. And I don't love anyone here. No one trusts me and I don't trust anyone. I need you."

"You trust me? After what I did to you?"

"I trust you. Because of what you did to me."

Søren took a deep breath. Kingsley felt his chest rise and fall.

Kingsley sensed Søren's reluctance to pull away, but pull away he did.

"I'll help your girl," Kingsley said. "I know people. I'll make sure she doesn't go away."

"Don't hate her. You'll want to hate her, and we both know why. But try to keep your heart open."

"How long have you been back in the United States?" Kingsley asked.

Søren seemed taken aback by the question.

"A few months," he said.

"You've been to the city before?"

"Yes."

"But you never came to see me."

Søren didn't say anything. Kingsley hated him for that silence.

"You weren't planning on seeing me ever again, were you?" Kingsley asked.

"I thought about seeing you again," Søren said. "I wasn't sure if I should. For the obvious reasons."

"Your little girl got herself in trouble, and that's what it took to bring you back to me? How can I hate her?"

Søren nodded. It looked as if he had something else to say. Whatever it was, he decided against saying it.

"I'll come back tomorrow," Søren said. "I've been up all night, and it looks like you have, too. We'll talk more after we've both had some sleep."

"Good." Kingsley was so relieved to hear he'd see Søren tomorrow, he was almost ashamed of himself. He could have cried from relief. "I have a car. It can take you home."

"It's fine. I have a way back."

"Please, don't tell me you're taking public transportation. I can handle the vow of celibacy better than that."

Søren laughed—a joyful new morning laugh. Joyful? He hadn't expected joy. Søren was happy in his new life? That was good. Kingsley wanted him happy. At least one of them was happy. Better than nothing.

"I promise, no public transportation."

Kingsley followed Søren out on to the sidewalk. From the two-foot gap between his town house and the house next to him, Søren wheeled out a black motorcycle—a Ducati.

Kingsley whistled.

"If this is standard-issue transportation for Jesuits, no wonder you joined."

"It's a bribe, actually," Søren said, pulling on a leather jacket and zipping it up. He slipped his white collar out of his shirt and pocketed it. Just like that, Søren ceased looking like a priest and became himself again in Kingsley's eyes.

"Priests take bribes?"

"We have a long history of it. Ever heard of indulgences?"

"My entire life is an indulgence."

"I'm starting to see that," Søren said, looking the town house up and down. "But this bribe was my father's doing. He assumed—wrongly—that I'd drop out of seminary so I could keep it. Jesuits hold all property in common. If I accepted the bike and stayed in seminary, I'd have to give it up to the order. They often sell large expensive gifts and use the money for more important things—like food and books."

"What happened?"

"I told my superior at the province. He told me to take the bike, become a priest and let my father go to hell. That's the sort of spiritual counsel I can live with."

"Your father must hate you."

"Almost as much as I hate him."

Søren started the engine. Before he could drive off, Kingsley stepped in front of the bike.

"Don't forget the favor. Don't leave me again," Kingsley said.

"Again? You seem to be forgetting something," Søren said.

"What?"

Søren looked him deep in the eyes. And in those gray

depths Kingsley caught a glimpse of something. Fury—old, cold, but still burning.

"Eleven years ago, I didn't leave you," Søren said. "You left me first."

And with that, Søren put on his helmet, revved up his bike and rode off into the street.

Funny. Kingsley had forgotten that.

He had left Søren first.

6

THE THINGS KINGSLEY DID FOR LOVE.

Kingsley took a breath, walked up the steps into the East-side Rifle and Pistol Range. He was on time, but Robert Dixon was already there. Dixon caught Kingsley's eye, nodded at him, then raised his pistol and shot six bullets into the target. Kingsley stood safely behind him and watched. Dixon could shoot. Kingsley had to give him that. Six bullets, six hits. He'd peppered an erratic circle around the target's heart.

Dixon, aged forty and looking every day of it, took off his earmuffs.

"Your turn," Dixon said to Kingsley. "Impress me, and I'll hear you out."

With another sigh, Kingsley put on his earmuffs and safety glasses, aimed his 9mm and shot six rounds into a fresh target. Two in the head between the eyes, two in the heart and two in the groin just to make Dixon think twice.

Kingsley pulled off the earmuffs, turned around and faced Dixon.

"Where'd you learn to shoot like that?" Dixon asked.

"French Foreign Legion."

"I thought all the French military knew how to do was surrender."

"You'd be curtsying to the Queen of England if it wasn't for the French."

"What do you want? A thank-you note?"

"Just a favor. We'll call it even between France and America then."

Dixon looked him up and down. "Let's go talk. Keep your hands off your gun."

"Your idea to meet at a shooting range," Kingsley reminded him.

"I shoot better than anyone I know."

"Not anymore."

"I'm pretending I don't know you," Dixon said. Kingsley didn't blame him for that.

They left the shooting lanes and found a quiet corner near the lockers. Dixon pulled on his jacket, stuffed his hands in his pockets and waited.

"I need your help," Kingsley said.

"You're fucking my wife, and you come to ask for a favor. I almost admire that."

"I wouldn't have to fuck your wife if you weren't too busy fucking your wife's sister."

Dixon's eyes widened. Kingsley smiled.

"Go on," Dixon said. "What do you need my help with?"

"A girl was arrested in Manhattan last night. She's being charged today with five counts of grand theft auto."

"A girl?"

"She's fifteen."

"We better throw in a charge for driving without a license then."

"You're funny," Kingsley said, and mentally put two bullets in Dixon's head. "I need the charges dropped."

"Not gonna happen."

"How much to make it happen?"

"I can't get the charges dropped. That's a big fucking red flag, and I'm not prepared to wave it."

"Can you get them reduced? I want to keep her out of doing any time."

"Who is this girl?"

"Friend of a friend," Kingsley said.

"You have friends who are friends with fifteen-year-old girls?"

"I have interesting friends."

"I didn't know you had any friends, Edge," Dixon said with a wide grin. Kingsley put two more bullets in him—center of his chest this time. "Or do fuck buddies count as friends these days?"

"Are you going to help her or not?" Kingsley asked.

"I'll consider it. What's her name?"

"Eleanor Schreiber. She lives in Wakefield, Connecticut."

"Schreiber? Yeah, they're looking for the father right now. They want her to roll on him and anyone else she can."

"She'll roll on him."

"Who's the friend?"

"Why does it matter?"

"I put my job on the line helping a fifteen-year-old girl get out of going to juvie for multiple counts of car theft, I want to know the story."

"Fine. Short story. An old friend of mine is a Catholic priest now. Her priest. He asked me to help her. I owe him a big favor. This is the favor."

"You're friends with a priest?"

"Trust me, no one is more shocked by that than I am."

"Is he fucking her? The priest?"

"What?" Kingsley asked. Did Dixon already know something about Søren?

"It's all over the papers," Dixon said. "Every damn day

there's a new story about a Catholic priest fucking some kid. Boston's exploding. Phillie, Detroit, Chicago… I get caught helping a priest with the underage girl he's fucking and—"

"He's not fucking her."

"How do you know?"

"Because I'm fucking her," Kingsley said, coming up with the quickest cover he could think of.

"You're fucking her?"

"I went to visit his church. I saw her. I fucked her. I thought she was eighteen."

"You thought she was eighteen," Dixon repeated.

"Oops." Kingsley shrugged.

"Now this is making more sense to me. I can't see you doing a favor for a friend out of the goodness of your heart. I can see you fucking a fifteen-year-old girl."

"Guilty as charged." Kingsley raised his hands in mock surrender. "She's looking at hard time. Can we get her community service?"

"You want her out of juvie so you can keep fucking her?"

"Not easy to fuck through iron bars. Possible, but not one of my kinks."

Dixon went quiet. Kingsley waited. He couldn't stand being around this man another thirty seconds. Dixon did favors all the time for the mafia and still went to church with his wife and kids every fucking Sunday.

"It's not my case, but I can make something happen," Dixon finally said. "There's a judge who's soft on teenage girls. Gives them community service in most of his cases, even violent ones. If I grease the wheels of justice, we can make it one of those cases."

"How much grease?"

"Fifty thousand."

"Done," Kingsley said, not even bothering to negotiate. He didn't negotiate where Søren was concerned.

"That was easy," Dixon said. "You must really like this little girl."

"Le cœur a ses raisons que la raison ne connaît point," Kingsley said.

"What was that?"

"I said, yes, I really like this girl. Call it destiny."

"Let's hope my wife doesn't find out about you and your little destiny. She likes you."

"Let's hope your wife doesn't find out about a lot things," Kingsley said with a smile. "I'll send someone to your house later. Or maybe I'll just drop it off next time I'm there."

"You son of a bitch."

"My mother was a saint," Kingsley said. "I'm the only bitch in the family."

He patted Dixon on the shoulder and walked past him. As soon as he was out of the front door, he stopped, leaned back against a brick wall and closed his eyes. He breathed for ten whole seconds as the tension left his body. These pissing contests never got easier. Dixon was stupid and powerful, and it was a terrifying combination in an enemy. Why did he even have enemies anymore? Wasn't he supposed to be retired? Isn't that why he'd left France, left the job, taken the money and run?

Then again, he was only twenty-eight. Who retired at twenty-eight? And if he wasn't making trouble for someone, then what was the point of getting out of bed in the morning?

Kingsley rubbed his forehead, felt the weariness in his bones. He needed a better reason for getting out of bed in the morning.

Kingsley walked four blocks and found a pay phone.

"It's me," Kingsley said when Søren answered. He spoke in French. No need for names.

"What's the verdict?" Søren asked.

"She'll get community service. Good enough?"

He heard a pause on the other end, and Kingsley lived and died in that pause. Just like old times.

"Thank you," Søren said. "That is more than I'd dared to hope for."

"Let me ask you something. If I hadn't been able to help your little girl, what would you have done? What was Plan B?"

"I think she and my mother would get along quite well."

Kingsley shook his head and laughed to himself. "I'm glad I could save you from the necessity of kidnapping a minor and transporting her across international borders."

"*Kidnapping* is such a strong word. I prefer the term *rescuing*."

"You really love her."

"You will, too."

"What's so special about this girl you're willing to commit felonies on her behalf?"

"Truth?"

"Truth," Kingsley said.

"She reminds me of you."

"That's why you love her?" Kingsley asked, hoping the answer was "yes" but knowing it wasn't.

"That's why I'm trying to help her."

Kingsley heard the pointed note in Søren's words.

"I don't need help," Kingsley said.

"Are you certain of that?"

"Yes," Kingsley said, and hung up the phone.

As he walked away, he had a fleeting thought.

What was the penance for lying to a priest?

7

"HIT ME," KINGSLEY SAID AS HE TAPPED THE TABLE.

"I'm not going to hit you," Søren said.

"You have to do what I say. And I say hit me."

Søren glared at him. Kingsley glared back.

"You have an ace and an eight," Søren said.

"Which means I have nine or nineteen. I'm calling it nine. Hit me."

"You want another card because you want to say 'hit me' to me as many times as possible tonight."

"I'm not disagreeing with that." Kingsley tapped the table again. "Hit me."

Søren gave Kingsley another card—a second ace. Now he had twenty or ten, depending on how he wanted to play it. He and Søren weren't playing blackjack for money, so he didn't care much if he won or not. In fact, he didn't care at all. But he couldn't deny the fact he was enjoying himself. Kingsley needed time to stop and stop completely. He hadn't felt this… He couldn't even find the right word. He hadn't felt this *something* in years. Whatever it was, he didn't want to lose it, and he'd found it the instant Søren had stepped through his front door.

"Kingsley?"

"I'm thinking."

"You have twenty. You should stand."

"I'm not going to take the strategy advice of my enemy."

"I'm the dealer, not the enemy."

"When did you start playing blackjack anyway?" Kingsley demanded as he perused his cards again. One more ace and he'd have blackjack. "Do they teach this in seminary?"

"Cards were an extracurricular activity. An entire household full of men who aren't allowed to have sex? We find other hobbies."

"So, blackjack?"

"Among other things."

Kingsley gave him a searching look.

"Care to tell me what these other hobbies of yours are?" Kingsley asked.

"They're on a need-to-know basis. You don't need to know," Søren said, fanning the cards in front of him.

"I need to know everything," Kingsley said. "If I'm going to keep you from getting excommunicated or going to prison for seducing and/or kidnapping a teenage girl—"

"Seduce her? I haven't even seen her for a full month."

Kingsley cocked an eyebrow at Søren.

"She quit church?"

Søren cleared his throat and sat up a little straighter.

"She's grounded."

Kingsley dropped his head on to the table.

"Why didn't I defect to Russia when I had the chance?" Kingsley sighed.

"Are you going to make a decision about your cards, or are we going to be here all night?"

"We're going to be here all night." Kingsley sat up again. Søren shook his head in disgust. "Don't look at me like that. I'm not the one with a girlfriend young enough to be grounded."

Exhaling with exasperation, Søren swept up his cards and Kingsley's. With his agile pianist's fingers, he shuffled the cards one-handed. Kingsley watched the display of casual grace and dexterity with envy and longing. Once, those skillful hands had owned every inch of his body. He'd never wanted to be a deck of cards so much in his life.

"Let's try this again, shall we?" Søren dealt the cards.

"King?" came a woman's voice behind Kingsley. Without looking back, he raised his hand and beckoned her into the dining room. A beautiful young woman in a forties-style skirt and blouse stood next to his chair and waited.

He wrapped an arm around her hips and dragged her down to his lap.

"You're interrupting," he said to her. "Can't you see how busy I am?"

"Oh, forgive me. I didn't mean to interrupt your—" she glanced down at the table and back into Kingsley's eyes "—card game?"

Kingsley pointed at Søren.

"Blaise, I would like you to meet my oldest and dearest friend…" He paused and looked at Søren when he realized he didn't know if he was allowed to tell anyone Søren's name. Out in the world Søren had gone by the name his father had given him—Marcus Stearns. Even now he was *Father Marcus Stearns, SJ,* according to church records. Søren was the name his mother had given him, and few called him that.

"Who the hell are you again?" Kingsley asked.

Søren stretched out his hand and took Blaise's.

"Søren. Kingsley and I went to school together."

"I'm Blaise," she said, and gave Søren her brightest smile and the most unapologetic bedroom eyes Kingsley had ever seen. So unfair. Why did Søren always turn every head in the room? Kingsley looked at Søren who today wore normal clothes. Normal? Black slacks, a fitted black long-sleeve T-shirt. They'd be normal clothes on anyone but Søren. In them, Søren looked like something out of a fever dream. He couldn't blame Blaise for looking at Søren the way she did.

But he did wonder why Søren looked at her the same way.

"Blaise, might I inquire what you're doing interrupting this incredibly important card game of mine?"

"Against my better judgment, I answered the phone and took a message for you. But don't get any ideas that I'm your new secretary, although you need to get a new secretary—"

"I will, *chouchou*. I promise."

"You said that last week."

"I got a new secretary last week."

"Where is she?"

"She quit."

"Did you fuck her?"

"I didn't mean to. It was an accident."

Blaise turned her attention back to Søren.

"Can you please tell your oldest and dearest friend to stop seducing his secretaries so they'll stop quitting on him when they catch him fucking someone else?"

"Kingsley," Søren said, shuffling the cards again. "Stop seducing your secretaries so they'll stop quitting on you."

"Thank you." Blaise gave Søren a smile.

"My pleasure," Søren said. Kingsley mentally slapped them both.

"Don't pretend you don't like playing secretary," Kingsley said.

"That's different." Blaise shook her head. "If I'm pretending to be your secretary so you'll fuck me on your desk—that's one thing. But I don't actually want to *be* your secretary."

"Just give me the message," Kingsley said, running his hand up her thigh and caressing the bare skin above her flesh-tone stockings.

Blaise reached into her nearly translucent pale pink blouse and produced a folded note from inside her lace-trimmed bra.

Kingsley unfolded the note, still warm from her body, and read.

Tonight at nine. —Phoebe

Kingsley tensed when he read the words and briefly considered lying his way out of the situation. But no...Phoebe was not the sort of woman one said no to.

"I have to go," Kingsley said to Blaise and Søren. "I won't be gone long—an hour or so. You'll keep my guest company, won't you?" he asked Blaise.

"Happily." Her thousand-watt smile brightened a few more watts. With her on his lap, he could feel the heat emanating from between her legs.

"Good. You two have so much in common, so much to talk about. Blaise, tell Søren what you do."

"I run a nonprofit," she said, leaning forward on the table and resting her chin on her hand. The move allowed everyone in the room to get a much clearer view of her soft, ample cleavage.

"A nonprofit?" Søren continued shuffling the cards while never once looking away from Blaise.

"Tell him what it does." Kingsley pinched her on the thigh, and she shuddered in pleasure. "Our Blaise is *très* altruistic."

"It's called Slut Pride. We educate people about women's sexual freedom, especially in regards to women's participation in BDSM activities. Some people like to tell us that it's not feminist to enjoy being flogged. I say it's not feminist to tell a woman what she can and can't do. But enough about me. What do you do?"

"I'm a Catholic priest."

Blaise said nothing. She gawked at Søren with her full red-lipped mouth agape. And then she laughed, a warm throaty sound that filled the room.

"You're terrible," she said. "You had me there for a second."

Søren winked at Kingsley. Kingsley had never guessed Søren had this flirtatious side to him. Back in their school days Søren had been feared and envied by all the other boys, and Søren had almost never spoken to anyone but the other priests. Kingsley realized that, other than his sister, he'd never seen Søren around a beautiful woman before. Interesting. The man was human after all. Even if he was a priest.

"I must be off. You two chat, become friends. Blaise, *peut-être* you should take my friend upstairs and show him what BDSM looks like in action. I'm sure he'll find it fascinating."

"I'm sure I will," Søren said. "We'll be fine, Kingsley. Have a lovely evening."

Kingsley patted Blaise's shapely bottom, and she stood up and let him out. On his way from the dining room he heard Blaise asking Søren, "So what do you really do?"

"You wouldn't believe me if I told you," Søren answered.

Kingsley chuckled on his way upstairs. He needed to grab a few things. That was it. Think about what he needed to take with him, not what he had to do. Just a job. He'd done hundreds of jobs in his life. He'd get a file, a mission, a plane ticket, a target. This was child's play in comparison.

Digging his keys out of the pocket of his jeans, he opened a locked box in his closet and took out his Walther P88. He removed the clip and pulled the slide, checking that no bullets remained in the chamber. He snapped the clip in, shoved it into his holster on his jeans and pulled on his leather jacket.

Kingsley left the house and neither hailed a cab nor took a car. On foot he made it to the apartment in twenty minutes. He rang the doorbell, and a housekeeper let him in without a word. No words necessary. The look of disgust and disdain said everything. Fuck her. Kingsley wasn't here to make the housekeeper happy.

He raced up the stairs right as Phoebe Dixon stepped into the hallway in her long silk bathrobe. She had a towel to her wet hair and walked toward her bedroom at the end of the long hall. She didn't look back or speak. She hadn't seen him.

Good.

Kingsley took a quick and silent breath and pulled his gun out. Careful of the creaking floor, he stalked her down the hall. When she reached for the door handle to her bedroom, he put the gun to the center of her back.

"Don't scream," he ordered as he slapped a hand over her mouth. "Not if you want to live."

8

PHOEBE'S ENTIRE BODY STIFFENED LIKE A CORPSE. She whimpered but didn't scream.

"Open the door. Now."

She opened it, and he pushed her inside, pushed her so hard she landed on the floor, her bathrobe coming open to reveal her naked body underneath.

He grabbed her by the arm and shoved her into the floor again.

"Don't…" she begged, her voice breaking with tears. "I have children."

"Are you offering them?" he asked, ripping the robe from her body and wrenching her to her feet.

"Please, don't kill me. My husband's an attorney. He has money—"

"Keep begging. It won't work," he said as he bent her over the bed and kicked at her ankles until she parted her shaking thighs. He pressed the barrel of the gun into her throat. "But I like how you do it."

Tossing the gun aside, he opened his pants and slammed inside her. Her body clenched around him tighter with each thrust. Despite her pleas and her protests, she grew wetter the more he rammed into her, the harder he worked her. But he couldn't come, not yet. Although he wanted to get it over with as soon as possible. Sex with Phoebe was business, not pleasure, and he hated the work.

As she moaned underneath him, crying against the intrusion, Kingsley closed his eyes and disappeared to another place, another time. The elegant and well-appointed bedroom he stood in disappeared and dissolved. The hunter-green walls and the modern art prints faded away and rough wood took their place. The king-size bed adorned with silk sheets and pillows was gone, and now a small cot sat on the floor near a fireplace. And Kingsley lay on his side facing the fire.

"You have a bruise on your neck under your ear," Søren said, touching the sensitive spot with his fingertip. "It'll go above your collar."

"If someone says anything, I'll tell them a tree hit me."

Søren laughed softly and kissed the bruise.

"I don't think they'll believe a tree hit you. Maybe they'd believe you hit a tree."

"Why would I hit a tree? A tree never did anything to me."

"Perhaps it likes being hit." Søren kissed Kingsley's neck again, his shoulder, his throat.

Kingsley remembered this night. It had a been a Sunday. Everyone at their school went to bed early on Sunday nights. They'd woken early for Sunday Mass and had to wake early again for Monday morning classes. Once everyone had gone to bed, he and Søren had sneaked out to the hermitage to spend a few perfect hours alone together.

"Aren't you worried someone will find out what we're doing out here?" Kingsley asked as he covered Søren's roving hand with his own.

"They'd never believe it even if we told them."

"What? They'd believe I'd sleep with a teacher, but they

wouldn't believe you'd sleep with a student?" Kingsley tried to sound outraged. He wasn't sure if he pulled it off or not.

"Precisely."

"Because I'm a slut, and you're perfect?"

"Because you have friends, and no one likes me," Søren said.

Kingsley sat up and looked down at Søren.

"I like you," Kingsley said.

"No, you don't," Søren said with a half smile. "You want me. There's a difference."

"You don't like me, either," Kingsley chided. He ignored the unwelcome pang of sympathy Søren's placid "No one likes me" declaration gave him.

"It isn't that I don't like you," Søren said with a playful sigh. "It's only I like me so much more than I like you that, in comparison, it looks like I dislike you."

"I might suffocate you tonight with a pillow," Kingsley said.

"You'll have to teach my French classes, then. Lesson plans in my desk."

"Forget it. You get to live."

"I thought as much."

Kingsley collapsed on to Søren's chest with a sigh. Søren lifted Kingsley's hair and pressed a kiss under his ear.

"Well, I'm worried they'll find out about us," Kingsley said, turning on to his side away from Søren. Søren wasn't deterred. He ran his hand down the center of Kingsley's back and pressed a kiss to the top of his spine. Kingsley relished these moments, after the fire of Søren's sadism had burned itself out. The gentle touches and kisses hurt almost more than the blows from the belt and the cane did. They hurt his heart, and yet he treasured the ache. It was his favorite pain.

"Why are you worried? We're always careful. No one ever sees us together. I don't care if they find out about me. I have places I can go. But I don't want you…"

"Don't want me what?" Kingsley asked.

"I don't want to embarrass you," Søren said, and Kingsley laughed out loud at the abject absurdity of that statement.

"You don't want to embarrass me? An hour ago, you stripped me naked, told me to get on my knees and confess to you the most shameful sexual fantasies I've ever had in my life, and you say you don't want to embarrass me?"

"That's different. Who we are in private has nothing to do with who we have to be out there. Do you want people to know what you are?"

"Your lover?"

"Not that."

Kingsley thought about the question. Alone with Søren he became a slave, a slut, a groveling nobody who submitted to sexual torture and said thank you for the privilege. Having sex with another boy didn't embarrass him. It was everything else that did.

"*Non*, it's true. I don't want people to know I like being hurt. They wouldn't understand it, and they wouldn't understand you. They'd think you were a monster."

"I am a monster," Søren said as he bit the center of Kingsley's back.

"Yes, but no one knows that but me. It's our secret. But…" He sighed heavily and pressed his back against Søren's chest. "I'm afraid they'll find out soon enough anyway."

"And why is that?" Søren demanded.

"Well, you see…" He braced himself for Søren's wrath. "I'm pregnant."

Kingsley bit his bottom lip to keep from laughing as Søren sighed so heavily with disgust the cot vibrated. Then Kingsley felt something in his back, something that felt like a foot.

That foot pushed, and Kingsley landed hard on the floor right on his ass.

"Oh, no," he said as he hit the hardwood beneath him with bruising force. "I lost the baby."

When he looked up over the edge of the mattress, he found Søren's face buried in the pillow. He'd never seen Søren brought to tears by laughter.

"Don't cry," Kingsley said, rubbing Søren's heaving shoulder. "We'll try again."

Kingsley couldn't hold off coming anymore. Surely enough time would have passed by now. He came inside Phoebe with such force he grunted in near discomfort.

He pulled out of her and grabbed her robe from the floor to wipe himself off.

"Hey, that robe cost a thousand dollars," she said as she stretched out on the bed, naked and happy. One hand teased her own nipples while another slipped between her legs. His semen dripped out of her, leaving a wet stain under her hips. If she didn't care about the silk sheets, he knew she didn't actually care about the robe.

"Now it's a thousand-dollar cum-rag." He tossed it back on the floor as he zipped himself up.

"You're terrible."

"You're welcome," he said, and she lazily sat up. "I hope that was to your liking."

"I like that you laughed."

He grabbed the gun and shoved it in the waistband of his pants again.

"What?"

"I said…" She left the bed and came to him, putting her arms around his neck. "I liked that you laughed while you were fucking me. It made it feel dirtier, like you really were some psycho maniac raping me." She grinned up at him. He should have found her attractive, this thin, graceful beauty who looked twenty-five but had probably said hello and goodbye to thirty-five a long time ago. Once upon a time he found her attractive, but today she repulsed him. He wanted to take her arms off him, but it wouldn't do to upset her. He needed her. More accurately, he needed her husband. Robert Dixon was working his way up. He'd be mayor someday if he continued on his current career trajectory. Kingsley would love to have a mayor in his pocket.

So he smiled at her, played nice and let her kiss him.

"I laughed because I was remembering something."

"What were you remembering?"

"I don't remember," he lied.

She went to a chest of drawers, opened the top drawer and pulled out a leather makeup case. She opened it and laid out two lines of cocaine. She'd probably been on it while he'd fucked her. Would explain why she couldn't shut up now.

"I heard you and Robert went shooting together," Phoebe said.

"I had to discuss something with him."

"Me?" she asked with a saccharine smile.

"Work," Kingsley said. "Just work. Your name didn't come up."

"Good," she said. "Just checking." She handed him the rolled up bill. "Have some. We'll go for round two."

Kingsley tried to look enthusiastic about the prospect of fucking her again. She laid out two more lines for him. He hated coke, hated how much one hit made him want another hit half an hour later. But maybe if he couldn't get it up again for round two, he'd have the drugs to blame.

Phoebe got on her knees in front of him and took his cock in her mouth. He breathed deep and tried to think of the most erotic images he could conjure, anything to get him back in the mood. For some reason all that came to mind were memories of Søren and those stolen nights together when they were teenagers. Luckily that worked, and he felt himself starting to grow hard again.

"Mom?" A small boy's voice called out in the hallway. Phoebe pulled back and exhaled with frustration.

"Give me a minute, Cody. Mommy just got out of the shower."

"I got sick at Tyler's. They brought me home."

"Wait there, baby. Mommy's coming."

Phoebe rolled her eyes.

"He's supposed to be with friends tonight. Sorry," she whispered to Kingsley as she stood to her feet. She started to pick her robe up off the floor but then noticed the semen stain. She grabbed a terry-cloth bathrobe from inside her closet and pulled it tight around her.

"I'll go. It's fine," Kingsley said, relieved to have such an easy out.

"I'll call soon. I promise."

"Take your time," he said, wishing she'd never call him again.

"You're amazing." She gave him a long deep kiss that Kingsley returned with no enthusiasm whatsoever. "The sexiest man on earth. See you soon? Please?"

"Bien sûr."

"I love the French. Rape me in French next time." She kissed him again and pointed at the nightstand. "It's in there. I'll call."

She left him alone in the room. Kingsley waited until the voices disappeared from the hallway. He opened the drawer she'd pointed to, and he found the envelope. He slipped out the door, down the stairs and grabbed a cab. All he wanted to do was take a quick shower, wash Phoebe off him and get back to his blackjack game with Søren.

He raced up the stairs to his front door, his heart pounding as the coke hit his bloodstream.

When he strode through the foyer, he noticed two well-turned ankles shod in a pair of beige pumps resting on the arm of his sofa in his sitting room.

"Blaise?" He peered over the back of the sofa and found a rather euphoric-looking Blaise laying supine and looking sublime. She had a bowl of strawberries balanced on her chest.

"*Bonne soir, monsieur.*" She gave a tired happy laugh and popped a strawberry in her mouth. Her usually perfectly coiffed hair was now mussed, and it appeared she'd gotten undressed and redressed at some point. "I love your house. It's the best house in New York. Have I ever told you that?"

He narrowed his eyes at her.

"Are you stoned?"

She shook her head and giggled. "Nope. This is all afterglow."

"Afterglow?"

"You know what's amazing, King? He didn't even lay a hand on me. But that was easily—" she made a huge sweeping gesture with her arm "—*easily* the best pain I've ever experienced."

"Pain?"

"A little B, a little D and a lot of S&M. I was the M."

"You were the M, were you?"

"It was *amazing*. Your friend is a god of pain."

"Who? Who's a god?"

"Your blond friend. Søren."

Kingsley glared down at her.

"You had sex with Søren while I was gone?"

"No, Silly. I said he hardly touched me. He didn't have to. His soul touched me. His pain touched me."

"You're out of your mind. How did this happen?"

"I don't know." She raised both hands in the air to stretch. "After you left he asked me how I spelled my name. I said like Blaise Pascal, and then he told me about how Blaise Pascal, he was a mathematician who—"

"He hated the Jesuits. Wrote all sorts of slanderous, and therefore *true*, things about them."

"That. Anyway, we were talking, and then I did what you said I should do and I took him up to the playroom—the one with the Francis Bacon painting over the bed—and suddenly I'm getting flogged and whipped, and then I had an orgasm from the pain alone. Then I was down here with my skirt on backward. I raided your fridge. You know kink makes me hungry."

She lifted her bowl of strawberries and offered him one. Kingsley ignored them.

"Do you think you and your friend would tag-team me someday?"

"No. Eat your strawberries. I need to talk to the god."

"Tell him I want to kiss his feet. Again."

"I'll pass that along."

She waved her hand, shooing him from the room.

"Søren?" Kingsley shouted as he ran up the stairs.

"I'm in my room," Søren called back. Kingsley had given him his own guest room to stay in whenever he wished. So far he hadn't slept any nights in it.

"All rooms are my room." Kingsley threw open the door to the guest room. Søren stood on the opposite side of the bed, an open silver suitcase in front of him.

"Very well, then. I'm in *your* room."

"Can I ask you one question?"

"Ask."

"What did you do to Blaise?"

Søren looked up at him.

"I'm not going to answer that."

"Did you fuck her?"

"That's two questions, and no, I didn't. Are you upset we played? She said she's allowed to be with anyone she wants."

"I don't care who she plays with. I want to know why she's lying on my couch in a stupor claiming you gave her the best pain of her life?"

"The best? I'm sure that's an exaggeration, but I'm pleased she enjoyed herself." Søren smiled as he dug through the suitcase of kink toys Kingsley kept under every bed in the house. "I certainly enjoyed her."

"So all that about not breaking your vows was, *quoi*?"

"There was no sex, and I didn't marry her. Nor did I take money from her or refuse to obey a direct order from the pope."

"What about—" Kingsley made a specific hand gesture.

"Well," Søren said. "I did do that, of course."

"Of course."

"But we Jesuits aren't nearly so hard-line or heavy-handed as the Curia when it comes to masturbation. My God, there are at least three puns in that last sentence. Entirely unintentional."

"Stop joking. This is serious."

"It's not serious. Calm down, Kingsley."

"I'm perfectly calm."

"You're speaking in tongues, Kingsley. I heard French and English, and some Spanish mixed in, and you're speaking them all at the same time."

"You're a priest. A Jesuit priest. And I left the house for one hour and come back, and I've got a girl with afterglow on my couch eating strawberries claiming my ex-lover who is now a Catholic priest gave her the best pain of her life. I can't ever leave my house again."

"You know from personal experience it's in the world's best interest I beat someone on a regular basis. I spoke to my confessor, and he gave me leave to deal with this side of myself as long as I don't break any vows. So there."

"So there? No, not there. We're not there yet. You—" Kingsley pointed at Søren. "You're in a good mood all the time. And you talk. And you're...*nice*. Well, nicer." The word *nice* hurt coming out. "You've changed."

"Kingsley—"

"It's the girl, isn't it? The Virgin Queen. I should have known."

Søren eyed him with suspicion. "Kingsley, are you—"

"Give me a second." Kingsley paced the room. His mind reeled. What had happened under his own roof? He reached into his jacket pocket and pulled out tobacco and rolling papers.

"What are you doing?"

"I need a cigarette to calm my nerves. They're frazzled."

"You're not a dowager duchess. You shouldn't have frazzled nerves at twenty-eight," Søren said. "And you shouldn't be smoking, either."

"My house, my rules. It's a smoking house. Everyone has to smoke in my house. I won't quit smoking, and if you stay here you have to start." Kingsley quickly rolled a cigarette and licked the rolling paper to seal it.

"Then I'll go back to the rectory."

Kingsley flicked his lighter, lit his cigarette, took a long drag and glared at Søren.

"How do you give someone the best pain of their life without touching them?"

Kingsley raised the cigarette to his lips again.

He heard a snapping sound, and the cigarette no longer had a flame.

For a long time he looked at his cigarette before slowly turning his head toward Søren who held a bullwhip in his hand. Casually Søren coiled it.

Cigarette lit.

Bullwhip snap.

Cigarette not lit anymore.

He held the stub in his hand split in two.

"Any other questions?" Søren asked with an arrogant lift of his eyebrow.

Kingsley pointed at the whip, pointed at his hand, pointed at Søren...

"Can you teach me to do that?"

"I'll answer your questions if you answer mine."

Søren threw the whip down on the bed and came around to Kingsley. He raised his hands to Kingsley's face and lifted his eyelids.

"What are your questions?" Kingsley asked, trying to blink.

"Why do you smell like a brothel? Why do you have a gun in your pants? And most importantly, what drugs are you on right now?"

9

WHEN IN DOUBT, KINGSLEY FUCKED.

And ever since Søren had caught him taking drugs, he'd been drowning in self-doubt. Now he was drowning in Blaise's body, a vastly superior body to drown in. She'd made the mistake of looking much too attractive today when she stopped by his office to say good morning. But she hadn't complained when he'd slipped his hand under her skirt, and she certainly wasn't complaining now that he had her straddling him in his large leather desk chair.

"You're in a good mood today," Blaise said as she unbuttoned his collar. She dipped her head and kissed his lips, his neck.

"I have you on top of me. Of course I'm in a good mood." He skimmed his fingers down her throat and into the V of her blouse.

"If you were inside me, you'd be in an even better mood."

"Are you sure about that?" Kingsley asked. He slid his hands under her skirt and massaged her soft thighs.

"Only one way to find out, isn't there?" Blaise bit his earlobe and whispered. *"S'il vous plait, monsieur."*

"Since you ask so nicely..."

Blaise laughed as Kingsley stood up without warning and

sat her down hard on the edge of his desk. He hiked her skirt up to her hips, and Blaise tensed.

"Something wrong, *chouchou*?" he asked.

"I love this skirt. Just don't tear it. Please?"

"If I did, I would replace it for you."

"It belonged to Bette Davis."

"You and your outfits…"

Kingsley dragged her off the desk and turned her back to him. Carefully, so as not to tear the vintage fabric, he pulled the tiny zipper down and slid the skirt down her legs. She stepped out of it, and he laid it over the back of his chair.

"Are you wearing anything else that belongs to a dead actress?"

"Everything else on me or in me is fair game."

"Good." Kingsley tore her panties off but left her still wearing her stockings and garters. Then he spanked her hard on her bare bottom, hard enough she yelped. He did love that sound. He swatted her again even harder this time, then snapped her garter against the back of her thigh. Her skin pinked beautifully. But he preferred red, so he spanked her again.

"You're evil," Blaise said as she hung her head and panted in pain. "How do you make a spanking hurt that much?"

"Practice," Kingsley said, and swatted her again. "You know you love it."

"I hate it."

"Are you sure about that?" Kingsley pressed her legs apart and pushed a finger inside her. "This doesn't feel like hate to me."

She was wet inside, very wet, and hot.

"My pussy loves you. Every other part of me hates you right now."

"Every other part?" He brought his arm around her waist and found her swollen clitoris. He kneaded it gently.

"Okay…maybe not every other part," Blaise said breathlessly, her lips parting. She braced herself against his desk while he touched her, one hand inside, one outside. He pushed a third finger into her vagina and opened her up for him. Blaise let out a groan of pleasure that was likely heard by everyone in the entire house. Good. He hadn't bothered to lock his office door. Blaise's inability to stay quiet during sex worked better than any tie on a doorknob.

"Where's my camera when I need it?" Kingsley asked as he pushed deeper into her body until her inner muscles flinched around him. "You make quite a picture right now."

"How's this for a pose?" Blaise parted her legs even more, giving him a better look at all her assets.

"*Très jolie,*" he said with appreciation. "But this would make a better picture."

"What would?"

Kingsley picked her up and sat her on top of his desk. He stripped her of her blouse and bra and pushed her thighs open. She had nothing on now but her stockings, her garters and a pair of high heels. Kingsley admired her body so open and ready for him.

"*Parfait.*"

Kingsley unzipped his pants and stroked himself to his full hardness. He let the wet tip of his cock rub against Blaise's clitoris. She moaned and lifted her hips.

"You're going to make me beg for it, aren't you?" she asked.

"Don't I always?"

"Always," she said. "Please, fuck me."

"Not good enough."

Blaise sighed heavily. "Please, monsieur, fuck me. You're the most beautiful man in New York City and maybe the entire tri-state area."

"That's a new one."

"I love your hair, how soft it is, and your dark eyes. And you have the sexiest hands on any man ever."

"Hands?"

"I like hands," Blaise said. "It's a girl thing."

"Anything else?" he asked.

"Um…I love your accent, and your cock is magnificent, and if you don't put it in me soon I will cry and it'll ruin my makeup and it'll be all your fault, so please fuck me now, right now, this second, or I swear to God I will forget I'm the submissive in this relationship."

Kingsley penetrated her with one hard stroke. Blaise's head fell back, and she lifted her hips off the desk taking him all the way into her. With a jerk of his hips he pulled out and slammed into her again. He grasped her breasts in his hands and squeezed them, lightly pinching her nipples as she writhed beneath him. She was burning up on the inside and wet enough he could hear it as he moved in her. He watched himself fucking her. With the pad of his thumb he rubbed her where their bodies joined. Blaise stiffened with pleasure and grasped the edge of his desk to steady herself. Her skin flushed red, and her nipples hardened. Inside her and all around him she pulsed with her building climax.

He was nothing now but a body. Nothing now but sex. He didn't think, didn't remember, didn't need, didn't doubt himself because he didn't exist—not when he was fucking. He'd fuck constantly if he could. Anything to keep the *memoire* at bay. Anything to keep the world at bay.

With a quick yank of his hands, Kingsley dragged Blaise closer to the edge of the desk. He pushed her thighs back, wider and closer to her chest. When she was as open for him as she could be and he as deep inside her as possible, he ordered her to come for him. She grabbed his wrists and squeezed them to the point of pain the way he liked, and she came hard, her shoulders rising off the desk, her hips moving wildly against him, her voice nothing but a series of sharp desperate breaths. When she was done, Kingsley wrapped his arms around her, pulled up and pressed her chest against his. She kissed him and he kissed back, a desperate hungry kiss between lovers who knew exactly what the other one wanted. He fucked her as he kissed her, fucked her without mercy, and she took every thrust like his good girl should. He had to come, but he didn't want to, not yet. He wanted to stay inside her hot wet hole all day and all night and until he'd died fucking her, and then he'd never have to think or remember or feel anything but the welcoming inside of a woman's body again.

So much pressure...he could barely breathe... His thighs were shaking from the endless thrusting, his cock so sensitive it ached... In his ear Blaise whispered erotic encouragements. *Come inside me, my King...I want it dripping down my thighs all day...as hard as you want...as hard as you can...*

As hard as he could was hard enough that his eyes watered from the force of his own orgasm. He came with a rush, with a fierce deep spasm, and a rush of hot fluid inside her. In the back of his mind somewhere he heard Blaise crying out in what sounded like pain.

Far too quickly he came down from the high of his climax. He rested his head on Blaise's shoulder. She wrapped her arms around him and laughed.

"You're laughing at me?" Kingsley asked, slowly disentangling himself from her arms.

"I am. Look." She raised her shoulder to show the bite mark on it. "You vampire."

"I don't remember doing that. My sincerest apologies." He kissed the wound. He'd broken the skin but only a little.

"Don't apologize. I love it when you give me presents."

He pulled out of her and collapsed into his office chair.

"Your turn to handle cleanup." He waved his hand at her, shooing her off his desk. She hopped off and pulled a box of tissues out of his desk.

"It's always my turn to handle cleanup."

"You're so good at it."

"Well, I can't argue with that." She knelt in front of him and used her tongue to gently lick him. It hurt. It always hurt to be touched after an orgasm. Pleasure and pain all in one act. He wasn't satisfied until he'd had both.

When Blaise finished, she cleaned herself off with the tissues in his desk, got dressed and kissed him goodbye.

"That was fun. Want to go for round two tonight?" she asked.

"Please."

"You'll be sober?"

"No promises."

Blaise rolled her eyes, kissed him again and left him alone in his office. Kingsley finished straightening his clothes and pulling himself back together. And then it happened the way it always happened. Thoughts. Memories. Things he wanted to forget but couldn't all came rushing back into his mind. Life would be so much better if he could keep the blood in his cock and out of his brain all the time.

Kingsley unlocked the bottom drawer of his desk—the large one made to hold files—and took inventory of its contents. Eleven bottles of bourbon, two grams of cocaine, one ounce of marijuana, two bottles of pure codeine, ninety pills—one-hundred milligrams each—and one bottle of ketamine, because sometimes only a tranquilizer made for horses and the magical Wonderland it sent him falling into would do.

He reached for a bottle of the codeine, but his office door opened. Kingsley slammed the drawer shut and sat back in his chair.

"Do you never knock?" Kingsley asked.

"The moaning and groaning had stopped, and the walls have stopped rattling," Søren said. "I assumed the coast was clear."

"Clear for what? What are you doing here?"

"Fulfilling my end of the deal, like I said I would."

"Are you here to yell at me again?" Kingsley asked as Søren walked in.

"I didn't yell," Søren said, taking a seat opposite Kingsley's desk. "At no point did I raise my voice at you."

"It felt like yelling."

"Even the lightest touch can hurt an open wound. You can't blame me for being worried about you."

"Stop worrying. You aren't my father."

"I should hope not," Søren said, furrowing his brow. "If so, my infant self has some explaining to do."

"You aren't my priest, either," Kingsley said, although Søren didn't look like a priest today. He wore his usual off-duty uniform of a long-sleeved black T-shirt and black pants.

"Why, Kingsley, aren't we looking very defensive today."

"Leave me alone."

"I can't do that. You asked me to teach you the whip trick. Here I am."

"I asked you to teach me a whip trick?"

"I can't say I'm surprised you don't remember."

"I remember." Kingsley narrowed his eyes at him. Now that Søren had reminded him about it, he remembered.

"I can go if you've changed your mind," Søren said, standing up.

"No. Sit. Don't go."

Søren looked at him and sat back down.

"I don't do coke very often," Kingsley said. "I was having a bad night. That's all."

"How many bad nights do you have?"

"One or two. Not many," Kingsley said.

"I know I gave you the money with no strings attached. But I never suspected you'd use it for drugs."

"You want the money back?"

"No. I want you to take better care of yourself. That's all."

"Take better care of myself? An interesting statement coming from the man who used to beat me black-and-blue on a regular basis. I see you've found some new whipping boys."

"Whipping girls."

"Only girls these days?" Kingsley asked.

"Only women. I'm less likely to go too far."

"I loved it when you went too far."

"And now," Søren said with a smile, "you know why I don't play with you."

Kingsley lowered his head and rested his chin on his crossed arms.

"Kingsley?"

"What happened to you? You're different," Kingsley said.

"You want to know the truth?"

"I asked."

"Her name is Magdalena."

"Secret girlfriend?"

"She's the madam of a Roman brothel. She and her employees cater to a very specific clientele."

"Masochists?"

"Mostly."

"That's where you've been going to…" Kingsley waved his hand.

"It is."

"Normal men join a gym to work off their extra energy," Kingsley said. "So I've heard."

"I'm not normal men. And don't pretend you are, either."

Kingsley rolled his eyes, waved his hand again. "So she's your friend and…?"

"My first two years of seminary were difficult. I'm not sure I would have made it without Magdalena. I owe her, but she refused to accept any form of remuneration from me."

"I've known a lot of prostitutes. Never heard of one refusing money from a john. Of course, it's you, and I'd pay you money for another—"

"Kingsley, she and I never slept together. We were friends. I learned from her."

"You learned how to knock a cigarette out of someone's mouth with a whip?"

"One of the first skills she taught me, yes," Søren said.

Now Kingsley knew what Søren's "other hobbies" were. He'd learned the art and science of sadism over the past decade. Sounded far more useful to Kingsley than a degree in theology.

"I traveled a great deal while in school," Søren continued, "but when I was in Rome, not a week passed that I didn't find myself at her home."

"She let you hurt her?"

"She did," Søren said. "Although she herself is a sadist. And a very good one."

"How good?"

Søren looked away and smiled at something before looking back at Kingsley.

"She was very mean to me," Søren said.

Kingsley pointed at him. "Good. Someone needs to be. Is the reason for all this…" He waved his hand again.

"This what?"

"Good behavior?"

"I just told you I went to a brothel every week in seminary

to learn sadism from a madam. You have an interesting definition of good behavior."

"When I started at St. Ignatius, everyone was terrified of
you. Everyone. *Tout le monde.* Even the priests were afraid of
you, and they liked you. You didn't even speak to other students. You were this impenetrable blond fortress, and everyone hated you—for good reason. What happened?"

"I grew up," Søren said. "I'm not in high school anymore.
That does wonders for a person."

"I don't like it," Kingsley said.

"You don't like me?"

"No. Yes. I don't know," Kingsley admitted. "When we
were in school, we were all like scared puppies, and you, you
were a wolf. I don't like seeing you…"

"What?"

"Domesticated. They even put a collar on you."

"I put on my own collar."

"You used to scare me."

"Have you considered the possibility that the reason I don't
scare you now is that you aren't a puppy anymore?"

Søren waited.

Kingsley looked at Søren and barked. Søren only looked at
him. Maybe he should try a bite next time.

"If it makes you feel any better," Søren said, "the wolf is
still there, but he's on a stronger leash."

"You let the wolf off the leash with me."

"Which is why I needed a stronger leash."

"I don't know if I want to pay this Magdalena person for
making you boring."

"What she did was make me take myself less seriously,
which is, as you know, the first of three miracles she'll need
to qualify for sainthood."

"I envy her," Kingsley said. "She had you in her life. I never thought I'd see you again."

"We wouldn't be having this conversation if it wasn't for her," Søren said. "I wouldn't have been able to face you without her help."

"Then I suppose I owe her, too. Even if you do yell at me."

"I don't yell."

"What's her address?" Kingsley asked.

"Why?"

"I'll send her a check. If she's the reason you're here right now, then I owe her and you both."

Søren sighed, picked up a pen and a scrap of paper off Kingsley's desk and wrote the address. He held it out, and Kingsley reached for it. Søren pulled it back out of his grasp.

"I know what you're doing," Søren said.

"What am I doing?"

Søren glanced to the right and looked pointedly at Kingsley's filing cabinets.

"Blaise has a big mouth," Kingsley said. "One of her better qualities. Usually."

"Here," Søren said and gave Kingsley the address. "You should visit her. She could help you like she helped me."

"I'm fine," Kingsley said. "You act like I'm falling apart."

"You were shot last year and almost died."

Kingsley shrugged. "Worked out well for me, didn't it? Someone came to my death bed and left me an 'I'm sorry' gift."

"It wasn't a gift. And it wasn't an apology. It was a payment."

"Payment? For what?"

Søren reached into the pocket of his trousers and pulled out a tiny clear plastic tube. He sat it on Kingsley's desk.

"What is this?" Kingsley asked as he picked up the small tube. A few flecks of metal danced in the afternoon sunlight.

"If you were a cat, that would be one of your lives."

"This is my bullet?" Kingsley asked in shock.

"What's left of it."

"Why do you have it?"

"I wanted it," Søren said. "I took it. I paid you for it. So now you don't owe me anything."

"They gave it to you in the hospital?"

"I asked for it."

Kingsley spun the tube, pretending to study the shrapnel. In truth, he couldn't care less what it looked like. All that mattered was that Søren had kept it. Why? Was it a talisman? A memento? A reminder of the last time they'd seen each other? Kingsley thought about reaching into his pocket. In it was a small silver cross on a broken silver chain—the one memento he'd keep from his first night with Søren. The cross and the memories.

"You kept this? All this time you've had my bullet with you?" Kingsley asked.

"I have. If you want it back, you'll have to pay for it."

"I will never understand you," Kingsley said.

"Then stop trying." He held out his hand, and Kingsley dropped the tube with the bullet fragments into his palm. He liked the idea of Søren having this piece of himself in his possession. Was there an object in the world more intimate to a victim than the weapon that had nearly killed him? These bullet fragments had been inside Kingsley's body and had almost destroyed him. Instead of ending his life, that shot had changed his life. No wonder Søren felt such a kinship to those deadly remnants. They had much in common.

Søren pocketed the tube that held Kingsley's bullet fragment.

"Are you ready?" Søren asked.

"Yes. For what?"

At that Søren smiled—a devilish sexy smile that made Kingsley completely forget for a moment that it was a Catholic priest who sat in his office and not the Søren of old who had used him as a human target on a regular basis.

He lifted his hand, crooked a finger at Kingsley.

"Now?" Kingsley asked.

"You had plans?" Søren asked. "My free time is limited, as you know."

"Hosting an exorcism tonight?" Kingsley asked.

"Worse. Couples' counseling."

"Same thing," Kingsley said. "It's all your fault. No one told you to get a real job."

Kingsley stood up and came around the desk.

"I like my job," Søren said as he followed Kingsley from the office. "You should think about getting one, too. You'll be surprised how enjoyable it is to be useful to society."

"You know what else is enjoyable?"

"What?"

"Not having a job."

Kingsley led Søren to his personal playroom.

"This is my real office," Kingsley said, opening the door. He had a St. Andrew's Cross, a rack, an X-bar, several spreader bars, all the bondage cuffs and equipment one man could ever need.

"Like it?"

"It'll do," Søren said, although Kingsley could see Søren eying everything with interest.

Every one of the bedrooms in the house had kink equipment in it. Vanilla sorts were not welcome in his home. And on the rare occasion they did infiltrate the town house, they were not vanilla after they left.

"How often do you play?" Kingsley asked.

"Whenever I can," Søren said. "When it's safe. If I go longer than a month, I get... What's the word I'm looking for?"

"Lethal?"

"Unpleasant. You?"

"As often as I can. Once a day at least."

"Once a day? Who's the lucky recipient of that honor?"

"Trust me, you don't have time for the list of people I play with. I've probably fucked every submissive in Manhattan. I may have to move to Brooklyn."

"Only submissives?"

"Only submissives."

"That's unusual for you, isn't it?" Søren crossed his arms over his chest and looked at Kingsley.

"Why? Because I bottomed for you, I have to do it for the rest of the world?"

"Not the rest of the world. One person at least. I remember."

"What do you remember?"

"How much you needed it, wanted it."

"I needed you, not it."

"You loved submitting to pain. Why the change?"

"I don't bottom anymore. *Fin*," Kingsley said. "The end."

Søren studied Kingsley's face as if looking at an alien specimen.

"Are you going to teach me the whip trick or not?" Kingsley demanded.

"I will, but this conversation isn't over yet, whether you *fin*-ed it or not."

"Show me the trick."

"There's no trick to it," Søren said as he scanned the rows of single-tails on the wall. He took one down, pulled it taut, coiled it again and hung it back on the wall. A second single-tail whip proved more to his liking. "It takes a great deal of practice. And I'm not the teacher Magdalena is. She could have you flipping quarters in midair with a single-tail in two weeks."

"Then why isn't she teaching me?"

"She's in Rome. Have you used a whip before?"

"On the back—large target."

"Then you'll need to practice on a smaller target. Not a person." Søren had one of Kingsley's business cards in his hand. He stabbed it over a hook on the wall.

"You want me to hit that?" Kingsley asked. "A business card?"

Søren put his hand on the center of Kingsley's chest and pushed him back…back…back until he was against the wall.

"No," Søren said. "I'm going to hit it. You're going to watch. From a safe distance."

Søren stepped away, coiled the whip, put his right foot before his left foot and then released the whip with a quick snap. With the tip of the whip, Søren cut the business card neatly in half.

Kingsley applauded as he walked up to the card. The cut sliced the card right down the middle between the word *Edge* and *Enterprises*.

"Such a good trick," he said, impressed.

"Whips are multipurpose," Søren said. "Good for pain. Good for bondage."

"Bondage?" Kingsley asked, reaching for the card.

Søren lightly flung the whip at him. It wrapped around Kingsley's wrist. He laughed even as it tightened, and Søren tugged on it, pulling him closer.

"Nice," Kingsley said, his breath quickening. "What else?"

"Wrists," Søren said, taking Kingsley's other wrist and wrapping the supple leather whip around his hands. "Ankles even. The neck, too, but you have to be careful. Do you want to see Magdalena's favorite trick?"

"Show me."

Søren had left an eight-inch length of whip between Kingsley's right wrist and left wrist. He spun Kingsley around quickly and pulled his back to Søren's chest, bringing the whip hard against Kingsley's throat.

The world fell out from under Kingsley.

He blinked, and the walls turned to black, the temperature dropped and when he breathed in he smelled sulfur.

He dropped to his knees and yanked at the chain around his neck. If he could get his fingers between the chain and his throat he had a chance. The air went out of the room. He could hear nothing, see nothing. But he could feel, and what he felt was a wet-hole cavern in his chest, bone shattering and a lung collapsing.

No air. None. No matter how he gasped, how he gulped, how he fought, he could get no air.

Someone spoke…Slovakian? Ukrainian? He couldn't tell. The voice was too far away…and it didn't matter.

He was dying.

He was dying.

A bullet in his chest. A chain around his neck.

He was dead.

"Kingsley."

He heard his name but didn't respond. Dead men don't scream.

"Kingsley, you're in Manhattan. You're home."

He wasn't home. He was bleeding to death on a shit-stained basement floor in Ljubljana.

"You're alive."

No, he wasn't.

"Open your eyes. Can you hear me?"

He heard something in his ears. A popping. It startled him. He jumped. His eyes flew open. The world was a haze. But he did see something, a gray light.

"You have to breathe."

He heard something other than the voice. A deep loud gasping wheeze. Over and over again.

Kingsley felt something on his back, a hand hitting him hard. It should have scared him, but instead the pain and the rhythm brought him back to himself.

"Kingsley, talk to me," the voice ordered. It was Søren. His voice. His hand.

"I'm fine," Kingsley said.

"Stop lying to me. You aren't fine."

Kingsley looked down. He sat on the floor of his playroom, his back to the wall. His shirt was sticky with sweat and his throat raw from wheezing.

"I'm fine," he said again.

"Was that a panic attack?" Søren asked, crouching in front of him. "Or a flashback?"

"It was nothing." Kingsley's body was tense. His hands shook. "I think I spaced out for a second."

"Two minutes," Søren said. "Not one second."

Kingsley tried to stand, but Søren put his hand on Kingsley's shoulder and held him in place.

"Stay down. Look at me."

"I don't want to look at you," Kingsley said.

"I don't care. Look at me." Søren took Kingsley by the chin, forcing the eye contact. "Tell me where you were."

"Slovenia."

"Why?"

"I was shot there."

"Is that all that happened?"

"I think so."

He glanced away. It hurt to be looked at like this, with such concern and pity. That wasn't how he wanted Søren to look at him. He wanted Søren to look at him with lust and desire and want and hunger.

He tried to stand up again, but Søren still wouldn't let him.

"I touched your throat with the whip, and you started wheezing like you were actually choking," Søren said. "You fell to your knees and wouldn't speak."

"I'm fine," Kingsley said for the third and final time.

Søren sighed and pushed a damp lock of hair off Kingsley's forehead.

"I didn't mean to scare you," Søren said, his tone almost, but not quite, apologetic.

"You didn't scare me. I'm not scared." His racing heart, his churning stomach made a liar of him.

"Well, this answers my question."

"What question?" Kingsley asked, dropping his head. He didn't want to look in Søren's eyes. He saw fear in them, not of Kingsley but for Kingsley. And something told him Søren wouldn't be touching him again for a very long time.

If ever.

"Now I know why you don't let anyone hurt you anymore."

Kingsley looked up at Søren from the floor.

"Get out of my house," Kingsley said.

"Kingsley?"

"You said I don't owe you anything. Get the fuck out of my house."

Søren got the fuck out.

10

SEVEN DAYS AND SEVEN NIGHTS PASSED, AND SØREN didn't come back to Kingsley's house. He didn't call, didn't write, didn't visit and didn't once tell Kingsley he needed to get help. He was gone, gone, gone, and that was fine, fine, fine with Kingsley.

Except it wasn't. Because Søren had promised never to leave him again. And he had.

Promises, promises.

Kingsley took another swig from the bottle of bourbon, coughed a little, and laid back on the chaise longue. He crossed his feet at the ankles and watched the light from the swimming pool dance across the ceiling. He had no idea why he still had the pool down here. No one ever swam in it. He kept the doors locked to prevent any of his inebriated houseguests from turning up facedown in it by accident. A bad sign when the only person who got anything out of the swimming pool was the pool boy. And even he wasn't attractive enough for Kingsley to bother seducing.

But tonight he wanted to lie by the water while he drank. It was peaceful here. The pool wasn't large or deep—ten by twenty feet across and four feet to the bottom. The floor was Mediterranean tile, and red, yellow and gold murals of northern Italy covered the walls. The paintings reminded him of a little village in the south of France he and his family had gone to every August when he was a child. A village right on the Mediterranean. Beautiful place, restful. Water, hills, vineyards. A vintner's wife had seduced him there when he was twenty-two and hiding out while he recovered from his first gunshot wound. He had nothing but fond memories of the place. Being near water soothed his soul. If he had a soul. Did he have one? Didn't matter if he did or not. He and God weren't on speaking terms right now. And that was fine. Kingsley didn't mind. What did he and God have to talk about anyway? The only thing he wanted to ask God was why He'd called Søren to the priesthood. Could God have played a sicker joke on him?

"Knock, knock?"

Kingsley sighed. Blaise's gentle voice came from the door. He waved his arm tiredly at her, beckoning her in.

"He's not here," Kingsley said.

"I wasn't looking for him, I promise," Blaise said.

"Are you swimming?"

"And mess up my hair?" She tossed her honey-blond hair over her shoulder. "No, I'm checking on you."

Blaise crawled up on the chaise longue next to him. Kingsley looked her up and down as she settled in next to him.

"You've outdone yourself with this ensemble," he said. "You look like… What's her name? That pretty blonde actress. The dead one with the hair. River? Ocean? Pool?"

"Veronica Lake. And that's what I was going for. See?" She held up her leg to display her seamed stockings that disappeared under her pencil skirt. She had her hair coiffed in a forties peekaboo style.

"Why do you dress like this?" he asked. Every day she wore some new vintage outfit that put one in mind of old Hollywood.

"The world is sadly lacking in glamour. I want to be part of the solution, not part of the problem. And not all of us are as naturally gorgeous and eye-catching as you are, King," she said, tapping the end of his nose. "Some of us have to work for it."

"You like the attention. You're the girl in the room who dresses like she forgot what decade she's in."

"I'm trying to forget what decade I'm in. The nineties need to shape up fast. You know what people are wearing now? On purpose? Flannel. I saw it on MTV."

"I shudder."

"Me, too. Awful. There is nothing glamorous about flannel."

"You don't dress like this to be glamorous. You dress to be remembered."

"So? What's wrong with being memorable? Even if someone forgets my name, they still remember the girl in the seamed stockings."

"Nothing's wrong with being memorable. Except when someone's trying to forget you."

Blaise sighed and laid her head on his chest.

"I knew you were in a funk," she said. "You always get like this when you drink."

"I drink all the time."

"You're in a funk all the time. I thought it would get better when your friend turned up. Where is Søren anyway?"

"I pissed him off. He left."

"Well, un-piss him off. I like him."

"The last thing we need is a priest hanging around this house."

Blaise's mouth fell open.

"He's really a priest? That wasn't a joke?"

"I wish."

Blaise laughed so hard the chaise longue shook.

"I can't believe I did kink with a priest. I can't wait to tell—"

Faster than either of them expected, Kingsley rolled up, grabbed Blaise and put her flat on her back underneath him. He grasped both her wrists and slammed them down by her head.

"King—"

"Shut up. I mean it." He tightened his grip on her to the point of pain and stayed there. "Not a word to anyone that you did anything with a priest. Do you understand me?"

Blaise looked up at him in fear—real fear.

"Fuck, fine. I won't tell anyone."

"You've never seen me this serious before, have you?"

Blaise shook her head. "No."

"There's a reason for that. You will tell no one."

"Okay," she whispered. "I swear."

Kingsley held her down another few seconds, long enough to make her nervous and long enough to get him aroused.

"Good girl." He bent his head and kissed her before letting her go.

He rolled on to his back again, crossed his legs at his ankles again, watched the light dance again.

Blaise sat up and looked down at him.

"You scared the shit out of me." She put her hand over her heart.

"Good."

"For someone who says he doesn't like Søren, you're awfully protective of him."

"Love him or hate, he's one of us. We take care of our own."

"I can't get him in trouble, you know. I only know his first name."

"Actually, you don't." Kingsley laughed to himself. Søren had introduced himself as "Søren" to Blaise, not Marcus Stearns. There was no "Søren" on anyone's records anywhere. If she tried to find a Catholic priest in the United States named Søren, she'd be searching forever. So that's why Søren told her his real name? That fucking brilliant blond monster. Now it all made sense.

"He told me his name, remember?" She rolled her eyes. "Jesus, how much have you had to drink?"

"Enough to put me in the mood, but not enough to ruin it. Now I'm going to get very drunk so you should go unless you want to make yourself useful."

"Maybe I want to make myself useful," she said, lifting up his shirt. She pressed her lips into his stomach, and the soft curling tips of her hair tickled his skin. Yes. This. Right now he needed this. Distraction. Desire. Anything to keep from remembering. "I like it when you scare me like that."

"And that," he said, caressing her cheek, "is why you are my *chouchou*."

She kissed lower, deeper, and with one hand she unbuttoned and unzipped his jeans. He wasn't hard yet, but if she kept doing what she was doing, he would be any second now. She took him in her hand and massaged him lightly. When he stiffened, she bent her head and licked the tip. For a few minutes it was all she did, kissing, licking, teasing, focusing all her attention on that one part of him. Blood rushed through him, and he grew hard in her hand. He sighed softly as she stroked him before bringing her mouth down on to him.

Perfect… Her mouth was so wet and warm. She rubbed him with her talented tongue and sucked hard. The pressure built in him, and he lifted his hips into her mouth, small undulations that set every nerve inside him alight. He wove his fingers into her hair, seeking connection with the woman who did this erotic kindness to him.

She paused and used her hand on him, rubbing the shaft from base to tip, squeezing and stoking him to greater pleasure.

"I love your cock," she whispered before lapping at the wet tip. "I love how big it is. I love how it tastes."

"You're too kind. Keep it up, *chouchou*, and I'll give you the honor of swallowing."

Blaise grinned seductively at him. "You keep it up, and I'll keep it up." She gave him a dirty wink before resuming her task. She sucked even harder now, deeper, and he grew painfully hard. She swirled her tongue around him, up and down, over and over. With her gentle fingertips she eased his foreskin back and lapped at the tip so skillfully his back arched in the shock of pleasure.

A deep muscle tightened in his lower stomach. He felt blood pooling, pressure building. His heart raced, and his fingers dug into the fabric of the chaise lounge. For a few more seconds he held off, trying to prolong the release, wanting to put off as long as possible the return to bitter reality. Blaise sucked him, stroked him, coaxed him, pulled him to the depths of her throat. He hovered at the edge of orgasm, breathing through his nose as Blaise continued to work on him, taking ownership of him with her mouth. She took him deep and massaged his testicles with her tongue. She pulled back to the tip again, and Kingsley came hard into her mouth, spasm after spasm of pleasure washing over him as he spurted his semen into her welcoming throat.

Like the good girl she was, Blaise swallowed every drop of him before releasing him from her mouth. She kissed her way up to his lips, and he tasted himself on her tongue.

"Are you in a good mood now?" she asked, wiping her mouth with one of the towels stacked next to them.

"Better," Kingsley said. "For now."

Blaise groaned in frustration.

"You are the king of top drop."

"You're making up words again."

"Top drop. It's that funk dominants fall into after the scene's over. You brood."

"Brooding is my version of afterglow."

"Call the priest. You're in a better mood when he's around. He doesn't brood like you do."

"He invented brooding. He holds the patent on brooding. He gets royalties whenever anyone broods. You just haven't seen him do it yet."

"Call him," Blaise said, poking him in the chest.

"I don't want to. I don't like him anymore."

Blaise exhaled and shook her head in abject disgust.

"You lying French asshole. You called him your 'oldest and dearest friend' right in front of me. I was there."

"I was being sarcastic."

"Then what is he?" Blaise asked, annoyed. He did love to ruffle her glamorous feathers.

"My dead sister's widowed husband."

Blaise's eyes widened hugely.

"I didn't know you had a sister."

"I don't anymore. Told you, she's dead. He was married to her for a few weeks before she flung herself off a cliff, and her body broke into two pieces. Sheered her face off, too."

"Oh, Jesus." Blaise clapped a hand over her mouth as if she were about to be sick.

Kingsley picked up his bottle of bourbon.

"Doesn't matter," he said. "It was a long time ago."

"Kingsley…I had no idea."

"And now you know why I drink."

He took a sip, then a second one.

"I hoped it was because you loved the taste of bourbon."
She tried to smile at him, tried and failed.

"Love it? I hate this shit."

Blaise leaned over and kissed him again—not on the mouth but on his forehead like a mother kissing her child.

"I'm sorry," she whispered before slipping off the chaise and leaving him alone by the pool. A gentle and sensitive soul, she'd probably run off to cry somewhere. Good thing she left. Last thing he wanted to see was a woman in tears. He'd seen more than enough of that in his life.

Alone again with his bourbon he drank. He drank until he felt safe enough to sleep. The alcohol never turned off the nightmares, but it did mute them. Tonight, however, he hadn't drunk quite enough to achieve the desired effect. This time he was back in the hospital, his mind alive and active, his body motionless, inert, dying. If he could get a word out, then maybe someone would realize he was aware inside the tomb his body had become.

All he wanted to do was scream.

In his nightmare, his mind screamed, and his mouth remained mute.

He woke up covered in water.

Water?

11

KINGSLEY COUGHED AND SPUTTERED. HIS EYES FI-
nally flew open as water rose and thrashed all around him.

"What the fuck?" He wasn't sure if he spoke in English or French, wasn't sure he even spoke out loud.

"Kingsley. Look at me."

"Non."

"Kingsley. Right now. Do as I say."

"I don't take orders from you anymore." Kingsley sank down into the water before a strong hand hauled him back up.

Søren gripped his neck hard enough to penetrate the shield his body had become.

"What do you want?" Kingsley's eyes fluttered open again. He saw Søren waist-deep in the water. Søren grabbed Kingsley by the shirt and backed against the edge of the pool.

"I want you to live."

"That makes one of us." Kingsley tried to pass out again, but Søren shook him awake once more.

"Are you hearing anything I'm saying?"

"I hear you." Finally Kingsley had the strength to open his eyes and keep them open. He saw Søren again, saw his face. He looked angry and scared, almost human. He had his clerics on again, his white collar. "Why are you wearing that?"

"I'm a priest, remember? How many brain cells did you kill tonight?"

"Not enough of them."

A wave of nausea passed through him. He coughed again, and Søren hauled him up and over the edge of the pool. Into a large white towel, Kingsley threw up.

"Get it all out," Søren said calmly. Kingsley felt a hand on his back, rubbing the heaving muscles. He wasn't drunk enough to be sick from the alcohol. The dream had done it to him.

Kingsley's body complied with the order. For what felt like eternity, he threw up again and again. Søren held his hair back, rubbed his shoulders, offered encouragements that Kingsley could barely hear over the sound of his own wrenching sickness.

Finally Kingsley stopped. He knew better than to move, lest he get sick again. He shivered and took shallow breaths.

"You threw me in the pool?" Kingsley asked when the nausea finally passed.

"You were screaming and thrashing. I couldn't get you to wake up."

"Bad dream," Kingsley whispered. "I have them sometimes."

Kingsley pulled away from Søren and sat on the steps that led into the pool. He closed his eyes and tried to focus on the water that surrounded him. Water. Only water. It wouldn't hurt him. Nothing here would hurt him. Not even Søren. Not anymore.

"Why were you drinking tonight?" Søren asked, standing in front of him. He didn't seem to mind that he was fully dressed in his clerics and soaked to the skin. If Kingsley passed out and fell forward, Søren's chest would break his fall.

"Same reason I drink every night."

"Which is?"

"It helps me sleep."

"A sleeping pill would help you sleep. Tell me the truth."

Kingsley raked his fingers through his wet hair, slicking it back. He breathed into his hands before looking at Søren with a half smile.

"You don't want to know." He shook his head. "You think you do, but you don't."

"I know I don't want to know," Søren said. "But you need to tell me."

"Why do you care?"

"Because I care."

"That's a tautology. You like the word? I remember philosophy class at St. Ignatius." Kingsley released a weary, mirthless laugh.

"I care about you, because I care about you is a fact."

"You don't give a shit about me. I took her back to France alone."

"I offered to go with you, and you said no. You didn't want me with you."

"You let me go, and you forgot all about me."

"I never forgot about you."

"You did. You let me go to France and you forgot—"

"I never forgot you." Søren shouted the words. They echoed off the tile floor, off the walls, and slammed into Kingsley like a fist, sobering him up instantly. He'd never heard Søren raise his voice like that. Ever.

Kingsley smiled tiredly.

"Now you are yelling at me."

"You want me to yell at you? Fine. I will yell at you, Kingsley. Maybe if I yell, you'll finally hear me. I never left you. And when you went back to France, I tried to find you."

"You tried to find me?" Kingsley's eyes slowly focused on Søren's face. "When?"

"I waited for you to come back to school. When you didn't, I went to find you. I left two days after the semester ended. I didn't even tell my own sisters I was leaving the country. I packed, ran one very important errand and left for Europe. I went to Paris, Lyon, Marseilles—every city you ever told me you'd visited in France. I went to your old neighborhood. I found your father's former business partner. I hunted down every single fucking Boissonneault in France."

Kingsley blinked. Søren said "fucking"? He must be furious.

"You looked for me?" Kingsley repeated, not quite able to believe Søren's words.

"I looked everywhere for you. I looked for you before I even looked for my own mother whom I hadn't seen since I was five years old."

"You looked for me," Kingsley said again. This time it wasn't a question.

"And I didn't find you."

"Why didn't you tell me you looked for me?" Kingsley asked.

"What does it matter?" Søren was quiet now, but his voice still resonated. "I didn't find you."

"It doesn't matter that you didn't find me." Kingsley shook his head. "It matters that you looked."

"After six weeks of searching in five different countries, I gave up," Søren said. "I assumed you were hiding because you'd didn't want me to find you. I took it as a sign from God that I was supposed to become a priest like I'd dreamed of since I was fourteen. My last and final prayer to God the night before I entered seminary in Rome was, 'God, if this is not your will for me to become a priest, then let me find him tonight.' I didn't find you. I became a priest. And you..."

"I joined *La Legion*."

"I never considered you the military type. Although in retrospect, I should have. You were certainly good at taking orders."

"My commanding officers had nothing on you. You should have been in the army."

"And follow in my father's footsteps? No, thank you." Søren's voice was cold and bitter. "Why *did* you join the military?"

"I don't know. Maybe it was the next best thing to suicide." Kingsley laughed, although he wasn't joking. "Anyway, it was good not to have to think for myself for a while. I needed that."

"Believe it or not, I understand," Søren said. "The discipline of a religious order has the same comfort of routine. My own thoughts scared me after everything happened, after you were gone. It was better to let someone else direct my existence for a few years."

"I was too good at taking orders. And too good at hitting targets. And too good at speaking English without an accent. Someone in the government thought I'd be more useful working in a less official capacity."

"What did you do?" Søren's voice was even and calm, but Kingsley heard the smallest note of suspicion hiding under the surface of the words.

"Everything they ordered me to. I hunted who they told me to hunt. Spied on who they told me to spy on. Killed who they told me to kill. And then someone caught me. I was a prisoner for a month. See? I still have scars from the shackles."

He held up his wrists. Two matching swaths of scar tissue marred the skin on the sides of his wrists. They rubbed against the bone, the shackles had. Like a trapped wolf, he'd wanted to gnaw off his own hands.

"I was a prisoner," he continued. "I was tortured. And..."

"And what?" Søren's voice was gentle now, probing, but not demanding.

"It wasn't just torture."

He gazed up at Søren and met his eyes for one second before lowering them again in humiliation.

"Oh, God, Kingsley."

"I was unconscious," Kingsley said. "I guess you'd call it a blessing that I don't remember it happening. I only remember waking up and knowing it had happened."

"Kingsley..."

Kingsley raised his hands to his face, pressed his palms against his eyes. He couldn't bear to hear the pity and the sorrow in Søren's voice.

"It's funny." Kingsley's eyes burned. He wanted to blame the chlorine. "I loved Lawrence of Arabia as a boy. He was my hero. I read all the books I could about him. Now I can say Lawrence of Arabia and I have something in common."

"Two things in common."

"Two?"

"T. E. Lawrence loved a good flogging."

Kingsley opened his eyes but couldn't look at Søren.

"Is he dead?" Søren asked as Kingsley watched the water. "The man who hurt you?"

"Very dead," Kingsley said.

"Good."

"Good? Aren't you supposed to love your enemies?"

"Put me alone in a room with him, and I could conveniently forget that command."

"He's in hell now," Kingsley said. "Then again, so am I."

Søren took a long deep breath. Meanwhile Kingsley considered falling asleep. Falling asleep and never waking up. The dead don't dream.

"Can I touch you?" Søren finally asked.

"Toujours," Kingsley said, laughing again. Always.

Søren reached out and cupped the side of his face. Water ran down Kingsley's cheek. He hoped it was water from the pool and nothing more.

"It shouldn't have happened to you. You didn't deserve it."

Kingsley smiled. "You're good at this. They should make you pope."

"A Jesuit pope? It'll never happen."

Kingsley closed his eyes again, cupped water into his mouth and spit it out. He couldn't remember when he'd been this tired, and yet he never wanted to sleep again.

"There's something I never told you," Søren said. "Something I wanted to tell you, but never found the words or the reason to tell you."

Kingsley opened his eyes.

"What?" he asked.

"The semester before you started St. Ignatius, a visiting priest came to teach church history. I was in his class. He was a young priest, thirty-five. Charming, Irish, handsome. He taught me Gaelic in his free time."

Søren fell silent. Kingsley let the silence stand.

"Three weeks before Christmas we were alone in his office working on a translation of the *Fiannaidheacht*. In the middle of a sentence, Father Sean simply stopped talking. And he shut the door to his office and locked it. He knelt in front of me on the floor and begged me in the most hushed and desperate whispers to take him. He said 'Anything… You can do anything to me, Marcus. Anything you want. Anything at all.' He tried to touch me."

Kingsley had no words. His mouth was dry, and he couldn't swallow.

"I was almost seventeen then. It was growing more difficult all the time to control myself. I ran miles every day, worked myself into exhaustion, cut myself in secret trying to cool the fever in my blood. And I could have had everything I wanted right then and there with Father Sean. I could see in his eyes he would have let me destroy him right there on his office floor."

"What did you do?"

"I told him to stop touching me or I would kill him. It shames me to admit I meant it. If he touched me again, I would have killed him. I told him to stand up. I told him to find an excuse, any excuse to leave St. Ignatius, because if he returned next semester, I would tell Father Henry he'd tried propositioning a student for sex."

"You wanted him?"

"I wanted to hurt him."

"Why didn't you?"

"I didn't love him," Søren said.

"You hurt me. The next semester you—"

"I loved you."

"Well…" Kingsley said. "Now you tell me."

Kingsley met Søren's eyes. It was past tense, the word he'd used. *Loved*, not *love*. But it was enough. Tonight it was enough.

"Here's my confession," Kingsley said. "I fuck for money."

Søren looked at him in shock and dismay.

"Why?" he breathed. "You have all the money in the world."

"It's not the money. It's the paper trail. Makes it easier to blackmail people if I have the paper trail. That's where I was going when I left you alone with Blaise. A DA's wife. The DA I paid off to get your Virgin Queen her 'Get Out of Jail' card."

Søren didn't say anything at first. The silence was the purest hell.

"How much do you charge?" Søren finally asked.

"Why? You want to buy an hour with me? I'll give you the friends-and-family discount."

"I want to know what price you put on something I considered priceless."

"Sex isn't priceless."

"It was with you."

Kingsley's stomach cramped from guilt and sorrow. Søren laid a hand on the top of Kingsley's head.

"I absolve you," Søren whispered.

"I've killed people."

"I absolve you."

"I've fucked half of Manhattan and three-fourths of Europe."

"I absolve you."

"Absolve me? I'm not Catholic."

"I absolve you of that, too."

Kingsley laughed once more, a real laugh this time. Søren laughed with him. Then the laugh died, and the room was silent once more, silent but for the slight sloshing of the water against the side of the pool whenever Kingsley moved. Søren stepped even closer. Kingsley rested his forehead on Søren's chest, too tired to hold it up any longer.

"You have to stop punishing yourself," Søren said, cupping the back of Kingsley's head. "Judgment is for God alone. You're committing slow suicide with the way you're living. That is a sin I cannot absolve you of."

"I'm so tired," Kingsley confessed, ashamed to admit even this one small weakness. "The nightmares make me afraid to sleep. No matter how tired I am, I don't want to sleep. But if I have someone in bed with me, I sleep better. They expect me to fuck them first. Can't disappoint them, can I?"

"Are you at least being careful?"

"Not very often."

"Kingsley, you have to be."

"I'm getting a condom lecture from a priest."

"You'll get more than that if you're not careful. And you have to stop taking drugs. And you can't drink like this."

"I'm a *bon vivant*."

"You're the most miserable *bon vivant* I've ever met. Drinking is for celebrating, not for suicide."

"I have nothing to celebrate."

"I do. Celebrate with me."

"What are you celebrating?"

"For years I had no idea where you were, what you were doing, how you were living. And then you were shot and in the hospital and dying. And that's why they contacted me. That's how I found you. Now here you are, right in front of me. God brought me back to you, brought you back to me. I haven't stopped celebrating from that night I first stepped in this house and saw you again."

"You were angry at me."

"It breaks my heart to see you like this."

"I don't believe that. I don't believe you have a heart."

Søren pressed his hand to the side of Kingsley's face and with his thumb stroked the arch of his cheekbone. A gentle touch, a loving touch. He would have preferred a slap. It would hurt less.

"Do you remember all those notes you hid inside my Bible?" Søren asked.

"I wrote them in French so no one could read them."

"I still have them. They're still inside my Bible. I think the Kingsley I remember is still here."

"You kept my notes?" Kingsley asked. It was the last thing he expected to hear. The notes, the remnants of his bullet... What other pieces of Kingsley did Søren still have in his possession? Other than his heart?

"All of them."

"Why? You aren't in love with me anymore."

"I treasure the memory of what we had. And I pray we can have something even better, deeper now."

"What?"

"Friendship. A real friendship."

"You're never going to fuck me again, are you?"

"Could you be faithful to me if I did?"

"Is that a serious question?" Kingsley asked.

"Let's say it is. Let's say I would break my vows with you. Let's say I'd even consider leaving the priesthood for you. Could you be faithful to me?"

"Just you and I?"

"You. Me. Eleanor. The three of us, like we dreamed of that day."

"You aren't serious."

"Pretend that I am," Søren said with unbroken eye contact. And for a split second Kingsley almost believed him. "This will be the one time I make you this offer. You. Me. Eleanor. The three of us. Forever."

"Forever?"

"Eleanor agreed to forever. Can you?"

Kingsley closed his eyes. He could have Søren and the girl they dreamed of. And what? No one else? Ever? Forever was such a long time. And he'd been free of Søren for eleven years now. Only Søren? Only this girl he'd never met?

"I take it back," Kingsley said. "You're still a wolf."

Søren grabbed a towel off the stack by the steps. He took a corner of it and dried Kingsley's face. If Kingsley could fall asleep right here, right now, when Søren was taking care of him, he could fall asleep and never wake up. If he died now, maybe he could die almost happy.

"Can you remember…" Søren began as he squeezed water

from Kingsley's hair. "Was there ever a time when you felt like you were doing what God put you on this earth to do?"

"Once."

"When?"

"When we were lovers."

"Kingsley, be serious."

"I mean it. You were so alone," Kingsley said. "I've never met anyone more alone than you were back then. Everyone was afraid of you. No one ever talked to you. They treated you like a leper. You wanted them to."

"You didn't."

"I was scared. But I loved you more than I feared you. I had to know you. And that night in the hallway when you said you wondered why God had made you the way you are, you wondered what the reason was…"

"Je suis la raison," Søren repeated. "That's what you said to me."

"I am the reason," Kingsley whispered.

Søren nodded.

"That was it," Kingsley said. "That night I felt like God put me on earth to show you why he created you like He did. You needed me as much as I needed you."

"I did. Until you, I thought I was the only one who wanted the things I wanted."

"You never hurt me. Do you know that? Even when you hurt me you never hurt me. I loved it. It wasn't until you stopped that I felt the pain."

"It hurt me, too." Søren ran his fingers through Kingsley's hair. Eleven years since their last night together, and yet Søren still knew exactly how to touch him in the way he most needed. "I was wrong. I shouldn't have married Marie-Laure. I thought I was solving all our problems. It was arrogant and foolish, and I realize that now."

"It was fucking stupid is what it was," Kingsley said. "Your Virgin Queen was right. You are an idiot."

Søren dropped his hand into the water and splashed Kingsley in the face in punishment.

"Good to know you're still as much a bastard as always," Kingsley said, grabbing the towel and swiping his face with it.

Kingsley tossed the towel on the floor and looked up again.

"I don't know what to do," Kingsley said, watching the light dance once more on the ceiling. It danced faster now as he and Søren set the water moving.

"Now? Tomorrow? Forever?"

"With my life. I don't have to work. You saw to that. I don't know what to do with myself. I make enemies as a hobby. I drink to kill time. I fuck to forget."

"I can't tell you what to do with your life," Søren said. "That's between you and God. But first you have to know that you do want to live. Once you're certain you want to live, you'll find your reason for living."

"I don't know if I want to live. I look at the future, and I see nothing. It's all black. I have no dreams, no visions, no hope. And you don't even want me anymore like you used to."

"If that beautiful, proud Kingsley Boissonneault who chased me down the hall and watched me sleep and confessed he thought of me all the time and yelled at me for breaking the rules of a game without rules… If he walked into this room right now, then I would be tempted to break my vows. That boy was a king, which is why I took so much pleasure in making him kneel. But this self-pitying, self-loathing, self-destructive Kingsley Edge in front of me? There's no honor in breaking someone already broken. There's no fun in it, either."

"I want to be him again. But I can't. He's gone, he's dead. I've done too much. I've seen too much." He closed his eyes and raised his hands, wanting to push away the visions in his mind—the crimes, the corpses, the missions into war zones. He'd taken a wrong turn somewhere and found himself wandering the back alleys of hell.

"You can be a new man, Kingsley. If he's dead, then he's dead. But you don't have to live the rest of your life walking around inside his corpse. You can have a new life."

"It's so easy for you to say and so hard for me to do."

"It's not hard at all. You only have to want it. You have to want the life where you're doing what God created you to do. If the one time you felt like you were fulfilling your destiny was by helping me, then go find the others like us and help them, too."

"How?"

"I don't know. You're one of the most intelligent men on this earth. You can figure it out."

"I don't even know where to start on a new life."

"Do you truly want one? Do you want to give up all this self-destructive foolishness and do something worthwhile? Do you want to be a new man?"

Kingsley paused and thought about the question. It seemed too good to be true. It sounded like a magic trick. *Voila.* New man. New life. But he wanted that magic even if it was an illusion. What he wouldn't give to feel that way again, feel the way he felt when he and Søren had been lovers, when his mere existence gave Søren reason for hope. When Søren's existence gave him hope.

"Oui." Kingsley met Søren's eyes. "I want it. What do I do?"

"You die and then you're reborn. New life."

Kingsley rolled his eyes.

"I die? That's going to take some doing. I've been trying to die for ten years now. No luck."

"With this I can help."

"How? Are you going to kill me?"

"Yes." Søren grasped Kingsley by the front of his shirt and dragged him to his feet.

"Life." Søren looked straight and deep into Kingsley's eyes.

"What?"

"Death." Søren pushed him underwater.

Immediately Kingsley thrashed and jerked, trying to fight off Søren's iron grip that held him under the surface of the water. He was drowning, couldn't breathe, couldn't get back up. He knew how drowning worked. He knew he would be dead in a minute. The water covered his head and face, and he couldn't get traction, couldn't get air. He looked death in the face and clawed at its eyes. He'd kill death before he'd let death kill him.

He fought back, fought hard.

He would not die tonight. He would live even if he had to kill Søren to survive.

Søren pulled him back up, and Kingsley spit out water, his throat and lungs burning.

"Resurrection."

The water settled. Kingsley panted. The word *resurrection* echoed around the room, reverberating into the innermost chamber of his heart.

Søren took a step back.

"I did my part by coming back to you," he said. "God did His part to keep you alive long enough for me to get here. Now you do your part and make yourself worthy of the second chance you've been given."

"You tried to drown me."

Søren smiled.

"It's called baptism, Kingsley. Welcome to the Kingdom."

Søren walked up the stairs, grabbed a towel and left him alone in the pool. Kingsley wordlessly watched him leave.

He could still taste the vomit in his mouth. His clothes were soaked, he looked like hell. And yet, he felt clean.

Welcome to the Kingdom.

The Kingdom.

In that moment he stood sick and shaking and cold and wet, Kingsley knew exactly what he would do with his life. Once upon a time, he'd made Søren a promise. He'd made a promise and now he would keep it. He saw it before him, and it seemed so real he could touch it, feel it. He saw a building, old, Gothic, crumbling, like he was—awaiting rebirth. And people filed into it, people with secrets. They needed him, needed his protection, needed his knowledge. They needed to kneel. They needed a king. He heard their cries of ecstasy, saw their hunger and devotion. He would take them all and give them to one more worthy.

And he'd never seen anything more beautiful in his life.

A promise made long ago… A promise he would keep.

A king must have a kingdom after all.

12

May

"YOU'RE PLANNING TO BUILD A WHAT?" SØREN ASKED.

"A BDSM club," Kingsley said. He leaned forward at his desk and held up photographs he'd taken at a dozen different clubs. "I've been all over the world the past three weeks looking at what's out there. I took these pictures in LA. It's more a nightclub than a kink club, but it has a few dungeons. I went to this club in Germany—it's as terrifying as it looks. This one was New Orleans. A brothel and a club, probably like your friend's in Rome. And this is Chicago. Did you know the old Playboy clubs gave a key to every member? We'll do something like—"

"Kingsley, stop." Søren met his eyes across the desk.

"What?"

"Are you on drugs again?" Søren asked.

Kingsley tossed his photographs down.

"I'm sober, and I have been for two weeks." He wasn't merely sober, he was wildly sober, willfully sober and blissfully sober. His head was clear, his eyes bright and the bone-deep exhaustion he'd been living with for a year had evaporated. He was alive and happy about it for the first time in as long as he could remember. "I'm trying to tell you I know what to do with my life."

"And that is…?"

"I'm going to build the biggest, most exclusive, most impressive S and M club in the world."

Søren said nothing at first. But he did look up to the ceiling and addressed a few words to it.

"I suppose it wouldn't have occurred to you to call him to join the Peace Corps, Lord," Søren said, still gazing upward. "It had to be this?"

"Who the hell are you talking to?" Kingsley demanded.

"God. I was criticizing Him, so perhaps it's for the best you interrupted. This is your grand calling in life? Your ultimate purpose? An S and M club?"

"No," Kingsley said, shaking his head. "Not *an* S and M club. *The* S and M club. And you're going to help me, because it's your fault I'm doing this."

"My fault?" Søren repeated, pointing at himself. "What leaps in logic did you take to lay this at my doorstep?"

"You turned me kinky," Kingsley said.

Søren paused.

"I want to argue with that assertion," Søren said.

"Oui?"

"I said I wanted to argue with, not that I could." Søren took a breath, sat forward in the chair and clasped his hands. "I have to say I am pleased to see you enthusiastic about something that isn't drinking yourself to death before thirty."

"Drinking yourself to death before thirty is so nineteenth century."

"Whatever the reason for this change of heart, I'm grateful it happened. If I can help you in any way, I will. But, please, recall I am now a Catholic priest, so I'd prefer not doing anything particularly illegal if it can be helped."

"Nothing illegal. I just don't know where to start. You're the smartest man I know, and your friend Magdalena had a club. How do I do this?"

"I suppose you'd start with a location. Magdalena's club was her home, her home her club. But I assume the town house isn't zoned for commercial enterprises."

"And it's not big enough. And neither is the Möbius. But, yes, you're right. We'll need the perfect location. Lots of rooms to play in. A big room for a big dungeon. A bar, too, but we'll keep the alcohol consumption in check. More or less."

"More," Søren said.

"You're a Catholic priest. Aren't you all drunks?"

"If I wasn't before, being back in your life might drive me to drink. Between you and Eleanor it's a miracle I'm even lucid."

Kingsley pointed at him. "I take that as a compliment."

"You would."

"Maybe an old hospital," Kingsley said, turning back to his photographs and flipping through them. "Are there any old abandoned hospitals lying around Manhattan? Or a mental asylum?"

"A mental asylum might send the wrong message," Søren said.

"Oh, you know what they say," Kingsley said with a wide grin at Søren. "We're all mad here."

"Who's mad?" Blaise asked, as she strode into the office without knocking first. She had what looked like a newspaper in her hands. Not a good sign where Blaise was concerned.

"My girlfriend is mad for interrupting us when we're working," Kingsley said, feigning disapproval, which was Blaise's favorite form of foreplay. The more peeved he was at her, the harder she worked to get back into his good graces.

"I told you, I am not your girlfriend," Blaise said. "I am your submissive."

"She has a point," Søren said. "They're quite different concepts."

"Thank you, Father." Blaise gave Søren a curtsy, which was an act of submission and exhibitionism, as her pale green kimono-style robe barely made it past her hips. At least she had underwear on.

For now.

"What, pray tell, are you doing in my office when I told you not to interrupt?" Kingsley asked, grabbing Blaise by the arm and pulling her down on to his lap. In addition to sternness, she also adored a good manhandling.

"I need ten thousand dollars, please," she said.

Kingsley looked across his desk at Søren.

"She's right. She's not my girlfriend. She's my ex-girlfriend."

"This is serious, King." Blaise scrambled out of his lap and sat on his desk facing him. "It's for a good cause."

"Oh, God, not another cause." Kingsley collapsed back in his office chair and groaned. "No more causes. That's an order."

"Listen to me, you French fascist," Blaise said. "I need to picket a church."

"*Chouchou*, you know I adore you, but you can't picket God," Kingsley said.

"You can picket God," Søren said. "No prohibition against that in the Bible, to my knowledge."

"Thank you. I appreciate the support," Blaise said. Without smiling she looked back at Kingsley. "Listen to me. This is a bad church. They're the ones who are always on the news with the 'God Hates Fags' signs and 'Abortion is Murder' signs. And they're coming to our city. *Your* city. Read it."

Kingsley grabbed the newspaper from her hands. He took his glasses out of his desk and put them on.

"Oh, don't do that," Blaise said with a purr in her voice.

"I can't be mad at you when you have your glasses on. You look too sexy. Doesn't King look sexy in his glasses?" she asked Søren.

"I am overcome," Søren said. Kingsley glared at him over the top of his glasses.

"Just read it, King. There's a church called The Way, The Truth, and The Life, and they're trying to take over Manhattan. Those people who have been protesting at the Möbius are part of that church."

"Are you sure?"

"Yes, I asked them last time I was there. They tried to tell me strip clubs exploit women."

"What did you do?"

"Flashed them."

"Don't reward bad behavior," Kingsley said, wagging his finger at her. "If they think they'll see your breasts again, we'll never get rid of them."

"We won't get rid of them. That's what I'm trying to tell you. They're trying to take over the city. The guy who runs it is a piece of shit. He's this big fire-and-brimstone preacher, and he wants to make sodomy a federal crime, outlaw strip clubs and pornography in every form, ban public schools from teaching evolution, and make having an abortion punishable by jail time. Also, they hate Catholics. They think the pope is the Antichrist."

"What does that have to do with us?" Kingsley asked. "I mean, other than you're a feminist, he's a Catholic priest and sodomy's my favorite hobby?"

"You are not listening to me," Blaise said, snapping her fingers to get his attention. "The governor of New York is Reverend Fuller's best friend. His wife and the mayor's wife go shopping together. This guy even says the opening prayer at all the state functions in Albany. The church is rich, it's powerful and it wants to take all our freedoms away. Reverend Fuller's like an evil Billy Graham on acid, and we have to stop him."

"I met Reverend Graham once," Søren said, putting his feet up on Kingsley's desk. "A good man. I'm currently trying to imagine him on acid. Makes for quite a thought experiment."

But Kingsley wasn't listening. He was staring…studying… gazing…seeing…

There it was. Right there.

Kingsley reached into his desk and pulled out a bundle of cash bound with a paper band.

"Here," he said, handing the money to Blaise and removing his glasses.

Blaise threw her arms around his neck and kissed him on the cheek.

"Merci, monsieur," she said. "I promise I will earn every penny of this in bed tonight. And tomorrow night. And the night after…"

"Consider it a finder's fee," Kingsley said.

"For what?"

"For this." He held up the newspaper to display the black-and-white photograph. "I found our club."

Kingsley was gratified to see Søren's eyes widen.

"What is it?" Blaise asked.

"This church bought a five-story condemned hotel from the city," Kingsley said. "The paper says they're turning it into their new church headquarters. It has a ballroom, a bar and fifty hotel rooms. Complete with attached parking garage. This is our club."

"You intend to buy that building for your club?" Søren asked, sounding dubious.

"Fuck, yes, I do," Kingsley said.

"Are you serious?" Blaise asked. She sounded awed and aroused. He could probably talk Blaise into submitting to anal sex tonight—lots of it. He should go on anti-church crusades more often.

"Deadly serious," Kingsley said. He couldn't stop staring at the picture in the paper. It looked like everything he'd dreamed right before his eyes. He hadn't felt this sense of destiny, this rightness about what he was doing since the day he first laid eyes on seventeen-year-old Søren sitting behind a piano in a chapel in Maine twelve years ago. The hotel was his. It belonged to him. And he could shut down a toxic church in the bargain—killing two birds with one flogger.

"But the sale already went through," Blaise said. "The church owns the building now."

"I don't care. I'll buy it from them or steal it from them. But I need to know more about this church before I try either. You know them?" he asked Søren.

"I have heard of them," Søren said. "What I've heard certainly gives me pause. The church is politically active—a fullfledged member of the Religious Right. I'm a firm believer in the separation of church and state. Better for the state. Better for the church. Better for everyone. This particular ministry seems determined to turn America into an evangelical Christian theocracy, which, as you can imagine, doesn't sit any better with Catholics than it does with heathens like yourself."

"You should ask Sam about the church," Blaise said. "She's the one who showed me the article in the paper. She knows all about them."

"Sam? Who's Sam?" Kingsley asked.

"Sam works at the club," Blaise said. "At the Möbius. Your Möbius?"

"Sam. Is she new?" He couldn't picture a bartender named Sam.

"She started a month ago."

"How do you know this and I don't?" Kingsley asked.

"Because you don't pay any attention to the club except when you want to sleep with one of the dancers."

"You may have a point. So, who is Sam?"

"Sam's the new head bartender. And she's amazing. Really smart and funny. She has history with Fuller's church—bad history."

"How bad?"

"She didn't tell me much, just that if Fuller's church moves in, she's moving out. Which would be sad, because she gives me free drinks whenever I go in."

"Because you're my girlfriend?" Kingsley asked. "Submissive? Whatever you are?"

"No, silly." Blaise rolled her eyes. "Because she likes me."

"Likes you?"

Blaise gave him a wide-eyed and pointed look. "She. Likes. Me."

"Kingsley, I believe your ex-girlfriend, current submissive is attempting to tell you your bartender is a lesbian."

"Why are you in my office?" Kingsley demanded.

"You summoned me," Søren reminded him.

"When did you start doing what I asked you to do?"

"I promise, it won't happen again," Søren said, standing up. "If you have no further need of me in your divinely inspired quest to build the largest kink club in the world, I have a homily to write."

"Go," Kingsley said. "You've done enough. You—" he pointed at Blaise "—you don't leave the house. I'll be back in a few hours, and your presence will be required in my bed."

"Where are you going?" Blaise asked as Kingsley grabbed his jacket off the back of his chair and headed for the door.

"The Möbius," Kingsley said. "I have a lesbian bartender to seduce."

13

KINGSLEY ENTERED THE MÖBIUS THROUGH THE front door, not the back like he usually did. He wanted to be inconspicuous, and entering through the employees-only door would compromise his anonymity. He'd pulled his neck-length hair back into a ponytail, and instead of a suit he wore jeans, a black T-shirt and black jacket. The stage flashed with red lights and female flesh, but he kept his eye on the bar.

He didn't see her at first. No one worked the bar tonight except for a slim young man with short shaggy hair. Once seated on a stool, Kingsley saw how mistaken he'd been. The young man was a young woman. She had a woman's delicate features, smooth skin, high cheekbones and straight small nose. But she was dressed like a man. She wore straight-leg pinstriped trousers, a white shirt with the sleeves rolled to her elbows and a pinstriped vest. It even appeared she had spats on her shoes.

"What can I get you?" the woman asked as she placed a napkin on the counter in front of him.

"Information," Kingsley said, suppressing his French accent. It would give away his identity immediately.

"Information? I don't serve that here," she said with a tight smile.

"Just on your clothes. Where did you get the suit?"

She narrowed her eyes at him.

"You want to know where I got my suit?"

"I like your suit," he said simply.

"Are you insinuating something?"

"Only that I like your suit." Kingsley could see Sam was already on the defensive. No doubt she'd fielded her fair share of unpleasant inquiries about her clothes, hair, gender and orientation more than once in her life.

"I have a tailor," she said. "And you have to order something if you're going to sit at the bar."

"A bottle of champagne."

"A whole bottle? Are you celebrating something?"

"Not yet, but I plan to," Kingsley said.

"Then congrats on your future whatever," she said, and pulled a bottle from the wine refrigerator under the bar. "Sixty for the bottle."

He put a hundred down on the counter and told her to keep the change. She looked at the bill with suspicion.

"You from out of town?" she asked.

"You could say that."

"Well, here in New York, the standard tip is a dollar a drink."

"I bought the whole bottle."

"That's six drinks. Six dollars."

"I'm not usually this generous. You should take the money."

"I don't take advantage of drunk guys."

"I'm sober."

"I don't take advantage of them, either."

"You have integrity."

"You say that like it's a bad thing," Sam said.

"It's inconvenient, but I won't hold it against you."

"You're too kind," she said. "So, where are you from? You look Greek, but you don't sound it."

"I'm—"

"Sam? We're low on ice." The club manager, Mack, leaned over the bar. Before Mack could see him, Kingsley pulled back out of the light, hiding from view. "Get your shit together."

"We have plenty of ice."

"Go grab a forty-pound bag."

"That's twice as much as we need for the night."

"You want to play like you're a man, then you can carry a big fucking bag of ice like a man."

"Fine. Happy to." Sam put on a stunningly fake smile and walked into the back. She returned a few seconds later carrying a large bag of ice.

"Good boy," Mack said to her as she ripped open the top of the bag and poured ice into the cooler. "I'd say there's a man in that suit after all, but I'm guessing you've never had a man in any part of you."

Sam grabbed the ice pick from under the counter. Mack's eyes widened momentarily. Sam smiled again and jabbed at the ice to break up the clumps.

"Jesus, why did you make me hire her again, Duke?" Mack asked the other bartender. "Her? Him? It?"

"Shove it, Mack. She's the best bartender in the city," Duke said as he loaded up a tray with drinks.

"The Duke and the Dyke. What a pair. I miss Jason."

"All the girls hated Jason," Duke said.

"I liked Jason."

"Jason was a sexually harassing prick who treated the girls like shit," Sam said. "Holly was about ready to file a lawsuit from what she told me."

"Ah, Holly…" Mack said, and spun on his bar stool to ogle the stage. "That's a real woman." He pointed at Holly, who wore nothing but a black thong and knee-high leather boots. Currently she had her knees around the neck of a man Kingsley recognized as the youngest son of a Mafia don. "Men should dress like men, and women should dress like women. And *that* is how women should dress."

Kingsley watched as Sam's grip on the ice pick tightened even as her fake smile widened. Mack turned around, winked at Sam and went on his nightly ramble through the club.

"The Duke and the Dyke." Sam sighed. "You know he was up all night thinking of that joke."

"He's going to be patting himself on the back for the next week," Duke said. "Fucking hate that guy."

"I'd like to nail his balls to the bar with this ice pick."

Duke took his tray of drinks out to the floor. Sam turned in his direction.

"Sorry," she said. "Bad night."

"He has an interesting definition of 'real women.'" Kingsley pointed to the stage. "I'm fond of Holly myself, but if she's not forty-percent plastic by now, I don't know women. And I know women."

Sam studied Holly and tapped her chin in faux earnestness. "The tits are fake," she said. "And the nose. I think she said she had lipo, too. So…more like twenty-percent plastic?"

"Is your boss always like this?"

"You mean a total asshole?" she asked. "Yes."

"Why don't you quit?"

"Someone has to keep an eye on the girls," she said. "He's worse to them than he is to me. And Duke only works two nights a week. I look out for them."

"So you're fucking one of them?" Kingsley asked.

"No, I'm not."

"Really?"

Sam gave him a smile, a real smile this time.

"I'm fucking all of them."

Kingsley laughed. "I like you, Sam. I'm going to do something for you."

"Look, you already over-tipped me. What—"

"You need a better boss," Kingsley said and hopped off his bar stool.

He could feel Sam's eyes on him the entire way across the floor. He slipped down a back hall and into the locker room where he was greeted, as usual, with inordinate displays of affection and enthusiasm, which he didn't let go to his head. He did own the place after all. When he mentioned to Raven and Shae what he had in mind, they threw themselves into helping him. Anything to get back at Mack, they said. Anything at all.

In ten minutes he was ready. The music started, and Kingsley walked out onto the stage to the accompaniment of "Sweet Transvestite."

Kingsley looked at Sam who was in the process of flipping a bottle of vodka. She barely caught it in time. He had on high heels, black stockings, black underwear—turned around backward for extra room—and a black corset. Plus a feather boa, of course.

"I heard someone say tonight," Kingsley intoned in his French accent into the microphone, "that women should dress like women and men should dress like men. I'm a man. And this is how I dress. Like it?"

All the dancers and waitresses had gathered round and were standing on chairs and tables, applauding and cheering. The men stared in silence, a few booed and a few cheered, too drunk to know what the hell was happening.

"I'll take that as a yes," he said, and scanned the crowd as he stalked across the stage in long, confident strides. This wasn't his first time in heels, and he wasn't afraid to show it. "Now where is Mack?"

"Over there, King." Raven pointed at a table. Kingsley

jumped lightly from the stage to the top of a table, stepped from one table to the next until he stood looming over Mack. Kingsley squatted down and smiled at the man.

"*Bonjour*, Mack," Kingsley said. "Do you like my outfit?"

"No," Mack said, looking pale and pasty.

"*Non?* The girls like it. Don't you, ladies?"

Every woman in the place, including and especially Sam, yelled their approval at the top of their lungs.

"Now, Mack, I have a question for you," Kingsley said. "The question is very simple. Who am I?"

He held the microphone out.

"You're Kingsley Edge."

"Very good. And why do I get to take over the stage whenever I want?" Kingsley asked.

"Because you own the club," Mack said, swallowing audibly. He looked terrified now, and Kingsley was pleased to see it.

Kingsley looked over at the bar and saw Sam's eyes widen to the size of wineglasses.

"Since I own this club, you work for me," Kingsley said. "And since you work for me, you have to do whatever I say. And I say you have to go backstage, dress like this—" he pointed at himself "—come back on stage and let all these lovely ladies put a dollar in your garter. Or…"

"Or what?" Mack demanded.

"Or you can get the fuck out of my club, you piece of shit. And never come back."

"I'm out of here, fag," Mack said, every word dripping with disgust.

"You won't be missed. *Au revoir.*" He waved his feather boa. "*Adieu.*"

He stepped off the table onto a chair and then to the floor. He strolled right over to the bar and hopped up on the counter.

"And now," he said into the microphone. "I'm going to kiss the most beautiful woman in this club. Wonder who she is…"

He placed his hand over his eyes and pretended to scan the crowd.

Raven and Shae, Holly and Ivy, and every other woman in the place waved and pointed at themselves.

Instead, Kingsley spun to face Sam. She stood up straight in surprise.

"May I kiss you, mademoiselle?" he asked.

Sam grinned broadly. "I await the kiss with antici…"

He bent over the bar and kissed her, a quick one on the lips.

"Parfait," he said and sat back up again. "Now everyone— back to work. The floor show is over."

He turned the microphone off, tossed it to Raven and dropped down on to a bar stool.

"You're the boss?" Sam asked.

"*Le grand* boss," he said with a wink.

"Has anyone ever told you that you have killer gams, Toots?" Sam asked. "Seriously, best legs I've ever seen on a man or a woman."

"The heels really bring out the muscle definition in my calves, don't they?" Kingsley asked.

"And the thighs. You dress like this often?"

"When necessary," Kingsley said with a shrug. There wasn't much he hadn't done in his twenty-eight years for business or pleasure. "You always dress in men's clothes?"

"I'm a woman. If they're my clothes, they're women's clothes," Sam said. "I'm not a cross-dresser. I'm a good dresser."

"You are. The spats are a nice touch."

"When you work in a strip club that's a front for a bath-house, you need the extra shoe protection. Speaking of shoes," she said, pausing to tap her chin and point at him. "Where did you get shoes big enough?"

"I stole them out of Petra's locker."

"Petra? Oh, Peter. Our Thursday-night drag queen. Should have known. Anyway, thank you for getting rid of Mack. I'll buy you a drink as long as it's not an entire bottle of champagne."

"I don't need a drink. I wasn't kidding earlier. I do need some information."

"Ask," she said. Kingsley was pleased to see his little stunt had gained her confidence.

"Do you know a woman named Blaise?"

Sam slapped a hand over her heart.

"Blaise? Blaise of Glory Blaise? The future mother of my children Blaise? Hair like Rita Hayworth, eyes like Ingrid Bergman, dresses like Lauren Bacall?"

"You know her, then."

"Know her? I worship her. If there is a God and if that God loves me, I will wake up tomorrow morning with no work to do, no place to go and that perfect piece of ass in my bed. I'd tie her down spread-eagle and turn her inside out. I'd make her come so often she'd forget how to go. I want to spend so much time inside that girl I'd have to get my mail forwarded to her pussy. So, yes, I know her."

"So do I. We're sleeping together."

Sam opened her mouth and closed it again.

"Well, bully for you," she said at last.

"I'm a lucky man."

"I guess I should apologize for saying I'd forward my mail to your girlfriend's vagina."

"Don't apologize. I feel the same way. I did have my mail forwarded there until she started complaining about paper cuts. Women," he said.

"You're a very understanding boyfriend. So, what information do you need?"

"Blaise mentioned you told her about a church that's moving into Manhattan."

Sam paused long enough to let Kingsley know he needed to tread lightly on this topic.

"Yeah, The Way, The Truth, and The Life Ministries. I saw in the paper they'd bought an old hotel. They're turning it into a church and office complex. It's supposed to be the new WTL HQ."

"This pissed you off?"

"I'm not a fan of them, no."

"Is it personal?"

"Kind of personal, yes," she said.

"So you know the Fullers?"

"Never met them. But I know a lot about them, a lot about the church. I know enough to not enjoy chatting about them in a bar on Friday night."

"Then let me ask you a different question—why are you working here?"

"Why? A bartender tends bar. I came here a couple times to see friends dance. The last head bartender was an ass. He hit on all the girls. All of them. Constantly. They told Mack either he goes or they do. So he fired him. Duke told him to hire me. No straight guys hit on me, and the women feel safe around me."

"They must feel more than safe around you if you're fucking them all."

"They have needs. And I have needs. I have the need to meet their needs. We get along well."

"*Intéressant,*" he said. "You have no interest in men?"

"I like men. I get along great with most men. I don't fuck men."

"Ever?"

"Ever."

Kingsley tapped the bar, thinking.

"Are you going to stay in that get-up all night?" Sam asked him. "Just wondering."

"You don't like it?"

"You look amazing," she said. "And I'm not kidding. You're sexier than Tim Curry in *Rocky Horror*, and that's saying something. But you're in a strip club full of men."

"They're only jealous I look better in a corset and heels than they do in their suits. I have fantastic shoulders, don't I?" He tossed his hair playfully.

"To die for."

"Let me ask you something, Sam. Do you love working here?"

"I like working here. I can't say I love it. I'm good at it."

"What would you rather be doing?"

She sighed and shrugged her shoulders.

"Using my brain more often. Getting into trouble more often."

"You like trouble?"

"I love trouble."

"Then let me make you offer."

"What's the offer?" Sam asked.

"Come get in trouble with me."

14

"TROUBLE?" SAM REPEATED.

"I'm offering you a job. Work for me."

"Work for you? Doing what?" Sam asked Kingsley as he threw a leg on to the bar and straightened his stocking.

"I need a personal assistant," Kingsley said, tilting his head to let Holly and Raven kiss him on the cheek. They tried to steal his boa, and he slapped their hands away.

"Personal assistant? How personal?" she asked, sounding cautiously curious.

"You can live in my house for all I care, as long as we get the work done. And I do have a very nice house."

"What's the work?"

He didn't answer her. Instead, he looked around the club. He caught Duke's eye and waved him over.

"I'm taking Sam with me. Can you handle things without her?" he asked Duke.

"Sure. Carla's here now. No problem," Duke said.

"Good. Sam? This way, *s'il vous plait*."

Sam followed Kingsley through the club and to the street. What a pair they made—he in his corset and stockings and she in a three-piece suit, black Oxfords with white spats. Some drunk teenagers across the street whistled. Kingsley waved his boa at them.

His silver Rolls Royce waited behind the club. His driver hopped out of the Rolls and opened the door for them. Gia gave Kingsley a little smile of approval and a slap on his ass as he got in the car. Women—did they ever stop thinking about sex?

"So, where are we going?" Sam asked as the car pulled into the street.

"To a hotel."

"Why?"

"Before I answer that," Kingsley said, "let me ask you a question."

"Ask."

Kingsley stretched out his leg and put his high-heeled foot on the seat next to her.

"Have you ever had sex in the back of a Rolls Royce?"

Sam furrowed her brow at him and leaned forward.

"Look at me." She pointed at herself. "What part of 'I'm a lesbian' do you not understand?"

"You said you were fucking all the girls at the Möbius, *oui*?"

"*Fucking* might be too strong a word. But I've gotten them all off at one time or another."

"They aren't all lesbians."

"Yeah, but I'm really good at what I do."

"So am I. Care to find out?"

"No. No I wouldn't. And you can let me off right here."

"Let you off? Or get you off?"

"Not funny. Let me out of the fucking car," she said, reaching for the door handle.

Kingsley tapped on the window that separated him from the driver. The window rolled down an inch. Kingsley ordered the driver to pull over. As soon as it stopped, Sam reached for the door. Kingsley put his high-heeled foot on the door to block her.

"Let me out," Sam ordered.

"You passed," Kingsley said.

She crossed her arms over her chest and raised her chin.

"Passed what?" she asked.

"The test."

Sam eyed him warily. "What test?"

"I have a problem," Kingsley said, and he sat back. Sam remained on her guard. "I need help. I'm doing something with my life. Finally. Something important. It might even be the most important thing I've ever done. And I can't do it alone. But I fuck my assistants. Then when they realize I'm not in love with them, they get pissed and quit."

"This is why I fuck straight girls. No commitment."

"Forgive me for upsetting you. Please. I only wanted to see if you had any inclination, any interest in me. You don't."

"Not a bit," she said. "But don't take it personally. I mean, I see the appeal. You look great in drag, and you have amazing legs. And you've got the sexy hair and the Greek thing going—"

"The French thing."

"French. Right. Sorry," she said, and he noted her biting back a smile. "I mean, *pardonnez-moi*."

"*De rien,*" he said.

"All that being said…you're darn cute. I'm just not attracted to you. I hope that makes sense, and your ego isn't too bruised."

"My ego enjoys the occasional bruise." Among other parts of him. "And you don't have to apologize for not wanting to have sex with me. I consider it a mark in your favor. Especially if you're my assistant."

"What exactly would I be doing for you as a personal assistant?"

"Let me show you something."

Sam raised her eyebrow.

"It's a building," he said. "I promise."

"Good. Just checking."

When they arrived at their destination, the driver held open the door for them. Sam exited the car first and then held out her hand to Kingsley.

"Might I assist you, ma'am?" Sam asked.

"Who said chivalry was dead?" Kingsley took her hand, and she pulled him—high heels, corset and all—out of the car.

Side by side they stood on the sidewalk in the light of a lamppost, in the shadow of a ghost.

"What are we doing here?" Sam demanded. "This is the hotel Fuller's church bought, isn't it?"

"It is."

"Why are we here?"

"Because I want it."

"The city sold the place to them two weeks ago. It's not on the market anymore."

"I've fucked more married women than I can count," Kingsley said. "If something's worth owning, it's worth stealing."

"You are an interesting man, Kingsley Edge," Sam said, watching him as he scanned the exterior of the hotel. "I'm not sure if that's a compliment or not."

"You seduce straight girls in order to make them question their sexuality. Jury is still out on you, too," he said. "And for the record, I have had sex with lesbians before."

"Yeah, how did that happen?"

"One was on an 'orientation vacation' as she called it. The other didn't know she was until after we had sex."

"Ouch," Sam said.

"There were no hard feelings. Especially after she told me she was gay."

They walked up and down the sidewalk in front of the building. It was boarded up and chained. Yellow caution tape warned passersby away. Signs and notices declared it condemned and closed.

Kingsley was undeterred.

"What did the newspaper say about this place?" Kingsley asked.

"According to the *Times*, it was called The Renaissance. Now it's The Nothing since it's been closed for ten years."

"Why does a church want a hotel?"

"Reverend Fuller wants to expand his empire of conservative family values into the heart of New York City blah blah bullshit et cetera," Sam said. "In the interview in the paper he said something about how, unlike the righteous Lot who fled from Sodom, WTL Ministries will infiltrate the city of New York and save it from within."

"The righteous Lot fucked his own daughters," Kingsley said. "I wonder if Reverend Fuller remembers that part."

"You know the Bible?" Sam asked.

"I went to an all-boys Catholic school."

"How did you survive that?"

"By sleeping with a teacher."

"Was she hot?"

"He was, yes."

Kingsley made a circuit of the exterior of the building. For all the dirt and decay, it had beautiful old bones. Twelve fifty-foot high lancet windows adorned the main floor. The top two floors were decorated with jutting corbels that look like the beaks of birds. The entire building, with its dark exterior and stone plumage, gave off the impression of a great stone raven, hunched over in the cold and sleeping.

"Maybe we can find out who sold the place," Sam said. "I'm sure we could get the real estate agent to show us the inside. Maybe they can show us another building like this one but not already owned by a cult."

"Or we can look inside it now and see if it's worth stealing." Kingsley strode to a boarded-up door and kicked. The door flew open.

"Damn," Sam said.

"I know." Kingsley frowned. He held up his shoe. "I broke a heel. Petra's going to kill me."

He took off both shoes and stepped barefoot into the building. Sam followed.

"What the hell am I doing?" Sam asked herself as she walked in behind Kingsley. "I've never met you before tonight, and here I am, breaking and entering a building owned by the creepiest church in America."

"I told you I'd get you into trouble," he said. "I'm keeping my promise."

"You know we could get arrested for this," Sam said.

"I have a DA's wife in my pocket," Kingsley said. He reached out and flipped a wall switch. Surprisingly the lights worked. The church must have had the power turned back on already. Overhead a dusty chandelier cast dingy hexagons of light onto the seedy carpet. "And the DA, too."

"You must have big pockets."

Kingsley turned and faced Sam.

"What do I need to know about you?" he asked.

Sam stuffed her hands in her pockets. "There's not much to know about me."

"What's your full name?"

"Samantha Jean Fleming. I'm twenty-six. I'm a lesbian."

"You don't say."

"Shut up," she said, laughing. "You have no room to talk, Dr. Frank-N-Furter."

Kingsley flipped another light switch.

"What else?"

"Nothing much else."

Kingsley gazed at her.

He touched her chin, tilting it up to meet his eyes.

"Can I trust you?" he asked.

"I hope so. And if you're against Fuller's church, I'm on your side. I don't know if that answers your question or not."

"It's a good answer. On my side is where I need you."

"After what you did for me tonight at the club, I'm yours," she said. "Just not in a sexual way. Every other way."

"So, what do you think of the place?" Kingsley asked.

"It's definitely a wreck," Sam said as they wandered down the hall. "The newspaper said the church got a deal on it because the city was about to condemn the place. But you can tell it was beautiful once."

"I like that it's not beautiful anymore. I like that it's been hurt."

"It's kind of big for a BDSM club. Most kink clubs I know are little shitholes."

"Well, my club will be a big shithole."

They entered what had been the lobby of the hotel and found moth-eaten furniture, fading Persian rugs, layers of grime on a curved bar—grime and grim everywhere they looked. Once, the decor had been blue and red and gold, but now everything had faded to a dull gray. Kingsley opened a set of double doors, and Sam peered over his shoulder.

"It looks like an old concert hall." Sam pointed up at the ceiling. "Or a dining hall. Hard to tell."

She and Kingsley walked through the dining room, stepping over broken chairs, breathing in dust-filled air.

"Is that an elevator?" Kingsley asked.

"Looks like it." Sam pointed upward. "There's some kind of landing up there. I guess the bigwigs got to eat their dinner looking down on the little wigs."

Kingsley stood in the middle of the grand hall and turned slowly in a circle.

"Let's see the rest," he said. Together he and Sam wandered for an hour through the now-defunct Renaissance. A madman must have designed the building. The layout made very little sense. One hallway of guest rooms was hidden behind the dining room. There were secret doors all over the place that led to other hallways. Guests must have gotten lost all the time trying to find their way back to their rooms. No wonder it had gone out of business.

"I think M.C. Escher must have been the architect on this place," Sam said.

"I hate to think what Fuller would do to a building this unique."

"He'll probably turn it into a church like his other churches—a big ugly warehouse with beige carpet."

"This place…it's been through many transformations." Kingsley stood in one of the larger suites. "Many incarnations. Now it doesn't know what it is anymore. It only knows that it's been abandoned. I know how it feels."

He reached out and laid his hand on an ornately carved door frame like a doctor feeling for a heartbeat. "This place is perfect," Kingsley said. "Everything I dreamed of."

"You have weird dreams."

"These suites are what I need for our pros."

"Pros? Like hookers?"

"No hookers. I'm not a pimp. I mean professionals. Professional dominants."

"Dominatrixes?"

"One or two. The best in the city."

"Mistress Felicia? You want this club to be special, you want her."

"Isn't she still in prison?" he asked. Last he'd heard the notorious Mistress Felicia was still locked away in Danbury for ignoring a subpoena to testify in a high-profile divorce case.

"She got out last month. She says she's retiring, but she might come out of retirement for you," Sam said with a wink.

"I'm not a submissive," Kingsley said.

"I mean for the club. She's the best in the city. You should woo her."

"You know a lot about kink in this city."

"Everyone tells the bartender everything. Plus, I'm kinky. Does this come as a shock to you?"

Kingsley looked her up and down.

"Not at all. I want people like us at the club. I want all of our kind welcome here—gay and straight, bi, as long as they're kinky. We'll need professional male dominants, too. A few bouncers."

"Then you'll need some of the leather guard," she said. "What else?"

"Pro-submissives—male and female."

"Those will be harder to find. There's ads for dominatrixes in the goddamn phone book, but pro-subs? How many people do you know who want to get the shit beat out of them for a living?"

"Enough of them do it for free. They might as well get paid for it."

"What else?" Sam asked. "If it's an S and M club, I guess we'll need some sadists."

"I have one sadist already. Not on the payroll, but he'll certainly bring the pain, out of the kindness of his heart."

"Is he good?"

"He can slice a lit cigarette in half with the tip of a whip. But we'll need more than one. There are more masochists in this city than you would believe."

"With rent as high as it is, I'd say we're all masochists."

He stood in front of her and looked at her without smiling.

"This might get ugly," Kingsley said. "I do ugly things in my work sometimes. If you work for me, you'll get your hands dirty."

"I like dirty."

"Illegal things may or may not happen."

"I have an amazing ability to look the other way."

"I'll never put you in harm's way, but I will put myself there."

"You're a grown-up," she said. "Just make sure my paychecks don't bounce."

"I pay in cash," he said.

"This is the greatest job ever. Let's do it."

"This is our kingdom." He waved his hand, indicating the hotel. "Or will be when I'm done with it."

"But Fuller beat us to it. It's sold."

"I'll buy it from him. And if he won't sell, I'll steal it."

"That's not a good idea," Sam said in a stern voice. "Seriously. Politicians suck up to Reverend Fuller all the time just so he'll tell his TV flock to donate to their campaigns. He's famous. He's important. And he will not be happy if you fuck with him."

"Do you want his church in this town?" Kingsley asked.

"No," she admitted. "I hate his church."

He looked at her through narrowed eyes.

"Tell me why you're on my side," Kingsley ordered. Sam didn't answer at first.

Finally she spoke.

"The Fullers... Their church... They run reorienting camps."

"What are those?"

"It's where they send gay kids to try to turn them straight."

"That can't be legal," Kingsley said, eying her with horror.

"It's legal. There are hundreds of kids at those camps right now."

"That gives me even more reason to fuck with him."

Sam sighed. "I was afraid of that."

"Sam, I dreamed of this building. I recognized it the second I saw the picture in the paper. This is fate."

"Fate is a bad thing. Fate is why Oedipus screwed his mother and lost his eyeballs."

"My mother is dead. I'll get a guide dog. I always wanted a dog."

"You're crazy. You're going to buy his church from Reverend Fuller and turn it into an S and M club?"

"You know you love this idea. Admit it."

"Get back at Fuller and his fucking church? Let's do it."

"Keep that bottle of champagne I bought tonight."

"Why?"

"We'll drink it together, you and I, on opening night."

"I serve at your pleasure, Your Majesty." She gave him a mock bow.

"Good," Kingsley said. "Now let's build a kingdom."

15

KINGSLEY WAS DISAPPOINTED BUT NOT SURPRISED when Fuller's ministry refused to sell the Renaissance to him. He upped his offer, and they turned it down flat. He tried buying the building through one of his more legitimate fronts, a fake travel agency he "owned" as a way to manage excess cash flow, and Fuller still wouldn't sell.

Time for Plan B.

"What's Plan B?" Sam asked as she flipped a page on her clipboard. For a week, she'd been working for Kingsley, and so far she'd done everything he'd told her to do in a timely and efficient manner. He'd told her to go buy a computer if she wanted one. Instead, she kept his entire life in order on her clipboard.

"Plan B is blackmail," Kingsley said as he took a seat behind his desk. "We need dirt on the Fullers. Real dirt."

"What kind of dirt?"

"Any dirt will do as long as it sticks. Do you know any-thing incriminating about the church?"

"Um…well, they're very fundamentalist. They believe women should submit to their husbands."

"That's terrible. What if the husband's the submissive?"

"Kingsley, be serious. A lot of the men in the church beat their wives because of that mind-set."

"I believe it, but as horrible as that is, that's dirt on the church, not the Fullers. We need to find out if Fuller is beating his wife. Or cheating on her. Or laundering money. Or anything. But whatever it is, it has to be something he is directly involved in. We don't need a bullet. We need a bomb."

Sam sighed and ran her hands through her hair. Her warm hazel eyes shone with deep intelligence, and he'd been impressed by how quickly she'd learned names in his house.

"A bomb? That's not going to be easy. The Fullers have been around forever," she said. "I think Reverend Fuller inherited the ministry from his father."

"Bizarre."

"What is?"

"Inheriting a church from your father. My only experience with religion is with the Catholic church. Priests have sons sometimes, but they don't go around handing the keys of the church over to them."

"I don't know much about Catholics. I'm pretty comfortably agnostic. What are you?"

"I'm French," Kingsley said.

"I'm asking about your religion."

"That *is* my religion. And fucking with Fuller is my new religion," Kingsley said.

"Are you sure about this? I want to fuck with Fuller, too, but he's powerful. More powerful than you are."

"That hurts."

"You said you have a DA and his wife in your pocket. Fuller has the governor in his. And the mayor."

"I don't care who his friends are. I don't care how big his church is. I'm not going to let him turn this city into his playground, Sam. This is my city," Kingsley said. The thought of

some Bible-thumping preacher bringing his message of hate
to New York turned Kingsley's stomach. He could imagine
what Fuller would have to say about him and Søren and what
had passed between them back at school. Kingsley knew in his
soul—if he had one—that nothing he and Søren did had been
a sin. Fuller and his kind could go fuck themselves.

"So what do you want me to do?" Sam asked.

"Get me everything you can on Fuller and his church."

"King, I've looked through everything there is on him
already. I haven't found anything. He's an ass, don't get me
wrong. Pompous and preachy and completely bigoted. But
that puts him in line with every other televangelist preacher
out there. No rumors of adultery, no rumors of wife-beating,
no rumors of kid-fucking."

"There's something. There has to be something."

"What if there isn't?"

Kingsley stood up and came around the desk.

"I'm going to tell you something, and you're going to keep
it between you and me. It won't always be a secret, but for
now it is."

"What?" she asked.

"At the hotel, I told you I knew a world-class sadist who
could cut a lit cigarette in half with the tip of a bullwhip.
What I didn't tell you is that he's also a Catholic priest. Look
in my eyes, Sam."

She looked into his eyes as ordered.

"There is always something," Kingsley said.

"Okay," she said, taking a deep breath. "I'll look again.
What are you going to do?"

"Nothing you need to know about," he said.

"No hints?"

"It starts with an A," Kingsley said.

"Assignation? Audition? Ass…sex? They all start with A."

"I'm going to audition someone for an ass-sex assignation. I'll see you later," he said, standing up straight. The scar tissue on his chest was painfully tight today.

"Are you okay?"

"Of course I am."

"I saw you wince. Are you in pain?"

"Don't start worrying about me." He shook his finger at her. "Once you start that habit, you'll never stop."

"That worrisome, are you?"

Kingsley raised his hands and ticked off numbers on his fingers as he spoke.

"One. My parents died in a train crash when I was fourteen. Two. My sister committed suicide when I was seventeen shortly after marrying the man I was in love with. Three. I used to kill people for a living for a secret organization inside the French government. Four. I have pissed off dangerous men with long memories. Five. My closest friend is a Catholic priest, the aforementioned sadist, who is in love with a girl in his congregation whose father has a rap sheet as long as your leg and some very nasty mob connections. And that, Sam, is only the beginning of the list of reasons you might want to worry about me."

"Six. You're in pain."

"I have an old injury that's healing slowly. It's nothing to worry about. I'm nothing to worry about. So, don't worry."

"You should see a doctor."

"I hate doctors."

"I don't care. See one anyway."

"You forget I'm your boss. Not the other way around."

"And I'm your assistant. I'm assisting you. You need to see a doctor."

"I'm leaving now. Goodbye." He patted her on the shoulder as he walked past her.

"I'm making you a doctor's appointment," she called out after him.

Kingsley paused in the door, turned around and came back to her.

"You are insubordinate," he said.

"You hired me to help you," she said, turning her bright eyes up to him. "Let me help you."

Kingsley sat on the edge of his desk and looked down at her.

"I could align the planets using your nose as a sextant," he said, tapping the end of it. "It's that straight."

"It's the only straight part of me. Now stop trying to distract me and tell me how I can help you."

"Stop dressing like that."

"I dress like a man. No apologies. I don't feel like myself in skirts and dresses. Okay?"

"I don't care about that. I don't care if I never see you in a dress or a skirt as long as I live." He waved his hand to indicate his own attire of jeans, T-shirt and jacket. "But you dress nicer than I do, and I'm your employer. You'll have to tone it down."

"Maybe you should tone it up."

"Tone it up?"

"You said you wanted to be a king of your own kingdom, right? You should dress like one."

"I'd have to dress in a top hat and tails to outshine you."

She tilted her head back and looked him up and down.

"You'd look incredible in a tuxedo."

"You think?"

"Like a sexy French penguin," she said.

"I'm leaving."

"Bon voyage," she said. "I'll make the appointment."

"No doctors," he called back.

"I meant with my tailor."

Kingsley had a smile on his face as he left Sam in his office. The smile faded by the time he exited the house. His driver, Gia, waited for him with the car, but he waved her off, telling her he'd rather walk today. It was a nice May day after all. The walk would do him good. Of course the real reason he didn't want Gia to drive him was because he didn't want anyone knowing where he was going. He walked four blocks and then caught a cab. He still couldn't believe Søren had talked him into doing this. He hadn't belonged to Søren since he was seventeen, and yet, here he was, following Søren's orders like those eleven years had been eleven days. It had been so long since he'd felt as if it mattered to someone whether or not he lived or died that he couldn't help but give in when Søren pushed him to come here.

The cab let him out in front of a two-story Brooklyn brownstone with nothing to distinguish it but the brass plaque on the front door. He paused at the steps and heard the roar of an Italian motorcycle engine. Of course. Of course he'd be here.

"I told you I would do it," Kingsley said to Søren as he pulled off his helmet and stepped onto the sidewalk. "You don't have to babysit me."

"I'm not babysitting you, and I knew you would do it if you said you would do it."

Kingsley wasn't sure about that, but he appreciated the vote of confidence.

Thankfully, Søren wasn't in his clerics today. He looked like any other six-foot-four twenty-nine-year-old blond god out for a sunny late-May motorcycle ride.

"Then, why did you follow me here?"

"Even a deviant like you needs a priest sometimes. Especially a deviant like you."

Kingsley's throat tightened. He swallowed the knot.

"Fine," he said. "You can come in. But don't embarrass me in front of cute nurses."

"I wouldn't dream of it."

He strode up the stairs, Søren at his side.

Once inside Kingsley gave the nurse his name. She handed him a clipboard covered in forms.

"I don't fill out forms," Kingsley said.

"Give them to me," Søren said with a put-upon sigh. The nurse raised an eyebrow and led Kingsley back immediately. Without Kingsley asking him to stay or go, Søren followed him inside.

What a ghastly place—posters covered in dire warnings and pictures of people with diseases hung on the walls.

"I wish I had a medical fetish," Kingsley said, looking in horror at the décor of the doctor's office. "Then I might enjoy this."

He opened a drawer at the end of the examining table.

"Oh, speculums…"

"Will you please behave?" Søren said as he took a seat in a chair under a Warning Signs of Lyme Disease poster. Kingsley sat on the examining table feeling as if he were a boy again, at the doctor's with his father to get vaccinated. He remembered how proud his father had been of him, not once flinching at the needles. He was more scared today than he was twenty years ago. And he missed his father.

"When was your last physical?" Søren asked.

"Two years ago. And what the hell are you doing?"

"Your intake form."

Kingsley ripped the clipboard from Søren's hand. In his neat, Catholic school handwriting, Søren had not only filled in most of the blanks on the form, he'd filled them in accurately. Full name, height, age, birth date, address, social security number…

"Someone else to fill out the health forms…" Kingsley said, nodding his appreciation. "Now I know why people get married."

"Now I know why people *don't* have children," Søren said, taking the clipboard back. "Now sit down and behave yourself."

"Yes, Father."

Kingsley sat on the paper-covered examining table and tried to ignore his racing heart.

"Why are you here?" Kingsley asked. "Really?"

Søren fell silent and glanced away.

"After our first time…" he began and paused once more. "I should have come to you in the infirmary when you were there. I have always regretted not coming to you."

Kingsley shook his head. He remembered those first few days after that night with Søren in the forest when he was sixteen, remembered the almost religious ecstasy he'd fallen into. He had been bruised and bloody and broken, and none of it had mattered. He'd never known such peace. All he wanted then was to be well once more, so it could happen again, so he could be broken again.

"No…if you had come to me, they would have known it was you who put me in there."

"I know, and that's the excuse I used on myself. But the truth is I was afraid to find out if you hated me for what I did to you."

"I loved you for what you did to me."

"I was equally afraid of that." Søren gave Kingsley a look of concern. Maybe he'd learned how to make that face in seminary. "Are you scared?"

"Terrified," Kingsley admitted. "As you can imagine. Or not." Kingsley laughed to himself. "Keep forgetting you're a priest."

"I wasn't always a priest."

It was a simple statement of fact. Of course Søren hadn't always been a priest. But Kingsley heard something else in the words, something under them.

"Did you..." Kingsley stopped and reconsidered his question. "I know you didn't catch anything from me."

"My father had mistresses," Søren said, his voice devoid of emotion.

"Your sister Elizabeth got something from your father, didn't she? She gave it to you?"

Søren silently nodded.

"What did you have?"

Søren raised his hands and clapped once.

Kingsley would have laughed if it wasn't the most horrible thing he'd ever heard. Søren, at age eleven, had contracted gonorrhea, the clap, from his sister during their tortured adolescence.

"A Benedictine sister worked at the hospital where they took me after my father broke my arm," Søren continued. "She was my nurse. I've never forgotten her kindness. We all need kindness every now and then."

Søren started to say something else, but then the doctor came in—an intelligent-looking woman in her late thirties—and the words were lost.

"Kingsley, this is Dr. Sutton," Søren said. "She attends my church. Dr. Sutton, this is my brother-in-law, Kingsley. He is a reprobate. You've been warned."

"I've had my fair share of reprobates. They keep me in business." Dr. Sutton smiled in that placid seen-everything way doctors always smiled. "How are you, Kingsley?"

"I hate being here, so, please, get this over with as soon as possible," Kingsley said.

"As you can tell, Kingsley is also charming and pleasant."

"It's all right, Father Stearns," Dr. Sutton said, giving him a motherly pat on the knee. "I've had worse. Now, Kingsley, we're getting tested?" she asked, pulling up a wheeled stool.

"I don't know what *we're* doing," Kingsley said. "But I'm getting tested."

Søren gave him the "behave yourself" glare.

Dr. Sutton rattled off a long list of questions that Kingsley answered without making eye contact. Yes, he'd had the clap and syphilis. Yes, he'd been treated. No, he had no current symptoms. When she asked how many sexual partners he'd had, she did a double take at the answer.

"I think that's a record," she said, writing the number down.

"I'm French," Kingsley said.

"That's your excuse for everything," Søren said.

"It's not an excuse. It's an explanation."

"You're half French," Søren reminded him with a scowl.

"Yes, and if I was all-French that number would be twice that."

"Is there anything in particular you think you've been exposed to?"

"Yes," Kingsley said, staring at Søren who'd forced him to do this stupid testing. "Catholic guilt's a venereal disease, *oui*? I wonder who I caught it from."

He expected another glare from Søren. Instead, he received something far worse—a look of compassion mixed with pity.

"Tell her the truth," Søren said.

"The truth?" the doctor asked. "You can tell me anything. Whatever you say is confidential. Doctors are like priests in that regard. We can kick him out of the room if you'd like."

Kingsley turned away from them both and stared blankly at a yellow smiley-face poster.

"I was doing some work in Eastern Europe last January," Kingsley finally said, his tone as casual as possible under the circumstances. "Don't ask me what I was doing, because I'm not allowed to say. But I was taken prisoner and shot. At the hospital they said…they said I'd been assaulted. While I was unconscious, I mean."

In his peripheral vision he saw the doctor studying his face.

"You were sexually assaulted?" Her tone was neutral, calm. He appreciated that.

"Very likely," he said.

"Do you have any lingering pain or symptoms?"

"I have flashbacks sometimes. Nightmares. No memories."

"Sounds likes post-traumatic stress disorder," Dr. Sutton said. "I can refer you to someone who is an expert in that field."

"No therapists," Kingsley said. "I hate them even more than doctors."

"When were you last tested?" Dr. Sutton asked.

"I was tested in the hospital, and I was supposed to get tested again six months later. I didn't."

"Why didn't you?"

He turned his head and met her eyes.

"Told you—I hate doctors."

She smiled at him.

"I hear that a lot," she said. "So…after what you went through, I take it we're testing you for…"

Kingsley took a nervous breath.

"Everything."

16

DR. SUTTON TOOK HIS VITALS, TWO VIALS OF HIS blood, made him piss in a cup and then did something with a Q-tip that men routinely paid upward of five-hundred dollars for a dominatrix to do to them. She told him the results would come back in two weeks.

"Two weeks?" he repeated. "I have to wait two weeks?"

She gave him a look of deepest compassion.

"I know. It's the scariest two weeks of anyone's life waiting on the lab results. And they might come sooner, but two weeks is average. Try not to think about it."

"That's not going to happen."

"I'm advising you not to have intercourse until your results are in."

"Not possible," he said.

"It is possible," Søren said. "I'll chain you to the floor if I have to."

"I've had sex chained to the floor before. Remember when—"

"Kingsley."

"You have to think about your future," Dr. Sutton said. "You're putting your life at risk. You're putting your fertility at risk. Even if you don't want children—"

"I do."

Søren looked up sharply. Kingsley had no idea where those words came from. Did he just say he wanted children? He did? When was he planning on telling himself that?

"Then you should use protection," Dr. Sutton continued. "Every time. Until, of course, you're ready for children."

"No other options?" Kingsley asked.

"You could try celibacy," Søren suggested, and Kingsley flicked a tongue depressor at him.

"Unnatural," Kingsley said. "No one should be celibate."

"I agree," Dr. Sutton said, and winked at Søren.

Dr. Sutton promised to call as soon as the results were in. He and Søren walked out into the sunshine.

"She's your doctor, too, yes?" Kingsley asked.

"She is."

"And she goes to your church?"

"She does."

"And she doesn't believe priests should have to be celibate?"

"Now you know why she's my doctor." Søren grinned. The smile faded, and he put his hand on Kingsley's shoulder. "Whatever happens, I'll be here."

"Two weeks. I'm going to die while waiting to find out if I'm going to die."

"You don't have my permission to die."

"I'll never make it. What do people who don't have sex do with their time? Other than plan their suicide?"

"I don't have sex. Do I seem suicidal to you?"

"What do you do in your free time?"

"I'll show you. Meet me at Central Park on the North Meadow at three."

"Don't you have a job?" Kingsley demanded.

"I said morning Mass at ten. I took the rest of the day off for you. Come to the park. Wear clothes you can run in."

"I don't want to run."

"North Meadow. Three."

Søren held up three fingers.

In response, Kingsley held up one finger.

Once Søren was gone, Kingsley stopped at a pay phone and called Sam.

"You paged me?" he asked as soon as Sam picked up his office phone.

"You have messages. Most important message—Blaise wants you to escort her to some fund-raiser Friday night."

"Do I have to?" Kingsley asked.

"If you don't take her, I will," Sam said with an amorous tone in her voice.

"I'll take Blaise to the thing. You're not allowed to steal my *chouchou*."

"We need to renegotiate my terms of service, then."

"What else?" Kingsley asked.

"An Officer Cooper called. He's at the twenty-sixth precinct. I don't know what this message means, but he said 'Tell King I've got a live one for him.'"

Ahh…that sounded promising.

"I'll go right now," he said.

"What's a live one? Who's a live one?"

"I told you we needed professionals—dominatrixes, dominants, submissives. I have some contacts keeping an eye out for me for anyone who might fit in well at the club."

"A beat cop is one of your contacts?"

"Cooper puts the beat in beat cop."

He hung up on Sam and hailed a cab. He was almost as fond of police stations as he was fond of doctor's offices. He'd already been to the doctor today, so he might as well go play with the police, too. If today continued along this trajectory, he'd be attending Mass by nightfall.

All of this was Søren's fault—getting sober, getting an assistant, getting tested, working. Fucking priest. He was so glad he'd come back to him, Kingsley could barely breathe thinking about it.

Officer Cooper, twenty-five, black, tall, muscular and handsome, met Kingsley in the lobby. He didn't speak a word until they were halfway to the holding cells.

"Who is she?" Kingsley asked.

"Name's Irina Harris, born Irina Zhirov. Age, twenty-two."

"A Russian, eh?"

"Came to the States as an eighteen-year-old mail-order bride," Officer Cooper said. Kingsley laughed. "I'm serious, King. We see it a lot. Russian women so desperate to get out of the country they marry American men, total strangers most of the time. They hook up through matchmaking agencies. Sometimes it works out and they live happily ever after. Sometimes the lovely bride tries to poison his dinner."

"She poisoned her husband?"

"That's the charge."

"You brought me down here to meet a murderess?"

"Attempted murderess. I don't know. You know what I like," Officer Cooper said. "And I like her. I get that feeling about her. Want to meet her?"

"A Russian mail-order who tried to kill her husband? Of course I want to meet her."

This day was looking up.

"I don't have any excuse for bringing you down here, so if anyone asks, lie and say you're her translator or something."

"Da," he said in Russian. "Моё судно на воздушной подушке полно угрей."

"Whatever you say," Cooper said, nodding. "And you've got ten minutes before I have to get you back out again. Good luck."

Kingsley slapped Cooper on the arm. They'd met at a party, and Cooper claimed he was such a good submissive, he could pick out a dominatrix in a lineup of five other women simply by listening to her voice. "It takes a sub to know a domme," he'd said. Now they would find out if he was right.

A woman sat alone in a cell on a gray metal bench. She had her back to the door and didn't turn around when Cooper let Kingsley in the cell.

Cooper left them alone together.

From the back he could see she had black hair, stylishly coiffed, and she wore designer clothes. He walked around to stand in front of her and found her staring into the corner of the room, refusing to make eye contact.

"My name is Kingsley," he said in Russian. If his fluency surprised her, she didn't betray it with so much as a blink. "You're Irina Zhirov."

"Harris," she said, in thickly accented English. "I'm married."

"I heard someone tried to poison your husband."

"I'm a bad cook. His stomach overreacted."

Interesting answer. Kingsley studied her as she picked at her nail polish. She had an elegant profile, undeniably Russian, undeniably lovely. But she had a hard set to her mouth, as if she hadn't smiled in so long her lips had calcified into a pale tight line of bitterness.

"Does your husband overreact often?"

Irina met his eyes before looking away again without speaking.

"I'm not with the police," Kingsley said. "And I'm not a lawyer. I'm not a translator."

"Who are you?" she asked in Russian, finally meeting his eyes.

"A friend," he said. "If you need a friend."

"I need a lawyer."

"I can help you get a lawyer. Tell me more about your husband overreacting."

She cocked her head, tried to look innocent. "He's a man. They all overreact. A man you've never met before smiles at you, and now you're sleeping with him. You don't do his ironing right, so you hate him. You cook the food bad, and you're poisoning him."

"Your husband sounds like a little poisoning would be good for him."

"A lot of poisoning would be better for him."

She had a hard cold voice. Her dark eyes sparked like struck flint when she spoke. The anger in her went all the way to her toes. He could work with that.

Kingsley knelt on the floor in front of her. Her eyes widened in surprise, but she made no objection. A good sign that she had no issue with men kneeling in front of her.

"Did you poison him?" Kingsley asked, studying her face and neck.

"I didn't want him to fuck me," she whispered. "If he's sick he can't fuck me. I wanted to make him sick. That's all."

"Most wives I know like getting fucked by their husbands."

"Those wives aren't married to my husband."

He raised his hand and lifted her hair off her neck. She closed her eyes as Kingsley examined four small black bruises that marred the otherwise unblemished skin under her hairline.

Kingsley positioned his hand until his fingertips lined up with the bruises. "He tried to choke you. Was this in bed or out of bed?"

"He does it all the time," she whispered. "I think…someday he will kill me."

"Why do you stay with him?"

"I'm not a citizen," she said. "Not yet. I'd rather die than go back to Russia. My father's worse than my husband."

Kingsley sighed heavily.

"How tall are you?" he asked. Irina gave him a puzzled look.

"Five foot ten."

"Are you very strong?"

"Stronger than I look."

"I believe that. How would you feel if I kissed the tip of your shoe?"

Irina narrowed her eyes at him. "Why would you do that?"

"Why not?"

"Kiss it, then. I don't care."

"I would if we weren't in a holding cell. Against my will, I find I have a new lease on life these days," he said. "I'd hate to catch something."

She smiled, and that one little smile transformed her face. In an instant she was rendered unspeakably lovely.

"You can kiss it later, then," she said, an imperious look on her face. It was there an instant and then gone again. But he'd seen it—arrogance, self-importance, power. Cooper was right.

"Did you ever want to fight your husband off?"

"Every time," she said. "I wanted to break him and beat him into the ground. But he had the money, and if he divorced me, I wouldn't be able to stay here."

"You like the thought of hitting men."

"Most men need a good beating to teach them how the world really works."

She smiled as she spoke, a dark dangerous smile.

"You might be surprised to find I agree with you."

She looked at him now, full-on at him, and for the first time, it seemed she noticed his existence.

"Who are you?" she asked again. "What are you doing here?"

"I told you, my name is Kingsley. I own a club in town, a strip club. But I'm starting a new club. I need people to work the club. Special people. People like you."

"Like me?"

"Like you."

"I don't know anything about working in a club," she said.

"I can teach you everything you need to know."

"What would I do?"

"Beat the shit out of men. Some women, too, but mostly men."

Irina looked at him as if he'd grown a second head.

"Does that pay well? Beating up men?"

"It can, if you do it well enough."

"Sounds like a dream come true."

"Can you be brutal?" he asked.

"I am brutal," she said. "My husband will be in the hospital for a week because of what I gave him last night. I couldn't stop laughing while he was sick."

"You monster." Kingsley grinned at her. "I like you already."

"You're nice," she said. "And you're handsome. And you make me laugh. But I'm going to prison. I'll be deported. My husband has friends. He'll see to it."

"I have better friends than he does. I can help you out of this."

"Why would you do that?"

"I told you—I need you. If you agree to come work for me, I promise that, from now on, you will be doing all the beating. Do you like the sound of that?"

Kingsley stood up and looked down at her. She gazed up at him without smiling.

"I love the sound of that."

He held out his hand to shake. Instead of shaking it, Irina lifted up her foot and put it in his palm. Flexible. Also a good sign.

Kingsley bent and kissed her boot at the ankle.

"Don't speak to anyone," he whispered. Detective Cooper waited for him at the door. "I'll take care of this."

He left her alone in the cell, and Cooper locked it behind them.

"Well?" Cooper asked.

"You were right," Kingsley said.

"Told you so."

"How do you know Russian?" Cooper asked, clearly impressed.

"I used to hunt there."

"No shit. You're a hunter? What's there to hunt in Russia? Bears?"

Kingsley smiled. "KGB."

Upon leaving the police station, Kingsley headed back to the town house to change clothes. He found Sam in his office.

"You have your checklist?" he asked her.

"Always," she said, picking up a pen.

"Check off one dominatrix."

"Check," she said. "Is she good?"

"She'll be perfect when I'm done with her."

"Mistress Felicia?"

"Not yet. I'm still working on her."

"She won't return your calls?"

"Not a one." Kingsley sighed. "But I'll keep trying. You keep digging on Reverend Fuller. I have to leave again."

"Again? Where to this time? More secret sex missions?"

Kingsley sighed heavily. "If only."

Kingsley changed clothes and made it to the North Meadow of Central Park by 3:05 p.m.

He stood there by the grass feeling foolish. Here he was, notorious club owner and underground figure, standing in Central Park in a white T-shirt and black-and-red running pants. He had work to do, professionals to hire, bigoted televangelists to blackmail, a Russian husband-poisoner to get out of jail. He was building a kingdom. He didn't have time for—

Balls.

A soccer ball sailed toward Kingsley's head. He grabbed it out of the air before it made impact.

"Keeps your balls out of my face," Kingsley said as Søren jogged over to him. He wore black track pants, a black T-shirt and sunglasses. Even in casual attire he still looked like a fucking priest.

"You almost ended up with a black eye," Søren said. "Pay more attention."

"You're kidding me, right?" Kingsley looked down at the ball in his hand.

"I thought you'd want some retribution for the day I scored on you in school."

"I don't have time for this," Kingsley said.

"You can't have sex for two weeks. That has to give you at least a spare ten minutes a day," Søren said.

"Ten minutes? Ten? You know I can last longer than ten minutes."

"Do I? I seem to recall having to punish you a few times—"

"I was sixteen. And I'm leaving. Sam needs me to help her with the files."

Kingsley turned around, intending to head back to the street.

"Coward," Søren said.

"What did you call me?" Kingsley turned back around.

"You heard me. Are you intimidated because I'm taller than you are? Or is it because I've been living in Italy where the best football players in the world live?"

"France. The best football players in the world are in France."

"I heard Denmark had a better team this year." Søren dropped the ball and juggled it with a few deft kicks on his foot.

"My high school team could have beat Denmark this year."

Søren kicked the ball three feet in the air. Kingsley caught it.

"You're trying to get me to play with you. It won't work," he said.

"Why not? Scared I'll beat you?"

"You forget, I like it when you beat me. But you're very arrogant and proud of yourself," Kingsley said. "And I'm fully capable of destroying you right now, and I'm not sure you'll ever recover from the blow to your massive blond ego."

"We seem to have acquired an audience," Søren said, glancing around. Kingsley noticed at least a dozen young women in shorts and barely-there T-shirts had gathered round, trying to look inconspicuous and failing miserably.

"He's a Catholic priest," Kingsley yelled at them. The girls booed.

"He's not." Søren called out to them.

The girls cheered.

"I can't have sex for two weeks," Kingsley reminded him.

"You know you can spend time with someone you're attracted to without having sex with them."

"You really have lost your mind."

"Try it. I dare you."

"Drop the fucking ball," Kingsley said.

"That's our goal." Søren pointed at two trees that stood three feet apart forty meters away.

"That might be your goal," Kingsley said. "But *my* goal is to do something I've wanted to do all my life."

"And that is?" Søren dropped the ball between them. Before Søren moved an inch, Kingsley turned and, with all his strength and the muscle memory formed from playing thousands of hours of soccer as a teenager, kicked the ball in a high perfect arc toward the two trees. The ball passed down the middle of them with the precision of a whip tip through the center of a business card.

Goal.

He turned to Søren and smiled.

"Beat the shit out of you."

17

NOT THAT ANYONE HAD EVER ASKED, BUT IF THEY had, Kingsley would have told them he bought the town house because he fell in love with the bathtub. Grand in size, porcelain with gold accents and claw-foot, it was a bathtub built for a king. He could live in it. If he kept playing football with Søren he would have to live in it. He needed the heat and the water to loosen up his chest where the scar tissue was healing too tightly. He arched his back to the point of pain and let the water seep into his scars. He tried to take a deep breath, but the scar restricted his movements.

Yet for all the agony, it couldn't wipe the smile off his face. He'd done it. He'd scored on Søren ten times to his six today. Not quite the rout he was hoping for, but defeating Søren, even in a game of Central Park soccer, was exactly what the doctor ordered. Unfortunately, the exertion had resulted in tonight's renewed aches and pains. But it was worth it. For the bragging rights alone, it was worth it.

While soaking his sore muscles, he put on his glasses, picked up a book he'd bought yesterday and opened to page one. A few minutes later he heard a knock on the bathroom door.

"Come in," Kingsley said.

Sam opened the door with a hand over her eyes.

"Number one or number two?" she asked from the doorway.

"Number…I don't know. I'm taking a bath."

"Bubble bath?"

"I'm not a girl," Kingsley said.

"Okay, I'm keeping my eyes covered, then," she said. "Which is not going to work, because I have messages to read to you."

"Turn your back and read them to me," Kingsley said. "Or look. I don't care."

Sam peeked over the top of her hand.

"What the hell are you doing?" she demanded. "You're wearing glasses."

"I'm farsighted. I can hit a target at five hundred yards, but words six inches in front of my face are blurry."

"You're reading in the bathtub. Are you sure you're not a girl?"

Kingsley glanced down into the water.

"Fairly sure," he said.

"What are you reading?"

Kingsley closed the book and showed Sam the cover.

Designed to Serve: A Guide to Becoming The Wife God Wants You To Be by Lucy Fuller.

"You're reading a Christian marriage guide?" Sam asked, wide-eyed with horror. Real horror, not amused horror. "Why?"

"I want to save my marriage," Kingsley said, turning a page.

"You're not married."

"Someday my prince will come." He turned a page. "Preferably on my back."

"Do you really think you're going to find any dirt on the Fullers in a Christian marriage guide? I mean, in our world being vanilla is a sin, but not to them."

"I want to know more about Fuller's family life. Lucy Fuller has written five of these fucking Christian self-help books. Christian dating, Christian marriage, Christian sex, Christian parenthood, Christian cooking. Do fundamentalist Christians eat different food than we heathens do?"

"I'm surprised you didn't get the book on Christian sex."

"It didn't have any pictures," he said. "She's cute, no?"

He flipped the book over to show Sam the author photo on the back. Lucy Fuller was ten years younger then her reverend husband. She was thirty-five years old, had fake blond hair, a bright smile, gleaming teeth and dead eyes, which was exactly how he expected a televangelist's wife to look.

"She's a helluva lot better-looking than her husband."

"You are a harsh critic," Kingsley said, *tsk-tsk*ing at her. "You should read this. It's full of good advice. She says if I want to make my husband happy, I have to dress modestly."

"You were wearing a very modest corset and heels the night we met."

"Chapter three tells me I have to be attuned to my husband's needs and anticipate them before he has to ask. Do you think she's talking about blow jobs? I hope she's talking about blow jobs."

"I doubt James Fuller has ever gotten a blow job in his life."

"Chapter Seven," Kingsley said, flipping through the book. "The importance of waiting until marriage for sex. You're right. This book is bullshit." He closed the book and tossed it on the floor.

"Total bullshit," Sam said.

Kingsley narrowed his eyes at her.

"You know this church well, don't you?" Kingsley asked.

"We have history," she said. "Nothing exciting. Just unpleasant."

"Tell me," he said, looking at her expectantly. "Please?"

Sam crossed her arms over her chest and looked away into the corner of the room.

"I grew up in a fundamentalist church. My parents called me their 'tomboy.' That's the way fundies make lesbians disappear. 'Just a tomboy…she'll grow out of it.' Mom made it her personal mission to make a lady out of me. Makeup. Pretty long hair. Dresses. Girl stuff. Her lessons didn't take. It was humiliating," she said, and he heard the anguish in her voice. "I don't like talking about it. Sorry."

"I understand. There are things I don't like to talk about, either. But sometimes I have to."

"I know," Sam said, and she gave him a forced smile. "I told you they run reorienting camps. My parents sent me to one of those camps."

"I see," Kingsley said, fighting a wave of rage that someone had done that to his Sam. "I assume it didn't take?"

"No. It didn't take. And it was the worst month of my life. And I've had some bad months."

"Did you hear anything about the Fullers that we can use?"

"Not that I know of. Some of the kids there hated him. Some didn't know him from Adam. Some thought he was their personal Jesus. I wish I knew more. I want to see that church go down in flames as much as you do."

"I'll find something on him. There's always something. Towel?"

Sam grabbed a towel and tossed it to him.

"Turn around," he said. "I'm getting out."

"Oh, now you're getting modest?" Sam asked, glaring at him.

"Chapter two," Kingsley said. "Only my husband is allowed to see me naked."

"Fine. I'm not looking at you," she said. "I'm looking at my clipboard."

"Why aren't you looking at me?"

"You're a dude and you're my boss. I don't want to see you naked."

"I'm very pretty," he said as he pulled himself out of the water and wrapped the towel around his waist.

"Will it make you happy if I check you out?"

"I wouldn't recommend it actually." Kingsley took off his glasses and set them aside. "Since you're a worrier."

But it was too late. Sam had looked.

"Oh, shit."

Kingsley sighed.

"I was afraid of that," he said. "It's not as bad as it looks."

Sam dropped her clipboard on the floor and walked over to him.

"I'm looking," she said, and whistled to herself. "God damn, that must have hurt. What did that?"

"Bullet plus the surgery to dig it out."

"Can I touch it?"

"I'm wet and wearing a towel, and you want to touch me?"

"Yup."

"Look, Little Lord Fauntleroy, the reason I hired you to be my assistant was so that we could have some…" He paused and searched for the right word. "*Distance* between us."

"I'm not giving you a blow job. I'm touching your scars."

"Blaise gives me blow jobs. She doesn't touch my scars."

Sam looked into his eyes. Kingsley was acutely aware of the closeness of her body. Without his clothes on, he could feel the heat emanating from her. She'd shed her jacket and vest after he'd ordered her to "tone it down." Suspenders held up her pin-striped trousers, and her white shirt was unbuttoned to the center of her chest. She might be dressed in men's clothing, but he couldn't deny how alluring and feminine he found her. At the V in her shirt he could see the slightest curve of her small but pert breasts. The last thing he needed was to get an erection and scare away the best assistant he'd found yet.

"Fine. I don't believe in touching someone who doesn't want to be touched." She raised both hands in surrender. "I am, as you see, turning my back on you."

She put one foot over the other and spun neatly around. "Now would you like to hear messages?"

"Not particularly. Do you think I should seduce Lucy Fuller?" Kingsley walked to his closet and dug for clothes. He heard something drop. When he turned around, he saw Sam picking her clipboard off the floor again.

"Seduce Lucy Fuller?" she asked, looking shocked and slightly disgusted. "Why?"

"It would cause a scandal if it got out she'd cheated on her husband. Might give us some leverage against Fuller."

"Or make him a sympathetic martyr to his whole congregation. You know people always blame the wife and never the husband."

"Good point," he said. "I didn't want to fuck her anyway."

"Why not?"

"She had an entire chapter in her book on marriage on why sodomy is such a crime against nature even married couples shouldn't engage in it."

"That's bizarre."

"Sodomy's not a crime against nature. Nature invented sodomy. If Mother Nature didn't want us engaging in it, she wouldn't have made it so much fun."

"I can't argue with your science. Poor Lucy. Her loss."

"Poor Lucy? She's richer than I am. Did you know that? Her books and videos fund the WTL empire."

"They always hit the bestseller list. God only knows why."

"The WTL empire is built on their perfect marriage."

"I have parents," Sam said. "I don't believe there's such a thing as a perfect marriage."

"My parents did. Until they died," Kingsley said. "Maybe it's for the best. They would rather have died than fall out of love with each other."

Sam gave him a long searching look that Kingsley tried to ignore.

"I'd rather fall out of love with someone than die," Sam said. "You can always love someone else."

"Easier said than done," Kingsley said, and his words sounded bitterer than he intended.

"So, who are you in love with you don't want to be in love with?" Sam asked.

Kingsley glared at her.

"Right," she said. "Distance. We're trying to keep some distance."

"If you please."

"Sorry. Okay, I'll get back to work digging around on Reverend Fuller."

"Let's divide and conquer. I'll handle Reverend Fuller. You focus on Lucy Fuller. They're making a lot of money off her books. Follow the money."

He pulled his pants on and grabbed a shirt from off the hanger.

"Now, what are my messages?"

"Are you dressed? Is it safe to turn around again? I don't want my delicate lesbian sensibilities overwhelmed by your incredible manliness. I might get the vapors, whatever those are."

"It's safe."

She turned around.

"Kingsley, you haven't buttoned up your shirt yet, and I can totally see your chest. You lied to me, and now I have the vapors."

"Come here," he ordered. She looked left and then right as if scanning the room for a trap. Maybe hiring Sam had been a mistake. All he could think about right now was getting her into bed and seeing the woman's body she hid under her men's clothing.

He took her by the wrist, raised her hand and laid it on the scar on the side of his chest.

"You're lucky to be alive. Is this why you were wincing in your office?" She pressed her palm gently against the scar.

"The scar tissue is tight. It hurts when I try to take a deep breath."

"You know you should listen to your body. Pain's an alarm. It says 'pay attention to me.'"

"I promise I'm paying attention to it. It's not getting better."

"I know what you need. There's a lady in Midtown who does amazing therapeutic massage."

"I don't need a massage."

"I can see if she gives happy endings."

"I might need a massage."

"Thought so. I'll make you an appointment. She's good with surgical scars and other wounds."

"How do you know so much about scars?" he asked, impressed more by her moxie than her knowledge. No one but Søren ever dared to challenge him. He liked it.

Sam let her hand fall from his side.

"You're not the only one around here with scars," she said.

"Show me your scars." He said "scars" but what he meant was "body."

"My scars? My scars are—" The phone rang. Sam grinned broadly at it. "I'll get it."

"That's my private line. You don't have to answer my private line," he said.

"The private line's the one I want to answer."

She jumped onto his bed and crawled across the red sheets. With a flourish she grabbed the receiver, held it to her ear and rolled flat on to her back.

"Kingsley Edge's Bed, Sam speaking."

With the phone at her ear and her legs dancing playfully in the air, she looked almost like a teenage girl in her bedroom. Kingsley took a deep steadying breath. *Lesbian,* he reminded himself.

"I'll see if he's in," she said. "Hold, please."

She sat the phone on the bedside table, pulled the covers back, and stuck her head between the sheets.

"King? You in there?"

"Who is it?" he whispered.

"He says he's your father," she said in a stage whisper of her own. "But that can't be, because you said your father was dead."

"Did he say he was *my* father or *a* father?"

Sam looked up at him.

"I'll ask." She grabbed the phone again. "Are you *a* father or are you Kingsley's father? Kingsley's father's dead, and Kingsley is not at home to ghosts. And if you are a ghost, are you like a Hamlet ghost or a *Ghostbusters* ghost?"

Kingsley sighed. He shouldn't be having this much fun with his secretary. He never had fun with his other secretaries. He just fucked them.

"You're not a father, you're a *Father*. Oh, so you're the priest King told me about. Hey, can you explain transubstantiation to me in twenty-five words or less?"

Sam tucked the phone under her chin and held two hands up in the air. She ticked off numbers on her fingers. Kingsley counted twenty-one.

"Wow," she said after a few seconds. "You're good."

"Give me that." He took the phone from Sam. "What do

you want?" he asked Søren in French. Whatever Søren was calling about, he didn't want Sam to be privy to it.

"This is your first of fourteen nightly reminders to not have sex with anyone until you get your test results back," Søren replied, also in French.

"Go fuck a fifteen-year-old."

"Her birthday was in March. She's sixteen now."

"I'm hanging up on you."

"I like the new secretary," Søren said. "Keep this one."

Kingsley hung up on him.

"Well, that was rude," Sam said.

"I hung up on him because he deserved it."

"No, I mean it's rude to talk to him in French. I couldn't keep up."

"He said he liked you," Kingsley said. Sam's eyes sparkled like a child's on Christmas morning.

"Then I like him. I've never met a kinky priest before. He has a nice voice. Stern but soothing. I want to call him 'sir' and serve him tea and crumpets and listen to him read *The Hobbit* to me."

"Everyone he meets wants to call him 'sir.' And his father's English, so he'd probably appreciate the tea. I have no idea if he eats crumpets."

"Do you think he'd read *The Hobbit* out loud to me?"

"Ask him that when you meet him. And make sure I'm there for the answer. Now, can you please give me my messages so I can kick you out of my bedroom?"

"I like your bedroom. It's cozy in a Gothic nightmare kind of way. Was V. C. Andrews your interior decorator? Your bed has bed curtains. I've never seen that in real life before."

"Messages?"

"Fine." She grabbed her clipboard, rolled over on the bed and read.

"Message number one—Signore Vitale will see you on June tenth at two for a fitting." She read the entire message in a cartoonish Italian accent.

"I don't know who that is. And what am I getting a fitting for? Please, tell me I didn't agree to go to a wedding."

"Vitale is my tailor, and you're getting fitted for a new wardrobe. You want to be a kingly king, right? Not just a king?"

"Right."

"Then you need a better wardrobe. Trust me on this. Vitale is a genius. Message number two—Officer Cooper said Irina's out on bail, and he gave me her phone number."

"Good. She's our new dominatrix in training. Call her and tell her she can move in this weekend. She's staying with us until her divorce is finalized."

"Is she nice?"

"She tried to poison her husband."

"Nice. Message number three—Luka says she'll be by tonight at nine."

"And who the hell is Luka?"

"Old friend of mine," Sam said. "Incredibly sexy. Her dad's Jamaican and her mom's Canadian. Weirdest accent ever. And she's a pain-slut."

"And I'm meeting her because…?"

"I think she could be our pro-sub. She's never done it for money before, but she said she was up for a meeting."

"A meeting or a beating?"

"That's between you two. And now, I'm out of here. Good night, King Kingsley. I'll see you in the morning."

She salaamed at him on her way out of his bedroom.

"Sam?"

She paused in the doorway and turned around.

"The meeting with Luka—you take it. If she's good, offer her the job."

"You don't want to meet her? Beat her? All that jizz?"

"I'll let you take this one. Meet her. Talk to her. If you think she's right for the job, hire her."

Kingsley did want to meet her and probably beat her, too. He'd also probably fuck her, and he'd promised Søren and Dr. Sutton he'd be a good boy for two weeks.

"Sure," Sam said with a shrug. "You busy tonight?"

"Very busy," he said. "I'll leave Luka to your good judgment."

"Thank you," she said. "Nice to be trusted. I won't let you down."

"I know you won't. Anything else?"

"No. Yes. I forgot. One more message. A woman named Phoebe called. She said nine o'clock tomorrow. Which I assume means someone named Phoebe wants you to fuck her tomorrow night. Am I wrong?"

"You're not wrong."

"Should I call her back?"

Phoebe Dixon. He hadn't seen her or fucked her in months. He assumed her husband had hinted that her extracurricular activities were no longer to be tolerated. Maybe Mister Dixon was out of town.

Out of town sounded like a very good idea right now.

"I'll handle it," Kingsley said. "Toss the message."

"You got it." She crumbled up the message and tossed it into his trash can on her way out of his door.

"Sam?"

"What?" she asked, her hand on the doorknob.

"You didn't show me your scars," he reminded her.

She smiled, but the smile looked both forced and faked.

"I don't show anybody my scars."

Sam walked out of his bedroom without another word.

Kingsley stood alone by his closet and tried to focus on getting dressed. But the message from Phoebe Dixon couldn't be ignored. He pinched the bridge of his nose, trying to think of a good enough excuse to get out of seeing her again. She only wanted him for one thing, and he was under orders from a doctor and a priest not to give that one thing to anyone for two weeks. Not that he was going to tell Phoebe or anyone else that. Telling her the truth wasn't an option. Telling her no wasn't an option. And pissing her off wasn't an option.

But if he was out of town…

Kingsley strode from his bedroom and found Sam in his office.

"Three things," he said. "First, call Phoebe. Tell her I'm out of town."

"Check."

"Second. There's a number in my desk for a man named The Barber—"

"Are you getting a hair cut? Please, say no. I love the long hair."

"He's not a barber. It's his nickname. He's a Mafia numbers guy. He combs through files," Kingsley said, wiggling his fingers like a comb at work.

"If he combs through the files, why don't they call him The Comb?"

"Have you met anyone in the mob? They aren't known for being brain trusts."

"Fine. I'll call The Barber. What do I ask him?"

"Tell him to dig through the Fullers' finances—church and personal."

"Can do. Anything else?"

"Third. I need you to book a flight for me."

"Where are you going?"

I'm not the teacher. Magdalena is. She could have you flipping quarters in midair with a single-tail in two weeks.

"Rome."

18

June

TODAY KINGSLEY FELT WHAT HE WOULD CLASSIFY AS a "new" pain.

And considering how much and how many types of pain he'd experienced in his life, this was saying something.

He lay naked on his side, a warm white blanket pulled up to his hip. Soothing music played in the background. And a masseuse named Anita talked to him as she kneaded the tough scar tissue in his chest. She worked against the grain, she explained, breaking up the tightness, opening up the tissue, forcing blood into the inert cells. Not even in the hospital had he experienced this level of raw pain. Unshed tears scalded his eyes, and his fingers held on to a pillow with a death grip.

"You should be a sadist," Kingsley said between gritted teeth. "I think getting shot hurt less."

Anita paused and wiped sweat from his forehead. Her touch was welcome and motherly, which made him feel a little guilty about his massive erection hidden under the blanket.

"You'll feel like a new man when I'm done with you, I promise. Do you need to stop for the day?"

Kingsley shook his head.

"No," he said, panting. "You said you'll make me feel like a new man. Then, make me feel like a new man."

"Has anyone ever told you that you have a very high tolerance for pain?" Anita asked.

"Yes. A priest I used to date," he said. Anita gave him the exact look he expected her to give him.

Anita returned to her work, and Kingsley mentally fired Sam in ten different ways for talking him into this. But he'd come home from Rome yesterday with a stiff back and tightness in his chest so severe he couldn't take a full breath. Sam had called Anita, the massaging miracle worker, and gotten him an emergency appointment.

Not even getting fucked raw by Søren had hurt this badly. He could come any second now.

"Breathe," Anita ordered, and Kingsley did as commanded. He breathed, she massaged, and every nerve in his body screamed.

The pain suffused him. He was awash in pain, bathing in pain, drinking in pain, breathing in pain. The pain from candle wax-play was something like this sort of steady persistent agony. When was the last time he'd felt the wax? With Søren, of course. They'd gotten wrought-iron candleholders out of storage at the school and brought them to the hermitage for extra light to play and read by. One cold quiet night, Søren had ordered Kingsley on to his stomach on the cot and tied his wrists and ankles to each bed leg. For hours Søren had sat at his hip and dripped the wax on him, burning him one drop at a time. No matter how Kingsley had panted, how he groaned, how he gasped and winced, Søren never let up. As Søren had scalded him with the wax, he'd asked Kingsley questions.

What do you want to do with your life?
Where do you want to go?

What do you dream about?
What do you love?
What do you hate?
And he'd answered the questions all truthfully.
I want to spend my life with you.
I want to go where you go.
I dream of you.
I love sex.
I love pain.
I love you.
I hate the nights I spend without you.

How small his world was back then. It had been the size of that hermitage. What if his sister, Marie-Laure, had never come to St. Ignatius? Would Kingsley's world still be that small? He would have willingly, joyfully and blindly devoted himself to Søren. He would have gone where Søren had gone, done what Søren had ordered, slept where Søren told him to sleep, eaten what Søren told him to eat and died by his own hand if Søren had decreed it. Was it possible that it was for the best Kingsley had gotten away from Søren for a few years? Was it possible leaving and going out on his own had been the right thing to do? Søren certainly seemed happier now than he did in high school. Maybe being apart from him had been good for Søren, too, although it rankled to entertain the very idea that Søren had been better off without him. Kingsley wondered…what would he answer now if asked those same questions?

I want to build a kingdom for our kind and keep us all safe.

I want to go to the Caribbean. I haven't been there yet. Trinidad, Dominican Republic, Haiti.

At night I dream about being choked, being shot. But during the day, when I'm awake, I dream about finding someone to share my life with and my kingdom with.

I love sex. I love women. I love men. I love this city. I love music. I love my house. I love Søren still. Always.

I hate...

What did he hate these days? Oh, he knew.

I hate people like Fuller, which is why I'm taking his church from him.

Very different answers from when he was a teenager. Better answers.

Kingsley would never know for certain what would have happened if they'd stayed together. The past was a corpse. He should stop trying to dig it up and reanimate it. He'd been clinging to it for years now because he had nothing else to hold on to. But now he had a vision, a dream, a hope for the future. And no matter what happened, he would see it come to life. Whatever it took.

Anita finished her work on his scar. He rolled on to his stomach, and she spent the next hour working the soreness out of his neck and shoulders. When she finished, she laid a gentle hand on the crown of his head.

"Kingsley, can you take a deep breath for me?" Anita asked, her words penetrating his thoughts.

He rolled on to his back, arched his shoulders and inhaled.

"Again?"

He breathed in again. His lungs expanded, his chest swelled and he took the deepest breath of his life.

And it didn't hurt.

"Dieu, merci..." He sighed and smiled.

"You feel better?" Anita asked.

"Like a new man."

Anita left him alone to dress. He said he would have Sam call and set up another appointment. Anita hugged him— hugged him?—goodbye and told him to enjoy the day, go for a walk, breathe fresh air.

He found a pay phone and dialed a number.

"Test results?" Søren asked as soon as Kingsley spoke.

"Not yet," he said. "I find out tomorrow."

"Do you want me to be with you?"

"No," Kingsley said. "I think I need to do this alone."

He didn't want to be alone, but if the results weren't what he wanted, Søren wouldn't have to see him fall apart.

"I can respect that," Søren said. "To what do I owe the pleasure of this call, then?"

"I wanted to tell you I went to Rome."

"So that's where you disappeared to. Sam wouldn't tell me when I called."

"She's overprotective," Kingsley said, smiling to himself. He liked that Sam didn't tell Søren where he was. The woman wasn't afraid to annoy Søren. He should give her a raise. "I met your friend Magdalena."

"What did you think of her?"

"She was very mean to me," Kingsley said, an understatement. She'd taught him types of kink he'd never known existed, lectured him on consent and safe kink practice and forced him to practice with a whip until he, too, could split a business card in half. He wished he could have stayed longer.

"I warned you about her," Søren said, laughing. "I'm glad you're home."

"Did you miss me?"

"I missed being mean to you."

"About that..." Kingsley said. "Are you busy today?"

"Why?"

"Do you want to beat me?"

"Kingsley, haven't we had this talk?"

"Beat me in football," he said. "I mean, do you want to play football with me again? *Pardonnez-moi*...soccer." He felt unreasonably stupid right now, like a nervous teenager asking the most popular girl in school on a date. He'd never done that. He'd skipped the dating and gone right to the fucking. "You're busy, aren't you? And—"

"Kingsley."

"Never mind. I forget you have a job."

"Kingsley. Focus."

"*Quoi?*"

"Yes. Come to my church," Søren said, and Kingsley was certain he could hear Søren smiling. "Sacred Heart in Wakefield. Be there at five."

"So, you do want to play with me?" Kingsley asked.

He heard Søren softly laugh. "I thought you'd never ask."

Still smiling, Kingsley hung up and headed back to his town house to change clothes. He hadn't seen Sacred Heart yet. He'd been waiting for an invitation, not wanting to force himself into Søren's world. Now he found himself unexpectedly nervous. What if she was there? The new love? The Virgin Queen? Eleanor Louise Schreiber, thief of cars and hearts.

"So, how was it?" Sam asked as Kingsley walked into his office. "Did Anita work her magic?"

"I thought she was going to kill me. I've never been in so much pain in my life. And I've been shot four times."

"So…"

"See if she can get me in again this week."

"I told you she was a miracle worker," Sam said.

"Speaking of miracles, I have to run. I have a date with a priest to play football."

"Real football or fake European football?"

"Fake European football."

"Soccer," she said, with a wink and a finger point. "Something came for you while you were out."

She handed him a padded envelope with his name on it and nothing else.

"Where did this come from?" Kingsley asked.

"Courier dropped it off. Why?"

"No reason," he said. He ripped the envelope open. A mini-cassette tape slid out into his hand.

He looked at Sam. She shook her head in confusion. Kingsley walked around his desk, pulled out his tape player and stuck the tape in.

When he hit Play he heard his own voice speaking.

"Friend of a friend."

"You have friends who are friends with fifteen-year-old girls?"

The other voice on the tape belonged to Robert Dixon. The tape continued.

"I have interesting friends."

"I didn't know you had any friends, Edge."

"Kingsley? What is this?" Sam asked. He raised his hand to silence her.

"I put my job on the line helping a fifteen-year-old girl get out of going to juvie for stealing cars, I want to know the story."

"Fine. Old friend of mine is a Catholic priest now. Her priest. He asked me to help her. I owe him a big favor. This is the favor."

"You're friends with a priest?"

"Trust me, no one is more shocked by that than I am."

"Is he fucking her? The priest?"

"What?"

"It's all over the papers," Dixon said. *"Every damn day there's a new story about a Catholic priest fucking some kid. Boston's exploding. Phillie, Detroit, Chicago… I get caught helping a priest with the underage girl he's fucking and—"*

"He's not fucking her."

"How do you know?"

"Because I'm fucking her."

Kingsley shut off the tape.

Sam stared at him.

"I'm not fucking a fifteen-year-old girl, Sam," he said.

"But—"

"That was a lie. I had to lie."

"Who is that on the tape with you?"

"A DA. I was bribing him to help someone."

"He recorded you. He's going to have copies of that."

Kingsley tapped the envelope. "Many copies."

"King, you're confessing to committing statutory rape."

"And bribing a public official, too. Don't forget that."

"Did you fuck her?"

"No, of course not. I've never met her."

"Then why did you confess—"

"It doesn't matter. What matters is that I've pissed someone off."

"Who?"

"It's a long list of suspects."

"What are you going to do about it?"

"Nothing tonight," he said. "I'll have a talk with Mr. Dixon tomorrow."

"Why's he threatening you?"

Kingsley shook his head.

"No idea. I know enough about him to ruin his career and his marriage. It might not be him."

"Then who—"

"I don't know. Don't worry about it."

"I'm worried," she said, looking stricken.

Kingsley walked up to her, put his hands on her face and stared into her eyes.

"Sam, listen to me. You think this is the first time something like this has happened to me? This is nothing compared to what I've handled before. This is what I do. This is the job."

Sam met his eyes. He saw fear in them, real fear.

"You really didn't have sex with a fifteen-year-old, did you?" Sam asked.

"I didn't even fuck fifteen-year-old girls when I was fifteen. Sixteen—bare minimum."

Sam laughed, and Kingsley tapped her under the chin.

"Okay," she said. "I trust you."

"I have to go. No worrying."

He kissed her on the forehead and left her in his office. He locked up the tape, changed clothes and by five o'clock he'd pulled into the parking lot of Sacred Heart. Kingsley Edge at a Catholic Church. He wasn't sure God existed, but if He did, He had a fucking sick sense of humor.

Since March, Søren's life as a priest had been something only theoretical to Kingsley. He'd seen the collar, the clerics, but had never seen him at work. Every Sunday he thought of Søren saying Mass in this little town. Did they have any idea who their pastor was? What he was? What he'd given up so he could say Mass in this little town to these little people who had no inkling their priest had walked away from wealth and power to serve them? Of course not, and that's how Søren wanted it. His money was tainted by his father. Power was too easily abused, and Søren's father was proof of that. As Kingsley stared at the church, a Romanesque pile of stone and stained glass, Kingsley had to wonder…

Had Søren become a priest because he loved God, the Father?

Or had he become a priest because he hated his own father?

Or both?

"Good. You're here," Søren said. He had emerged from a side door of the church into the parking lot and was striding toward Kingsley. He had on black track pants and a black T-shirt. "We're going to be late."

"Late for football?"

"Late for practice."

"Practice?" Kingsley asked as they headed down a side street. "I thought we were playing. Just you and I."

"You're too good. You need to be on a team." Søren pointed ahead of them to a soccer field behind a small school. He saw about twenty-five people milling about on the field, kicking balls back and forth. Most of them looked to be teenagers—boys and a few girls. But a few were their age, in their twenties and thirties. One girl with a swinging ponytail wearing short shorts and knee socks jogged past them and waved at Søren.

"What are you doing to me?" Kingsley asked.

"Congratulations, Kingsley. You're the new striker on our intermural church league team."

"Were you this weird back in high school?" Kingsley asked. "Or is this a side effect of prolonged celibacy?"

"You can't say no. We've already ordered your T-shirt."

"Definitely weirder since high school."

"The wisest thing my confessor ever told me was that I could be a priest and have fun."

"Church league soccer is your definition of fun?"

"It is when you win. But First Presbyterian slaughtered us last week. We lost four to one."

"Aren't Presbyterians Calvinists?" Kingsley asked. Søren hated Calvinism.

"Now you know why I need you to help me destroy them."

"If I help you destroy the Presbyterians, what do I get in return?"

"My gratitude?"

Kingsley stayed silent.

"My eternal gratitude?" Søren upped his offer.

Kingsley still said nothing.

"A night with Eleanor once she's old enough?"

Kingsley narrowed his eyes at Søren and stroked his chin while considering the offer.

"You and her both? My bedroom?"

Søren paused.

"If you're clean," Søren finally said, "and if you behave, don't get yourself killed between now and then, and if she's amenable to the idea."

"Agreed," Kingsley said.

"Then it's a deal."

Kingsley took the soccer ball out of Søren's hands.

"First Presbyterian will never know what hit them," Kingsley said. Side by side they ran on to the field, and in short order, Kingsley had taken command of the team. The team assumed, rightly, that being European, Kingsley could play better than they could, and they willingly followed his direction. The younger players especially were in awe. For a perfect two hours Kingsley didn't think once of his impending test results, not once about Robert Dixon's tape, not once about taking out Fuller's church.

And not once did he think of Søren as anything other than an annoyingly good player on his team.

When practice ended, they walked back to the church sweaty and tired. But it was a good sweaty, a good tired.

"Admit it, you had fun," Søren said. "Fun that didn't involve sex, drugs, or blackmailing and/or bribing a district attorney."

"I don't bribe DAs for fun. That was a favor to you."

"And I appreciate it. So does Eleanor, even if she doesn't know what you did on her behalf."

"She'll make it up to me someday," Kingsley said, attempting to goad Søren and succeeding.

"I said *if* she's amendable to the idea. She might not be."

"You can't even say that with a straight face."

"I admit it's unlikely."

"You know," Kingsley said, taking his keys out of his pocket. "I would have joined the team without you giving me a night with your girl."

Søren smiled and turned away, heading to his church. In French he called back.

"I would have given you a night with her without you joining the team."

Kingsley laughed. Maybe there was hope for that priest yet.

19

"DO YOU WANT A STRAIGHT PIN THROUGH YOUR future children?"

"No." Kingsley sighed.

"Then, young man, I'd suggest you hold still."

"I am holding still," Kingsley said, rolling his eyes. First Magdalena, and then Signore Vitale. Kingsley decided he had more than fulfilled his quota for suffering the abuses of irascible Italians for the century.

"Hold more still," the little white-haired man at his feet said.

"King," Sam said, tapping her foot in annoyance. "Hold the fuck still."

"When I have a man on his feet in front of me, it's usually considered an insult if I hold still," Kingsley said.

"Don't flatter yourself. You aren't my type." The tailor, Signore Vitale, looked up from the floor.

"Are you straight?" Kingsley asked. He was everyone's type. Except Sam's.

"No, but you are French."

"Italians…" Kingsley shook his head. "Look, I'm no fan of Napoleon, either. But it was a hundred-and-ninety years ago."

"Italians have long memories."

Kingsley forced himself to stop moving, stop breathing, stop thinking.

"Better," Signore Vitale said. "Much better. Soon we'll have you looking like a new you."

"I thought the old me looked good."

"You dress like a gay hobo," Signore Vitale said.

"That's not true," Sam said, coming to Kingsley's defense.

"Merci," Kingsley said.

"He dresses like a bisexual hobo."

Kingsley glared at her.

"For the record, I consider myself pansexual."

"Does that mean you like to fuck cookware?"

"It means I like to fuck everything."

"Typical *francese*." Vitale sighed.

"Am I paying for these insults to my heritage?" Kingsley asked.

"Yes," Vitale said. "Five percent surcharge for French clients."

"Make it two-and-a-half percent. I'm only half French."

In his twenty-eight years, Kingsley had had many a man kneeling before him at crotch level. Signore Vitale would win the award for the oldest and least appealing of all the men who'd ended up in this position. He tried not to look down as Vitale made the most minor of adjustments on his trousers, pinning the fabric and marking it with chalk.

"Good. You're finished." Vitale clapped his hands once and, with Sam's help, rose off the floor. "You can take those off."

With a sigh of relief Kingsley walked behind the changing screen where he'd left his regular clothes. He should never have let Sam talk him into getting a new wardrobe. She had taken over his entire life in a month. Sam had gotten all his files in order. She'd hired a housekeeper—a woman who'd once worked at a pornography studio and was thus unfazed by anything that happened under Kingsley's roof. And after one session with Anita, the pain in his chest had lessened considerably.

Kingsley pulled off the jacket but paused when he noticed something on the wall. He walked to it, stared at it, studied it…

"King, what it is?" Sam asked, standing at his side.

He pointed to the cross on the wall. A small pretty thing, six inches tall, six inches wide. He hadn't noticed it at first because the golden color blended into the green-and-gold wallpaper.

"It's a Huguenot Cross," Kingsley said. "See? The top is a Maltese cross—the four points are the four Gospels, the eight ends are the eight Beatitudes. The dove at the bottom, he's the Holy Spirit."

"Don't touch that," Signore Vitale said as he came back into the fitting room. "That was my grandmother's."

"Your grandmother was descended from the Huguenots?"

"She was, yes," Vitale said, seemingly taken aback by the question. "I told you we have long memories. What of it?"

"My father's family is descended from them, too. Supposedly we hid out in Italy for three generations before returning to France."

Vitale craned his neck and studied Kingsley through his small rounded spectacles.

"You have Italian blood in you," Vitale said. "I can see it now."

"My grandmother was from Amalfi."

"That's where my family is from."

"Beautiful city," Kingsley said.

Vitale looked Kingsley up and down and for the first time seemed to see him.

"Why do you want a new wardrobe, monsieur?" Vitale asked. Monsieur, he'd said. Not "young man."

"My name is King. I want to live up to my name."

"He needs something special," Sam said. "Something regal. Something royal."

Vitale narrowed his eyes and looked Kingsley up and down again.

"My family fled to England when Mussolini took power. I was two years old," Vitale said. "We moved back after the war ended. But while in England my father apprenticed at Benson & Clegg. Do you know it?"

"I've heard of it, of course."

"My father once measured King George VI for a suit. Now, he was a king who knew how to dress like a man. A real man. Wait here…"

Vitale disappeared again. Sam and Kingsley looked at each other. When Vitale returned he had a book in his hand—large, leather-bound, stuffed with yellowed papers.

"You see this?" Vitale opened the book. "This was my father's. All the patterns, the measurements, the finished product." He turned the pages and there he was—King George VI in all his royal glory. "He was a military man. Navy first. Then air force. A pilot. Are you a military man?"

"French Foreign Legion," Kingsley said.

"What rank?"

"Captain," Kingsley said.

"You were a captain in the French Foreign Legion?" Sam asked, obviously flabbergasted.

"You're surprised?" he asked, amused by her wide-mouthed shock. He chucked her under the chin.

"I'm not," Vitale said. "He's got the good posture. A soldier's posture. So did King George."

He flipped a page in the book to a picture of a man, handsome, midthirties, in an officer's uniform and knee-high boots.

"Nice," Sam said. "You should dress like that, King."

"I was never in the Royal Air Force."

"I meant the boots."

"Hessian boots," Vitale said. "Excellent for riding."

Sam took the book from Vitale and flipped carefully through the pages.

"Damn, check out these suits," Sam said, eyeing the pages of pictures and patterns. "Morning jackets, frock coats, double-breasted overcoats, breeches, boots, military jackets... Those are my favorite. All those brass buttons. You'd be the sexiest man in the city in suits like these, King."

"Sexy? Nonsense," Vitale said, scoffing. "Sexy is for beer commercials. A king should be arresting, powerful. Everyone should notice when he walks in a room."

"You dress like that," Sam said, pointing at a picture of the king in a long military coat, "and even I'll want to sleep with you."

She smiled at him with shining eyes. Kingsley turned to Vitale.

"I'll take them," Kingsley said.

"Take what?" Vitale asked.

Kingsley shut the book and put it in Vitale's hands.

"All of them."

"All of them?" Vitale repeated.

"And one for her, too," he said, nodding toward Sam. "Whatever she wants."

"Those are five-thousand dollar suits, King," Sam said in wide-eyed shock.

"Pick whatever you want," he said, slapping her on the back. "Daddy's buying."

The fitting ended, and Kingsley put in an order for twelve new suits in various vintage and royal styles including Regency, Victorian and Edwardian. Sam insisted on the Regency. She blamed her childhood love of romance novels for her breeches fetish.

"Can I have your old shirt?" Sam asked as she gathered up his clothes. "You know, after you get all your new shirts."

"That is not a good idea."

"It's really nice," she said. "I love Brooks Brothers. That shit lasts forever. This would be perfect to sleep in."

She held out the shirt he'd worn to the fitting, a white button-down, and pulled it on over her vest.

"Sam, don't." Kingsley walked over to where she stood by the mirror.

"You're that attached to this shirt?" she asked, smiling at him. "You have two dozen new ones being made for you."

"It's not the shirt, it's the principle of the shirt."

"Your shirts have principles?" She buttoned the three middle buttons.

"You don't know anything about men, so let me fill you in on a little secret," he said, standing in front of her. "When a woman wears one of our shirts, one we've worn, one we've lived in, it's as if she's saying 'He is mine.'"

"And that's bad?"

"It's very good under the right conditions. But you wearing my shirt and sleeping in it and keeping it is the female equivalent of me coming on your back. It's like marking your territory. Do you consider me your property?"

Sam met his eyes, and he saw surprise in them.

"No," she said. "Of course not. You're my employer, Captain." She saluted him.

Kingsley raised his hands and unbuttoned the shirt.

"I know you aren't attracted to me," he said as he slid the shirt off her arms and pulled it back on. "But I am attracted to you, and I'm doing my best to not think of you like that. You wearing my shirt isn't helping me."

"I'm sorry," she whispered. "I didn't... I honestly didn't even think about that."

"It's fine. No harm done."

Kingsley glanced up at the clock in the fitting room and sighed.

"Are you okay?" Sam asked.

"I have to go," he said. "I'm running late."

"Where are you going?"

"Nowhere."

"How can you be late to nowhere?"

"Sam, please. I'm not in the mood right now."

"King? What's going on?" she asked and gave him a concerned look. "Talk to me."

Kingsley paused and weighed the costs and benefits of telling Sam. If he didn't tell her, she'd continue to worry without knowing the reason. If he did tell her, she'd have a reason to worry. Either way, she was going to worry. Might as well get it out.

"I have an appointment," he said. "I had some tests done, and I'm getting the results back."

"Tests? What kind of tests?"

"The kind of tests a twenty-eight year old man who's had sex with half of Europe has to have on occasion."

"Oh, fuck. Those kinds of tests. I wish I could empathize, but the only disease lesbians get from sex is lockjaw."

Kingsley laughed. God, she was good at making him laugh.

"It's fine. I've been thinking about it nonstop for two weeks, so no matter what, at least I'll know."

"We'll know. I'm going with you."

"You don't have to come with me."

"I don't have to," she said. "But I want to. And you want me to. No one wants to be alone for this stuff. Not even you."

"You are too good to me," he said, taking her hand and kissing inside her wrist.

"Stop stalling."

"I'm not stalling, I'm flirting."

"You're a man flirting with a lesbian. That is the very definition of stalling. It's not going to work. I have a lock on my pants, and I threw away the key."

He looked down.

"I don't see a lock."

"It's an invisible lock."

"I'll hire an invisible locksmith."

"I'll put that on the checklist. Now come on. Whatever the news is, better to get it over with."

"If it's bad news, I'd prefer to put it off indefinitely."

"Then I guess you don't want to see this bad news?" She pulled a piece of paper out of her jacket pocket.

"What is it?"

"The bill from Signore Vitale."

He took it from her and glanced at the total. He whistled at the figure.

"Good thing I'm rich."

"How does a captain in the French Foreign Legion get rich?"

"Catholic guilt," Kingsley said.

"You can make money off that?" Sam asked.

"Apparently so."

"How do I get in on that action?"

"Have you ever heard the phrase, 'if you marry money, expect to earn every penny'?"

"You married money?"

"My sister. But she's dead, and now I'm rich. Funny how the world works."

"Yeah," Sam said without laughing. "Hilarious."

They arrived at the clinic, and Sam got out of the car first. She held the door open for him and stuck her hand inside.

"Take it," she said, waving her hand. He took it with a sigh. "I'm feeling chivalrous again."

"I'm not wearing heels today."

"Yeah, but I needed an excuse."

"An excuse for what?"

Sam twined her fingers around his.

"To hold your hand."

20

AS THEY WALKED INTO THE CLINIC, SAM REFUSED TO let go of Kingsley's hand. Even when he sat in Dr. Sutton's office, Sam stood next to him, her hand still in his. Or perhaps it was his hand in hers. She'd twined their fingers together so tightly he couldn't tell who held on to whom.

Dr. Sutton entered with a file in her hand.

"No speeches. No preliminaries," Kingsley said before Dr. Sutton could say a word. "Tell me right now—good or bad."

"Kingsley…" Dr. Sutton took a seat, and Sam clutched his hand even tighter. It was bad. He knew it was bad.

Was he going to die?

What did he have?

Had he given it to anyone else?

He was never going to have children. He was never going to do anything ever again.

Would Søren miss him after he was gone?

Would anyone miss him at all?

Dr. Sutton smiled.

"Good," she said.

Kingsley's shoulders slumped, and he breathed out two solid weeks' worth of terror. Had he ever felt so relieved? So happy? So grateful?

Sam took his face in her hands and kissed him on both cheeks. When he looked at her, he saw tears in her eyes.

Dr. Sutton gave him the lecture on sexual health and responsibility to end all lectures, scheduled him for follow-up testing in six months and then six months after that. Half an hour later he and Sam, still holding hands, left the office. The sun was shining. The birds were singing. The street people weren't pissing on the sidewalk anywhere near his shoes. A perfect day.

"I'll admit, I got a little worried when you said you've had sex with half of Europe," she said. "I'd settle for half of Chelsea. Or all of Chelsea if she's cute."

"You disapprove?"

"I'm impressed."

"You might not want me, but other people do."

"I think you're very pretty," Sam said, and patted him on the arm.

"Thank you. Now tell me I have a good personality."

"Oh, get over it. You can have every other woman in the city."

"You're right, I can," he said, grinning ear to ear. "I can fuck again."

"You couldn't fuck before?"

"I had to wait until I got my results back."

"Is that why you went to Rome for two weeks?"

"Among other reasons."

"What did you do in Rome?"

"Learned the art of sadism from a notorious Roman madam."

"Please, tell me you have vacation slides."

The car pulled up to the curb, but Kingsley stopped Sam from getting in.

"I want you to do something for me," Kingsley said.

"Anything for you," she said.

"You take the Rolls and go back to the house. Call everyone in my red book and invite them over tonight. Then go buy a week's worth of condoms."

"I've never bought condoms before. What's a week's worth?"

"I don't know. A hundred? Wait. We're having a party. Better make it a thousand."

"What else?"

"Get big ones," he said. "Since I'm—"

Sam stuck her fingers in her ears.

"La la la," she sang. "Not listening…"

He pulled her hands from her ears.

"Call for food. Call for alcohol. We're having a party."

"What kind of party?" she asked.

Kingsley grinned.

"Gotcha," Sam said. "That kind of party."

Sam took her marching orders and marched. He was glad she hadn't asked him where he was going. Since she hadn't made any progress digging for dirt on Reverend Fuller, he decided to take matters into his own hands.

He hailed a cab and gave the driver an address in Queens. He'd learned from Sam that Fuller had a small satellite office in the city. They'd move into their larger quarters once The Renaissance was remodeled.

The driver let him out at the end of the block and Kingsley quickly found the WTL offices. They were housed in a three-story brick building wedged between a school and a run-down apartment complex. Kingsley entered it warily feeling like a soldier encroaching on enemy ground. In fact, everywhere he looked he saw signs and posters warning of the dangers of sin, the inevitability of judgment.

Are you ready to meet your Maker?

The way is narrow.

All have sinned and fallen short of the glory of God.

Flee from the wrath to come.

He studied another poorly designed poster that depicted human beings stretching their arms toward heaven in supplication even as their lower bodies burned up in a fire.

"Cheerful," Kingsley said to himself.

He caught sight of another poster—an aborted fetus lying on a bloodied blanket—with the words *I formed you in the womb* underneath in a melodramatic font. A grotesque image, it did nothing to change his opinion about abortion and did everything to make him want to lose his lunch on the church carpeting. Did people truly find comfort or enlightenment in a place like this?

He'd found comfort and acceptance back at St. Ignatius Academy, the Catholic school where he'd met Søren. He wasn't Catholic, never had been, but the Jesuits at the school had been hard-drinking, open-minded intellectuals. Jesuits were notoriously liberal, at least by Catholic standards. He remembered one brave boy in a social ethics class asking Father Henry under what circumstances an abortion could be permitted. Father Henry had answered, "Never on an empty stomach," and the class had been too shocked to laugh for a full five seconds.

Something told him abortion jokes wouldn't be welcome in this church.

"Awful, isn't it?" Kingsley turned and saw a young woman standing in the door to an office at the front of the church. "That poster."

Kingsley took the necessary two seconds to reorient his brain, so he could speak without any trace of his French accent.

"It is awful," Kingsley agreed. "My religion forbids engaging in propaganda."

"Excuse me?"

Kingsley gave her a placid, nonthreatening and therefore entirely fake smile.

"I was wondering if Reverend Fuller was in. I'd like to speak to him."

"He's not here," she said with a nervous lilt in her voice. The girl was pretty and could have been beautiful if she wasn't hiding under a shapeless floral dress. She looked young, twenty or twenty-one, and she had a sweet innocent gleam in her eyes. "The WTL headquarters are in Stamford. He doesn't stop by here very often. He's a busy man."

"I hear he's also a very godly man."

The girl smiled broadly.

"He is. So inspiring. Reverend Fuller truly loves the Lord, and his church loves him."

"No one loves men of the cloth more than I do."

"My name is Chastity. Could I do something for you?"

"No, Chastity does nothing for me."

"Sir?"

"Actually you might be able to help me," he said, walking up to her and putting the bare minimum of socially required distance between them as possible. "I have a friend. She has a serious problem."

"What sort of problem?"

"She's a lesbian."

Chastity's eyes widened.

"That is a problem. Have you talked to her about it?"

"I have. She's unrepentant." He exhaled heavily in faux disappointment.

"Those people often are. The heart of the homosexual gets hard the longer they stay in their sinful lifestyle."

"Yes, her heart is very hard. So hard it makes me hard."

"Oh, no, you can't let your heart get hardened. God loves a soft heart."

"So I should be soft?"

"You should. Soft and open to God."

"Are you soft and open, Chastity?"

The young woman blushed a little. When she spoke she'd developed a slight stammer.

"I try to be. For God." She coughed and took a small step back. "So, you're here because you're worried about your lesbian friend and the life of sin she's living?"

"I heard that Reverend Fuller's church has programs to help people like her. Camps, even. Is that true?"

"Yes, we do have some programs. There's the New Paradise program. It involves intensive reorienting therapy."

"New Paradise? Sounds promising."

"It's a program that helps homosexuals return to an existence like that of Eden and the Garden of Paradise."

"So, it's a nudist colony?"

"No, silly." Chastity blushed and giggled. Then she slapped a hand over her mouth to silence herself. "In Eden it was Adam and Eve, not Adam and Steve."

"Poor Steve. He can stay with me."

"Sir?"

"The New Paradise program?" Kingsley prompted.

"Right. Yes," she said, clearly relieved to get off that train of thought. "In the New Paradise program she'll undergo intensive therapy to help her understand a woman's place in the world."

"Which is?"

"Underneath men."

"Women belong underneath men?"

"Of course. Women are submissive to men. That's the biblical model of the family."

"I'm a man," Kingsley said. "And you're a woman. So you should be under me?"

"In a biblical way," she said, stammering again.

"That's my favorite way." Kingsley stepped closer, close enough he could feel her body trembling with nervousness. But this time she didn't take a step back. "I'm worried this therapy won't be enough for my friend. She loves to seduce straight girls."

Chastity's blush deepened.

"She is in deep sin, then."

"So very deep," Kingsley agreed. "She has short hair and dresses like a man."

"That's awful. A woman's femininity is a gift from God. Women shouldn't even wear pants as they disguise her womanliness."

Kingsley glanced down at the shapeless dress she wore. Sam in her suits looked more womanly than this girl in her house dress.

"I agree. I try to get her to take off her pants, but I haven't made any progress yet."

"Shameful. She should take her pants off for you. I mean, she should wear dresses. All women should wear dresses or skirts. That's what I mean."

"Skirts do make it easier for me."

"I'm sorry?"

"Tell me more about the camps. I might be able to trick her into going to a camp."

"Well," the young woman began. "There are a few of them, and they run for twenty-eight days. There are three sessions every summer. We have camps in Texas, Colorado, Ohio and Pennsylvania."

"None closer than that?"

"There was one upstate," she said, lowering her voice as if imparting a secret. "But it closed down ten years ago."

"Upstate New York would have been perfect. Why did it close?"

The young woman raised her empty hands. "I heard…"

Kingsley leaned in close, very close, as close as this poor plain virgin girl had probably ever been to a man.

"What did you hear?" he asked, putting his mouth at her ear and letting his breath tickle her neck.

"I heard a camper died there," she whispered. "Suicide. It wasn't Reverend Fuller's fault at all. The investigation cleared him and the church of any wrongdoing. You see, suicide is nobody's fault but the person who commits it. But still, they shut the camp down."

"That's too bad."

"But there's still Pennsylvania. Do you think your friend would like to go to camp in western Pennsylvania?"

"I think she would like it as much as I would like it." Kingsley would rather have his testicles soldered to his eyeballs than go to a sexual reorienting camp in western Pennsylvania.

"Oh, good." Chastity smiled broadly. "Then wait here. I'll get you some brochures."

She walked off, and Kingsley pondered the possibility of seducing her. Fucking a girl named Chastity—how poetic. It would probably be good for her, give her a taste for what the world had to offer outside the walls of her church. Then again, why set her up for a lifetime of unreasonable expectations?

Chastity returned with a sheaf of brochures and a hardcover book.

"I brought this for you," Chastity said. "*Miraculous Womanhood* by Lucy Fuller. Wonderful book. Changed my life. Maybe it'll help your friend."

"You can keep it," Kingsley said. "I've already read this one."

Out on the street he found another taxi, and once inside he

flipped through the brochures the girl had given him. One detailed the work of the ministry. Reverend Fuller's church focused on personal sin and accountability. Kingsley took that to mean the church didn't actually do anything to improve the world. Lots of programs for people to quit adultery, quit drinking, quit smoking even, and programs for girls who were pregnant out of wedlock. He assumed they talked them out of abortions, had them give up their babies for adoption and then promptly forgot the mothers existed. He didn't see anything about soup kitchens or homeless shelters. Søren would likely have something to say about that.

He should call Søren. He spoke over a dozen languages. Maybe one of them was fundamentalist Christian.

Back at the town house, he found Sam making phone calls with his red book of names open in front of her.

"We will need vast quantities of alcohol," Sam said into the phone. "The good shit."

Kingsley snapped his fingers to get her attention. "Who's coming tonight?"

She held up one finger.

"One person is coming?"

She pointed at him. Of course he was coming tonight. Several times.

"You should come, too," he mouthed. She held up a sheet of names, confirmations for the party. In red she'd circled the names of half a dozen women. He raised his eyebrow at her in a question.

"Targets," she whispered.

Kingsley laughed, and Sam handed him the list of names. It would be a packed house tonight. Good. For the first time in a long time he felt like celebrating. On his way out the door he heard Sam snapping her fingers. She put a hand over the receiver.

"Your priest called. You're supposed to call him back," she said before returning to her own phone call. As he walked out of the room he heard her on the phone with the caterer.

"We're having an 'I Don't Have AIDS' party tonight, and we need food for a hundred people. Caviar? Good call."

In his bedroom he found that Signore Vitale had a suit and some shirts delivered. Sam had put them on his bed with a note that said, "Wear the suit and even I might consider spreading for you. I won't do it, but I might *consider* doing it." She had underlined *consider* three times.

Even her considering spreading for him was better than not considering it. He'd wear whatever Sam liked if it made her happy.

He sat on his bed and picked up the phone.

"Tell me it's good news," Søren said when Kingsley greeted him.

"It's good news," he said. "All good."

Kingsley could hear the relief in Søren's breath all the way from Connecticut to Manhattan.

"*Gratias tibi, Deus,*" Søren breathed in Latin. "I have been praying nonstop for two weeks. If you ever scare me like this again—"

"I won't," Kingsley said. "I have to get tested again in six months. And six months after that."

"And?" Søren prompted.

"And I have to use condoms unless I'm monogamous, which I'm not." Kingsley sighed heavily.

"Exactly."

"Anyway, thank you. For making me get tested. And for being there."

"It's always a pleasure forcing you to do things you don't want to do."

"I like it better when you force me to do things I want to do."

"Kingsley. You know—"

"I know. Forget it. I need to ask you something. Have you heard of these camps where they send gay teenagers to be re-oriented?"

"God loves you the way you are, Kingsley. You are created in His image and are fearfully and wonderfully made."

"It's cute when you think you're funny," Kingsley said. "Now, what do you know about them?"

"Not much except they don't work. Reorienting therapy works as well as trying to turn a left-handed person into a right-handed person. You're fighting nature tooth and nail. It's far more likely to turn a person suicidal than straight."

"It would have made me suicidal."

"Do I want to know why you're asking?"

"Long story," he said. "Does your church have posters of aborted fetuses hanging up?"

"There was one in the narthex when I arrived here in March. I made them take it down."

"How did that go over?"

"I told the objecting church members they weren't allowed to post any signs that featured dead children as that seemed to convey the opposite message intended regarding the sanctity of life. And might I ask where all these questions are coming from?"

"I talked to someone from the WTL church today."

"Please, don't tell me I inadvertently turned you into a fundamentalist when I baptized you."

"That was an attempted murder, not a baptism."

"Tell me what's going on."

"Fuller has an office in the city. I stopped by and talked to an assistant. The church runs reorienting camps. I found out today someone committed suicide at one of them, but the church was cleared of any responsibility. No charges filed."

"You sound angry. Are you taking this personally?"

Kingsley paused before answering.

"Sam was sent to one of those camps."

"I see. And this upsets you."

"Sam's perfect. Yes, it upsets me."

"Kingsley, don't look now, but you have a crush on your secretary."

"I do not have a crush on my secretary."

"Methinks the Frenchman doth protest too much."

"My secretary is gay, remember?"

"I'm straight, remember?"

"You told me that once before. I think it was after you'd fucked me so hard we broke a spring in the cot."

"Are you finished with me? I have to check on Eleanor. We have an Ursuline sister here this week, and Eleanor is giving her a tour of the church property."

"This is a cause for concern?"

"Eleanor asked the sister if she wore hole-y underwear. And if that wasn't bad enough, she asked the sister if she also had, and I quote, 'a hard-on' for Captain von Trapp."

"I need to meet this girl. And soon."

"That is the opposite of what needs to happen. I'm hanging up now."

"Don't go yet. I have one final question to ask you. It is *très importante*."

"Fine. What's the question?"

"Will you come to my party tonight?"

21

THE PARTY WAS TO START AT NINE, AND AT EIGHT fifty-five, Kingsley stood in his bedroom trying to decide if he would fuck three girls tonight or fuck one girl three times. He concluded it would be best to split the difference. He would fuck one girl twice and a second girl once. But the question remained, which girls? Knowing Sam, they might end up in a fight over one.

He heard a soft knock on his bedroom door.

"Come in," he called out, and Sam entered holding a large box. He would have paid more attention to the box except Sam looked so arresting he couldn't see anything but her.

"Like it?" she asked. "I'm a sexy not-French penguin."

Kingsley walked to Sam and took a turn around her. She wore a well-tailored tuxedo. The vest was cut low and went under her breasts, drawing exquisite attention to them. The jacket was cinched in at her waist, and she wore 1940s-style black-and-white brogues on her feet.

"You aren't a penguin," he said.

"I was going for penguin."

"You have failed. Instead, you are the most beautiful woman in the city."

Sam exhaled in obvious exasperation.

"What?" he asked.

"Will you please stop telling me that you think I'm beautiful?"

"I have never told you I think you're beautiful. I told you that you are beautiful. There's a difference, *non*?"

"Non," she said.

"Does it bother you?" He stepped back and sat on the bed. She placed the large box on the floor and stood in front of him.

"Sort of," she said. "Mainly because I'm not used to it. You know, from men."

"I can't believe that. All the lovers you have—"

"It's different coming from women than it is coming from you."

"Why?"

"I don't know." She looked up at him through her thick long eyelashes. Her hair had more wave than usual, and he longed to capture a lock between his fingers and kiss it. "But it is."

"Sam?" He put both hands on her shoulders and forced her to face him. "You know I want you, right?"

She said nothing at first and then slowly nodded her head.

"It won't go away anytime soon," he said. "So if it truly bothers you that I feel this way about you, then it might be we can't work together. I don't..." He squeezed her shoulders before pulling his hands away. "I don't want to hurt you or make you uncomfortable."

"It doesn't upset me," Sam said. "Except the thought that I'm hurting you hurts me."

"Trust me, hurting me is not anything you have to worry about."

"But I've never loved a job more than this. I love working with you. I love the work we're doing. Especially the part of the work where we make Reverend Fuller's life a nightmare."

"Still working on that part. But we'll get him. Eventually."

"I know we will. I have nothing but faith in you." Her words made his heart soar.

"You'll have to forgive me. I'm a man who loves both men and women. You give me a woman who dresses like a man, and it's…" Kingsley paused. "What was the thing that crippled Superman?"

"Lois Lane's pussy?"

"Kryptonite," Kingsley said. "A woman in a suit is my Kryptonite."

Sam grinned, and that smile of hers turned the night back into day.

"If it makes you feel any better," she said, "I'll tell you this. If I were going to be with any man on earth, it would be you. No one but you. Feel better?"

"Much." He didn't know why, but those were the words he most needed to hear from Sam. He adored her, loved her humor, her playfulness, the way she took care of his home as if it were her own, taking care of him as if he were her own. That's all he needed to hear—if she was ever going to go to bed with a man, it would be him. He needed to be special to her, as special as she was to him.

"Good. But you really do have to stop telling me I'm beautiful all the time. I'm vain enough as it is."

"I'll stop saying it, then," he promised. "But I won't stop thinking it."

"You're the beautiful one." She crossed her arms over her chest. "You put anyone in a room to shame—man or woman."

"You won't think that when you meet *le prêtre*. He puts all men to shame."

"Who? Oh, the priest? He's that hot?"

"Even you'll be tempted."

Sam gave him a searching look, and he feared she was about to ask a question he didn't want to answer.

"What's in the box?" he asked before Sam could ask her question.

"Present for you," she said. "A thank-you gift for this job."

"You don't owe me any gifts. Everything you do for me has been a gift."

"Fine, then." She picked up the box. "I'll keep them."

"I didn't say you could do that." He grabbed the box from her. "Mine."

He took off the lid, and inside he found a pair of black knee-high boots, gleaming leather, polished to the highest shine.

"You can't dress in a suit like that without boots like these. I ran out and got you the most perfect pair I could find. You have huge feet, by the way."

"I have normal feet for a man. If you want to see something huge you should see my—"

"Ego?"

"Exactement."

"Have you ever worn riding boots before?" she asked, taking the boots out of the box.

"I don't ride. Not horses anyway."

"Well, these are like Hessians. They're special, and they take a little getting used to. You don't zip them or lace them or step into them like cowboy boots. You have to use boot pulls to get them on. Once you wear a pair for a few days, though, they'll feel like a second skin."

Sam dropped to her knees in front of him.

"What are you doing on the floor? You're wearing a tuxedo."

"By your leave, my lord," she said, smiling up at him. "Consider me your valet."

"How many romance novels did you read as a girl?"

"Hundreds," she said. "That's the only type of book my mom had in the house. She hid them from my father much better than she hid them from me."

"That's the first time you've ever mentioned your family without wincing."

"We're not close anymore," she said, smiling at Kingsley. "They didn't want a daughter like me."

"If I have a daughter someday, I hope she'll be like you."

Sam blinked hard, like an invisible hand had slapped her.

"What?" he asked, narrowing his eyes at her.

"Nothing." She took his ankle in her hand. "Nobody's ever said anything that nice to me before."

"I'll never do it again," he promised.

"Good. Now, shove it in as far as it'll go."

Kingsley looked down at her.

"Your foot," she said. "Shove your foot in."

"You're kinkier than I thought."

Kingsley shoved. Sam took two thin curved sticks and slipped them in the small eyelets inside the top of the boot.

"Stand up and push your foot down while I pull up." He stood. She pulled. The boot was on. "Okay, one more time."

It took thirty seconds of pushing, pulling and trouser rear-ranging, but then it was done, and Sam, still on the floor, sat back and looked him up and down.

"God damn," she said.

"Good God damn?" he asked.

"The best God damn."

He reached down and helped her off the floor. With her hand in his, she dragged him over to the cheval mirror.

"Now that's a sight to behold." Sam leaned against him, and they stood shoulder to shoulder—his shoulder a mere four inches higher than hers.

Kingsley pulled her in front of him, his arm across her chest

like a shield over her heart. She rested her chin on his forearm, and the small gesture of feminine surrender sent a surge
of possessiveness through him.

"That's an even better sight to behold."

"I do look damn good in a tux."

Kingsley smiled but didn't speak. He'd meant the image of
Sam in his arms was the better sight to behold. She must not
have understood. Or perhaps she did understand and didn't
agree.

"I like the boots," he said, letting her go before he got too
used to holding her.

"I don't."

"You don't?"

"I love the boots. I want you to wear them every single day
until they're a part of you."

"I will," he said. Easy enough to do since they were a gift
from her. They were already a part of him.

"I'll help you put them on every morning. It'll be our routine. I'll help you put on your boots, and you can give me
my orders for the day. Then we'll drink coffee and figure out
who to blackmail next."

"Sounds like paradise." Sam's face being the first one he
saw every morning? He could get used to that.

From outside his bedroom came the sound of laughter.
Someone from somewhere in the house—Blaise from the
sound of it—called his name.

"Party time," Sam said. "Have fun fucking half your guests."

"What are you going to do?" he asked as they headed to
his bedroom door.

"Fuck the other half."

The house was almost full by the time he and Sam made it
to the main floor. Thirty minutes later, they had a full house
and then some. Sam had done a masterful job with the food

and wine, especially given what short notice she'd had. Apparently working as a bartender for six years had put her in contact with the best people in the business. They ate. They drank. They laughed.

And of course, they fucked.

Not Kingsley. He walked from room to room with a glass of wine in his hand. For two weeks he'd been fasting from sex. He wanted his first meal to be a feast, not a snack. He needed someone delectable, succulent, mouth-watering...

Søren walked in.

Kingsley rolled his eyes.

"Not you," Kingsley said to him.

"Hello to you, too," Søren said, glaring at him. "I'm here for five seconds, and you're already upset with me."

"Yes," Kingsley said. "I'm trying to pick out someone to fuck, and you're blocking my view."

"Forgive me. I had no idea you were prowling."

"When am I not prowling?" He handed Søren a glass of Syrah off a passing tray. Søren often wore his clerics when he stopped by the house, but tonight he'd come incognito—black pants and black jacket, but a white shirt. "I can't believe you actually came tonight."

"I hadn't planned to."

"What changed your mind?"

Søren reached into his jacket pocket and pulled out an envelope.

"This."

He gave it to Kingsley who opened the envelope.

He found a minicassette tape inside.

"Fuck," Kingsley said.

"It was delivered to the church two hours ago. I listened to it." Søren spoke in French now, a wise move considering they were surrounded. "You seem to be confessing to sleeping with my Eleanor. Which is an impressive feat since you've never met her."

"I lied because—"

"I know why you lied, and I appreciate it. But someone clearly does not appreciate it."

"I'll handle it," Kingsley said, and took the tape from him.

"Is this something I need to be concerned about?"

"*Non,*" Kingsley said. "It's mine to deal with, not you."

"Do you know who sent it?"

Kingsley shook his head. "I talked to the man on the tape— Robert Dixon. He swears it wasn't him. I believe him, but he's not telling me everything. He admits to taping us, but he tapes everything out of paranoia."

"You'll let me know if this situation gets out of hand?"

"It won't get out of hand," Kingsley said. "But just in case…"

"What?"

"Pack a bag for Denmark."

Søren started to say something, but Sam picked that inopportune moment to interrupt.

"Is this him?" Sam asked. Even without the Roman collar, Søren had a priestly air to him. It was no wonder Sam had known who he was without an introduction. "I'm Sam. You must be Our Father Who Art in Connecticut."

"A pleasure," Søren said, and kissed her hand.

"No. Stop." Kingsley took Søren's hand away from Sam's. "Take two steps back right now. She's my secretary. You aren't allowed to flirt with her."

"I wasn't flirting," Søren said. "Merely being polite."

"He's worried because he thinks you're prettier than he is," Sam said to Søren.

"He is prettier than I am," Kingsley said. "It's the eyelashes."

"You do have unusually dark eyelashes for a blond," Sam said, studying Søren. "How do you do it?"

Søren answered, "Mascara."

"No offense, Padre, but between the two of you, Kingsley would win the pretty boy competition."

"I'm not the least offended," Søren said.

"It's the long hair. All boys should have long hair." She pulled his hair, and he slapped her hand away. She slapped back.

"Children," Søren scolded. "Behave."

"Sorry. I love the hair," Sam said.

"He certainly wears it to his advantage. I approve of the wardrobe change, as well. Your doing?" Søren asked Sam.

"All my idea. He wants to be a king. He should look like a king."

"You've succeeded," Søren said. "He looks positively majestic."

"See?" Sam said. "I win. You lose. You have to dress like this forever."

"I surrender," Kingsley said.

"So, let me ask you two a question." With her glass of wine, Sam pointed first at him and then at Søren. "How are you going to get away with the fact that he's him and you're a priest? I mean, is it safe for a priest to be in the house of a strip club-owning, S and M club-creating, blackmailing blackmailer, Kingsley the Edge?"

"Of course I can be in Kingsley's home without any fear of censure," Søren said. "I have a very good excuse."

"What's the excuse?" Sam asked.

Søren answered before Kingsley could stop him.

"We're related."

Sam's eyes went laughably wide.

She eyed Kingsley. Then Søren. Then Kingsley again.

"You're both white boys. You're both good-looking. You know, for men. Other than that, I don't see the resemblance."

"Related by marriage," Søren said. "I was very briefly married to Kingsley's sister before she passed away."

"Oh," Sam said, nodding. "But Kingsley, you said your sister married—"

Kingsley glared at her. He'd told Sam his sister had married the man he was in love with. Tonight was not the night to dredge all that up.

"Married who?" Søren asked, looking from Sam to Kingsley and then back at Sam.

"I told Sam my sister married a pompous arrogant self-important overeducated pretentious bastard."

"That would be me," Søren said, raising his glass.

"Gotcha. Well, I'll leave you two bros-in-law to catch up. There are women in this room who have never had a multiple orgasm. They need me. I have heard their cries in the night."

"Go answer the cries," Kingsley said.

Sam bowed to them both and stalked off.

"What was she going to say?" Søren asked.

"Nothing," Kingsley said. "Nothing at all."

Søren watched Sam as she disappeared into the crowd.

"What do you know about her?" he asked.

"Everything I need to," Kingsley said.

"That's an excellent nonanswer."

"Why do you ask? She's my secretary, not yours."

"I could spend the next two hours telling you everything I know about my secretary, Diane. I know where she was born, where she grew up, where she went to school, who she's dating, who her parents are... Can you say the same about Sam?"

"Why do you care?"

"She knows I'm in Connecticut. She knows about your sister. Did you tell her my real name?"

Kingsley stalled by taking a sip of his Syrah.

"Kingsley?"

"She needed to know," Kingsley said. "If anything happened to me, someone needs to be able to find you."

"I understand that. And I don't object to you telling her anything you need to tell her if you have good reason for trusting her so implicitly. If you do have good reason, I have no issue with it. I'm curious *why* you trust her so implicitly when you know so little about her."

"I told you, I know what I need to know about her."

"Someone knows quite a bit about the both of us," Søren reminded him.

"I trust Sam. You can trust her, too."

"Are you in love with her? Is that why you trust her?"

"I'm not in love with her," Kingsley said truthfully. What he felt for Sam was different than love. Or maybe it was love but a different sort than what he felt for Søren.

Søren raised his glass of wine to his lips.

"Good."

"Hello, Father," Blaise said, appearing out of nowhere. Kingsley had never been so glad to see the girl in his life. She rose up on the tips of her toes to kiss Søren on the cheek. "How's my favorite kinky Jesuit priest?"

"He's still kinky," Kingsley said. "And still a Jesuit. Boggles the mind, doesn't it?"

"So I have to ask, what is a Jesuit?" Blaise said.

"We're an order of priests founded by St. Ignatius of Loyola," Søren said. "We began as a missionary order."

"He says missionary. I say military," Kingsley said with a wide grin. "They did so much political maneuvering in the 1700s, the order was disbanded by the pope."

"I still haven't forgiven Pope Clement the Fourteenth over that one."

"So Jesuits are bad priests?" Blaise asked, seeming pleased by this revelation.

"They are," Kingsley said. "Naughty priests, then and now."

"At least we aren't the Legion of Christ."

"Stop me if you've heard this one," Kingsley began. "A man walks up to a Franciscan and a Jesuit and asks, 'How many novenas must you pray to get a Mercedes-Benz?'"

"I'm stopping you," Søren said.

"So the Franciscan," Kingsley continued, "asks the man, 'What's a Mercedes-Benz?' And the Jesuit asks the man…"

Kingsley waited. Blaise looked up at Søren expectantly.

"'What's a novena?'" Søren finished, his tone dripping with disdain. "For the record, every Jesuit I know can tell you what a novena is."

"What is a novena?" Blaise asked.

"Take her upstairs and tell her," Kingsley said to Søren. "Give her a good hard Catholic schooling."

"I did spend ten years in seminary," he said. "It would be a crime to waste all that training."

"With your permission, monsieur…" Blaise looked at Kingsley with pleading eyes.

"Have a fun scourging, *chouchou*," Kingsley said. Blaise kissed him on the cheek. She then took Søren's hand and led him through the crowd and up the stairs. Kingsley looked into his half-finished glass of wine and fought the urge to take it down in one swallow. Where did Søren get off questioning him about Sam? Sam was none of Søren's business. And who cared if he didn't know much about her? He knew what he needed to know. Sam cared about him. She was on his side. Whatever her secrets, that wasn't one of them.

Irritated with both Søren and whoever the fuck it was sending the tapes, Kingsley left the party behind and headed upstairs to his bedroom, taking the steps two at a time. He'd throw the tape into his wall safe, change clothes and find Dixon. He would beat the man into a bloody coma if he had to, but before this night was over, Kingsley would have answers. As he strode down the hall to his bedroom he heard cries of pleasure and pain emanating from within the rooms he passed. Sometimes pleasure and pain came from the same room. He ignored them. He was a man on a mission.

Kingsley threw open the door to his bedroom. A woman stood by the foot of his bed. She was dark-skinned, thin and regal. Her boots, corset, skirt and opera gloves—all leather. Her shoulders were bare, and ample cleavage spilled out over the top of the corset. She wore a lace choker around her neck, and her thick braided hair was coiffed in an elegant knot, and behind her right ear she wore a pale pink rose.

In her hand she held something long, black and thin. He recognized it immediately.

A riding crop.

Kingsley waited in silence, waited for the domme to speak.

"I received your lovely messages," the woman began in a posh English accent. "And the flowers."

Kingsley's eyes widened.

He'd sent only one woman flowers lately. Twelve dozen red, white and pink roses in the hopes she would take his interest in seeing her seriously. Apparently it had worked.

"Mistress Felicia," he said at last.

"I do have a fondness for flowers from men who aren't afraid to beg."

Mistress Felicia Tryst had been all over the newspapers when he first came to the city. She'd been named as the offending party in a divorce between a business magnate and his socialite wife. The story had been a bloodbath, a feeding frenzy. Salacious reporters couldn't get enough of the white American billionaire who was sexually enslaved to a black

British dominatrix. Mistress Felicia had risen above the fray and refused to testify on the grounds she never spoke about her clients. She'd languished in prison and kept her vow of silence until the parties settled out of court. He'd once seen her photograph in the *Post*, but it did not do this dark beauty justice.

"To what do I owe the honor?" Kingsley asked.

"You wanted to speak to me about working in your new club, yes?" she asked.

"Yes. Is that why you're here?" he asked. They could have had this conversation in his office. Why was Mistress Felicia in his bedroom?

"I'll admit to an ulterior motive."

"Ulterior motives. Care to enlighten me?"

"I saw you downstairs. And as soon as I saw you, I knew I wanted to beat you and fuck you. How is that for an ulterior motive?"

Kingsley's groin tightened at the sight of the beautiful woman and her riding crop. And everyone who knew anything about kink knew this woman was the most notorious sadist in the city. She could likely give Søren a run for his money.

"Well?" Mistress Felicia asked.

The tape could wait.

His cock couldn't.

22

"HOW DO YOU KNOW I WOULD LET YOU BEAT ME?" Kingsley asked.

"You might not let me. You might be nothing but a dominant after all, and the thought of submitting to a woman may hold no appeal." She strolled toward him, the riding crop swishing behind her like a tiger's tail. "Then again, it might."

"Did anyone see you come in here, *Maîtresse*?"

"No one was in the hallway before I came in."

Kingsley sighed with relief. "Good," he said. "Please, don't be offended—"

"I have many clients who would prefer not to have their proclivities announced to the world. You don't have to explain. I am nothing if not discreet."

"Your discretion is the stuff of legend, *Maîtresse*."

She raised her eyebrow at him. "I was warned about your accent. They were right."

Kingsley desperately wanted this woman, but he'd rather die than have the whole city know about the other side of his sexual proclivities—the submissive masochistic side.

Mistress Felicia walked to him, walked slowly, taking her sweet time, making every step toward him a lesson in patience.

"I compliment his accent and he stops speaking. Typical switch. Can't stop playing mind games for a second, can you?"

"Tell me what to say, and I'll say it," Kingsley said.

"Tell me you want me to beat you and fuck you, Kingsley."

Yes. God, yes. Yes, he wanted her to do everything to him. But...

"I would like that," he said. "But, you see, I—"

She laid her palm on his chest.

"Your heart is racing," she said. "Are you scared?"

"I have a problem," he said.

"I can see you're burdened by something. Tell me your burdens. Tell me how I can ease them," she said, touching his face, his forehead, his lips. She smelled like roses, like an English garden.

"I was shot," he said, focusing on the delicious scent of her instead of the memories. "Last year. I was with a dominant recently. I had a flashback."

"What triggered it?" she asked, apparently not the least bothered by his revelation.

"Someone touched my throat with a whip."

"Your throat," she repeated, looking at him but also into him.

"I was choked once."

"I see," she said, her voice quiet and serene. "I won't touch your throat. And I'm not afraid of your flashbacks. If you have one, you have one. If you don't, then...well, more time to play then, isn't it?"

Mistress Felicia ran a gloved hand through his hair. She grabbed a fistful of it at the nape of his neck, forcing his head back.

Kingsley didn't speak.

"I will hurt you the way you like being hurt tonight,"

Mistress Felicia said. "And in no other way. Tell me what you like."

"I will, *Maîtresse*."

"Do you like this?" she asked, tugging harder on his hair. "Do you like being treated like property?"

"*Oui, Maîtresse*," he said.

"Do you like pain?"

"More than anything."

"How much pain?"

"All the pain," he said.

"You're a masochist?"

"You could call me that."

"What don't you want?"

"I don't want a collar," he said. "I hate them."

Mistress Felicia laughed and pulled harder on his hair. His eyes watered from the pain. She was good, very good.

"I won't put a collar on you. Nothing on your throat. Nothing but my kisses." She brought her lips to his neck and bit the skin over his jugular vein. The bite turned into a kiss and back into another bite. "Your neck is too delicious to cover it up with anything but my mouth. And besides, there are other ways to enslave men that don't require collars."

She tossed her riding crop onto the bed and took him by the wrist, bringing his hand between her legs. She wore nothing beneath her leather skirt. He cupped her there, the base of his hand against her clitoris.

"One finger," she whispered. "One."

He slipped one finger between her folds and inside her. So warm, so wet. He closed his eyes.

"You like it inside me?" she asked.

"Yes," he breathed.

"If you survive the pain I'm going to inflict on you, I'll let you inside me again. I might let you put your cock in me. If you take everything I give you."

"I promise, *Maîtresse*, I can take it."

"What's your safe word?" she asked as Kingsley continued to stroke inside her body with one finger.

"I don't have one."

"Choose one."

"I don't need one."

"You have flashbacks from recent trauma. You need one."

"If I have a flashback, consider that my safe word."

Mistress Felicia laughed, and Kingsley felt her muscles gripping his finger. Two weeks... He was dying to be inside her. The wait would almost kill him. But for all that, he wanted the pain she had to offer even more than the sex. It had been so long since he'd let himself have the type of pain Søren had given him when they were teenagers. He hadn't planned on submitting to anyone tonight. But now that Mistress Felicia was here, he realized submission was what he most wanted.

Kingsley nearly groaned aloud in disappointment when she took his wrist again and moved his hand from her. But then she opened his pants.

"Don't get hard," she ordered.

"It would help if you left the room, *Maîtresse*."

"You're a big boy. You have self-control. Use it."

Kingsley focused his mind on things unlikely to arouse him—politics, airplane crashes, a bad case of the shingles, vanilla sex.

"Good boy," she said, slipping two fingers between her breasts and from her corset producing a leather strap.

"Fuck." He sighed.

"Eventually," she said, and wrapped the strap around his testicles and the base of his penis. Cock ring. Pleasure and torture all in one.

"You have a beautiful cock," she said, massaging it with both hands. The leather of her gloves abraded, and he quickly grew hard from the bite of the seams against his most sensitive skin. She grasped his cock by the base and slid her hands up and down the shaft. Fluid appeared on the tip and dripped onto her gloves.

"Eager, aren't you?"

"I haven't had sex in two weeks," he confessed. "Eager is an understatement."

"It's such an impressive erection, I'd hate for you to lose it before I had time to enjoy it."

"You'll enjoy it," he promised, as she traced the edges of the leather strap. Blood pooled and pumped into the shaft, and he closed his eyes tight.

"Does it hurt?"

"A little," he said.

"Good." She grinned at him. "It's a start anyway. Now stand there, don't move. I'm going to take your clothes off. I've heard rumors that Kingsley Edge had one of the better male bodies in the city. Time I find out for myself."

She pulled his jacket off his shoulders and pushed it down his arms. When she had it off, she walked to the armchair and laid it carefully over the back. He knew better than to think she was showing respect for him by showing respect for his clothes. No, he had a cock ring on and a painful erection. She would undress him as slowly as possible, dragging the process out until he was in agony.

"When was the first time you submitted to erotic pain?" she asked as she unbuttoned his vest.

"Eleven years ago."

"You're so young," she said. "How old were you when you started doing kink?"

"Sixteen."

"Domme?"

"Sadist," he said. "Male."

"Sixteen's awfully young to be submitting to a sadist."

"He was seventeen, *Maîtresse*."

Mistress Felicia laughed. "I wish I had gone to your high school instead of mine."

"You couldn't have. It was an all-boys Catholic school."

"Catholic," she said as she removed his shirt. She didn't flinch at the sight of the scars on his chest. She'd likely seen worse in her work. "I should send the pope a check. I get half my clients from his church."

Lifting his feet to let her tug his boots off sent pain shooting into his stomach. He hated cock rings. He could keep his erection without one. But the pain did what pain always did to him—cleared his mind, pulled him out of the past, obliterated the future. There was nothing but now, right now, and the pain that held him in place, unable to think, unable to dream, unable to want anything but more pain.

Mistress Felicia tugged his pants down, folded them neatly and laid them across a chair with his other clothes. He appreciated that she treated his clothes with respect, unlike Søren who'd taken perverse pleasure in dropping them on the floor and traipsing over them.

Kingsley focused on her face as she moved. A lovely woman in her late thirties, she had an imperious air to her, a proud set to her face and no mercy in her eyes. In that regard she reminded him very much of Søren.

"When did you start dominating people, *Maîtresse*?" he asked, curious what else she and Søren had in common.

"I'm going to punish you for speaking out of turn."

"As you should."

"But to answer your question," she said, standing in front of him, "I was eight when I started bossing around all the boys in my neighborhood, fifteen when I tied my first boyfriend up and nineteen when I took on my first client. He was my college chemistry professor."

"You had good chemistry, then?"

"I was going to be gentle with you," Mistress Felicia said. "Because of that joke, I'm afraid now I'll have to destroy you."

Kingsley's heart galloped in his chest. The cock ring had made him hard. The threat of pain made him harder.

"Good."

Mistress Felicia bent down and from a long leather bag produced two sets of leather cuffs.

"You haven't had sex in two weeks?" she asked.

"The two longest weeks of my life."

"I'm going to leave two weeks' worth of bruises on every inch of your body. It'll take them that long to heal, which will give you two choices. You can either not have sex for another two weeks until they're gone, or you can come to me every day and serve at my pleasure until they're gone. And then, if you beg nicely, I'll give you more."

Two weeks as the property of Mistress Felicia? It was June, wasn't it? Had Christmas come early?

"I'll take the second option," he said.

Mistress Felicia took a step forward and grabbed him roughly by the right forearm, pressing his hand to her chest. She strapped the cuff on his wrist and buckled it.

She released his right arm, and buckled his left. From her bag she produced a long metal clip. She ordered him to raise both arms. As soon as they were up, she cuffed his wrists over the top bar of the bed canopy. Once cuffed into place, he could do nothing but wait, not moving, and want her.

Mistress Felicia stood so close to him now that he could count her eyelashes. She had the tiniest beauty mark under her right eye. He longed to kiss it. He longed to kiss her, to taste her full lips, her skin, her body inside and out.

"You want to kiss me, don't you?" she asked.

"So much, *Maîtresse*."

"Your mouth has to earn it." She raised her riding crop and slipped it between his teeth. He bit it and held it in place. "I'm going to bruise the front of your body first. You keep the crop in your mouth the entire time, and you'll get your kiss."

He nodded his understanding and clamped his teeth even tighter on the crop. As sadistic as this task was, he appreciated the consideration. With the crop in his mouth, he wouldn't be tempted to cry out. And the last thing he wanted was for anyone in the house to know what he was doing right now. He needed this city to fear him. If they saw him like this— tied up, naked, vulnerable—he would never be seen the same way again.

From her bag she produced a cane—two feet long and made of rattan.

She raised her arms and brought them high. With a quick and vicious flick, she struck Kingsley's forearm two inches under the cuff. She hadn't been kidding. She intended to bruise his entire body from his wrists to his ankles.

Down his right arm she worked, striking him in even intervals, one inch and then lower an inch, and then lower an inch. The pain surprised him every time. Sharp, stinging and deep... He knew he'd have red welts for a day from the cane and bruises for at least a week if not longer.

From his right arm she moved to his left, hitting him again with controlled but brutal strikes. Søren had never hit him or struck him on this part of his body before, on the smooth skin from his elbow to armpit. But he'd cut him there one night, short shallow slices with a razor blade on the inside of his upper arms and inner thighs. They'd fucked afterward, face to face, chest to chest…it was one of the few times Søren hadn't tied him up before sex. Kingsley remembered wrapping his arms around Søren's shoulders, his legs around his back. Blood had covered them both. When it was over Søren even had a streak of it on his face. He'd looked primal as a wild animal with the slash of crimson across his cheek and the firelight glowing behind him—a wolf in a cave unafraid of fire. In that heated, sacred hour, with his eyes nothing but pupils, his hair slick with sweat, Søren had appeared to him like a beast, a demon, or a god. Kingsley hadn't cared which as long as he could worship at the altar of the blood-stained being who'd made a sacrifice of him.

"You do love pain, don't you?" Mistress Felicia asked, her voice low and sensual. As he had the crop in his mouth he couldn't answer in words. His ragged breathing and erection surely told her all she needed to know. "I can tell. You lose yourself in the pain."

He leaned his head back and closed his eyes as she ran her fingers over the welts on his arms, renewing the pain.

"Lose yourself, then," Mistress Felicia said. "Go wherever the pain wants to take you—into your mind, into your past, into your darkest dreams. Go as far away as you need to. I'll come for you, and I'll find you and bring you back."

If he could have spoken he would have thanked her. They were the words he most needed to hear, especially now as she worked his chest over, striking even the scar tissue left by the bullet wounds. She had no fear of the damage done to him by the violence of other men, and for that he would have kissed her feet could he have reached them.

He closed his eyes and let himself fall away into the crucible of pain. It burned. He burned. Everything burned. And through the fire he walked, barefoot and heedless of the flames. The path of the fire led him into his past, back to the first night Søren had him. When he came through the flames, he was sixteen again and running through the woods outside his school. He heard twigs breaking under his feet, the crunch of leaves, the soft thud of his soles on bare ground. And Søren was behind him, gaining on him. Why did he run? For eleven years he'd asked him that question. Yes, he'd run in fear. When he'd seen the look in Søren's eyes, he knew what was coming. But what Søren intended was everything Kingsley wanted.

Why did he run?

He ran for the pleasure of being pursued. That Søren wanted him so much that he would run after him even through the minefield of sharp hills, quick descents, grasping tree branches, tearing thorns. But was that why he ran? The true reason?

The fire caught up the half truths and burned them to ashes.

And then Kingsley remembered something he'd forgotten ever since that night. He'd wrenched himself from Søren's grip and taken off again. But he'd paused once, turned around and smiled at Søren. Come and get me, that smile had said.

Søren had come and gotten him.

"Where are you?" Mistress Felicia whispered in his ear. She took the crop from his mouth. "Tell me where you are in your mind."

"A forest," Kingsley said. "I'm sixteen. And I'm running, and I don't know why."

"You know why."

"He's chasing me."

"Who?"

"The boy I love."

"The sadist."

"Yes."

"If you love him, why are you running?"

"I want him to catch me."

"Has he caught you before?"

"No…the night in the forest was our first time."

"You wanted it?"

"More than anything," he said, speaking the truth from his heart. "So, why did I run?"

"Because you weren't running from him. You were running to you. The real you."

The words sank in to his soul.

"I was," he breathed.

"Good boy…" Mistress Felicia said, taking his erection in her hands again and stroking him. "Now, run to me."

Slowly he opened his eyes. It took a few seconds for the haze of the past to clear completely. He smiled.

When he looked down he saw that the entire front of his body had turned red. He had welts on his chest, welts on his sides, welts on his hips and stomach. A hundred welts decorated his legs in a pattern like tiger stripes. Mistress Felicia had been merciless with him. His skin throbbed from the injuries she'd inflicted on him. No wonder she could command billionaires to kiss her feet. Pain like this was worth any price.

She took the crop from his teeth and laid both her hands on either side of his face. She tilted his head so that his eyes met her eyes. For a long time she did nothing but hold the eye contact, forcing him to see her. In her eyes he saw power and strength, intelligence and compassion. Compassion? For what? For his suffering? Yes. He saw that. But which suffering? The pain she'd inflicted on him? Or all his other pain that she sensed he carried within? It didn't matter why he moved her that way, only that he did. For when she kissed him, he felt real tenderness, affection. She kissed masterfully, her lips teasing his, her tongue caressing his tongue. She didn't force the passion. She roused it. She bit his bottom lip and drew blood. He tasted the copper and swallowed it.

"I never kiss my clients," she whispered against his lips. "I never fuck them. But you're not a client."

"What am I?" he asked.

"Tonight," she said, "you're mine."

And tonight he was.

23

MISTRESS FELICIA UNHOOKED HIS CUFFS AND TURNED him so that he faced away from her now. She bent him over and cuffed his wrists to the footboard of the bed. Once again she gagged him with the crop. More pain came then. A cane that battered his thighs. A flogger that cut into his back. A whip that bit from his shoulders to his knees.

He glanced at the clock before she began her beating. He glanced at it again when she finished. She'd beaten him for a solid hour—an hour that had passed in seconds. His lungs burned from how hard he'd breathed during the beating. When Mistress Felicia touched his lower back, he flinched. His skin was so raw even the softest touch burned.

She laughed at his flinching, no doubt enjoying his pain. Any true sadist would. She kissed his neck above the tendon of his shoulder as she unlocked his wrists from the footboard.

Mistress Felicia took the crop out of his mouth again. "Do you need water?"

"Please."

She brought him water in a wineglass, but when he reached for it, she shook her head.

"On your knees."

He dropped to his knees, and Mistress Felicia cupped the

back of his head. She brought the glass to his lips and bade him to drink. His male pride loathed this childish dependence even as his hunger for surrender and submission gloried in being treated like a dog at the mercy of his master.

The water cooled his burning tongue, though it did nothing to alleviate the pain that suffused his entire body. Mistress Felicia took the glass from his lips, set it aside and returned to him. She wove her fingers through the long hair at the base of his neck and let him rest his head against her stomach.

"I've never known anyone who took pain as well as you do," she said, now massaging his neck. "You've pleased me more than I can say."

"Thank you, *Maîtresse*." Finally he could trust his voice to speak.

"And I've never had a more beautiful man at my feet before. You are a prize."

He closed his eyes. These were the words his soul needed. Once Søren had whispered similar words to him. It was like drinking a single sip of the finest red wine and forever chasing that taste in every glass he raised to his lips.

"*Merci,*" he whispered. She caressed the side of his face. With the same hand that had hurt him, she comforted him. She reached up to her hair, and from the knot by her ear she pulled out the rose.

"This is a Felicia rose," she said, tickling his lips and cheek with the petals. "Lovely, isn't it?"

"It is, but not as lovely as you."

"Well, what could be?" she asked, arrogant as any dominant he'd ever known—himself included. "All roses are traps, you know. The blooms are so beautiful everyone is drawn to them. And yet if you try to take one, and you aren't careful…"

She turned the rose and let the short stem brush his cheek. One single thorn scratched, but did not break, his skin.

"If you want the petals," she said, putting the bloom to his lips, "you'll have to bear the thorns."

She stepped away from him, reached into her bag, and from it pulled a square of folded wine-colored velvet. She carried the velvet to the side of his bed, unfolded the cloth and gathered its contents in her hand. With a toss of her hand she sprinkled something on top of his bedcovers.

"Come to me," she said, and beckoned him with her hand. He stood and walked to her and saw what she had done to his bed.

A thousand rose thorns, sharp and shining, lay scattered across the sheets.

"Lie on your back," she said. "If you want me, that is."

He wanted her. He crawled over the bed and felt the bite of the thorns into his knees and palms. He lay diagonally across the bed wincing as they pricked at his bruised and battered skin. Once he settled into the sheets, Mistress Felicia raised a hand to her neck and took off the black lace choker. She reached down and removed her boots. She stripped herself of her skirt, then her corset. Off came her stockings and garters. And when she finally stood naked, she took the knot of her hair down.

Now she crawled to him.

"The thorns," he warned as her hand touched the sheets.

"Have you ever met the rose who was afraid of her own thorns?"

She knelt at his side and took his wrists in her hands, pressing them into the bed by his head. The compassion was gone now, replaced by passion.

"Kiss me inside," she said against his lips before moving to straddle his head. He grasped her waist. Her skin was so warm and soft. She pushed her hips forward so that her clitoris was at his lips. He licked it and kissed it, sucking it between his lips and teasing it with the tip of his tongue. Mistress Felicia let out the softest sigh of pleasure. He pulled her harder on to his mouth. He tasted her heat and wanted more of it, so he grasped her hips and moved her on him, opening her up with his mouth, lapping at every part of her lips, outer and inner, seeking the core of her while she gasped and moaned on top of him. She covered his hands with hers and squeezed his fingers as she orgasmed. Fluid rushed out of her and coated his lips and chin, and he drank her wetness. He couldn't get enough of her.

When her shuddering ceased, she sat back on his chest and reached to the table at the side of the bed. He knew she reached for a condom, but he took his chance to capture her nipple in his mouth and suck on it. He circled her aureole with his tongue and sucked her breast deeper into his mouth. Two weeks… It seemed like a year since he'd had a woman's body in his bed. He had to taste all of her.

She let him kiss her breasts, offering up to his mouth first her right nipple and then her left. As he sucked her, he ran his hands up and down her smooth back. She was thin but shapely, tall and lissome as a flower but with strength rippling under her skin.

At last she pulled away, moved down his body, removed the cock ring and slipped the condom over his straining erection. She straddled him again. He watched as she gripped him and put him inside her. She took him in slowly, working him into her wet body inch by inch. Her orgasm was recent and her vagina tight from it. He felt that tightness straining to take him all, the size of him pushing against her narrow inner walls. It pleased him to fill her, to see her wince as her body struggled to accept all of him. She tilted her hips forward and took him all the way in. Ecstasy—white-hot and blinding—permeated him as she moved on him, riding him, each thrust of her hips taking him deeper inside her. She placed her hands on the sides of his chest, covering the scar with her palm. Her eyes closed, and he watched her move on him. Her hair swayed about her shoulders, her breasts rose and fell with every breath. She came again, and he could feel her tight inner body convulsing around him.

He wanted to come, too, but not yet. Not quite yet.

Mistress Felicia lifted off him and crawled to the head of the bed. She put her hands on the headboard and spread her legs in an invitation. He needed no other instruction. He mounted her from behind in one swift stroke and wrapped an arm around her waist. His other hand gripped the headboard to hold them both steady. Then he let loose with his need, pounding into her with all his pent-up need and desire. His hips beat against her soft rounded bottom, his cock pummeled and hammered deep inside her. He watched himself disappearing into her hole, reemerging from each foray wetter and wetter. She made no protest, gave no order to slow or stop. Whether she enjoyed it or not didn't seem to matter to her. He'd earned this privilege of fucking her as hard as he needed.

Blood throbbed in his thighs. Without mercy he pushed into her. Without complaint she received him. His climax built painfully in his back and hips. He'd been hard for so long, too long. His thrusts grew wilder, more desperate, more bruising. And when he knew neither of them could take anymore, he came and he came and he came, a hand clamped on her shoulder so hard she would share in his bruises tomorrow.

He pulled out of Mistress Felicia and lay on his back again. He knew the thorns were there, but he could no longer feel them.

She crawled on top of him and took a lock of his hair between her fingers. She lifted it and kissed the tip.

"You were sixteen," she said. "You let a boy inside you."

Kingsley whispered his yes.

"You'll let me inside you." It wasn't a question. Still, he whispered his assent.

She left the bed to retrieve her harness, and he rolled on to his stomach. Since coming out of the hospital he hadn't let anyone inside him. The knowledge that he'd been violated like that while unconscious had made him afraid to let anyone in him lest he remembered something he far preferred to forget. But Mistress Felicia had hurt him in the way he needed to be hurt, and tonight he could deny her nothing.

She prepped him well, and he felt nothing but pleasure as she pushed inside him. He closed his eyes and received, not merely the phallus she used to penetrate him, but received the comfort of her touch, as well, and the words she whispered into his heart.

Beautiful...she whispered into his ear. *Brave...virile...strong... powerful*...and a hundred other words that bound his wounds.

The litany kept him with her. He didn't go into his past, didn't leave her or the bed. And when he came soon after, they were both pleasantly surprised. She even laughed and kissed his cheek, called him her new favorite slut.

He asked her to stay the night, and she agreed. He worshipped her body all night long, fucking her on her back, on her side, in the shower. He gave her orgasm after orgasm with his hands and his mouth, his cock and the toys he kept under the bed. He obeyed her every order, indulged her every whim and took pride in how readily her body responded to him.

After they'd worn each other out with kink and sex, Felicia massaged warm oil into every inch of his body. He hadn't felt this sated in years. Not since Søren.

"You're a masterful sadist." Kingsley sighed contentedly.

"Merci beaucoup," she said, putting on a feigned French accent. Kingsley laughed.

"Did you come out of retirement just to fuck me?"

"To fuck you…and fuck with him by coming out of retirement to work at your club."

"Him? Oh, him." Kingsley knew immediately who "him" was—the billionaire whose divorce had landed Mistress Felicia in jail for two months. "Is he the jealous type?"

"Very much so. And he hates the idea of me with anyone else, even if I won't see him anymore. But you know what they say, hell hath no fury like a woman scorned." She lightly traced the welts she'd left on his chest. "As you can see."

"The female of the species is always deadlier than the male."

"Always?" Felicia asked.

Kingsley sat up in bed, a realization hitting him like Felicia's crop on his back.

"Always," he repeated. He turned around and kissed her. "I have to go. With your permission, *Maîtresse*."

"Tell me where you're going, and I'll consider it."

"Someone's been threatening me and I know who it is."

"Are you going to destroy him?"

"Her," Kingsley said.

Mistress Felicia grinned.

"You'll come to my house tonight?"

"I'll come to your house, in your house and on your house if you order me to."

"Permission granted."

Kingsley scrambled out of bed and threw his clothes on.

Five minutes later he was walking out his front door.

And twenty minutes after that, he stood at another front door.

He knocked and waited.

Phoebe Dixon opened the door. When she saw him, she

tried to slam it in his face. Kingsley stopped the door with his hand.

Kingsley smiled at her, and she took a fearful step back. "We need to talk."

24

"I HAVE NOTHING TO SAY TO YOU." PHOEBE GLARED at him as he pushed into the house and shut the door behind her. "I'll call the police if I have to."

"And tell them what exactly?"

"That you broke into my house."

"Call them. I'll tell where you hide all your drugs from your husband."

"You bastard, what do you want?"

"I want to know why you're threatening me with that tape."

"What tape? What are you talking about?" she asked, a crack in her voice betraying her guilt.

"You know exactly what I'm talking about. I know it's you. I don't need a confession. I only want to know why."

"I have to tell you why? You don't know?"

"I wish I could say I did. The last time I saw you I gave you exactly what you wanted."

"And then you dumped me without a word," she said. "Not one fucking word."

"So this is how you punish me? By threatening me and my friends?"

"I didn't send the tapes. I just... I gave one to someone."

"Who?"

"I don't know."

Kingsley sighed heavily.

"Phoebe, I'm a very busy man. We can play the back-and-forth game all day, or we can skip the part where you play dumb and get back to the part where you tell me the truth, so we can both move on with our lives."

Phoebe crossed her arms over her chest.

"Two can play this game," he reminded her. "Do I have to send that tape to the reporter I know? The tape of your husband accepting a bribe?"

She lifted her chin but remained silent.

"I can also tell my friend on the police force who you buy your drugs from, and then you'll have to find a new supplier."

"I don't know his name," she finally said. "He came to see Robert and asked about you. I overheard them talking. Robert kicked him out, but he left his phone number."

"And you called him?"

"You had your fucking secretary call me to blow me off. Your *secretary*. You couldn't pick up the fucking phone and call me yourself?"

"This is your payback because I didn't call you? I'd hate to see what you'd do if someone really tried to hurt your poor little feelings."

"I don't talk to secretaries."

"You should. They're some of the best people I know. Now tell me everything about this man who wanted information on me."

"I told you, I don't know his name."

"Who does he work for?"

"I don't know that, either. All he said was you were annoying his employer."

"Who does he work for?"

"I don't know."

"You have to know something."

She shook her head and raised her hands to her temples.

"He said... I don't know. Something about a building. Those were his words, 'All this bullshit over a fucking building.'"

"See? That wasn't so hard." Kingsley raised his eyebrows and tapped her under the chin.

Phoebe crossed her arms over her chest and glared.

"I don't know who you pissed on, but they're talking to everyone you know. Someone's going to break."

"Someone did," he said with a cold smile. "Now are you going to be a good girl and stop causing me trouble?"

"I didn't appreciate talking to your secretary."

"You have my sincerest apologies. It will not happen again."

"Good. Thank you." She walked toward him and put her hands on his chest. "So...if I forgive you and you forgive me, maybe we can go make up in my bedroom?"

He gently grasped her wrists and kissed the back of each hand.

"I would rather go to prison labeled as a sex offender than spend one more second in your company."

Phoebe slapped him.

Kingsley laughed. "If I knew you had this side to you..." he said. "No, I still wouldn't want to fuck you ever again."

He turned and strolled from her house and walked back to his. He needed Sam and he needed her now. Phoebe might be crowing that she'd scored some sort of victory against him, but Kingsley saw it differently.

If Fuller had put someone on Kingsley's trail, knew who his friends were, knew who his contacts were, knew who he was fucking...that meant they were on to something. Kingsley scared Fuller and Fuller was fighting back. He and Sam needed to get to work right now digging as deep as they could. One of them—either him or Sam—was getting closer to the truth. No backing down now. It was the two of them up against Fuller and his massive army of Christian fundamentalists. He liked those odds.

Hopefully Sam had spent the night at his house. She'd promised that she alone would be his valet, putting his boots on for him. On the off chance she was up and about, he went in search of her.

On the second floor he heard her voice, and he followed it to a bedroom. The door stood ajar, and he glanced inside.

And there he saw Sam giving someone a kiss. She was dressed. The person she kissed was dressed. But the sheets were wild, which told him her night had been wild. And it should have been nothing seeing them kiss. He shouldn't have cared. He shouldn't have seen it, but it shouldn't have mattered. But it did matter. And he did look, and he couldn't look away. Although it hurt to look. God, it hurt to look.

Because Sam was kissing a man. And that man wasn't him.

25

July

THE SUN HAD SET AN HOUR EARLIER, BUT THE CITY
still smoldered in the summer heat. Reluctantly Kingsley abandoned Felicia's Bedford cottage. The two-bedroom house was
hidden behind a veil of trees and offered the sort of privacy
only money could buy. For the past month, it had become
Kingsley's second home as he and Felicia owned each other's
bodies night and day. But as good as the kink and the sex had
been, Kingsley knew the main reason he stayed with her was
his desire to avoid seeing Sam. But Felicia had to leave him
to see a client in London, Blaise had gone to Washington and
Kingsley knew he couldn't hide forever.

Back at his town house he found Sam in his office, sitting
behind his desk with a stack of invoices. She looked up from
her work and smiled at him.

"Look at what the pussy dragged in," she said. "Have a
good night? And day? And night? And week? And month?"

"I need you to reschedule my appointment with Anita,"
he said.

Sam glared at him. "Again? This is the second time you've

rescheduled. I've never known anybody to cancel a massage. I mean…it's a massage."

"Reschedule it," he said. He owed her no explanations, none at all. "I'm going to bed. You should go home, too."

"Soon as this is finished."

"You won't see me much tomorrow," he said on his way out of the office.

"Getting used to that," she said half under her breath, half audibly.

Kingsley turned around in the doorway.

"You have something to say to me?" he asked, trying to keep his voice even.

Sam sat back in his desk chair. "I said I was getting used to not seeing you. You've been a ghost for the past month, which would be fine if you were busy and happy. But you don't seem happy, and something tells me you're avoiding me. It's a little hard to be an assistant when you have no one to assist."

"I don't need assisting right now."

"Don't need assisting? You have this grand plan to open an S and M kingdom before the end of the year, and we don't own a building for it yet. We don't have renovation plans yet. We don't even have a fucking name for it yet. And you're telling me you don't need assisting?"

"What's with the 'we'?" he asked. "It's *my* club, not *our* club. There is no 'we' here."

"*Your* club is never going to exist if *you* don't start doing some work on it."

"I'll do what I want when I want to do it. And I don't have to explain myself. To you or anyone."

He walked away from her toward his bedroom. He should have fired her. Why hadn't he fired her? He had every reason to fire her. No, he had no reason to fire her, which is why he hadn't. She'd told him a comforting fiction when she'd said if she would be with any man it would be him. How many times had he whispered those sorts of seductive nothings into a woman's ear before? *You're the best lover I've had…the most beautiful woman I've been with…if I could stay with you I would stay with you…* He had no reason to be this angry still even after a month. And yet he was.

Alone in his bedroom he undressed and crawled into bed. He hated sleeping alone, but his exhaustion was profound. He ached all over from lack of sleep. He'd sought refuge in the pain Felicia gave him from the pain Sam had given him. What hurt worse than anything—worse than Sam's lie and worse than Felicia's erotic brutality—was the simple terrible fact that Søren had been right. Kingsley didn't know anything about Sam. He'd been too quick to trust her. And now he regretted it.

He fell asleep the second his head hit the pillow, but terrible dreams poisoned his rest. In one dream he was a prisoner in his own bed, and it burned all around him. In a second dream some faceless enemy had Søren trapped in a labyrinthine prison, and Kingsley had sixty seconds to find him and save him before he was shot. The dream morphed a final time, now he was the prisoner, and a man stood before him with a chain in his hand. He wrapped the chain around Kingsley's throat, tightening it until he couldn't speak, couldn't fight, couldn't breathe.

He woke with a cough that wrenched his lungs and his stomach. He gasped for air and couldn't get enough of it. Finally the coughing fit ended, and on shaking legs he got out of bed. It was midnight according to his clock. He'd slept an hour and a half, and yet it seemed like days as his nightmares had been so vivid and brutal. The images stayed with him even as he dragged on his pants. He tried to banish them with other thoughts, but the panic stayed with him. He almost called Søren to reassure himself the dream of Søren's captivity and imminent death had been nothing but a dream.

Alcohol. That's what he needed. He hadn't had more than a glass of wine or two a day since meeting Felicia. He'd been drunk on her body and her pain for a month. But he should drink now—heavily.

He pulled on a shirt but didn't bother buttoning it. He walked down the back servants' staircase to the wine cellar behind the kitchen. Wine might not be strong enough tonight, but he discovered all the hard liquor in the house had disappeared. Søren's doing? Or Sam's? Both of them treated him like a fucking child these days. He wouldn't put it past either of them to hide the liquor. Fine. He'd drink wine. A bottle of pinot would put him to sleep and subdue his restless mind.

With the bottle in his hand he headed back through the dark kitchen. He flinched when light suddenly infiltrated the room.

"Ah, *merde*," he said, raising a hand to his eyes. "Who is it?"

"Me," Sam said. She quickly came into focus. "I heard footsteps and… Oh, my God."

Fuck. Kingsley sat the bottle on the kitchen table and started to button his shirt. But it was too late. Sam had already seen him, seen the bruises and welts Felicia had left on him.

"It's nothing," he said. "What are you still doing here?"

"It's not nothing. Who the hell did that to you?"

Sam reached for his shirt, and he caught her wrist in his hand. His head had cleared completely now, and he saw the look of fear on Sam's face. Fear? Of him? Or for him?

"Nobody," he said. "And you didn't answer me. What are you doing here?"

"Still working," she said. "I got the financials from your friend The Barber. I've been digging."

"Find anything?"

"I'm not having this conversation with you until you tell me why you look like someone beat the shit out of you," Sam demanded. She looked tired, too, as tired as he probably looked.

"Non," he said. "Forget you saw anything."

"Okay, maybe you'll answer this—where have you been for the past month?"

"Staying with Blaise," he said.

"Well, that's interesting."

"Nothing is interesting." He took his wine bottle and pushed past her.

"It's very interesting because Blaise has been in DC for the past two weeks with the NOW," Sam said, following him out of the kitchen and down the hall. "You want to tell me another lie?"

"You accuse me of lying?" Kingsley asked as he started up the stairs. "Very amusing accusation coming from you."

"What the fuck do you mean, coming from me?" She took two stairs at a time to keep up with him. "I have never lied to you. Do I want to talk about my past? No. But not talking about something isn't the same as lying about it. Don't you dare call me a liar when you can look me in the face and tell me you were with Blaise when we both know you weren't."

On the second landing, Kingsley turned to face her so fast she took a step back from him.

"You want to talk about lying to someone's face. You told me the night of the party that if you were going to be with any man it would be me."

"Yeah, I said that. So what?"

"So what? So I went to find you the morning after the

party, and I saw you with a man. You were kissing, the bed was a wreck, and I saw it all."

Sam turned her back to him. Her shoulders shook. Then she laughed—a big, loud, shocked laugh that filled the whole house.

"What? You think this is funny?"

"Hilarious," she said, turning back around. "Hysterical. So that's why you're so pissed at me? Why you've been avoiding me for a month? You think I had a sex with a man?"

"I know you did." He turned and strode up the last set of steps to the third floor. "And Søren was right about you."

"Wait one fucking second here." Sam raced after him. "What do you mean Søren was right about me? What's he got to do with this?"

"He told me not to trust you. I should have listened to him."

"I have given you no reason not to trust me."

"Here's a reason. You pretend I mean something to you when…" Pain choked him with unforgiving hands. He wanted to the throw the wine bottle against the wall and watch the red liquid flow like blood. "When I don't."

Sam followed him all the way down the hall.

"Kingsley, stop. Please, stop. I have to tell you something."

He stopped outside his bedroom door.

"What?" he asked, ready to be done with this conversation.

"Yes, I had sex with someone the night of the party. But no, it wasn't a man."

"I saw him." Even now, a month later, the feeling of foolishness hadn't dissipated one jot. He made a practice of trusting no one except himself and Søren, and yet for some stupid sentimental misguided reason, he'd trusted Sam. "Don't tell me I didn't see what I saw."

Sam put her hand to her forehead.

"It's hard to explain," Sam said.

"Try me."

"The man you saw me with is named Alex. Four years ago, Alex was Allison, and Allison was my girlfriend. Allison told me one day she was a man trapped in a woman's body, and she couldn't live like that anymore. Now she's gotten hormone therapy, has a five-o'clock shadow and a voice two octaves deeper. Alex or Allison didn't really matter to me that night. I just missed her. I mean, him. Alex-son."

Kingsley narrowed his eyes at her.

"So, Alex…?"

"Right," Sam said. "Let me rephrase my promise to you. I've never been with a dick, Kingsley. But if I'm ever going to be with a dick, you'll be the dick."

Kingsley let out a breath that he'd been holding in for an entire month. The breath turned into a groan.

"I am such a dick." Kingsley sighed.

"You are," Sam said. "But I forgive you."

"I thought the man you were kissing was a little on the short side. And thin."

"I like my men the way like I like my women—with vaginas."

"You can slap me if you want. I deserve it." He pointed at his cheek and waited.

Sam raised her eyebrow. "Looks like someone beat me to the beating. Now that you know I'm not a lying liar, are you going to tell me what the fuck is going on and who the fuck beat you up and where the fuck you've been and why the fuck you're drinking wine in the middle of the night and why the fuck I can't stop saying fuck?"

Her words were light, but her eyes were shadowed with concern.

He exhaled heavily. This was not a conversation he wanted to have tonight. Or ever. But he'd been such an idiot, been so cold to her for the past month that he knew he owed her.

"Come in," he said. "I'm not going to talk about this in the hallway."

He let her in the bedroom and set the wine bottle by the bed.

"Damn," she said, looking at his bed. "You get in a wrestling match with your covers?"

"I have nightmares sometimes," he admitted. "I had them tonight."

"Is that what the wine's for?"

"It helps me sleep."

Sam leaned across the bed and straightened his wild sheets.

"What sort of nightmares?" She fluffed a pillow and laid it back on the bed.

"The sort you have when you used to have the job I had. The sort of nightmares you have when you've been shot four times."

"So your nightmares aren't the showing-up-naked-at-school type?"

"I have dreams where I'm naked at St. Ignatius. They aren't nightmares."

Sam laughed, and the laugh turned into a sigh, and the sigh turned into her wrapping her arms around his shoulders and holding him close. He hesitated before returning the embrace. He buried his face in the crook of her shoulder and inhaled her scent, sandalwood and cedar. She was the only woman he knew who wore men's cologne. And yet, against her soft skin it smelled utterly feminine and alluring.

"I'm sorry you had bad dreams," she said.

"All my nightmares are of my own making."

"Do you have them every night?"

"If I have someone in bed with me, I usually don't dream."

"And here I thought you fucked someone every single night because you were a nympho."

"That, too," he said.

Sam laughed and rubbed her forehead.

"Okay," she finally said.

"Okay what?"

"Okay, get into bed. You give me the answers to my questions, and I'll give you someone to sleep with tonight so you won't have any more bad dreams."

She walked to the bedroom door and locked it.

"You're sleeping with me?"

"Just sleeping," she said. "I mean, we're sleeping when we're done talking."

Sam kicked off her shoes and yanked off her socks. Yes, it was happening. Sam was taking her clothes off in his bedroom. He must still be dreaming. And having a good dream for once.

"Do you have something I can sleep in? I usually sleep in a T-shirt and boxers. I get cold."

She pulled off her jacket, unbuttoned her vest. And when she started in on her shirt, Kingsley did the only thing he could do.

He took off his own shirt and offered it to her.

"King." It was all she said.

"Take it."

"This is one of your new fancy shirts from Vitale."

"It is."

"And you're going to let me sleep in it?"

"I'm asking you to sleep in it."

"What happened to that whole thing about how a woman wearing your shirt is like a man coming on her tits?"

"I said 'back.'"

"Tits are sexier."

"Wear it. Sleep in it. I won't come on your tits or back."

"Face guy, eh?"

She took the shirt into his bathroom, an act of modesty he found unbearably endearing.

"I sleep naked," he called out to her when she closed the door behind her. "Does that bother you?"

"What? Is all your underwear in the dirty laundry?"

"I don't own any," he admitted.

"I should have known." Sam sighed.

Kingsley stripped out of his clothes and climbed back into bed. Sam emerged seconds later wearing his white dress shirt. On her bare feet she padded across the carpet, came to the bed and slipped under the covers. He hadn't failed to notice her long bare legs and the tantalizing skin of her chest. They glowed in the gentle lamplight, and he dug his fingers into the sheets, a reminder not to touch her.

Sam rolled on to her side to face him.

"Naked?" she asked.

"Completely."

"You're enjoying this."

"More than I should," Kingsley admitted.

He smiled but Sam didn't. Instead, she reached out and touched his shoulder where the crack of a cane had left a two-inch black bruise.

"What happened to you?" she asked. "Please, tell me this was consensual."

"It was consensual. And all your fault."

"How is this my fault?"

"You're the one who told me to woo Mistress Felicia. I sent her flowers. She showed up in my bedroom the night of the party."

Sam's eyes went comically wide. He had to laugh at her.

"You're subbing for Mistress Felicia?" she asked. "Seriously?"

He reached out and covered her lips with one finger.

"It's a secret," he said.

"Why? Everyone knows you're bi. How is this different?"

"A man who likes to fuck other men scares straight men. A man who likes to get the shit beat out of him is a laughingstock." Their world could spout of all it wanted about sexual freedom and acceptance, but male submissives carried a stigma and he wanted no part of it.

"I think it's sexy," Sam said. "I like a man who isn't afraid to be vulnerable. It's how women feel all the time. And if it makes you feel any better, I guessed you might have a little masochistic streak in you when I found out it was Søren you were in love with."

"I didn't mean for you to know that. You're too easy to talk to. It all came out."

She ran her hands through his hair, tenderly and carefully, as if afraid to hurt him more than he already was.

"You can tell me anything. I don't care what Søren says—you can trust me."

"I want to. But you don't make it easy with all the secrets you keep."

"What secrets do you think I'm keeping?"

"You went to that camp the Fullers run and you won't talk about it."

"Do you like talking about when you got shot and ended up in the hospital?"

"Only if it'll get me laid."

Sam laughed.

"Would it really make you feel better to know about my ugly past?"

"I want to know you," Kingsley said. "All of you. And you know so much about me."

"Your secrets are sexier than mine," she said. "I don't have any bullet wounds or secret lovers."

"What kind of secrets do you have?" Kingsley asked.

Sam didn't smile, which scared him. Sam almost always had a smile for him.

"Ugly ones."

26

KINGSLEY WAITED WHILE SAM SETTLED HERSELF INTO the covers. She rolled on to her side to face him, and as Kingsley gazed at her, he made the troubling discovery that he loved seeing her in his bed. She looked so small and defenseless in his grand red bed, almost like a little girl with her pixie cut mussed and her hands under her chin like a child.

"My family failed miserably at turning me into a girly girl. So my church talked to my parents, and they decided to send me to summer camp. It wasn't the usual sort of summer camp. It was this place upstate where gay kids got sent to get their brains fixed."

"Sam…" Kingsley wanted to reach for her, but he held back. If he touched her, she might stop speaking, and he realized now he'd been starving to know the truth of her.

"I met a girl named Faith on the bus to this camp—this nasty awful camp where God wouldn't go if you paid Him. Faith had gotten caught in bed with someone at her church, someone important, and they shut Faith up by sending her to that camp."

"Where was this place they sent you?"

"Pleasant Valley Camp and Nature Center. Can you believe that's what they called it? What bullshit. There was no canoeing, no archery, no nature walks. Instead of that, there were 'prayer sessions' where they made us kneel for hours and pray out loud for God to take our sin away and heal us so we would desire men the way God intended. And there were fun 'therapy sessions' where we had to watch slide shows and were given electric shocks whenever the picture of a pretty girl appeared on the screen. Not electric shocks on the arms or the legs. No—electric shocks on our nipples and clits. But the best part was the drugs."

"Drugs?"

"They'd give us campers vomit-inducing drugs and make us watch lesbian porn. Cunts on the screen. Puke on the floor. We campers called it 'movie night at Caligula's.'"

Kingsley tried to take Sam's hand in his, but she'd curled up her fingers so tightly he could do nothing but place his hand on top of hers.

"Even though we were so busy with all these delightful and wholesome camping activities," Sam continued, her voice dripping with sarcasm and barely restrained fury, "me and Faith did what we could to keep each other strong and sane. Whenever we'd see each other we'd whisper our code words—*More weight*."

"More weight? What did that mean?"

"Some fundies consider lesbianism a kind of witchcraft. I'm not kidding. Just ask Pat Robertson. So when I heard that, I decided to learn about witchcraft like your typical disaffected queer teenager."

"I was a disaffected queer teenager."

"What did you do?"

"Slept with another disaffected queer teenager."

"Why didn't I think of that? Oh, wait, I did." Sam laughed and it was good to hear it. Then she spoke again, and neither of them laughed anymore. "I read this book about the witch hunts in colonial times. The law said a person couldn't be put on trial until they'd entered a guilty or not-guilty plea. This man, Giles Corey, was accused of witchcraft, but he refused to put in a plea. The court had a method for getting people to enter pleas. They'd lay them on a board, put a board on top of them, and they'd pile on weight, slowly crushing the person. They did this to Giles Corey. On went the weight, they'd stop, ask for his plea—guilty or not guilty. And his response was 'More weight.' He said it again and again and then finally 'More weight' were his last words. They killed him, but they never got him to say 'Guilty.' When me and Faith said 'more weight' that meant 'Bring it on. The pain. The tortures. We don't care. They'll never make us plead guilty. We didn't do anything wrong. They were the guilty ones.'"

Kingsley wanted to speak, wanted to stay something. But Sam's strength had humbled him into silence.

"After a month at the camp, they told us our progress was 'unsatisfactory,' and we would have to stay another month. Faith had an idea, and I thought it was a good one. We broke into the clinic and found all the pills we could find…"

Kingsley gave up on Sam's hand and instead pulled her to him, dragging her bodily against him. She rested her head against the center of his chest, and Kingsley put an arm around her shoulders. They were trembling.

"We held each other until morning," Sam said. "Just like you and I are right now. I don't know why we decided to wait until dawn. Maybe we wanted to see a sunrise one last time. But at dawn we swallowed the pills and washed them down with mineral water—like you do. Ten…twenty…thirty pills. And we shivered and burned and it felt like our skin was on fire. And then we slept. Two girls fell asleep. One girl woke up."

"You woke up," Kingsley said.

"The cops came," Sam continued. "They were the first people I spoke to when I woke up in the hospital. To this day it pisses me off when I hear people talking shit about cops. Those cops were the first noncrazy adults I'd talked to in weeks. This detective, Detective Feldman, said this camp sounded like it was run by Josef Mengele. I didn't know at the time what he meant by that, but I knew he was on our side."

"What happened to you? Were there charges filed?"

Sam took a heavy breath.

"Faith Spencer's family blamed me for her death. She'd taken more pills than I had, so they said I'd tricked her into killing herself. The truth was we took whatever we could find. We didn't count the pills. We just swallowed."

"What happened after?"

"Nothing much. I got sent to a state-run psychiatric facility for thirty days. Faith Spencer got buried. WTL paid for Faith's funeral expenses as a 'gesture of Christian charity.' Leave it to Fuller to turn a suicide pact into a public relations win for WTL. The church closed that camp, but they still have others. There are kids there now, right now at those camps. More weight... They're all getting crushed."

"Sam..." Kingsley rubbed her shoulders trying to get her to relax. Instead of relaxing, she pushed back from him and sat up in bed.

"This is why you have to make the club happen," Sam said. "The kingdom you want to build—you have to do it. You have to stop Fuller and WTL from building a church in our town. Faith Spencer is dead because of him and his camps, and he's a hero to his congregation because he threw some bills at her family to upgrade her coffin."

Kingsley stretched out his arm and touched her hair. She leaned her face into his hand and closed her eyes.

"I will build my kingdom," Kingsley said, "and the gates of Fuller's church will not prevail against it."

Sam grinned broadly, and tears lined her eyes. She had never looked so beautiful to him.

"You're going to hell for that," she said.

"I'm taking you with me."

"I go where you go," Sam said. "Someone has to take care of your boots."

She rolled back down and lay once more on his chest. Her head hit a bruise, and Kingsley flinched before he could stop himself.

"Shit, I'm sorry," she said, and tried to pull away.

"No, no, no, you stay. If I like pain enough to have these bruises, then I like pain enough to feel you against them."

"Are you sure?"

"I'm a masochist, Sam."

"Like…a real masochist?"

Kingsley hesitated before answering. He far preferred to keep secrets than to share them. But this was Sam, and he trusted her.

"Nothing arouses me more than pain and fear."

"Your pain?" she asked. "Your fear?"

"My pain. My fear. And the only things that arouse me as much as my pain and my fear are someone else's pain and fear. I didn't know the word *switch* until four years ago when I found a club in Paris. That's what I am. A switch."

"I thought you'd been doing kink since you were a teenager."

"I was doing kink before I'd even heard the word *kink*. We didn't know what we were doing or why we were doing it. We only knew it was what we needed."

"We? We as in you and Father Eyelashes?"

"He wasn't Father Eyelashes when we were together. He

was a student like me. The first time we were together he was a student," Kingsley corrected. "The second time he was a teacher—Mister Eyelashes."

"So that was the teacher you seduced?"

"He was," Kingsley said with pride. He knew Søren would never have pursued him if Kingsley hadn't pursued Søren first.

"Did he hurt you like this?" She touched the bruises on his chest and shoulder.

"He hurt me much worse than this, which is why I loved him more than anyone."

"He hurt you worse than this?" she asked, sounding mildly horrified. "I'm going to be honest—right now I'm struggling with my warring feelings of burning hatred of Søren and total fascination with him."

"Welcome to the club. But don't hate him for beating me. I wanted him to. And there were fifty other boys in our school, all of them terrified of him. He was taller than them, stronger than them, smarter than them and had them all in his thrall. And he didn't touch any of them."

"So why you, then?"

"They were afraid of him. Some of them might of hated him but it was probably jealousy, not hate. I don't blame them. I didn't hate him. I wanted him, and I told him so," Kingsley admitted without shame. "I stared at him, followed him, sat with him—uninvited—in the library while he was trying to do his homework. I even kissed him. Also uninvited."

"You devil. Did he kiss you back?"

"He pushed me back on to the bed and held me down so hard I heard something pop in my wrist. It made masturbating one minute after he walked away from me painful. Not that it stopped me."

"Almost getting your wrist broken turned you on?"

Kingsley took a deep breath.

"It not only turned me on, it turned me on more than anything had ever turned me on before in my life."

"You were sixteen."

"I'd been having sex for years by that point."

"God damn, the French start young."

"Not young enough. All my first lovers were older by a few years. But nothing prepared me for him."

"He was your first guy?"

"First person to hurt me during sex, too." Kingsley laid his hand on the center of Sam's back and mindlessly rubbed up and down the length of her spine. "He's the reason I want to build my kingdom. He's the reason I have to do this."

"Oh, do tell." Sam snuggled in more closely to him. Snuggled? They were snuggling now?

"You really want to hear about the sexually deviant escapades of two teenage boys at a Catholic boarding school?"

"You had me at *sexually deviant*. And *escapades*. And *teenage boys* and *Catholic boarding school*. All of those."

Kingsley opened his mouth to speak, to tell the story, but the words wouldn't come out.

"Kingsley?"

"Forgive me," he said. "It's… They're powerful memories."

"I understand," Sam said. She traced circles around one of his uglier bruises with her fingertip. "I loved someone when I was a teenager. She smelled like apple. It was her shampoo, nothing mystical, but I think about her every time I smell anything apple-scented. I can almost orgasm from eating one."

"Søren…he smells like winter. Did you notice that?"

Sam shook her head. "I haven't gotten that close to him. He makes me nervous."

"You know when it first gets cold, bitterly cold, and the

air has that bite to it? That sting? And the world smells clean and pure? That's what he smells like."

"I'll sniff him someday."

"You should," Kingsley said, although he almost wished he hadn't told Sam about it now. To know the scent of someone's bare skin was to know that person in the most intimate, primal way. "I would breathe him in when we were in bed together. Drove him crazy. If he caught me doing it, he would pinch my nose and hold it. Bastard."

Sam rose up and smiled down at him. She pinched his nose and held it.

"You're in love with him, aren't you? Still in love with him?"

Kingsley nodded. She released his nose.

"I understand. Continue your story."

Kingsley wrinkled his nose. Sam had a vicious pinch.

"You have to know something about Søren," Kingsley began. "He had a bad childhood."

"Didn't we all?"

"I didn't," Kingsley said. "I had a beautiful childhood. My parents were in love with each other, and they adored my sister and me. There is no better city than Paris to grow up in. The City of Light? The City of Love? Nothing bad happened to me. Until everything bad happened to me. My parents died, and I was sent to live with my grandparents in Maine. It was bad. I hated my school. I stayed sane by sleeping with as many girls as possible."

"That's my recipe for sanity, as well."

Kingsley grinned. "My grandparents sent me to an all-boys school. No girls to seduce. And then I fell in love with a sadist who…"

"Who did what?" Sam asked.

Kingsley had almost said "put me in the infirmary" but

decided to keep that part a secret. He wasn't ashamed, wasn't protecting Søren. But that first night he and Søren had had sex, that night on the forest floor, had been the most important night of his life. He'd been having sex since age twelve, but in his mind, his heart, that was the night he had lost his virginity.

"A sadist who was the most beautiful thing I'd ever seen in my life. Love at first sight. Or lust. Hard to tell the difference when you're sixteen. Hard to tell the difference when you're twenty-eight."

"I have that problem, too."

"Søren and I had sex one time the first semester I was there," Kingsley said, summing up the most meaningful night of his life in a few words. "And then I went home for the summer. When I came back for the fall semester, he'd graduated and was teaching. We started sleeping together then. For the first month of school, it was once a week maybe. Then two, three, four times a week. We couldn't get enough of each other. I'd wait until the students in my dorm were asleep, then I'd sneak out and run for it. He'd already be there in the hermitage waiting for me. We had to sneak around all the time. Exhausting but worth it. We had to sneak around even more after my sister, Marie-Laure, came to visit."

"What did you do?"

"Got off campus one day. Søren had gotten a letter from his sister, Elizabeth, and he needed to take care of some family business. He asked Marie-Laure to take over his French classes that Friday so he could deal with it."

"That sounds ominous."

"When the teenaged sadist in the family is the relative you turn to for help, you know there's a problem."

Sam winced. "Sounds like it. What was the problem?"

"Elizabeth learned their father had gotten remarried, and

his second wife had another daughter. She asked Søren to warn the new wife what kind of monster she'd married."

"Dad was bad?"

"Søren had the father of all bad fathers," Kingsley said. A joke, yes, but neither of them laughed at it. "Since my sister was substituting for him that day, I skipped class and went with him. I couldn't believe he'd let me skip, but we'd had so little time together since she showed up. He said yes."

"Where did you all go?"

"New Hampshire, to his father's house."

"How did you get there?"

Kingsley grinned. Grinned hugely. Grinned ear to shit-eating-grin ear.

"His father had money. Lots of it. I didn't even believe he had so much money until that trip. Elizabeth sent a car for him to take him to his father's house. But not just any car."

"Oh, God, don't tell me," Sam said. "I see where this is going."

"It was a Rolls Royce."

27

KINGSLEY DIDN'T LIE, BUT HE TOLD ENOUGH HALF truths to Marie-Laure to constitute a lie. *He's meeting his father's new wife. Needs to talk to her about a family situation. She's never met him before, might not believe he is who he says he is. He asked me to go with him to vouch for his identity. You'll be fine without us for one day, won't you?* Oh, yes, she said. *Bien sûr.* Go with him. Anything for him, she said, already obsessed with Søren only a week after meeting him.

Kingsley barely slept the night before. He'd fought the temptation all night to go to Søren's tiny apartment in the priests' quarters. But that would have been pushing his luck. He still couldn't believe Søren had agreed to take him along on this trip. Trip? More like a mission, from the way Søren explained it. *I have to go to my father's house. He's finally out of state on a trip. This is my chance to meet his new wife and talk to her without him anywhere near. I have to get his wife and my sister away from him. I need her to believe me.*

"I promise I'll vouch for your sanity and good character," Kingsley said.

"Thank you," Søren said.

"Even if I have to lie."

The insult had earned him a quick hard slap to the back of the head.

At 4:37 a.m., Kingsley left the dorms with his bag over his shoulder and waited in the chapel. Everyone was still asleep, even the priests. He cracked open the front door and watched. Ten minutes later a streak of silver glinted into view, and even in the moonlit morning darkness, he could see Søren's blond hair as he walked from his building to the car. Kingsley walked out then, too, and got into the car as if it were the most natural thing in the world and no one could or should question why he did it.

The driver held the door open for Søren, but Kingsley entered the opposite side. He sat there on the leather bench seat vibrating with nervous excitement. Søren, as usual, was the picture of genteel sophistication. Through the window that separated the backseats from the driver, Søren calmly gave the driver his instructions. Søren was three weeks away from turning eighteen, and the driver must have been fifty, but he bowed and scraped to Søren as if he were royalty.

The driver closed the window. Søren closed the curtain. And now, here, at last, they were alone in a Rolls Royce. Kingsley hadn't remembered dying, but somehow he'd found his way into heaven. And heaven had a hand-stitched gray leather interior.

"Don't even think about it," Søren said as Kingsley pulled his coat and gloves off.

"I'm always thinking about it," Kingsley said. "I brought the lube."

"Kingsley, it's not even five in the morning yet."

"You beat me this early before."

"I was attempting to wake you up."

"With your alarm cock?"

"Go back to sleep." Søren unbuttoned his coat and removed it. "We have a long drive ahead of us."

"In a Rolls Royce? This is nice. You can pay for this?"

"My sister Elizabeth arranged this trip. She'd go herself, but I'd prefer our father blame me for this than her. For her sake, I hope he doesn't find out at all."

"What are you doing?" Kingsley asked as Søren reached into his distressed leather messenger bag. He pulled out a file folder and a red pen.

"Grading papers."

"Then I'm definitely sleeping." He couldn't think of anything more boring than watching Søren grade Spanish homework for the next five hours. Still, he'd do it if he thought he could get some sex out of the deal. Unfortunately, beating and fucking Kingsley didn't seem to be on Søren's agenda today.

Kingsley stretched out his legs and balled up his jacket like a pillow. But before he could find a sleeping spot, Søren grabbed him by his shirt collar.

He froze, his body going stiff—every part of it.

"Not there," Søren said. He dragged Kingsley across the seat and across his lap. "Sleep here. I need a desk."

"Are you serious?"

"Deadly," Søren said, his tone dry and light, which was far more unnerving than if he sounded threatening. Kingsley groaned and turned on to his stomach, giving Søren his back to use a desk. He stuffed his jacket under his head and tried to get comfortable.

The low purr of the car's engine and the early hour eventually lulled him into a deep and restful sleep even if he did have to contend with Søren's thighs against his ribcage and the scratch of the pen against his back. If he could admit it to himself, he liked playing Søren's desk for him. Søren always used him in bed. Being used out of bed was a pleasant change of pace.

When he woke up, the sun had risen, and pale winter sunlight filled the car through the tinted windows.

"Are we there yet?" Kingsley asked. He wasn't sure how long he'd slept, but he sensed several hours had passed.

"Almost," Søren said. And that's when Kingsley realized Søren's hand lay on his back under his shirt. Sometime while he'd slept, Søren had finished his work, but instead of waking Kingsley up and ordering him to move, he'd let him sleep. And now Kingsley felt fingertips on the small of his back. He didn't move, didn't want to move. He feared if he moved, Søren would stop touching him like that. Søren could be gentle and had been gentle with him, but only after the beating and the fucking. No beating or fucking this morning, and yet Søren lightly caressed Kingsley's back under his shirt, following the line of his spine all the way to his neck and back down again. He traced the edge of Kingsley's rib cage, the sides of his stomach, the sensitive skin between his shoulder blades.

"What are you doing?" Kingsley asked.

"Touching your back."

"Why?" he asked. *Pourquoi?*

"Because I can. I can do anything I want to you. Isn't that right?"

"Anything," Kingsley said, releasing a deep sigh of pleasure. "Can I ask a stupid question?"

"You just did."

Kingsley laughed, and he heard Søren sigh in mock disgust.

"Ask your question."

"Do you like my body?" Kingsley blushed before, during and after asking it.

"Not at the moment."

"You don't?" Kingsley was crushed.

"Not nearly enough bruises on it for my liking."

Kingsley grinned at the answer. "You can make any improvements to my body you want. Welts...bruises...cuts... burns..."

"You're trying to tempt me."

"Always. Is it working?"

"It might be," Søren said, running one fingertip down the center of Kingsley's back again. He shivered at the touch. "You enjoy that?" he asked. He sounded almost surprised.

"*Oui, beaucoup.*" Kingsley slid into French. "I like pleasure almost as much as pain."

"Do you wish I felt the same?" Søren asked.

"*Pas du tout.* I can find any girl to give me pleasure. Who will give me pain if you won't?"

Søren laughed softly. Kingsley loved making Søren laugh. Kingsley theorized the whole course of human evolution had led to Søren, and when he laughed, the world knew it had done a good job with its work.

"Turn over," Søren ordered, and Kingsley obeyed instantly. Now Søren teased the front of his body, his stomach and chest. With his fingertips, Søren lightly scored Kingsley's ribs, counting them up the left side and down the right. By the time he counted to twenty-four, Kingsley was fully erect.

"You like this, too?" Søren asked as he pushed Kingsley's shirt up to his armpits. Kingsley did him one better and pulled it all the way off.

"Every second of it. Do you?"

Søren paused. A sign he was thinking deeply, weighing his words.

"It's interesting, seeing how you respond to different types of touch."

"Can I touch you, too?" Kingsley asked. "Please?"

"If you insist. Although I won't enjoy it, so I don't know why you'd bother."

Kingsley heard amusement in Søren's voice. He loved detailing Kingsley's many inadequacies for him—Kingsley was a waste of Søren's time. He was too French, not Catholic, too sex-obsessed, not studious enough, not nearly obedient enough, and, of course, beneath Søren in every way—physically, morally and ontologically. Considering Søren said these sort of cruel nothings to him while they were alone together, kissing, touching, fucking, Kingsley questioned if Søren actually meant them. In fact, sometimes Kingsley got the distinct feeling Søren liked him. He had paid to bring Marie-Laure all the way to America to visit him at school. If that wasn't love—or at least affection—what was it?

"You might not enjoy it," Kingsley said. "But I will."

Kingsley sat next to Søren, facing him. Søren turned his head and looked at Kingsley without speaking. No doubt Søren expected Kingsley to touch him in some intimate part of his body. And Kingsley did.

He reached up and touched Søren's face. In shock or surprise, Søren pulled back an inch. Kingsley waited, reached out again and pressed his fingertips to Søren's cheek.

"You're too pale," Kingsley said. "Every time I touch you I think your skin will be cold like stone."

"It isn't easy to get a tan in Maine," Søren said. "Any other complaints about my appearance?"

"Your eyelashes are too dark." Kingsley ran the pad of his thumb over the tips of Søren's eyelashes. "Makes it hard for me to concentrate when I'm around you."

"I don't accept my eyelashes as an excuse for your bad behavior."

"Then you'll have to keep punishing me for it, then."

"I intend to."

Kingsley leaned forward, wrapped his arms around Søren's shoulders and kissed him. Søren returned the kiss with surprising tenderness and gentleness. Usually Søren's kisses were of the bruising variety, which Kingsley loved. But he loved this, too; Søren's hands on his naked back, their lips touching, their tongues mingling… And then, because the kiss was too perfect, Kingsley ruined it by laughing.

Søren pulled back and glared at him.

"I'm sorry," Kingsley said. "I never thought…"

"Never thought what?" Søren demanded.

"Never thought I'd make out with you in the backseat of a car. Can we go to a drive-in movie tonight, too?"

Søren glared at him.

"Put your shirt on."

"Don't stop. We were almost to second base," Kingsley said, stilling laughing. He didn't even stop laughing when Søren pushed him on to the floor of the car.

"We have to stop," Søren said, all amusement gone from his eyes. "We're here."

Kingsley scrambled on to the seat and pulled his T-shirt and jacket back on. He ran his hand through his hair and straightened his clothes.

"What are you going to do?" Kingsley noticed the tight set to Søren's mouth, the hard line of his jaw.

"Pray that God gives me the words," he said. "I hope she's here."

"Didn't Elizabeth say the new wife should be home?"

"I didn't mean the new wife. I meant my sister—the baby. Claire."

"You said she was three, *oui*? She's not a baby, she's a pre-schooler."

"When did you become an expert on childhood development?"

"I didn't, but even I know the difference between a baby and a preschooler." Kingsley scoffed, and Søren narrowed his eyes at him. Maybe he would get a beating today after all.

"How did your sister find out about the new wife?"

"Her mother hired someone to watch my father's activities. Elizabeth keeps me informed. We knew he'd gotten remarried. We didn't know until recently he'd had another child."

"Why would he keep that a secret?"

"Because he knows Elizabeth and I would do something like this."

The car turned a corner on to a long, tree-lined stretch of road, and a grand English manor came into view.

"That's it?" Kingsley asked.

Søren stared blankly out the window before inclining his head.

"That's a castle," Kingsley said. "You grew up in a castle."

"It's a house."

"It's a big fucking house." Grand, breathtaking, magnificent and imposing. Not unlike Søren.

"I hate it."

Kingsley sighed. Søren had told him about life in that house.

"I don't blame you, *mon ami*."

The car drove down the long stretch of driveway. Kingsley sensed Søren tensing as they neared the house.

"What can I do?" Kingsley asked. "To help you, I mean."

"Stay in the car. If I need you to vouch for my identity, I'll come for you."

The car stopped in the bottom of the U of the driveway. The driver got out and opened the door for Søren. A blast of frigid air slapped Kingsley in the face. It would snow soon. Kingsley hoped it would snow. Then he and Søren would have to get a hotel room—maybe stay in it for days...

"Hey," Kingsley said, and Søren turned around. "Can I meet your sister?"

"Claire's not even three years old. If you want to flirt with my sister, we'll have to visit Elizabeth."

"I wasn't going to flirt," Kingsley said, stung that Søren apparently thought sex was his only interest in life. It was his biggest interest, of course, but not his only one. "I like kids."

Søren narrowed his eyes at him and pointed at the seat of the car.

"Wait," Søren said, as if Kingsley himself were the preschooler here.

The driver got back in the car. Kingsley got out and stood in the frigid late-autumn wind. Søren's long coat whipped around his legs as he walked to the house. His head was high and his eyes stony, but for all that, he looked like a condemned man walking to his own execution.

He rang the doorbell and the door opened. A woman stood on the threshold. Søren's father would be in his fifties by now, but this woman looked barely thirty. Young and beautiful, dark-haired and shapely. What did they call these women? Trophy wives? He'd heard that somewhere. A young woman marrying a much older man for his money. Would she even care that her husband had raped his other daughter? Or would she consider that a risk worth taking for the chance to live in such opulence?

Whoever she was, whatever her name, she seemed willing to listen to Søren. She didn't invite him in, but she didn't slam the door in his face, either. Who would slam the door in such a face? It would be like spitting on Michelangelo's *David*.

A smaller face appeared in the doorway. A little girl with her hair in curls and something in her hand—a stuffed toy? She gazed up at her mother, and the woman put her hand on top of the little girl's head. Kingsley didn't know what possessed him to disobey Søren's order, but without thinking he walked to the house and stood behind Søren on the porch.

"Oh, this is my friend Kingsley," Søren said to the woman. "I brought him to affirm I am who I say I am. I know what I'm telling you is—"

"I knew who you were the moment I saw you," she said, her voice shaking. "You're just like him."

Kingsley sensed Søren recoiling inwardly at the comparison.

"Forgive me," she said. "I mean…you look like him. That's all. I can see you're his son. I'm Annabelle." She gave Kingsley a faltering smile.

"And this is Claire, my sister," Søren said, nodding at the little girl who looked up at the three people arrayed on the porch, her eyes great with innocent curiosity.

"She's a little shy at first," Annabelle said. "But once she starts talking, you can't get her to shut up."

"Sounds like you, Kingsley," Søren said. "Kingsley?"

Kingsley ignored him and knelt on the ground.

"I like your unicorn," he said, tapping the purple beast she clutched on the tip of its horn. "What's her name?"

"Claire."

"That's your name."

"I named her after me," Claire said in a small, proud voice.

"I should… I'll go pack our bags now," Annabelle said. She picked the girl up into her arms. "Would you like to hold your sister while I pack?"

"I…" Søren began and stopped. Kingsley had never dreamed he would hear Søren stammer in nervousness. "I've never been around small children. I'm afraid I'll hurt her."

"I'll take her," Kingsley said, and Annabelle passed Claire to him. She wriggled around in his arms until she found a comfortable spot.

"Come in, please. Both of you."

Søren and Annabelle disappeared up the stairs to talk more and pack some things while Kingsley played with Claire. Anything he did made her giggle, especially when he spoke English to her and French to her unicorn. She also liked it when he bounced her unicorn on top of her head. She snatched it from his hand and attacked him with it. He played dead, which sent her into a giggle fit.

Claire acted as a tour guide for Kingsley. She pointed at everything that could possibly be of interest to him—the fireplace, the logs, the chairs, the picture of her papa. Kingsley peered at the photograph—a black-and-white eight-by-ten of a regal-looking man in a British Army officer's uniform. Søren looked so much like the man in the photograph that Kingsley couldn't look away at first. Same strong jaw and nose, same intense eyes, same noble and aristocratic bearing. And yet for all the similarities, Kingsley knew in his soul that this man and Søren could not have been more different. The father had done a lifetime of damage to his eldest daughter, and here was the son trying to stop it from happening to the youngest.

Not ten minutes later, Søren and Claire's mother were loading suitcases into her car. He heard her saying something about going to her parents, and Søren replied with one word—*attorney*. No matter what she did, where she went, her first phone call needed to be to a lawyer.

When it was time to go, Claire wouldn't let anyone but Kingsley put her coat and shoes on her. Søren watched him while he tied her tiny laces and zipped her into her coat. He had to tell her five times to stop wiggling her fingers, so he could get her mittens on her hands. But finally she was dressed and warm, and he swooped her into his arms and carried her out to the car, Søren and Annabelle behind them.

Annabelle held the door open for them, and Kingsley buckled Claire into her seat. He made sure she had her blanket and her unicorn tucked in with her before tapping the end of her nose in a goodbye.

"Thank you," Annabelle said. Her face had a ghostly pallor. She seemed on the verge of tears, or worse—getting sick all over the place. He couldn't blame her. If someone showed up at his doorstep and said someone he loved was a child-molesting rapist, he might have trouble keeping his breakfast down, as well. She gave Søren a phone number—Kingsley guessed it was her parents where she would flee now with her daughter. Søren promised to keep in touch, and he asked her to write him at school and tell him about his sister. Annabelle pledged that she would and then swore to him with all her heart that she would make sure his father never knew he'd come to see her.

"He wanted a son and was beyond disappointed that I had a girl. He's been—" Annabelle stopped and looked panic-stricken.

"Are you pregnant?" Søren asked, not the question a teen-age boy would ever—should ever—ask a married woman in her thirties. But he asked it with authority, and bowing to his authority she answered it.

"No," she said. "I lied and told him I wasn't on birth control anymore. I'm not ready for another one. But he's dying for a son."

"I'm a bastard he legitimized," Søren said. "He'd prefer the real thing."

"I won't give him another child."

"He'll want to know why you're leaving him. Please, keep Elizabeth's name out of it. If you have to name someone, name me."

"No," Kingsley said, in a panic. "Don't do that."

"Kingsley, this is not—"

"It is my concern," Kingsley said, already knowing what

Søren would say before he said it. "You told me your father broke your arm when you were eleven. I don't want him to hurt you."

"I won't tell him," Annabelle pledged. "I won't put you in danger. I owe you…everything."

"Keep my sister safe. That's all I ask."

She rose up on her toes and kissed Søren on the cheek.

"You're always welcome to visit your sister," she said. "Always. You, too," she said to Kingsley. "I think Claire's in love with you."

"Then he's never seeing her again," Søren said. "I'm her older brother. She's never allowed to fall in love. Especially with him."

"Ignore him. She can call me Uncle Kingsley," he said.

Annabelle laughed—a scared, brittle sound. She put her hand on Søren's chest over his heart. "Thank you," she whispered before getting into the car and driving away.

"How much trouble am I in for getting out of the car without permission?" Kingsley asked.

"None," Søren said, and Kingsley was wildly disappointed. "Let's go. We can make it back to school by tonight."

Kingsley followed him back to the car. The driver opened the door for them. When they were alone again, Kingsley said, "Or…"

"Or what?" Søren demanded.

"Or we could find a hotel and fuck in a real bed for once."

"We're not on a date. And here I was wondering where the real Kingsley had gone."

"What do you mean?" he asked as the driver opened the car door for them. He slipped inside and Søren followed. They were on the road again before Søren answered.

"When you were with Claire—I wasn't sure you were the same Kingsley I know and barely tolerate."

"Why? Because I like kids?"

"You were good with her."

"Kids are fun," he said. What else was there to say?

"I never considered you would like children."

"Well…I do. So what?"

"Nothing," Søren said, laughing to himself. "Nothing at all."

"I know you see me as some kind of pervert," Kingsley said. "But believe or not, I am a human being. Yes, I like kids. I might want kids someday. I don't have much of a family any-more. If I want a family I'll have to make my own. Sometimes I have thoughts that don't have anything to do with sex. I'm not just your toy, you know. I have feelings and—"

His impassioned "I have feelings" speech ended abruptly when Søren grabbed him hard by the back of the hair and brought his mouth down in a brutal kiss. Kingsley almost pulled away so he could finish his tirade before realizing he wanted the kiss so much more than the fight.

Kingsley returned the kiss with equal and greater passion. Søren yanked Kingsley's jacket off him and threw it on the floorboard. Kingsley pulled his own shirt off and rolled on to his back on the bench seat. He'd remember the sensation of leather on his bare back all his life.

"Have you ever had sex in the back of a Rolls Royce?" Kingsley asked, trying not to rip Søren's shirt in his rush to unbutton it. He needed Søren's skin on his skin right now.

"No," Søren said. "But ask me that question again in an hour."

Before Kingsley could respond to that, Søren grabbed his wrists, pinned them over Kingsley's head and kissed him again—deeper, slower, but no less punitive. Kingsley groaned, and Søren slapped a hand over his mouth.

"Quiet," Søren said into Kingsley's ear. "We aren't alone, and I'll gag you until you choke if I have to. Understand?"

Kingsley nodded against Søren's hand. A curtain and partition separated them from the driver. He couldn't see them, but if they were loud enough, he could hear them. He'd disobeyed Søren's orders to stay in the car, he'd yelled at him and talked back. He was going to get it this time.

Good.

Søren kissed him again. Kingsley kept his sounds of pleasure to a minimum even when Søren reached between their bodies, unzipped Kingsley's pants, and stroked him hard. Every muscle in Kingsley's stomach tightened. He sucked in his breath sharply from the shock of pleasure. It took every bit of self-control not to moan audibly.

"You like this?" Søren asked.

"God, yes, so much," Kingsley said, lifting his hips against Søren's hand. He spoke in French and English. He was about to lose control of more than his language skills if Søren didn't stop touching him like that.

"I think you like it too much." Søren rose up on his knees and looked down at Kingsley.

"I don't. I really don't. I like it exactly as much as you want me to."

"You're pathetic when you're turned on."

"I am so pathetic right now."

"Kneel on the floor," Søren ordered and Kingsley obeyed. He faced away from Søren and rested his arms on the bench seat opposite Søren. It was good to be here, good to be on his knees for Søren. It had been too long since Søren had hurt him. When he thought about it, it made no sense to him that he felt the free-est and the strongest when on his knees and being hurt. But it didn't matter what he thought or how much sense it made. They didn't have to justify what they did to anyone but themselves. They lost sleep over what they did, but not to their consciences.

When they lost sleep it was only because they found something better to do.

Kingsley heard movement behind him—the sound of leather and metal. Søren had removed his belt and Kingsley braced himself for a hit. But instead Søren wrapped it around Kingsley's neck. He froze as the belt pressed against his throat. Carefully, as if the belt were a leash, Søren pulled Kingsley to him until he sat up, ramrod straight, his bare back against Søren's knees.

"I've wanted to do this to you for a long time," Søren said, bending to whisper the words in Kingsley's ear. "If only to shut you up."

And he pulled the belt tighter. Kingsley inhaled sharply but couldn't breathe out, not yet.

"You like this?" Søren's hands wound around the leather strap. Kingsley would have said yes if he could have. "Prove it."

With shaking hands, Kingsley stroked himself while Søren watched from above and behind him. He couldn't remember a time it felt this good to touch himself. His head swam. He felt light and euphoric. His cock was brutally hard and intensely sensitive. Even with the belt around his neck he still managed a voiceless moan.

As he grew closer to coming and closer to unconsciousness, he had a flash of perfect clarity. Here he was in a Rolls Royce about to have an orgasm while the man he loved with all his heart and all his soul and all his body held Kingsley's very life in his hands. And it was as it should be, Søren holding the power of life and death. Kingsley's parents had named him after kings, but it was Søren who should rule the entire world. Søren was Kingsley's king. Søren needed a kingdom of his own. Kingsley could give it to him, build it for him. A world of danger, of secrets, of sex, of pain. He didn't know how or when, but he would do it someday, give Søren a kingdom of his own.

"Come," Søren ordered into Kingsley's ear. Kingsley released hard, so hard he saw light and stars and the sun at night, and if he didn't stop coming he would die of the never-ending bliss of it all.

Kingsley slumped forward on the seat. He rested on the edge of consciousness, falling back and forth between the darkness and the light. And in that twilight world between life and death, he sensed Søren's arms coming around him, Søren's mouth caressing his shoulder, Søren's hands easing his pants down to his knees…and then he felt cold wet fingers on him and in him. Then Søren was filling him, holding Kingsley's slack body back against his chest and moving in and out of him endlessly. And there were words then, beautiful words, but all in Danish, and Kingsley had no idea what Søren said to him, only that he needed to hear it.

Søren came inside him, his hands over Kingsley's hands, their fingers locked together as tightly as their bodies. Kingsley went limp in Søren's arms, and they stayed there on the floor of the Rolls Royce together until they both remembered how to breathe again.

When it was all over and he was weak, drained and too tired to move, Søren helped him dress. Kingsley must have pleased him, for Søren allowed him the rare privilege of curling up at his feet and resting his head in his lap for the remainder of their trip back to school. Søren's hands shook for thirty minutes afterward. When Kingsley asked him why, Søren answered, "I didn't know if I would stop in time."

"You stopped. I'm fine. More than fine," Kingsley said, drunk on happiness and contentment.

"I could have killed you."

"Kill me if you want," Kingsley said, smiling up at him. "I'd die happy."

Søren closed his eyes and laid his hand on top of Kingsley's head. It felt like a blessing.

"I'm going to do something for you someday." Kingsley sighed.

"You do everything for me." Søren twined his fingers in Kingsley's hair and tugged it.

"I want to build you a castle."

Søren laughed, and Kingsley laughed, although he didn't know what the joke was.

"I've had my fill of castles, Kingsley," Søren said. "What I need is a dungeon."

Sam laughed in Kingsley's arms.

"What are you laughing at?" he asked, pinching her nose.

"So that's what this is about?" Sam asked. "The club? Your kingdom? You're building Søren the world's biggest dungeon?"

"He's earned it," Kingsley said. "His father was as rich as God, and Søren risked his wrath, risked getting cut off by telling the new wife what sort of monster she'd married. And he didn't care. I've never met anyone like him in my life. I hope I never meet anyone like him again."

Sam laughed again and wrapped her arm over his chest. She took a ragged breath.

Ragged?

"I remember that day like yesterday. It should be opening night for our club. November thirtieth—we can finish it in time."

But Sam didn't seem interested in talking about the club right now.

"You and Søren fucking in the back of a Rolls Royce."

Sam sighed. "That might be the sexiest story I've ever heard in my life."

"I have better stories," Kingsley said. "I'll tell them to you someday."

"Is it still *auto* erotic asphyxiation if someone else chokes you, but they do it in the backseat of a car?"

"Whatever you call it, it's dangerous. That was the last time he choked me. When he married my sister, that put an end to our trysts. She didn't know about us. But she's gone now, and I thought when he came here... I hoped, I mean..."

"You hoped you could pick up where you left off?"

"I did. But he's in love with someone else."

"Who?"

"A girl at his church."

"The girl you bribed someone to help?"

"Before you hate him anymore, you should know he hasn't laid a hand on her."

"I don't care if he lays a hand on her as long as he doesn't ship her off to some kind of reorienting camp, if they get caught together, like that pastor's wife did to Faith."

"If they get caught together, they're moving to Denmark," Kingsley said. "I think he's already planned for it."

"Will you go with them?"

"I tried to learn Danish once. Gave up trying. Russian was easier if that tells you anything."

"Good," Sam said. "Then you should just stay here with me."

She pushed her hip into his leg, and he felt the heat radiating from her body.

Heat?

"I have to say, the thought of you playing with a little girl and her unicorn? So stinking cute. My ovaries want to hug you."

Kingsley laughed. "I like kids," he said. Not that he would ever have them. Women tended to want marriage and commitment along with their children, something he didn't think he could give anyone. Yet, the hope remained.

"You're amazing." Sam ran her hand over his chest and kissed his shoulder. "I still can't believe you were jealous because you saw me kissing someone you thought was a man. That's adorable."

"I've killed people. I'm not adorable."

"You are. And you're very pretty, too," she said, running her fingers through his hair.

"Sam, you're flirting with me."

"I am, aren't I? That's a weird thing for a lesbian to do with a man."

"You are what you are," Kingsley said. "And I would never try to change you. But if you ever want to play with me, it would be my honor."

Kingsley rolled onto his side. Sam lay inches from him. She had a full lush mouth, a bow to her bottom lip and her eyes were hooded with the unmistakable look of arousal. Whether it was him that had done it or the story he'd told her, he didn't care. She was boyish and beautiful and brilliant and he had to touch her.

So he touched her.

Not wanting to scare her, he touched only her lips with his fingertips.

"I'm not used to men wanting me," she said. "Not men like you. Men who can have any woman they wanted."

"Get used to it."

"That story made me really turned on."

"Do you want to go play in my Rolls Royce?" he teased. "I'll bring a belt."

Sam giggled—a beautiful sound, girlish and innocent. She

took a fistful of sheet and raised it, covering the lower half of her face like a veil.

"Don't hide from me," he said, pulling the cover down.

"I'm hiding from me," she said. "And from that."

She looked downward with a meaningful gleam in her eyes. Having Sam lying in his bed, wearing his shirt, draped across his chest, breathing his air and listening while he bared his soul to her had aroused him almost to the point of pain.

"I won't let it near you," he said.

"Promise," she said, peeking over the edge of her veil again.

"I promise. Does it make you nervous?"

Sam dropped the veil of her blanket and the mask of her feigned modesty.

"I have two brothers. Penises don't scare me, and they don't impress me. I have a whole collection of them back at my place. A couple of them even bigger than you."

"I can't win with you."

"You can't lose with me, either," she said, serious now. "The reason I'm not scared of your big naked self... I trust you."

"What do you trust me to do?"

"Will you touch me? Like he touched you in the car?"

"I would love to touch you," Kingsley said.

"Hand only," she said.

"I'll keep all other body parts to myself."

Sam paused before rolling on to her stomach. Kingsley slipped his hand under the back of her—his—shirt and tickled her.

The light touching turned into a light massage. Sam moaned in pleasure.

"You have such soft skin," he said.

"Thank you," Sam said. "Good line, by the way. I use it on girls, too."

Kingsley pulled the covers down so he could properly give Sam a fearsome spank.

"Shit, that hurt," she said, laughing. "I'm warning you, I know all the lines guys use to seduce women, because I use them, too."

"I don't use lines. Ever."

"*Have you ever had sex in the back of a Rolls Royce?*" Sam repeated. "How is that not a line?"

"It's not a line. It's a serious inquiry."

"Have you tried 'You have the sexiest blank of any woman I've ever been with?' Doesn't matter what you put in the blank—they spread for that line every time."

"I wasn't using a line on you. And what on earth are you wearing?" Her underwear was plain white cotton with writing on it.

"Days of the week underwear. Today is Friday. These are my Fridays."

"It's after midnight—it's Saturday."

"This is a problem with Days of the Week undies. If I sleep in them, I never know if I should wear the day I go to bed, or the day I wake up."

"If you slept naked, you wouldn't have that problem."

He traced the center of her back with his palm, grazed her shoulder blades and her neck... He couldn't believe how slight she felt under his hand. Her personality filled up an entire room. Big treasure. Small package. He knew what they were doing was beyond foolish. She was his assistant. He was her boss. They had to work together. Wouldn't it be awkward trying to work together if he and Sam had sex? Especially awkward considering she'd never had sex with a man before. And yet, nothing could stop him from wanting her, from wanting to be inside her. She wanted him, too. He knew what arousal looked like, and Sam was undeniably turned on.

Her skin was hot, her breathing rapid and ragged, and she'd licked her lips—twice.

He wanted nothing so much as to throw her Fridays on the floor and stay inside her until next Thursday. When had he become the sort of man who wanted to make love to a woman who wore Days of the Week underwear?

"You're laughing at me." Sam stretched out underneath his hand as if wanting more of him.

"I am not."

"I like it when you laugh at me." Sam turned over on to her back and Kingsley let his hand rest on her stomach.

"I'm smiling at you. It's a different thing."

"I like your smile."

"You do?"

"Of course. You have the sexiest smile of any man I've ever seen." She winked at him.

"You're going to get it now," he said.

"Oh, shit," she said, laughing and trying to pull away from him.

Sam squealed when he grabbed both her wrists and slammed them into the bed over her head.

"You're always the one in charge, aren't you? You top with women, don't you?"

"Every time," she said, a little breathless.

"How does it feel being with someone more dominant than you are?"

"Terrifying."

"Good terrifying or bad?"

"Both," she admitted, and Kingsley smiled down at her. He released her wrists but didn't move from his position over her. No part of him now touched any part of her. But if he lowered himself from his push-up position, he'd be on top of her.

"You look good in my shirt," he said. "And that's not a line."

"What do I have to do to keep it?"

"Pay for it," he said.

Her eyes widened hugely, and he felt an instant stab of regret.

"I'm sorry," he said, releasing her wrists. "I forgot—"

"Don't apologize," she said. "It's okay. You're a man in bed with a woman. I'm not complaining."

"You aren't?"

"I'm having fun," she said. "Promise. I like being in bed with you. How many women in this city wish they were here?"

"Most of them," Kingsley said.

"I'd tell you, you were arrogant, but that's probably true. I am the envy of the city tonight being here in your bed."

"I don't know," Kingsley said, caressing her stomach again. He could feel it quivering under his fingers. "Women who want to be in my bed aren't usually interested in hearing a story and going to sleep."

"I'm not, either," Sam said.

Kingsley arched his eyebrow at her.

"What do you want to do?" he asked.

"I get to decide?"

"I've been submitting to Felicia for a month now. I've gotten good at it." He tickled her rib cage with his fingertips. "You tell me."

"I want to pay for my shirt," she said. "That's what I want to do."

"You want me to come on you. You're a lesbian. Isn't this against the rules?"

"I don't care about the rules."

"You really want me to do this?"

"Yes, but not my back," she said. "Do it where it counts. You showed me your scars and let me touch them. You should see mine."

She raised her hand and unbuttoned her shirt…his shirt. She pulled it open and bared herself to him. Kingsley gazed down at her naked breasts with longing and desire coursing through his body. Lovely full breasts but not perfect. Both breasts were marred with old healed semicircle burn marks.

"I told you I had ugly secrets. These are souvenirs from that camp," Sam said, blushing pink. "I don't get naked very often with women. Do they look bad?"

He shook his head.

"Your breasts are beautiful," he said. "Do my scars make me look bad?"

"Your scars are sexy."

"So are yours."

"Thank you. Even if you're lying to me, thank you for being a good liar," she said.

"Not lying," he promised. He dropped his head and kissed one pale pink nipple. Then he moved his mouth and kissed the scar. He ached to touch her breasts, but he needed to touch himself more. Lowering himself, he positioned his knees on either side of Sam's hips. She didn't seem the least troubled by his nakedness, not even when he took himself in his hand.

Sam lifted her head and kissed the inside of his forearm before sliding her hand down her stomach and into her Fridays. She touched herself while he stroked himself. Sooner than he expected, she was moving beneath him, panting, her breaths hitching in her throat. Her pleasure stoked his, especially watching her nipples harden with her arousal and her skin flush. She took a sharp breath in and went silent. As she came he held back, although it pained him to do so. When her quiet shuddering was spent, she opened her hazel eyes and gazed up at him with undisguised desire. He stroked once more, twice more and then came onto her, covering her chest and breasts. He loved this, loved that she allowed him to do this to her, loved seeing his semen on her skin.

Sam closed her eyes and arched her back into his touch as he massaged his fluid into her breasts. Why was he doing this, marking her like this? He didn't know why. Who cared? He loved touching her. He took his time as her breasts felt so right in his hand. He rolled her nipples between his forefinger and thumb, traced circles around her aureoles.

"Nobody's touched my breasts in a long time," she said. "Forgotten how good it felt."

"Anytime you need it, my hands are here for you."

"So…do I get to keep the shirt?" she asked.

"Sam, you can have all my shirts."

With the greatest reluctance he pulled back and let her button his shirt up. He was gratified she didn't immediately run off to the bathroom to wash him off her. Good sign.

She lay flat on her back and looked up and away and anywhere but at him.

"Sam?"

"Give me a second. I've never fooled around with a guy before. I'm processing."

Kingsley sighed heavily and Sam grinned.

He sat up and leaned across her body.

"Kingsley, what are you doing?"

He pulled a small box from the drawer in the ebony table that sat at the side of his bed, took out rolling papers, a lighter and a small plastic baggie.

"Kingsley, is that—"

"It is," he said, grinning as he licked the paper and rolled the ends tight. "Here." Kingsley passed her the joint. "This will help you process."

Kingsley flicked his light, and Sam took a hit, held it in and blew it out. She relaxed against his pillow with a smile. She curled up on his chest and handed it back to him.

"Kingsley?"

"Yes, Sam?" He wrapped an arm around her, held her close and exhaled an artful smoke ring.

"You are the world's greatest boss."

28

KINGSLEY WOKE UP ALONE IN HIS BED. SAM HAD AL-
ready gone. She'd left his shirt on the bed in her place along
with a note. He unfolded the paper and read.

> *King-I didn't love you and leave you. I had an idea when we
> were talking last night, and I want to go look into it. I might
> be on to something with Fuller.*
> *Love,*
> *Sam*
> *P.S. You look like a little boy when you sleep. Almost inno-
> cent. I might have taken incriminating pictures.*
> *P.P.S. Don't forget you have a game at noon today.*
> *P.P.P.S. Thanks for the weed.*

He flipped the note over, making sure there were no further postscripts.

Game? Oh, yes, he did have a game today. Rematch with
First Presbyterian. If he missed it, Søren would kill him and
Kingsley was fairly certain the priest would do a more thor-
ough job of that than the last men who'd tried to do him in.

When he rolled out of bed he was met with a full-body
ache. A few days out of Mistress Felicia's bed would do him

good. He took a shower and dressed in his soccer clothes. He'd been scouted at age fifteen by Paris Saint-Germain Football Club, and here he was, suiting up to play church-league soccer. Still he laced on his cleats and pulled on his "Sacred Heart" T-shirt with his last name on the back and a number eight beneath it. The *T* in the Sacred Heart was even in the form of a cross. How quaint.

"Why did you make me number eight?" Kingsley had asked Søren when he'd been given his official "uniform."

"In Biblical mysticism, the eight symbolizes rebirth and new beginnings and Christ's resurrections."

"That's why I'm an eight?" Kingsley had been touched by the thoughtfulness.

"Actually, it was the only number between one and twenty we weren't using."

"I know seventy-two different ways to kill a man," Kingsley had said to Søren. "Three of them involve deploying T-shirts as weapons."

Kingsley finished dressing and pulled his hair back in a ponytail. He didn't need hair in his face when running on a field. He headed for the door of his bedroom but stopped when he heard his private phone line ringing. Five people alone had that number—Søren, Blaise, his lawyer, Sam and a "friend" on the police force—and none of them ever called him on that number for no good reason. Except Søren.

But it wasn't Søren on the line or any of his other private five.

"Mr. Edge?"

"Who is this?" Kingsley asked, instantly alert.

"This is Reverend James Fuller."

Kingsley stiffened, his grip on the phone tightening.

"How did you get this number?" Kingsley asked.

"Doesn't matter. I have it. And I'm using it to invite you to my office today. I think we should talk."

"I'm busy today," Kingsley said.

"Oh, yes, soccer game."

"Football," Kingsley said evenly, not letting his tone betray his surprise that Fuller knew so much about him. "I'm French. It's football."

"You're in America now, Mr. Edge. We do things differently here. When men have a dispute, they look each other in the eyes and talk about it."

"Well, I am half American. I can look you halfway in the eyes."

"Good. I'm in my office now. I'm sure you have the address in Stamford. Come see me. I won't take up much of your time. You won't even be late for your game."

Fuller hung up before Kingsley could answer. Good thing Stamford was on the way to Wakefield.

When he arrived, Kingsley walked through a side door and up the emergency exit stairs. He wanted to avoid being seen by secretaries and security guards alike. He quickly found Fuller's corner office. The door was open, but the room was empty. Kingsley took a moment to look around. Fuller's office was easily twice the size of Kingsley's. A CEO would have been comfortable in a room like this. Leather sofas, leather desk chair, desk the size of a boat. A wall of windows, awards on display, framed letters of praise and gratitude to "Reverend Fuller and Mrs. Fuller." And in the corner of the office, golf clubs. Of course.

Kingsley looked at the books on the shelves and noted their tight bindings and polished covers. The leather volumes were more likely for show than reading or research. He studied the framed photographs on the wall. Even they had brass plates

captioning Fuller's triumphs. One picture showed him lead-
ing a revival in 1990 before a crowd of ten thousand. Another picture captured him praying reverently at the Tomb
on the Unknown Soldier in Washington, DC. A lovely well-
staged photo op. In one other photograph he and his wife
stood with two dozen teenagers—"James and Lucy Fuller
at the First WTL Church, Hartford 1983." Everyone in the
photograph, teenage and adult, had a Bible clutched to their
chests and wide smiles on their faces. Their eyes were fixed
on the camera, giving the whole proceeding a look of eerie
sameness. Lucy Fuller had her arm around the shoulder of the
pretty dark-haired girl next to her. James Fuller had his arm
around the shoulder of the boy next to him. The very picture
of Christian love.

Kingsley tore his gaze from the photographs on the wall
and focused his attention on Fuller's desk. At first he found
nothing of interest—a calendar, a mug full of cold coffee, sta-
tionery and a few sermon notes. But under the coffee mug he
found an unbound sheaf of paper. Printed on the front page
were the words *Straight and Narrow—Bringing Homosexual Children Home to God.* The book was, unsurprisingly, authored by
Lucy Fuller, who had apparently exhausted all other topics of
Christian life. Curious, Kingsley leafed through it. One para-
graph jumped out at him.

*Homosexual teenagers are being influenced by demonic forces.
If enforcing a regime of constant prayer and fasting on your child
doesn't soften his or her heart, you might consider taking him
or her to a pastor to have the demons cast out. This is not exorcism in the Catholic sense but is rooted in traditional biblical
practices as found in the Gospels. Do not be deceived by your
child when she tells you she was "born gay" or has felt homosexual urges all her life. These are lies from the Devil and only*

the vigilance of loving and firm Christian parents can save these
children from the fires of Hell.

"Glad you could make it, Mr. Edge," came a voice from
the doorway. Kingsley looked up from the book and smiled.

"Your wife is quite the writer," Kingsley said, dropping
the book back on to the desk. "I didn't think women in your
denomination were allowed to speak in church."

"We're a nondenominational congregation. We let our
women speak and teach."

"Too bad," Kingsley said. "If my wife were spouting bullshit
like this, I wouldn't let her talk, either. Let me know if you
need to borrow a ball gag."

Fuller gave Kingsley a hard smile.

"I'm impressed you decided to show your face." Reverend
Fuller stepped into his office. Kingsley hadn't met him or seen
him yet, but he looked exactly like his photographs—gray
hair slicked back, oily smile and carrying twenty pounds too
many for his six-foot frame.

"You said you wanted to talk man to man," Kingsley said.
He dropped the book back on to Fuller's desk and walked
around to the other side. "So talk."

Kingsley didn't bother sitting. He wasn't going to be here
long. But Fuller sat behind his desk and smiled his greasy
smile at him.

"So…" Fuller began, "the infamous Kingsley Edge in person. Nice outfit."

"The T-shirt was free."

"Not your typical Saturday, is it? Playing church-league
soccer?"

"I'm the ringer," Kingsley said. "A certain priest I know
made me an offer I couldn't refuse."

"Yes, your brother-in-law's a priest. I guess celibacy doesn't run in families."

"Well, it wouldn't, would it?"

"Seems odd that he comes and goes so freely from your house, doesn't it?" Fuller's tone was casual, uncomfortably so.

"Odd? I wouldn't say that," Kingsley said with a casual air. "He's the only family I have. He likes to check in on me."

"He's a priest. And you're...not."

"Jesus was the Son of God, and he spent time with prostitutes. Something about not judging, not throwing stones. You know the verses, I'm sure."

"Wasn't it Shakespeare who said even the devil could quote the Bible?"

"It was, and he was right," Kingsley said. "I imagine the devil could even quote the Bible from a pulpit."

"Are you calling me the devil?" Fuller asked, his jaw tightening as his smile widened.

"After looking at that book, I'd say your wife is the more likely candidate."

Fuller raised his hand.

"We're not discussing my wife. We're talking man to man, remember?"

"About what exactly?"

"About women," Fuller said. "This is our fight, and we should fight like gentlemen. I know you want my building. I want you to go away forever. Let's keep our eyes on each other and leave the ladies out of this."

"Ladies, but not sixteen-year-old girls?"

"That was ten years ago. You're going to dig all that up?" Kingsley arched his eyebrow at him.

"I was referring to the girl on that tape you had sent to me and my brother-in-law."

Fuller shifted in his seat. "Of course. Her. Your teenage lover. Thought she was fifteen."

"She had a birthday. You know I've never met her, right? Are you planning on having me arrested for fucking a minor I've never met? Lying and bragging aren't illegal, last I heard. If they were every man I know would be in jail."

"No," Fuller said with some haste. "We're being men, you and I. We've agreed to leave the women and girls out of our dispute. Haven't we?"

"As you wish," Kingsley said. "But now I'm wondering, who were you referring to?"

"I'm sure you know by now of the girl who committed suicide at our camp. A tragic circumstance, but we were cleared of any wrongdoing."

"Money has a way of clearing things up, doesn't it?"

Fuller leaned forward, clasped his hands and gazed intently at Kingsley.

"Tell me something, Mr. Edge. What is it that you want from me?"

"I want your building. I want The Renaissance."

"You know I'm not selling to you, and yet you persist in pursuing this matter long after it's been closed. So, either you don't understand English well enough to know what *no* means. Or you want something else from me."

"My English is perfect," Kingsley said. "So it must be the other—I do want something else. I want you to keep your church out of my city, and I want you to stop torturing gay teenagers."

"That's therapy, not torture."

"Electrodes on the genitals? I've actually been tortured and they didn't even do that to me."

"I'm not a doctor or a therapist. I leave our licensed professionals to carry out their work. These therapies are tough, yes. But they work. And if you think you're going to stop us from helping these poor sick kids, you're as in need of therapy as they are."

"Can we compromise?" Kingsley asked. "I'll let you have the building for your church, and you shut the camps down?"

"Or how about you go back to your depraved lifestyle and leave our church alone to do God's work in peace. And I'll stop gathering information that could destroy you. That's my compromise."

"Destroy me? What could you possibly do to me that hasn't already been done?" Kingsley laughed openly. "You need a better threat."

"From what I can see, I have more on you than you have on me."

"I haven't given up looking. And unlike you, I'm not ashamed of anything you'd find out about me," Kingsley said, hoping Fuller believed that. He did have more than a few secrets he'd prefer to keep. "I don't think you could say the same."

"I have nothing to hide."

"Good," Kingsley said. "That will make it easier to find what I need."

"You're not going to find anything. And if you keep looking, so will I. And not only at you."

"My friends have nothing to hide, either."

"Even the priest in the family?"

"I'll tell you anything about him you want to know. Did you know he was abused as a child? Hospitalized after his father broke his arm? Did you know he killed a sexual predator at his school? He also gave up a huge fortune to become a priest after he was widowed at age eighteen. He spent several summers volunteering at a leper colony in India. How much time have you spent volunteering in leper colonies?"

Kingsley gave Fuller a long, pointed look. Fuller didn't answer.

"Take some advice," Kingsley said, "and keep your eyes on me. If you stare at him too long, you might learn something about what it means to be a man of God."

Fuller raised his chin.

"You can go now, Mr. Edge. I think we've talked man to man enough."

"I will. I don't want to be late for my game. My other game."

Kingsley gave a mock bow and headed out.

"Mr. Edge?" Fuller called out after him. Kingsley turned on his heel.

"Oui?"

"I have more money than you. And more contacts. And friends in higher places. Remember that."

"Quite the Goliath, aren't you?" Kingsley smiled once more. "When I get your hotel and turn it into my club, I'll fuck a man on opening night in your honor. By the way, do you have any sons?"

"Pardon my French, *Monsieur* Edge, but get the fuck out of my office."

Kingsley happily obliged the man.

He walked out of Fuller's building and to his car. Nothing productive had come from his meeting with Fuller. No secrets were uncovered. No truths revealed. And yet...

Fuller was scared and Kingsley had seen it. Fear meant one thing only—Fuller did have something to hide. And Kingsley was going to find it.

But something else had come of the meeting. Kingsley had a leak in his personal security. Five people had his private line number. Five suspects. Sam, Blaise and Søren were out. Sam hated the Fullers more than he did. Blaise was actively campaigning against them. And Søren wouldn't betray Kingsley to Fuller if someone put a gun to his head.

So that left his lawyer and his friend on the force. Kingsley would give them both a call very soon.

But not right now. He had better things to do with his time. And if not better, than certainly more enjoyable.

He made it to Wakefield an hour before the game started and found Søren working in his office. He had his collar and clerics on and had stacks of books piled high on the desk, note cards marking pages. The only photograph in the office was on Søren's desk—him in his white vestments standing next to a lovely blonde woman gazing on him adoringly. Søren and his mother on the day of his ordination. A small but elegant office. A sacred space devoted to learning and prayer. It couldn't have been more different than Fuller's. Not a golf club in sight.

"If you came for confession," Søren said, glancing up at him from his notes, "do it now. I will not be in a state of grace after this game if we lose."

"We aren't going to lose."

"Do you know what their pastor said to me after the last game? He said their team was predestined to win. Now I understand how holy wars get started."

Kingsley laughed and sat in the chair opposite Søren's desk.

"Can I ask you a stupid question?" Kingsley asked.

"You just did," Søren said, making a note on a white card.

Kingsley paused and laughed.

"What?" Søren glanced up from his writing.

"Déjà vu. Anyway, you didn't give anyone my private phone number, did you? Write it down? Give it to your secretary?"

"No. I have it memorized, and I'd never tell anyone unless it was a life-and-death situation. Why?"

"No reason. Are you ready to go?" Kingsley asked. "We should warm up."

"I suppose. It'll be a better use of my time than this." Søren slipped his legal pad into his top desk drawer.

"What are you working on?"

"My Ph.D. dissertation."

"I can think of a nearly infinite number of things that would be better uses of your time. And surprisingly, only half of them are sexual."

"Only half?"

"Two-thirds," Kingsley said. "Let's go."

"Going," Søren said. "I need to stop by the house and change. I'll meet you at the field."

"Do you have to wear the collar on Saturdays, too?"

"No. But it's for the best I do."

"Why is that?"

"Because Eleanor's here today, and I need as much armor as possible around her."

"She's here?" Kingsley sat up straighter.

"No."

"You just said—"

"Pretend I didn't."

"Can I see her?"

"Absolutely not."

"Why not?"

"She's busy, and I don't want you distracting her."

"She's sixteen. What's she doing that's so important?"

"Youth group."

"Is that as horrible as it sounds?"

"We have a seminarian here today. He's speaking to a group of teenagers about discerning God's will in their life. Eleanor's under orders to pay very close attention."

"You ordered your teenage girlfriend to go to youth group on a Saturday morning during summer break?"

Søren smiled fiendishly as he stood up and came around his desk.

"Sometimes the depths of my sadism surprises even me."

"That makes one of us," Kingsley said, standing to leave the office.

Søren replied with a swift slap to the center of Kingsley's back, making hard quick contact with a cluster of welts.

A flinch and gasp gave it away, and Kingsley had to grab the door frame to steady himself as pain washed over him.

"I remember that sound," Søren said, shutting his office door and locking it.

"What are you—"

"Hold still."

He hadn't belonged to Søren in eleven years, but an order was an order. Søren had said, "hold still." Kingsley held still.

Søren grasped the bottom of Kingsley's T-shirt and pulled it up and off of him. Kingsley heard a whistle of appreciation.

"Jealous?" Kingsley asked.

"Only impressed. You have bruises on top of bruises. Who did the work?"

"No one you know."

"What made these?" Søren traced half circles on Kingsley's upper back. The light touch on his abraded skin hurt enough to arouse him. He had to breathe to avoid getting a massive erection in a priest's office. He wasn't Catholic, but he assumed that was frowned upon.

Then again, maybe not.

"Electric cable looped in half," Kingsley said. "Feels like getting punched by fire."

"No cuts."

"Not with her. She prefers impact-play. A little candle-wax when she's in the mood."

"She?"

"She's a dominatrix I know."

"You know her intimately," Søren said, his voice low. The skin on Kingsley's back was so sensitive he could feel the breath from Søren's words brushing over his wounds.

"Very intimately. We're sleeping together." Kingsley turned around and showed Søren the welts on his chest.

"Good."

"Good?" Kingsley repeated, playfully aghast. "Did a priest just tell me it's good I'm engaging in sadomasochism and fornication?"

"I took the vow of celibacy, not you. And I'm pleased to hear you're feeling more yourself again. I can't imagine you being content to only top."

"You should meet her. You two can talk shop."

"Did you have a flashback with her?"

"A few times," he confessed, still embarrassed about the one he'd had in front of Søren. "They've mostly stopped. Not completely, but they aren't stopping me anymore."

Søren pressed the flat of his hand into the knot of welts on Kingsley's rib cage. He winced and inhaled sharply.

"It hurts coming back to life," Søren said. "It's a brutal, dirty business. Paddles on the chest pushing electric current into the dead heart, Dr. Frankenstein shooting lightning through his monster's corpse. Life is a force so strong it can blow a stone off a tomb. It's never easy—resurrection. It's violent and it hurts."

"It's better than the alternative, *non*?" Kingsley asked, turning around to face Søren. He pulled his shirt down. "Staying dead?"

"It's good to have you back."

"I've missed me," Kingsley said.

"You were always very fond of yourself."

"I charmed the pants off of me," Kingsley said as they walked out of Søren's office.

"I'll blame you if we lose today because you're bruised all over. There will be consequences, possible eternal."

"We aren't going to lose. Go, change. I'll meet you at the field."

When Søren was gone, Kingsley considered heading straight to the field. He considered it for one split second before deciding on an entirely different course of action.

Somewhere in this church was Søren's Virgin Queen. And Kingsley was going to see her.

Once outside the sanctuary Kingsley poked around until he found the breezeway that led to the attached annex. Once inside the annex, he heard voices—loud, obnoxious voices— and knew there were teenagers ahead. He found a door and peeked inside. About two dozen teenagers ranging in age from thirteen to eighteen sat in folding chairs arrayed in a semicircle around a very young and scared-looking man. Søren had called the man a seminarian, so he must have been a priest-in-training. Apparently his training included being subjected to a trial by fire. Kingsley nudged the door open a little wider and heard the seminarian attempting to talk over the din of three teenage boys who seemed determined to punish him for ruining their Saturday.

Behind the three rowdy boys sat a girl in black combat boots, a ratty denim skirt and a black low-cut shirt. She ran her fingers through her mass of wavy black hair and stretched luxuriously in her seat with the decadent unapologetic laziness of a cat that'd been forced out of bed too early. Had to be her, right? All the other girls looked like girls. This girl looked like a woman. She had a woman's curves, a woman's confidence and a woman's utter boredom with the boys who surrounded her. She wore gobs of black eyeliner, which gave her eyes a smoky, seductive look, and Kingsley couldn't stop staring at her.

He'd already mentally put the girl in his bed and made her come five times before he discerned that an argument had broken out in the room. One of the boys, a tall skinny punk in a *Terminator 2* T-shirt, was telling the seminarian that there was no reason for him to listen to a man who was never going to get married, have kids and wasn't even a real priest yet. What did he know about God's plan for his life or anyone else's? And the girl, that strange seductive girl with the creamy skin, was politely telling the Terminator to shut the fuck up and sit the fuck down. The Terminator ignored Combat Boots in favor of standing to give a high five to a boy two seats over.

That was a mistake.

Combat Boots gracefully raised her foot, hooked an ankle around the leg of the chair and swept it to the side as the Terminator went to sit down again.

With his chair gone, the boy hit the floor and landed on his back. He coughed as if the impact had knocked the wind right out of his lungs. Everyone gasped in shock, everyone but Combat Boots. She stretched out her legs and rested her feet on the center of the boy's chest. She leaned forward and smiled down at the now defeated Terminator.

"God's plan for your life is for you to shut the fuck up." Hers was a throaty voice thick as honey and drugging as wine. Sitting back, Combat Boots pointed at the stunned young seminarian and crossed her legs. She made certain to bounce her feet a time or two on the boy's chest. "You have our attention now."

If he'd landed a little harder, the boy might have cracked his skull on the hard floor. This possibility didn't seem to bother

Combat Boots in the least. She gave the boy on the floor a smile entirely devoid of apology or remorse.

"You little sociopath," Kingsley said under his breath. Not even Søren was so blithe about inflicting pain as this girl. "Fuck me until I forget I'm French."

There was no way, none, not a chance in heaven, hell or the purgatory they were living in right now that girl was a submissive. Søren had fallen in love with a baby domme who had a sadistic streak in her as wide as her smile. This girl would have men at her feet all her life by her will or theirs and whether they liked it or not.

Most of them would like it.

He walked—fast—away from her. If Søren were smart, he'd do the same. But no one in love was ever very smart.

Kingsley made it to the field before Søren did, but when Søren arrived, Kingsley couldn't stop smiling.

"What are you laughing at?" Søren asked as they ran laps around the field to warm up.

"I don't think you want to know..."

Even in the heat with the sun beating down on them, Kingsley couldn't suppress his grin.

"I think I do. In fact, I'm certain I do."

"If you must know, I'm starting to believe in God," Kingsley said.

"What brought this on?"

"I foresee a miracle occurring in the future."

"Which is?"

"You," Kingsley said as the team gathered on the sideline. "Being humbled."

"And what makes you say that?" Søren asked, sounding both imperious and skeptical.

Kingsley only smiled on and said three words.

"I met Eleanor."

29

"TELL ME TO CLOSE MY EYES AND THINK OF EN-gland," Kingsley said to Sam when she walked into the office holding a Styrofoam bowl in her hand.

"I've been to England. Great country, nice people. I tried to get Princess Di in bed." She sat on his desk in front of him and took a bite of whatever it was in the bowl.

"How did that work out for you?" he asked.

"My attempted seduction involved me staring longingly at Buckingham Palace until a man in a funny hat politely told me to move along. Do I want to know why you're closing your eyes and thinking of England?" she asked, taking another bite from her bowl.

"I think I have to seduce Lucy Fuller."

Sam screwed up her face in disgust.

"Oh, God, don't do that," she said. "There has to be a better way. I have to go puke up my ice cream now." She set the bowl on his desk in disgust.

"If I fuck her and get it on tape, I can use it as leverage to get Fuller to sell me his building."

"She's horrible, King."

"I know. She's got a new book coming out about how to turn your gay children straight. Forced fasting and prayer vigils. And if that doesn't work—exorcism."

"I don't think your dick is going to solve this problem," Sam said.

"Why not? It solves all my other problems."

"Can't you trick Fuller into committing a crime and get it on tape?"

"That's entrapment. That can blow back on us. What we need is a real crime. A scandal. A secret. He has to have a secret."

"I'm sure he does," Sam said. "And you'll find it. You stick to Reverend Fuller." She picked up her bowl again, held out her spoon, and Kingsley took a bite. He tried for a second bite but Sam wouldn't give it up. "I'll stick to Lucy Fuller. And this ice cream. I should have gotten the bigger size."

"Why are you so hungry today?"

"It's a secret."

"I'm in the business of secrets."

Sam narrowed her eyes at him and then took a seat in Kingsley's lap.

With unabashed pleasure he wrapped his arms around her and pulled her tight to him. She wore a new suit today—tight tailored white blouse, skinny tie, black trousers and suspenders.

"You want to know my secret?" she whispered in his ear. "I am bleeding like a stuck pig."

Kingsley groaned and pushed her off his lap. Laughing, Sam sat on his desk and picked up her ice cream again.

"You asked. It's why I'm craving chocolate. Seriously, I want chocolate more than pussy today. What I need is a pussy that I can put chocolate in. Sorry. I have thoughts like this when I'm on the rag."

"That's not the sort of secret I need to know."

"What? You don't swim the red river?"

"I have swum the red river. Swam? Swum? I hate English. *J'ai nagé la riviere rouge.*"

"Good. You get to keep your stud credentials. Only pussies are afraid of pussies."

"I am not afraid of pussies." Kingsley stood up and opened his mouth. She fed him another spoonful of her ice cream. "Speaking of pussies, Blaise is in DC again. Felicia has an overnight with a client. You want to sleep with me tonight?"

"Will you give me a back rub? I'm crampy today."

"Absolutely."

"Then I formally accept your invitation."

"Good." He snapped her suspenders, and she yelped. "I'll see you tonight."

"Where are you going?"

"To seduce Lucy Fuller."

She pushed him back, hard.

"Don't you dare."

"I was kidding," Kingsley said. "I'm reformed. These days I only fuck people I want to fuck. I don't fuck fundamentalist preachers or their wives. Catholic clergy only."

"It's good to have standards," Sam said, obviously relieved. "So, no fucking the Fullers. What about the money? Did you look through the financials The Barber sent over, too?"

"I did. Nothing there, either. The church is sitting on millions of dollars—most of it from the sale of merchandise and Lucy Fuller's books on how to be a godly wife."

"Please, stop reading those books," Sam said. "They're making you weird."

"They are not."

"Yesterday you asked me if we're spending enough quality time together."

"Are we?" Kingsley asked.

"Oh, my Jesus."

"Admit it, Sam. Our marriage has never been better," Kingsley said.

'I'm burning those books," Sam said.

Kingsley sighed. "I'm only trying to find something on these people. They're the Stepford Christians. No second homes, no secret islands, no lavish apartments for mistresses. The Fullers are rich, but so far that's their only sin." Kingsley sighed. "What about you? Did you find anything on your quest?"

"No," she said, not meeting his eyes. "Didn't really pan out. Still looking, though."

"Keep looking. It's there. We'll find it."

"Where are you going now?"

"An abortion clinic," Kingsley said.

"Is it mine?" Sam asked. "It's mine, isn't it? I knew I shouldn't have let you come on me."

Kingsley glared at her. "It's Fuller's. His protest, I mean. I want to talk to some people who go to his church. And Lucy Fuller, if she's there."

Kingsley tapped her under the chin and strode from the office. He heard footsteps behind him.

"King?"

He turned around and saw Sam wearing a rare expression of earnestness on her lovely face.

"You promise you won't go near Lucy Fuller?" she asked.

Kingsley narrowed his eyes at her.

"It bothers you, doesn't it? The thought of me with her. Why?"

"They run the camps that killed Faith. I know it was suicide, but she'd still be alive if it wasn't for them. Just...don't. Please?"

"I promise," Kingsley said. "But you owe me."

"Owe you what?" she demanded.

Kingsley took her ice-cream bowl from her and Sam glared at him.

"This will do."

The clinic was out in Brooklyn, so Kingsley took a cab. Before his driver had turned on to the street, Kingsley heard the shouting and the bullhorns. He got out at the end of the block and walked to the protest. As he approached the clinic, the sounds of shouting only grew louder and more shrill. He remembered something he'd read back at St. Ignatius, something C. S. Lewis had written. In heaven there is silence and music. In hell there is only noise.

This was hell.

Standing in the midst of two dozen people holding signs, marching and shouting, was the devil himself, Reverend Fuller, grasping a bullhorn and echoing their "Abortion is murder" chant. A bullhorn? Sam was right. This was a man who did not deserve to get fucked by him or anyone else. Seemed a veritable crime that Søren was supposed to be celibate, and yet this man could breed with impunity.

Kingsley stood in the shadows of an alley and watched as Fuller worked the crowd, shaking hands, thanking the protesters for their dedication and inviting them to his church. Nearby a man with a camera recorded everything—Fuller with the bullhorn, the handshakes, the stomping feet and the waving signs.

During all the glad-handing, a small car pulled into the clinic parking lot, a young patient inside. Kingsley wished he'd come armed. If any of these assholes tried anything with that poor girl in the car, he would shoot them.

Perhaps it was for the best he'd left the gun at home.

Before the woman could leave her car, a man emerged

from the clinic carrying a blanket. He looked about Kingsley's age—twenty-eight or twenty-nine—and had short dark hair and a heavily muscled build. Square-jawed, solid and handsome, even a few of the female protestors gave him appreciative glances. He walked swiftly to the car, unfolding the blanket as he went. August in Brooklyn. Why did he need the blanket? The woman got out of her car, and Kingsley discovered the answer. The blanket wasn't to keep her warm, Kingsley discovered, but to keep her identity hidden from the protestors and the man with the video camera. The clinic escort held the blanket open and stayed at her left side, imposing himself between her and the protestors as he led her into the clinic. The volume of the shouts increased as did the level of venom in the insults. The theoretical "Abortion is murder" became "You're a murderer." For all they knew, the woman was there for free birth control, but that didn't stop the abusive commentary.

Kingsley waited and watched until Fuller left the protestors and got into a waiting black Lincoln Town Car that pulled up to whisk him away back to his church or his golf game. Once Fuller had gone, a strange thing happened. The cameraman packed up his equipment and the protestors wandered away. Fuller had staged a protest for the cameras to show his congregation and his television audience at home that he was already doing God's work in New York City.

Kingsley stopped one of the protestors, a girl in her twenties.

"You look familiar," Kingsley said to her. "Have I seen you in anything?"

"I did a couple local commercials," she said. "One for a mattress company."

"Was this extra work?" Kingsley asked.

The girl shrugged. "Fund-raising video, they said. Gotta

make a living, right? That preacher guy's such a douche bag. Good thing he pays well."

"Right," Kingsley said and let the girl go.

But the clinic escort, he'd been interesting. Kingsley decided to wait and talk to him.

Five minutes passed. Then ten. But his patience was rewarded when the man emerged from the clinic alone.

"I hope they pay you well for what you do," Kingsley said as the man walked past him.

The man didn't turn around. Instead, he walked backward until he stood in front of Kingsley.

"Volunteer," the man said. "Got a problem with that, mate?"

"You're Australian. I didn't expect that. *Mon ami*." He added the "*mon ami*" in retaliation for the "mate."

"Yeah, and what the fuck are you?"

"French? American? Bisexual? Rich? Kinky? Pick one. Or all of them."

The man lifted his chin and cocked an eyebrow at Kingsley. The Aussie was sizing him up. The man was taller than him and had more overall muscle mass. But Kingsley was a trained killer and didn't sense anything threatening in the Aussie's posture.

"Australian," the man said. "Straight. Not rich. Not sure about kinky. It's only kinky the first time, right?"

"I had a feeling I would like you. What's your name?"

"Lachlan. Lockie, my friends call me. Not saying we're friends."

"I wouldn't dare presume." Kingsley nodded his head in polite and feigned submission. "I was impressed earlier. It must not be easy, doing what you do."

"I don't do it because it's easy. I do it because it needs doing.

I saw you earlier. You weren't protesting and you don't look pregnant. What do you want?"

"You," Kingsley said. "Not in a sexual way. You wouldn't by any chance be interested in a job, would you?"

"I have a job."

"A different job, then. I'm starting a club. Opens in November. I need someone to work as a bouncer of sorts."

"Of sorts? What the hell does that mean?"

"I'll have professional submissives in the club. They'll need a watcher when they're with a client. It would be a far more pleasant form of escort duty."

"I do important work here."

"You can still work here. The hours won't conflict, I promise."

Kingsley took out a silver case and passed his business card to the man.

"Kingsley Edge. Edge Enterprises," the man read aloud. "This is for real?"

"As real as it gets. I need a strong intimidating man who will be able to stand in a corner, keep his mouth shut and intervene if and only if a client crosses a line. He needs to be calm under pressure and able to face, let's call it…*unpleasantness* without getting unpleasant."

"I'm supposed to stand in a corner and watch someone beat up a woman without intervening?"

"Yes."

"She's getting paid for it?"

"Well paid. And she's consenting. And she enjoys it. All my employees enjoy their work. I see to that."

"And you're going to pay me to watch?"

"Good job, *oui*?"

"I can think of worse ways to make a living."

Kingsley smiled. "The club doesn't open until the end of

November. You call that number if you're interested. My secretary will bring you in for a more formal interview."

"I might be interested."

"There is one thing that might dampen your interest."

"What?" Lachlan asked, eyeing him.

"We'll have male submissives, too," Kingsley said, knowing most straight men wouldn't be comfortable watching two men engage in kink. "Male submissives with male or female dominants. They'll also need a watcher, a protector. That bother you?"

"I protect whoever needs protecting. I'm in this fucking city ten thousand miles from home because my sister married the world's biggest wanker. I'm not leaving until I can take her back to Sydney with me."

"Introduce her to me. I have a way of getting women to leave their husbands."

The man shook his head and laughed. The laugh transformed his expression from one of stony suspicion into boyish amusement.

"I might call your secretary. I might not. I might hunt down that arse with the bullhorn and shove it down his throat."

"Then this might induce you to come work for me," Kingsley said. "That arse with the bullhorn? I'm buying a building from him to turn into my club. Whether he likes it or not. And I promise, he doesn't."

"Then I've only got one question for you."

"Ask it," Kingsley said.

"When do I start?"

Kingsley shook hands with Lachlan and found a pay phone.

"Do you have your clipboard?" Kingsley asked Sam when she answered.

"Aye, aye, Captain? Who do we have now?"

He filled her in.

"You found a bouncer at an abortion clinic?" Sam asked.

"He's very cute."

"Speaking of cute, you have a message."

"What is it?"

"Mistress Felicia's home. And you've been summoned."

30

KINGSLEY LEFT THE CITY AT ONE O'CLOCK AND AR-
rived at Felicia's shortly before two. She'd given him his own
key, and he used it to enter through the patio door per her
instructions.

Felicia had a perfect retreat from the city out here in
Bedford—a classic New England cottage. He entered through
the side door into her dining room, a small intimate setting
with a table for two and a candelabrum in the center. The
first night he'd stayed with her, he'd made love to her on this
table, and she'd doused him with the candlewax after as a
thank-you. But it appeared they weren't to be dining today.
He locked the door behind him. On the table he found a box
with a white card on top. The card said two words—*Wear me.*

Inside the box, Kingsley found a black silk blindfold. Felicia was in a mood to play games today.

He tied the blindfold on and waited. He wasn't going to
take a step farther without instructions. Luckily he didn't have
to wait long for step two.

"It's a good look for you." Felicia's elegantly accented voice
came from the right where a doorway opened into the hallway. "You should wear a blindfold more often."

"It makes it difficult to find my way to you."

"You don't need your eyes today. Only your ears. Turn toward the sound of my voice."

Kingsley turned right.

"Good," she said. "Now two steps forward."

He took the two steps with surety, knowing her house as well as his own by now.

"What game are we playing?" he asked, knowing he was close to her because he could smell the heat of her body mingling with her perfume.

"The game where I blindfold you and make you do everything I tell you to do."

"Good game," he said. "What's my first order?"

"Kiss," she said. He felt her mouth on his mouth, and he kissed her with shameless hunger. Her mouth tasted sweet and warm, and he had to reach for her body. Before he could touch her, she pulled away. "I said 'kiss.' I didn't say 'touch.'"

"I changed my mind. Terrible game."

"Glad you like it. Now…" Her voice grew fainter, and he could hear she'd moved away from him. "Hands and knees. Crawl to me."

His pride rebelled at the order, but his erection gave into it immediately. He went down on his hands and knees and crawled toward the direction of Felicia's voice. He reached her quickly.

"Mistress?" he asked.

"Kiss again."

He started to stand but felt Felicia's hand on his head. She stoked his hair, his cheek, his lips.

"Not my mouth."

Kingsley paused long enough for her to know he was following her orders with the most extreme reluctance. He reached out with one hand until he felt her bare foot, her bare toes. He dropped a kiss on to the top of each of her feet.

"Ankles," she said. Ankles he kissed.

"Calves," she said. Calves he kissed.

Thighs. Hips. Stomach. Mistress Felicia was obviously naked, and he wasn't complaining. Breasts. Nipples. Neck. He was so hard now it hurt. Left shoulder. Right shoulder. Left wrist. Right wrist. If she didn't let him fuck her soon, he would not be held responsible for his actions.

"One more kiss for now," she said, and he felt something against his lips. The back of her hand. He pressed a kiss into her skin, and her hand shivered in his. Nice to know she was as eager for him as he was for her. He needed this day with Felicia. He needed her desire for him. He needed her attraction to him that she did nothing to hide. He adored Sam to the point it made his stomach hurt when he held her in his arms, but those nights in his bed holding her while they slept but doing nothing more were hard on his pride. And right now his pride was unbearably hard.

"Now I'm going to hide," Felicia explained. "And you'll have two minutes to find me. If you find me in that time, you can do anything you want to me for the next hour. If you don't find me in two minutes, I get to do whatever I want to you for the next hour. And you're not going to like it."

Kingsley's breath hitched in his throat. He had to have this woman—not two minutes from now, but two minutes ago.

"I'll start the countdown," she said from what sounded like twenty feet away. "Three…." Her voice receded. "Two…" Her voice grew ever fainter.

While waiting for the "one," Kingsley focused on his hearing. She'd led him down the hallway to the entryway of her home. Felicia had rugs all over her hardwood floors, but they still creaked ever so slightly when she walked. He searched for the sound of her movement. Left? At his left was her living room. Right? Right would take her either up the stairs or into a coat closet. Would she run to the closet? Hide in a bathroom? Slip behind a door?

When she said "one" he barely heard it. He came to his feet immediately, took a single step forward and found her arms around him. She ripped off the blindfold and grinned.

"I wanted you to win," she whispered.

Kingsley shoved her against the wall and devoured her mouth with kisses. She pushed her hips into his as his hands found her breasts. This was exactly what he wanted—this warm, beautiful woman wrapped all around him. He brought them both down to the rug. The front door stood five feet away. He almost hoped someone would walk in and see them coupling right on the floor of her entryway.

She made no protest as he pushed her thighs wide and opened her up with his fingers. He licked her, lapped at her, sucked her clitoris until she panted and squirmed underneath him. Nothing turned him on quite like making such a dominant and powerful woman lose control of herself in desire for him. She pumped her hips against his mouth and clutched his shoulders in need. Her dark hair spilled over the floor. He'd rarely seen a sight so erotic as her naked body lost in lust writhing beneath him on the floor.

Since she'd made him wait, he would take his time, although it killed him not to slam into her right this second. Instead, he pushed a finger inside her. Then two. Then three. He rubbed circles into her g-spot until she arched off the floor and groaned his name. He fucked her with his fingers, setting up a rhythm until Felicia panted in time to his movements. Then he turned his hand, pushed hard against the back wall of her vagina and was rewarded with her gasp of shock and pleasure. She said his name again, moaned it, breathed it, begged it. He needed to fuck her and fuck her now. She'd given him the entire hour to do whatever he liked to her and with her.

He'd have her this second and then would take his time with her. She had a large vibrator in her bedroom he'd use on her to force her to climax until she begged him to stop. But now he needed to be inside her.

He opened his pants, pulled off his shirt and put on a condom from his wallet in a matter of seconds. Then he grasped her by the knees, dragged her to him, letting the rug chafe her bare back. So what if it hurt her? Pain was their favorite toy.

With one smooth thrust he entered her, and she welcomed all of him inside her. She dug her heels into the rug and pushed up as he pushed in, meeting at the middle with a shared grunt of need. She twined her arms around his neck, her long legs around his lower back, and took his every thrust. He grasped her hair and forced her head back. He kissed the hollow of her throat, bit her lips and told her in no uncertain terms what he planned to do to her as soon as he'd come.

He pulled out and ordered her on to her hands and knees. "You should have expected this after making me crawl," he said as he entered her from behind. She didn't argue, didn't protest. Instead, she reached one hand under her body and between her legs and let her fingertips caress him as he moved in and out of her. He grew slick with her wetness, and her body opened up until he could bottom out in her. Her fingers moved from him to her clitoris. As she stroked herself, he clutched her shoulders, riding her with growing urgency. When she came, he felt her muscles clamping around him, fluttering and shuddering. With a few more long slow strokes he came, too, a cry of triumph and release escaping his lips.

For a few dozen breaths he stayed inside her as his heart calmed and her spasms subsided. He pulled out of her slowly, watching him leave her, knowing he'd be inside her again as soon as he was able.

He left her on the floor as he disposed of the condom, came back to her and offered his hand.

She rose to her feet, and off her feet he lifted her. Once again she wrapped herself around him as he carried her up the short flight of stairs to the master bedroom on the second floor. There he made good on his threat to make her come until she begged him to stop. Five orgasms later she claimed she could take no more. He wasn't finished, however. So he put her on her back, entered into her wet depths with one powerful stroke and held her breasts in his hands while he fucked her. He thrust into her as slowly and as leisurely as he could while she lay beneath him, receiving him, taking him, enjoying him.

He came again with a sigh before collapsing on to Felicia's warm, welcoming body. She held him close, kissed his shoulders, neck and lips and told him how much she'd enjoyed that. But since the hour was up, he had to be on his very best behavior.

Or else.

"I am an angel," he said, rolling on to his side. "A saint."

"And a liar," she said, facing Kingsley. She tugged a lock of his hair. "Now go get us two glasses of wine. White. I'll be waiting in bed."

"*Oui, Maîtresse.*"

When Kingsley returned with the wine, Felicia's two Russian blue cats had taken over his spot in her bed. He handed Felicia a glass before picking up one of the cats. It squeaked in protest.

"Hush, Severin," Kingsley said, scratching Severin under his chin. "You stole my pillow."

"That's Venus, not Severin," Felicia said.

"My apologies, *Maîtresse* Venus. All cats look alike to me." He winked at Felicia, and sat Venus-in-Fur down next to her twin. He got into bed, and the cats rearranged themselves into a yin-yang of thick gray fur.

"Don't tease my babies," Felicia said. "I missed them so much when I was gone to the bad place. Even though it's their fault I had to go away."

"The cats sent you to pris—"

"Shh…" Felicia said and covered Venus's twitching ears with her hands. "They don't know where I went. Someone else had to feed them for two months, and that's all they need to know."

Kingsley laughed. "How did your cats send you to…away?"

"Usually the wife finds out about the affair from the lipstick on the collar or by finding a strand of long hair on her husband's coat. Stephen gave me the kittens as a gift. He and his wife couldn't have cats because she was allergic. After leaving me one night he went home…and his lovely wife sneezed. 'The sneeze heard round the world,' the newspapers called it. Or, if not the world, the entire city."

Kingsley stroked Severin as the cat purred and preened.

"His wife found out about you, and you spent two months in prison, because Stephen Platt, a billionaire CEO, doesn't know how to use a lint roller?"

"Stephen is living proof that social Darwinism is a failed theory. You'd think a billionaire would be a little smarter."

"Men like him are arrogant," Kingsley said. "People assume the rich are smarter and better. They're just richer."

"They're certainly not any better. Most of my clients are millionaires and then some."

"They'd have to be to afford you."

"Aren't you glad I'm not charging you a cent?" Felicia leaned over the two cats and kissed him.

"Since you don't have sex with your clients, I'd say it was the best money I've never spent."

They kissed long and deep. He wanted her again already, but he would wait and recover so he could give her everything he had, not just everything he had left.

When the kiss ended, Kingsley lay on his back again. Severin stepped on to his chest in that imperious way cats had of making everyone their footstools and curled up on Kingsley's stomach.

"So, what's happened while I was gone?" Felicia asked. "Do you have my club ready for me yet?"

"Not yet," Kingsley said, sighing. Severin rose and fell with Kingsley's breath. "I can't find what Fuller's hiding."

"Trust your instincts. Stephen's wife knew that cat hair on his coat meant something more than Stephen stopped to pet a cat one day. She saw cat hair and looked for pussy."

"I'd look for pussy but Sam won't let me. I was thinking of seducing Fuller's wife, but Sam made me promise not to. She says Lucy Fuller isn't worthy of me."

"Your little secretary likes you too much. Hard to be objective with affection getting in the way. If Sam hadn't made you promise, would you go after the wife?"

"Absolutely. She's as bad or worse than Reverend Fuller anyway."

"Does he love his wife?"

"I don't know if he loves her, but he's protective of her. He swore he'd stay away from the women in my life if I stayed away from the women in his."

"How chivalrous."

"Yes," Kingsley said. "Uncharacteristically chivalrous. I saw him scream at a teenage girl through a bullhorn today."

"Maybe he isn't protective of his wife. Maybe he's protecting himself. Maybe he knows his wife would cheat with you. Maybe she's done it before."

"Peut-être," Kingsley said. "I did promise Sam I'd stay away from her."

"You promised me my club," Felicia said. "I'm your domme. You follow my orders."

"What are your orders, *Maîtresse*?" Kingsley asked, eager to follow any order that would get him back inside her body.

"Easy order," Felicia said as she lifted Severin up and off of Kingsley's chest. Then she put her foot against his hip, pushed hard, and shoved him out of bed on to the floor.

Why were his dominants always doing this to him?

"Go after the wife," Felicia ordered. "I need a club to play in."

With pleasure Kingsley answered, "Yes, ma'am."

31

KINGSLEY TOOK A SHOWER AT FELICIA'S, DRESSED
and drove to Stamford and the WTL headquarters. He'd timed
his arrival to coincide with one of the twice-weekly tapings of
Reverend Fuller's television show—*The Truth and Power Hour.*

The audience had already been admitted into the cavernous
sanctuary that doubled as Fuller's television studio, so Kingsley stood in the large foyer area and watched the taping on a
monitor that played in the lobby.

The music was abominable. Saccharine watered-down gos-
pel music sung by an all-white choir. When it stopped—
not soon enough—Reverend Fuller stepped to the pulpit and
smiled straight into the camera.

"Praise the Lord," Fuller said, and the crowd cheered as if
they were at a World Cup football match, not a church service. "I know you all aren't here to see me. I know who you
came for." The crowd's cheers turned to laughter. Kingsley was
going to hurt himself if he didn't stop rolling his eyes so hard.

"It's Wednesday night," Fuller continued. "And that's Ladies' Night. So I'll get out of the way now and let my beautiful wife, Lucy, take over. Lucy?"

Lucy Fuller might have been a beautiful woman if she had
anything behind her eyes other than religious zealotry. Her

dark eyes burned with God's fire, and the smile she aimed at the camera was fierce and flinty.

She and her husband exchanged a chaste kiss as he handed the pulpit off to her. The crowd applauded the kiss, at her wave to the masses, at her shy laugh at herself while she got behind the microphone.

"My handsome husband," Lucy Fuller said into the camera. "He's all mine, ladies. No one get any ideas."

Kingsley was getting ideas.

"I want to talk about something very serious tonight," Lucy Fuller began. "I want to talk to you all about something we don't talk about enough in this world. And that is sin."

The crowd got very quiet.

"We live in a dark world," Lucy continued. "And it's getting darker everyday. You only have to turn on the television to see it—pornography being sold to our children as music videos, movies that teach our kids it's okay to have sex whenever they feel like. And homosexuality is becoming increasingly accepted by society every day as if it was just another way to be and that's okay. Well, it's not okay. Not okay at all."

And the crowd went wild.

Lucy's tirade went on for the next thirty minutes. Nothing escaped her censure—books being taught in public schools that encouraged godlessness, politicians at the highest levels of office who cheated on their wives while telling everyone else how to live, network television for showing teenagers having sex without consequences, stores selling pornography, explicit music lyrics, people getting divorced, women having abortions left and right, kids painting their fingernails black and worshipping Satan.

This was a woman who needed to get laid.

As much as he had to grit his teeth to do it, Kingsley stayed for the entire sermon. When Lucy Fuller was finished calling out everything in the entire world that gave anyone the tiniest bit of pleasure or entertainment, she received a long, loving hug from her husband and a standing ovation from the crowd.

She ran off the stage in tears, overcome by her own message.

Kingsley slipped out the front and waited by the stage door in the back. He didn't have to wait long.

Ten minutes after the end of her sermon, Lucy Fuller stepped out the door into the alley. She'd changed from her navy blue power suit with its ankle-length skirt and white frilly blouse to a plain black skirt and blouse. She'd repaired her makeup from her crying jag and now looked calm and collected.

He didn't speak to her, didn't let himself be seen. But he did follow her. She walked purposefully, her high heels clicking on the concrete in a quick staccato. Where was she going in such a hurry? Kingsley had to know. Once he noted the make and model of the car she walked to, Kingsley headed back to his own. When she pulled out of the parking lot, he tailed her. He kept several cars between them, made sure she never noticed he took the same turns she took. After a few minutes he realized they were heading back into the city, back toward Manhattan. She was alone and in a hurry. All good signs she was doing something she shouldn't be doing.

In twenty-five minutes, they were in familiar territory. In a few more minutes, they turned on to Riverside Drive. Kingsley fell back as far as he could without losing her entirely. She got away from him for a minute, but then he found her again. She'd pulled up in front of a house.

His house.

Kingsley parked his car against the curb and watched.

He watched Sam walk out the front door carrying an envelope.

He watched Lucy Fuller roll down her passenger-side window.

He watched Sam toss something through the car window and walk back into the house.

He watched Lucy Fuller drive away.

Kingsley got out of his car and walked into his own house feeling as if he were entering the home of a stranger or an enemy.

He found Sam in his office, flipping through files.

"Hey," she said, giving him a smile. "I thought you'd be at Mistress Felicia's all night."

"How much are they paying you?"

"What?"

"How much are the Fullers paying you?"

Sam dropped the files she was holding on to Kingsley's desk.

"I asked you to stay away from Lucy Fuller," she said. "You promised me—"

"And you said you were on my side. We all make promises we can't keep."

"King, listen. I can—"

"How much are the Fullers paying you?" he asked again.

She paused, went silent. She seemed to be weighing her words, weighing her options. He couldn't remember the last time he'd been this coldly, bitterly angry. Not even when Marie-Laure had died. Not even then.

"More than you are," Sam finally said.

"So much 'more weight,' right?" Kingsley asked. "All that matters to you is more money."

"Suits like mine are expensive," Sam said.

And Kingsley replied with the only two words he could force out of his tight and clenched throat.

"You're fired."

32

"WHAT'S YOUR POISON?" THE BARTENDER ASKED, AND Kingsley answered, "Bartenders."

Duke raised his eyebrow and Kingsley laughed.

"I'm fine," Kingsley said. "I'm not drinking tonight."

"Prowling tonight?"

"Not that, either," Kingsley said.

"What can I get you, then?" Duke asked.

"Nothing," Kingsley answered. "You can't get me anything."

Duke gave him a look of sympathy and moved on to another customer. Meanwhile Kingsley stared at the bottles of alcohol arrayed behind the bar. Bourbon, whiskey, rum, vodka and rye. He wanted to drink them all. Every single bottle. Not that it would do him any good. He'd tried drinking again, but all it gave him was a hangover. No matter how much booze he'd poured into the hole Sam had left, it never filled up.

One good thing had come of Sam's betrayal and defection. It had hurt Kingsley so much he knew for certain he was alive again, as alive as he'd ever been and more. Knowing she'd taken money from the Fullers to feed them information about him had left him raging in every part of his being. Raging and grieving. He had never been so angry. He had never been so hurt. He had never felt more alive and wished more that he wasn't.

When his parents had died, he'd been angry, hurt, grief-stricken. But it had been an accident, and he'd had no one to blame.

When Søren married Marie-Laure and she died shortly thereafter, Kingsley had felt that same trinity of emotions—anger, pain, grief. But again, no one had tried to hurt him on purpose. Søren had married Marie-Laure so the three of them could be rich and could be free. And Marie-Laure had died in her own grief, her own hurt, her own pain. She wasn't trying to hurt him by dying. Surely not.

But Sam...she had betrayed him with wide eyes and a cold heart. It had been no accident, no act of God, no act of fate. She'd aimed a gun at his heart and fired.

And the hole was still there.

Kingsley wrenched his gaze from the too-tempting bottles of alcohol and looked around. Holly was sitting on the edge of the stage with her ankles around the neck of an elderly businessman. Cassandra was draped across the laps of five happy frat boys. Eden was holding the hand of a nervous groom-to-be and led him to the back room for a private show.

He walked away from the bar and strolled around the club. For the past five weeks he'd been coming to the Möbius almost every night, making his rounds, chatting with the girls, drinking nothing and leaving after half an hour. No one asked him why he made this nightly pilgrimage. He was the owner, so he could do whatever he wanted. But he knew why he did it, and that was bad enough.

Michelle strolled past him and paused long enough to kiss him on the cheek. He wouldn't have minded her company, but she was heading to the stage. Her turn to make her rent for the night.

Waste of time. Kingsley glanced around the club once more. He needed to stop coming here, needed to get on with his life, needed to stop living in the past.

Kingsley decided to leave and find something else to do. He hopped off his bar stool and turned to the door. He came face-to-face with a young man. He wore black jeans, a white shirt untucked and scuffed boots. He looked two parts scared and one part thrilled. But now all Kingsley noticed was his hair. His blond hair.

"Justin?"

"Wow," he said. "I can't believe you remembered my name."

Kingsley crooked his finger at Justin and stepped into a quiet corner of the club.

"What are you doing here?" Kingsley asked in a low voice.

"I left. I mean, I left everything. I had to. My parents found out."

"They didn't take it well?"

Justin didn't speak. The look in his eyes was answer enough.

"It's good you left. But why are you here?" Kingsley glanced pointedly at three naked girls on the stage.

Justin smiled sheepishly. "Honestly, I was hoping to run into you."

"I gave you my card."

"I didn't think you really wanted me showing up at your house. But if I ran into you here…"

Kingsley sighed.

"Sorry," Justin said, his face falling. "Stupid idea. It's just, I thought about you a lot. And as I'm saying this, I realize how pathetic it sounds—hanging out in a strip club hoping someone you're into shows up. Anyway, it's good to see you again."

"I thought about you," Kingsley said, surprised by the truth of the statement. Since that night in March, Justin had crossed his mind more than once, more than twice. It should have been a one-night stand. Rough and quick and then the good-bye, as rough and quick as the sex. But if he were honest with himself, Kingsley would have to admit he'd been worried about Justin and even a little ashamed of how he'd treated him.

"Is it? Good to see me again, I mean?"

Kingsley gripped the back of Justin's neck.

"You should have come to my house instead of coming here," Kingsley whispered in Justin's ear.

"Why?"

"It would have saved us the car trip."

He released Justin and strode to the door, pleased to hear the boy's feet following right behind him. His driver opened the door for them, and he and Justin entered the Rolls.

"Wow," Justin said again. "Nice."

"You like it?"

"Love it. I've never been in a Rolls Royce before."

"First time for everything," Kingsley said, and even in the low light he could see a faint blush on the boy's face.

"Have you ever... I mean, did you ever—?"

"Have I ever had sex in the back of a Rolls Royce?" Kingsley asked.

"That."

Kingsley smiled at him.

"Never."

Justin smiled back, then he laughed. And it was so good to see that smile and that laugh that Kingsley did something he hadn't done the first time they were together.

Kingsley kissed him.

Kingsley kissed the outside of Justin's mouth, his lips, along the tip of his tongue, and in and out and through him until

Justin clung to Kingsley's arms, panting from desire. Justin straddled Kingsley's lap, and Kingsley yanked his jacket off. They couldn't get home fast enough.

They broke the kiss when the car arrived at the town house. Once in his bedroom, Kingsley locked the door behind them and kissed Justin again. And again. And again. He couldn't get enough of his mouth, his trembling lips, the warmth and eagerness.

"I should have kissed you that night," Kingsley said as he unbuttoned Justin's shirt. "I should have kissed you all night."

Kingsley stripped them both naked to the waist and pushed Justin back on to the bed. The first time had been on a hard dirty floor. This time he would do it right.

He held Justin by the hair and kissed his throat and collarbone. When he bit the boy's shoulder, Justin gasped.

"You want pain again?" Kingsley asked. Last time he'd practically forced himself on Justin. This time he would do it right.

"Yeah, I do," Justin said as he ran his hands up Kingsley's bare arms. "I hurt myself sometimes. It turns me on."

Kingsley stared down into Justin's coffee-colored eyes. He touched Justin's pale hair, his lips, felt the pulse in his neck beating wildly. Kingsley had to will himself to calm down. He wanted this boy so much it hurt, wanted to hurt this boy so much.

"What do you like?" Kingsley asked. "How do you want me to hurt you?"

Justin laughed. "I get to tell you what I like?"

Kingsley ran his hand up and down Justin's chest. He couldn't get enough of the boy's smooth young skin.

"I should have asked that night," Kingsley said. "I wasn't in a good place then. I'm sorry."

Justin raised his head and kissed Kingsley. He hoped that meant he was accepting his apology.

"In all my fantasies," Justin whispered, "the sex is really rough. That's what I like."

"Rough sex," Kingsley repeated. "I think I can do that."

He moved on top of Justin and grabbed him by the wrists, pinning him to the bed. He kissed him hard this time, brutally hard, and bit his bottom lip until he broke the skin. More bites followed. Kingsley left a trail of bruises from Justin's ear to his bicep. Justin hadn't been exaggerating. He gasped in obvious pleasure as Kingsley dug his fingers into his hair and pulled his head back, exposing his throat. It felt so good to let go of all pretense of gentleness. If Justin liked it rough, Kingsley would show him rough.

Kingsley dug his thumb into the hollow of Justin's throat. With his free hand, Kingsley wrenched Justin's jeans open and shoved his hand into his pants. Justin was incredibly hard, and so Kingsley stroked him hard, painfully hard. Kingsley yearned to be inside him, but he was enough of a masochist that he forced himself to wait, to hold back as long as he could.

With a dozen vicious bites, Kingsley worked his way down Justin's body. When Kingsley took his cock into his mouth, Justin groaned and dug his fingers into the sheets. Even now Kingsley wasn't gentle. He made Justin gasp with the mix of pleasure and pain from the force of the sucking.

He pulled back before Justin could come and sat up on his knees. With his foot on Justin's hip, Kingsley kicked him onto his stomach. In seconds he'd stripped him completely naked.

Again he gripped his hair at the nape of his neck, pinning him into place.

"You like this, don't you?" Kingsley asked. "Being treated like property? Being used?"

"Yes," Justin whispered, his mouth against the red sheets.

"You want me to use you?"

"I want you to do everything to me you want."

"You want me to fuck you?" Kingsley demanded.

"Yes."

"Say it."

"Fuck me. Please…"

Kingsley heard the desperation in his voice.

"I might make you regret asking for that."

"I'll only regret what you don't do to me," he said. And for that sentiment alone, Kingsley decided to fuck Justin all night long.

He moved off the bed and pulled a case from underneath it. He unlatched it and pulled out a set of heavy stainless-steel handcuffs. He took out a plug and lube. Condoms were on the bedside table. Everything he needed for a night of sin.

Without asking permission first, Kingsley clapped the handcuffs on to Justin's wrists and locked them behind his back. The sight of this beautiful blond twenty-year-old boy in handcuffs naked on his bed was everything he could have asked for all wrapped up in a stainless-steel bow.

With two wet fingers, Kingsley pushed inside Justin. The boy groaned, and Kingsley smiled behind his back. He opened Justin up—first two fingers and then three. From three fingers to four. He inserted the plug to open Justin up even more. He pushed the boy on to his side and took him in his mouth again. Now he opened his pants and shoved himself into Justin's mouth. The boy choked a little at first but soon his throat opened, and he licked and kissed Kingsley as eagerly as Kingsley sucked and licked and kissed him. Lost in the mutual pleasure, Kingsley forgot everything. He forgot why he'd gone to the Möbius tonight, forgot what he looked for there, forgot the pain of knowing he didn't find it. He pulled back and knelt at Justin's head. Kingsley watched while Justin, with his eyes closed, sucked him deep. He'd promised to be rough with the boy, but it was a gentle hand that ran through his pale hair and caressed his face with his fingertips.

"Please," Justin whispered.

Without a word, Kingsley pushed him back on to his stomach, took the plug out of him and rolled on a condom. He entered Justin slowly, wanting to enjoy every second of sinking deep and being surrounded and held by his inner muscles. After a few strokes, Kingsley was all the way in. He gripped the boy's shoulders and pounded into him with all his strength. He thought of nothing, remembered nothing, but felt everything. His strokes were long and aggressive, his hands relentless. And beneath him Justin moaned and breathed and begged for more.

Kingsley bent low over him and pressed rough kisses into his shoulders and spine. Kisses and bites, bites and kisses. Pleasure and pain. Pain and pleasure. This was what he lived for, what they all lived for. His climax built and Kingsley didn't fight it. With his mouth against Justin's ear he came in silence, which increased the intensity of the orgasm. Once the spasms passed, Kingsley stayed inside him but only long enough to take the handcuffs off. He pulled out carefully, and Justin rolled on to his back.

"Come for me," Kingsley ordered. "I want to watch."

Justin took himself in hand and stroked upward. It didn't take long before his own semen spurted against his naked heaving chest. Kingsley was hard again from watching. After putting on a new condom, Kingsley pushed back into him and thrust again, slower this time, more carefully. Justin wrapped his arms around Kingsley's back and they kissed. Their tongues mingled and their lips met, and for now everything was right in his world. As long as Kingsley stayed inside this boy, everything was fine.

Kingsley stopped fucking long enough to pull the sheets down, undress completely, and settle Justin against his pillows. He wanted this erotic oblivion to last all night.

They fucked again, slower this time. And although it scared him, the desire overrode the fear, and Kingsley let Justin inside him. Afterward, Kingsley beat Justin raw with a flogger and cane. He took pain like a professional, like he was born for it. When their need and hunger for each other was finally spent, they stood in the shower together, Justin's back against the wall, Kingsley's mouth on his mouth as the burning water beat down on them and the steam soothed the soreness the sex had worked on them.

"Will you do something to me?" Justin whispered into Kingsley's lips.

"Anything."

Justin didn't tell him. He didn't have to. Justin knelt in the shower and offered his back to Kingsley. Not even Søren had been sadistic enough to relieve himself onto Kingsley. That made it all the more enjoyable for Kingsley to mark Justin as the hot water poured down on to both of them.

Kingsley sent Justin to bed after the shower. He smiled at the sight of that blond head on his pillow. For the first time Kingsley realized five whole hours had passed, and he hadn't thought once about Sam. A good sign.

Kingsley dipped his head and kissed him on the side of the neck. Justin stirred.

"Thank you," Justin said, half-asleep.

"For what?" Kingsley asked.

"Remembering my name."

Kingsley felt a knot in his throat.

"I would never forget it."

"I don't know what to do," Justin said. "With my life, I mean."

"What do you want to do?"

"I don't know. Never go home again."

"You want to work for me?" Kingsley asked.

"House boy?"

Kingsley laughed.

"Not quite," he said.

"Is there any money in being kinky?"

Kingsley smiled at him.

"You would be surprised."

33

KINGSLEY LEFT JUSTIN ALONE IN HIS BED. HE PULLED on his trousers, his shirt, and walked on bare feet to his office. In the bottom drawer of his desk, the only drawer he routinely locked, he pulled out Sam's clipboard. For five weeks he'd cherished a fantasy that Sam would show up on his doorstep demanding the return of her beloved clipboard. He'd rarely seen her without it in the months she'd worked for him. *Worked.* Past tense. He still couldn't get used to the past tense where Sam was concerned. In his fantasy she would show up and tell him she was wrong, that she shouldn't have taken the Fullers' money, but she needed it for something and she'd been too ashamed to tell him why. She'd beg him to forgive her and he would. He would forgive her and take her back. And everything would be okay again.

A stupid childish fantasy. It would never happen.

He picked up a pen and flipped to the checklist Sam had created for their club. In the little square beside the words "Male Submissive" Kingsley made a check mark. Justin needed a job that would let him afford NYC. Kingsley needed a male submissive for the club.

A match made in hell.

Today was September fifteenth. The club would open in

seventy-six days, and he still had no location for it. He'd put a tail on Reverend Fuller and sent both male and female prostitutes to tempt him into a scandal. So far...nothing. He was missing something. Fuller had an ugly secret and he knew it. He'd seen it in Fuller's eyes—the secret shame, the fear, the terror of discovery. It was there, but Kingsley didn't know how to find it. And he had to find it—not because he wanted the building so much anymore. But he wanted to destroy Fuller because Fuller had destroyed his love for Sam. And that was an unforgiveable sin.

He flipped through the notes she'd left on her clipboard. He loved her handwriting—loopy and playful even when writing out to-do lists for a BDSM club. But his Sam was always a creature of beautiful contradiction. She dressed like a man and yet was easily the most feminine woman he'd ever known, from her light and airy laugh to her pink-lipped smiles, her lithe, manicured fingers. And yet she had a teenage boy's libido and the ability to charm any woman—straight or gay— right into bed with her. And although she'd never indicated that she wanted them to be lovers, nothing had made her happier than hopping into bed with him, pulling his arm around her tight and being his "bed bug" as she called herself. She'd bite him on the arm or on the neck and then fall fast asleep.

No matter how much Blaise cajoled him to hire a new secretary, he couldn't bring himself to replace Sam. Not yet. Not while the wounds were still fresh and he could still conjure the scent of her in his mind, the sound of her voice and the memory of her sitting at his feet, pulling his boots on as if he was her king and she his valet.

Even looking at her notes hurt. And such banal notes they were. Mostly banal. *Square footage...call the dungeon outfitter... schedule K's massage...tell K you're pregnant with Søren's baby... stop reading my notes, King.*

He laughed so hard he almost cried. He could see her smiling at herself as she wrote those words, knowing he would get nosy someday and read her clipboard. At the bottom of the page she'd drawn a heart with a K in the center and a crown around the K. She'd put an arrow next to the heart and the words *Possible tattoo idea for left ass cheek.*

"God damn you, Sam," he said out loud. He threw the clipboard down on his desk and picked up his phone. But before he dialed her number, he hung the phone up again. She'd betrayed him and walked away with his heart in her teeth. She'd picked the Fullers' money over him, even though he'd opened his heart up to her time and time again.

He picked up the phone again, and this time he dialed.

"Kingsley, it's three in the morning," Søren said. He sounded more annoyed than sleepy.

"What are you wearing?"

"An angry scowl," Søren said.

"It's a good look for you."

"To what do I owe the pleasure of this call?" Søren asked.

"I almost called Sam to tell her how much I hate her. So I called you instead."

"Fine. Tell me how much you hate me."

"I don't hate you."

"Then you should hang up on me," Søren said.

"You'd like that too much. What are you doing still awake?"

"I'm reading."

"In bed?"

"In bed."

Kingsley couldn't stop himself from picturing Søren in bed. White sheet pulled up to his hip, naked chest, hand behind his head as he read. Divinity in repose.

"What are you reading?" Kingsley asked, trying to distract himself from the mental images.

"It's an erotic retelling of the Book of Esther."

Kingsley groaned. "You have to start having sex again. Please. I don't even care if it's with me or her. Anyone."

"I'm fine," Søren said, but Kingsley could tell he wasn't fine. His "I'm fine" sounded bruised.

"Do you miss it?" Kingsley asked. Not the question he meant. He meant "Do you miss me?"

"I'm twenty-nine, male and breathing," Søren said. "What do you think?"

"No one would judge you if you broke your vows. No one who matters."

"It would matter to me," Søren said. "I have reasons for doing what I do and not doing what I don't do. Reasons that have nothing to do with the church or being a priest. And reasons that also have nothing to do with you or Eleanor."

"I can call Blaise now. She'll be there in an hour. Would you like that?"

Søren didn't answer at first, didn't say a word.

"You're thinking about it, aren't you?" Kingsley asked and knew Søren was.

"I should have known better than to make friends with the devil."

Kingsley grinned. "Blaise is amazing in bed. You won't regret it. She can do this thing when she's going down on you where she takes your—"

"Kingsley."

"And goes so deep she can lick your—"

"Kingsley."

"It's amazing. Gift from God."

"Red."

"Red?" Kingsley repeated.

"I was attempting to safe out of this conversation."

Kingsley laughed softly.

"You'll need a better safe word than that with me, *mon ami.*"

"I'll find a stronger word. A few stronger words have already leaped to mind."

"If you don't want Blaise, I could come over," Kingsley said.

"I think you have more than enough lovers already," Søren said.

"We're not talking about what I need. We're talking about what you need."

"I need sleep and someone is keeping me from it."

Kingsley was undeterred.

"You know, it wouldn't have to mean anything. You can do whatever you want to me. Pain. Sex. More pain."

Søren fell silent again. What was he thinking? Feeling? Was he tempted?

Of course he was tempted.

"Tell me something...how long has it been?" Kingsley asked into the silence.

Søren sighed. "What day is it?"

"Friday."

"Then it's been...oh...eleven years. You?"

"Eleven minutes." More like an hour and eleven minutes, but why quibble? "You haven't been with anyone since me? Not even once?"

"No one since you," Søren said.

"And your Virgin Queen?"

"I made her a promise," Søren said, the irritation gone from his voice now. But Kingsley still heard the bruise. "I promised her I would give her everything. I intend to keep that promise."

"You made me a promise, too," Kingsley reminded him. "You said you'd share her with me."

"Another promise I intend to keep. I won't be enough for her, God knows. But I get her first."

"Why?" Kingsley demanded, smiling despite himself. "Because you saw her first?"

"Because I haven't had sex in *eleven years*."

"Fuck somebody, then," Kingsley said, half laughing, half yelling. "It offends me to know you're in your bed right now all alone reading erotic retellings of Ruth."

"Esther."

"You know I have to have *more* sex to make up for all the sex you aren't having. Someone has to restore the balance in the universe."

"The universe thanks you for your sacrifice. Now, may I hang up?" Søren asked.

"Not yet. I'm considering killing the Fullers—both of them."

"No, you aren't."

"It's crossed my mind. A quick painful death. Payback for making Sam betray me."

"No one made Sam betray you. If she did betray you, she did it of her own free will and for her own reasons. You started a war with the Fullers. They fought back. Now you know why I'm a pacifist."

Kingsley closed his eyes tight and wished he could close his ears to Søren's words, as well. All this time he'd been blind. He'd adored Sam so much he hadn't for one second considered the possibility she would turn on him. Now he'd seen her for who she really was and he wished he could, like Oedipus, blind himself.

"You can't win if you don't fight," Kingsley finally said.

"Tell me something, Kingsley. How did this fight start?"

"I wanted to buy The Renaissance Hotel from the Fullers."

"Why?"

"Because that building is mine. I knew it the moment I saw it."

"So you're fighting for it?"

"Of course. That's what you do when you want something."

"Do you remember the story in the Bible known as the Judgment of Solomon?" Søren asked.

"Why can't we have phone sex like normal perverts?" Kingsley asked.

"The story is found in 1 Kings, chapter three."

"So that's a no to phone sex?"

"God has asked Solomon what great gift he would most desire. Solomon answers 'wisdom,' and God grants him great wisdom. Shortly thereafter he's asked to settle a dispute between two prostitutes who live in the same house. Both women had given birth to sons within three days of each other. One child had died. The other lived. One mother claimed the living son was hers. The other mother said her son had been stolen and replaced with the dead child."

"I'd forgotten what a gruesome book the Old Testament is."

"It gets better," Søren continued. "The women demanded King Solomon make a judgment to determine to whom the living child belonged. Solomon declared 'Bring me a sword' and a sword was brought to him. He said he would cut the baby in half and give one part to one mother, another part to the other mother. Immediately one woman cried out 'Please, my Lord, give her the living boy, do not kill him.' And thus King Solomon knew the woman who was willing in an instant to give up the boy so that he might live was the true mother."

Kingsley sighed. "And your point is...?"

"The true test of love is not always 'Will you fight for it?' The real test of true love is often 'Are you willing to give it up?'"

Kingsley swallowed hard. "I can't give it up. I'm not strong like you are. I can't give up the things I want. I've lost too much in my life. I don't want to lose any more."

"The sacrifice is worth it," Søren said. "Try it sometime. You'll see."

"Spoken like a man who hasn't had sex in eleven years."

"I'm hanging up on you," Søren said.

"This is fun," Kingsley said. "You and me on the phone at night talking about girls. We should do this more often."

"Kingsley?"

"Oui?"

Click.

Kingsley laughed as he hung up the phone. He laughed until he couldn't laugh anymore. He laughed until he didn't feel like laughing anymore.

He stood up and took a steady breath. Right now a gorgeous blond boy who couldn't get enough of him waited for him in his bed.

He would go fuck in the present. The past could go fuck itself.

34

KINGSLEY DIDN'T HAVE HIS CLUB YET, AND HE DIDN'T have his kingdom. But he did have Irina and the promise he'd made her. For months he and Mistress Felicia had been training her in the arts of sadism and dominance. The training had transformed her from a cold, silent scared presence in his home afraid to step a toe out of line, into a proud fierce goddess of pain.

And lucky Blaise got to be Mistress Irina's very first victim. Not counting her soon-to-be ex-husband.

"Are you going to be a good girl for me?" he asked Blaise. They sat on the wooden throne in his playroom, she in his lap. "I need you to do everything I tell you to do."

"I will be the best girl for you, monsieur," Blaise said, putting her private-school French to good use. He lifted her chin and forced her to meet his eyes. She played the part of the scared little girl so well that it fooled even him sometimes. Or, more importantly, fooled his cock. She gave him her most innocent pouty face. Oh, yes, she would be the very best girl for him tonight.

"Wait here," he said to Blaise. She curtsied, and he left her standing in his playroom by the St. Andrew's cross. She'd worn her best tonight and looked like Rita Hayworth escaped from the silver screen and brought to modern Manhattan. She'd been pouting lately that Kingsley wasn't paying enough attention to her. Well, she would get all the attention she wanted tonight.

Out in the hall he found Irina waiting for him, pacing the hallway in her black-and-purple leather boots.

"My little girl is growing up," he said as he took Irina by the hands. She rolled her eyes.

"Can we get started?" she asked. Her Russian accent made everything she said sound vaguely menacing. Dominatrix was the rare profession where this trait gave her an advantage.

"In a hurry?"

"I've been waiting for this scene for months. Let me have her." A sadistic gleam shone in her dark eyes.

"Don't be too eager. Remember, your clients will be paying for your time. You are the one wanted, desired. You must be aloof. They should feel honored you are giving them your time and attention. They are beneath you. They want to be beneath you. Yes?"

"Yes." She exhaled heavily.

"Good." He kissed her quickly on both cheeks. "Now you may have her."

He followed her into the playroom. Blaise still waited by the flogger rack.

"This is a couples' session," Kingsley began, addressing his comment to Irina. "You'll have a few of these. What's the first rule about couples' sessions?"

"The woman books the session," Irina said. "Not the man."

"And why is that?"

"So we can cover our asses."

Kingsley laughed at Irina's answer.

"Technically that's true," he admitted as Blaise covered her mouth to stifle her own laugh. "I'd rather couch it in more chivalrous terms than litigious. Male dominants can be dangerously aggressive. We never want a woman involved in something she doesn't want to be involved in. So, what will you do in a case like this, Mistress?"

"Step into the hallway, please," Irina said to him. Kingsley kissed Blaise's hand, bowed to Irina and walked out. He could guess what they talked about while he was gone. Irina, like the good dominatrix she was, would ask Blaise if she was here of her own free will and fully consenting to this session. Once Blaise assured the Mistress that she was, Irina would ask her a few questions about what she enjoyed in a scene, what sort of pain she liked. Thudding? Stinging? Impact play that left welts and bruises? Bondage? Knowing Blaise, she'd answer "All of the above."

The door opened and Irina waved him back inside.

"She said you aren't holding her hostage and forcing her to do kinky things against her will," Irina said.

"Not tonight. Maybe tomorrow," Kingsley said, and Blaise winked at him. She'd played his willing victim many a night. She did put up a beautiful fight when they did rape-play. They'd had to establish two sets of safe words because her acting was so good that he hadn't been able to tell her feigned terror from real terror one night. It might have been the best sex they'd ever had.

"I'm thinking we should give your girl some souvenirs of this night," Irina said. "What do you think?" She walked a circle around Blaise, looking her up and down. He couldn't say who looked more alluring tonight—Blaise in her elegant 1940s pencil skirt and blouse or Mistress Irina in her leather corset and boots. They were a sight to behold, both of them. He wished Sam were still with him. He would have loved to tell her about tonight. But she was gone and would stay gone. Five weeks later and he still regretted what had happened. Regretted? No. He'd done the right thing. *Mourned*. That was the word he needed. *Grieved*. "Kingsley?"

"Oh, *oui*, souvenirs," he said, forcing his mind back to the present. He needed to stay focused for Irina's sake as much as Blaise's. "Blaise loves the flogger and the whip."

"She told me that," Irina said, gathering Blaise's hair into her hand and lifting it. She tugged lightly and Blaise's breath caught in her throat. "Didn't you?"

"Yes, Mistress."

"Good girl. Kingsley, you should undress your girl for me. Let me see what I have to work with."

Kingsley went to work taking Blaise's clothes off. He unbuttoned her blouse, unzipped her skirt, stripped her to her stockings, garters and high heels.

"In a session with a client," Kingsley said, "you'll do what before you start the play?"

"Make the client or clients undress," Irina said.

"And why do we do this?"

"It's a security measure. We're making sure our clients aren't carrying hidden weapons."

"Very good," Kingsley said. "You can frisk me if you like."

"I would, but you'd enjoy that too much," Irina teased.

When Blaise was naked but for her stockings, he took her wrists in his right hand and raised them, presenting her to Irina like a slave for inspection. He was taller than Blaise by half a foot, and she had to stretch to hold the position.

"Beautiful." Irina placed a hand on Blaise's chest. The Mistress caressed her breasts gently, carefully—but only at first. She pinched Blaise's right nipple then—pinched hard—and Blaise gasped. "Turn her."

Kingsley turned Blaise to face him so that Mistress Irina could see her back. At his command, Blaise hadn't done kink with anyone in the past week. He wanted her body to be a clean canvas for Irina's first session.

"Very nice," Irina said. "Beautiful skin. It will look better when I'm done with it. Put the cuffs on her."

Irina held out a set of leather cuffs. Kingsley lowered Blaise's arms and cuffed her wrists and ankles.

"What is the rule with couples?" Kingsley asked Irina as he handed Blaise over to her.

"The couple may touch each other as much as they want," Irina said. "They can have sex during the session."

"And you?"

"Dominatrixes don't have sex with their clients," Irina said, smiling. "Prostitution is illegal. S and M isn't."

"*Bon,*" Kingsley said. "But feel free to give Blaise an orgasm if you like. If she earns it."

"I'll earn it, monsieur," Blaise said, and Kingsley slapped her hard on the bottom for speaking out of turn.

Irina put Blaise on the X-shaped cross, face to the wood.

"What's your safe word, Blaise?" Kingsley said.

"*Casablanca.*"

Safe word established, Irina took a deerskin flogger off the wall. Good size. Good weight. Good heft. It would hurt like fuck, just the way Blaise liked.

"Start slow." He whispered the reminder.

He watched Irina take a steadying breath. She moved her feet into position, gripped the flogger by the tips of the tails and raised it over her head. Kingsley gave her a nod. And then Irina smiled, a wide, deep, dark sexy smile. She could play aloof all she wanted, but he could tell she was enjoying this scene as much or more than Blaise would. A true sadist—he did know how to spot one. Irina let the flogger go, and it struck Blaise in the center of her back. She raised it, let it go again—another center strike. For the next few minutes she dusted Blaise with the flogger, hitting her again and again—not too hard, not too light. Blaise's skin turned from creamy white to blazing red. She traded the deerskin for eel skin—a smaller, more vicious flogger. Blaise gasped and flinched as dozens of tiny welts raised on her back. The little flogger struck far more sharply, and soon it looked as if a dozen hands had clawed at Blaise's back with cruel fingernails.

As Irina rotated through four different types of floggers, he watched her work. She was sure-handed and dexterous. It was all too easy to aim wrong and hit a bound submissive in the back of the head. But Irina never missed her mark, and soon Blaise sagged in her bonds, panting from the pain and the arousal the pain inspired in her. Kingsley called a halt to it. He could see Blaise was nearing her limit.

"Did you enjoy your beating?" he whispered in her ear as he ran a hand over her burning skin.

"I did," she said, smiling. Her face was flushed with triumph. Blaise always looked her most beautiful after a beating.

"Do you think you earned an orgasm?" he asked her.

"Only if you think I did, monsieur."

"That's the right answer," he said, and Blaise beamed. When she was in the mood to submit, nothing made her happier than serving at the feet of a dominant man. Out in the real world, she single-handedly ran a controversial nonprofit group, lobbied the state and federal government and made weekly appearances at important society events to raise awareness of her causes—sexual freedom and other women's rights issues. But the powerful, competent, dominant Blaise disappeared the second she stepped into a playroom. It was all "yes, sir" and "no, sir" and "whatever pleases you, sir." And now, what would please him would be to please her while Irina watched and helped.

"I think," he said, "that you need more pain. A little more. What do you think?"

"I think you know best, monsieur."

"But I also think you need some pleasure with your pain. What do you think, Mistress?" he asked.

"I'm happy to supply the pain," Irina said, "if you'd like to supply the pleasure."

"An excellent idea." He unbound Blaise from the cross and led her by the wrists to the bed. He laid her on her back, and she winced as her skin touched the silk. "I'm thinking the rope? What do you think, Mistress?"

"Good choice," she said. "I'm thinking this."

She handed Kingsley a vibrator. He already knew what he'd do with it.

"She has been very good tonight," Kingsley said. "Haven't you?"

"If you say I've been good, then it must be true," Blaise said.

"You're so good at this, *chouchou*," he said to her with a wink.

He crooked his finger, indicating that Blaise should stand up again. She obeyed and let him lead her to the center of the room. He positioned her under a large sturdy metal hook that hung from the ceiling. Irina brought over a step stool and a length of black silk rope. She looped the rope through the D-rings on the cuffs and hoisted Blaise's arms over her head, tying her wrists to the hook.

Now Blaise stood tied in place, her arms above her head and no way to escape unless he or Irina untied her. And they would untie her. Eventually.

Irina stood in front of Blaise and, with deft hands, brought another length of rope around her back. For the next ten minutes, Irina looped and knotted, looped and knotted, until she'd made a corset of the rope, binding Blaise's chest, torso and breasts tightly.

Kingsley wrapped his arm around Blaise's hips and lightly pinched her clitoris between his thumb and forefinger.

"Do you have a preference?" he whispered in her ear. "Ass? Pussy? Both?"

Blaise laughed. "All of the above."

"Why did I know you were going to say that?"

"Because you know me so well, monsieur. Inside and out."

Kingsley lubricated both her holes thoroughly, and Blaise moaned from the pleasure of his fingers on her and inside her. He rolled on a condom and entered her from behind. As she was standing it took a few minutes to work past the tight ring of muscle that wanted to keep him out. But he pushed in while Blaise pushed back, and soon he was deep inside her. Irina handed him the vibrator, which he slid slowly into her vagina.

"Oh, God…" Blaise gasped—the last two coherent words she spoke for a while. Irina played with Blaise's bound breasts while Kingsley fucked her standing up. Irina squeezed and pinched, slapped and teased—inflicting pain both sharp and subtle.

He focused his attention on Blaise's body—the tightness of her around his cock, the smell of her long hair—jasmine— the scent of her skin—Chanel No. 5, Marilyn Monroe's perfume—the softness of her hips that he grasped, the sounds of her voice as she gasped and groaned and came, not once but twice in a row. He increased the speed of his thrusts and came, too, the orgasm almost painful in its intensity.

With a final kiss on Blaise's neck, he uncoupled their bodies. A few drops of her own wetness landed on the floor between her feet when he pulled the vibrator from her. He went into the bathroom and cleaned off while Irina untied Blaise. Like a good and sadistic dominatrix, Irina made Blaise clean up her own mess off the floor. He returned to find Blaise stretched out on the bed, flushed and happy, as Irina knotted up her rope.

"A good day's work," Kingsley said to Irina. "What do you think?" He pinched Blaise's toes.

"She's hired," Blaise said with a wide grin. Her eyes sparkled and her skin glowed. Was there anything more beautiful in the world than a sated woman? "That was glorious."

"Did I pass?" Irina asked Kingsley. "Am I ready for the real thing?"

"Your aim is excellent, attitude is perfect and you certainly played the part beautifully. You forgot one very important thing."

"What thing?" Irina scowled at him. "What did I do wrong?"

Kingsley reached into his pocket and pulled out ten one-hundred dollar bills. He held them out to Irina who reached for them. He pulled his hand back at the last second.

"Clients pay in advance." He put the money back in his pocket and walked out, certain Irina would never forget that detail ever again.

He walked upstairs to his office and collapsed onto the couch by the window. Good session. Great kink. Irina would make a world-class dominatrix. With her and Felicia as his top dommes, every man in the tri-state area who had even once fantasized about feeling a woman's boot on the back of his neck would come crawling to them, begging to be let into the club. A beautiful dream that might never come true. Fuller still wasn't budging. Kingsley still wasn't giving up. This staring contest had gone on long enough. One of them would have to blink.

Before Kingsley could finish his thought, Blaise burst into his office in her bathrobe.

"King—I need you. The cops are here."

"Cops? Why?"

"Irina. She's under arrest."

"For what?" Kingsley grabbed his jacket and pulled it on. He raced down the stairs and found Irina in handcuffs being escorted to a waiting squad car.

"What is this?" he demanded of the officer. "What's the charge?"

"She poisoned her husband," the officer said. "So I hear."

"That charge was dropped," Kingsley said, standing between Irina and the squad car.

"Looks like they picked the charge back up again. Excuse me. I don't want to have to arrest you, too."

"King, it's okay," Irina said. "You did your best."

"I'll get you out," he promised her. "Don't talk to anyone. Not a word. I'll call our lawyer."

She put up no fight as the officer shoved her in the car and drove away. He watched them disappear around the block.

"Mr. Edge?" came a voice from behind him. "Kingsley Edge."

Kingsley turned around and found a bike messenger waiting for him.

"Oui?"

"Delivery." The boy handed him two envelopes—one large manila envelope and one small white envelope. He rode off before Kingsley could say another word.

He opened the large manila envelope first and pulled out a sheaf of papers. He flipped through them while he walked back into the town house.

"King? What is it?"

"It's from the health department," he said, not believing what he was reading. "They're shutting down the Möbius for health code violations."

"Health code violations?" Blaise repeated. "Because of the... you know?"

The sex club in the back. Someone had tipped off the health department. And who worked at the Möbius? Who knew Irina was staying at his house?

Blaise ran her hands through her hair.

"King, what's going on? What happened?"

Kingsley closed his eyes.

"Sam happened."

35

"KINGSLEY, ARE YOU EVEN LISTENING TO ME?"

"What is it you do for a living again?" he asked, glancing around his still-empty strip club. Was there any place in the world more desolate or depressing than an empty strip club?

Maggie glared at him from across the table.

"I'm a lawyer. Specifically, your lawyer."

"Then, no, I'm not listening to you."

Maggie sighed and ran her hands through her hair. She was one of the highest paid and most respected attorneys in all of Manhattan. But right now she looked like a beautiful if exasperated ex-lover in a dark red suit. Which she also was.

"You remember you're paying me seven-hundred dollars an hour for this conversation?" she asked him, the toe of her red stiletto clicking on the floor in irritation.

"Now I'm listening. What's happening to my club?"

Maggie capped her pen and tapped her legal pad with the end.

"Nothing," she said. "Unfortunately. There is no organization in the city that works slower than the health department. And that's on a good day."

"And this is not a good day?"

"No, it's not a good day," Maggie said, ripping off a sheet

of paper and tossing it in the air. He did always adore her dramatics. "All the paperwork is 'in process,' which is their fancy way of saying 'we are doing nothing with this case, so sit there and shut up.' You must have seriously pissed someone off."

Kingsley stretched out his legs, threw his feet on to the seat of the chair next to Maggie, and crossed his boots at the ankle.

"It's possible."

"Oh, I know it's possible. I used to sleep with you, remember? You're the most infuriating man I've ever met and, considering the only people I know are other lawyers, and I'm using the term *people* loosely, that's saying something."

Kingsley narrowed his eyes at her. He'd met Maggie years ago when he'd been sent on a long undercover assignment in Manhattan. Older, rich, well-respected and powerful, Maggie was also a sexual submissive who loved nothing so much as spending all night on her hands and knees for a man. He'd taken great pleasure in giving her knees rug burn for two months straight.

"You miss me, don't you?" he asked her.

"No."

"Do you think if I hadn't gone back to France, we still would be together?" he asked.

"Kingsley?" Maggie reached across the table and snapped her fingers in his face. "Pay attention. Your club has been closed for a month. Can we talk about how much money you're losing and why?"

"I have plenty of money."

"Do you not care about the people who work for you who lost their jobs?"

"I'm still paying them."

"When did you become so altruistic?"

"I'm a very giving person. Orgasms, beatings, rug burn," he reminded her.

"I'm leaving. When you're ready to discuss your legal situation, call my office." She gathered her things and stood up. Kingsley took her by the wrist and pulled her back down to her chair. As he expected, she didn't put up a fight.

"I'm sorry," he said, moving his chair directly in front of hers. "I am. This is my own fault, which is why I don't want to talk about it. But I need to. I need you."

Maggie exhaled heavily. She took Kingsley's hands in hers. On her left hand she now sported a wedding band. His beautiful, servile, submissive Maggie, who had once spent twenty-four hours straight chained to his bed...was now married. And to a librarian of all things.

"Tell me what's going on. The truth," she said. "I can't help you if you won't tell me what's happening."

"I fell in love," he said.

She smiled at him sympathetically. "The root of all evil. Who is she? Or he?"

"She's a hotel called The Renaissance."

"Your strip club is closed. You're being investigated for tax code violations. And your friend Irina's being deported. And this is all about real estate?"

Kingsley nodded.

"Well," she said. "That's Manhattan for you."

"I want to open a new club," he began. "A club for us. For our kind. The world's largest S and M club. I found a place I wanted, but it's owned by Reverend James Fuller."

"Reverend Fuller? *The* Reverend Fuller? The Reverend Fuller who opens legislative sessions with prayers, held the Bible for the mayor when he was sworn in and baptized the governor's granddaughter? That Reverend Fuller?"

"The same," he said.

"Okay. Tell me everything."

He told her. He told her about Sam and The Renaissance,

about trying to buy it from Fuller and having his offer refused. He told her about the church, the camps and the teenage kids being tortured for being gay. He told her that while he could find another building for his club, he loathed Fuller so much he refused to give up.

"Maggie," he said, raising her hand and kissing it. "This is my city now. This is my home. I can't let Fuller bring his empire into my city. You know what I am. I was sleeping with another boy when I was sixteen. Fuller would have sent me to one of those fucking conversion therapy camps if he'd had the chance. Me and him. And Fuller's not sorry. He only closed the camp because two of the campers made a suicide pact."

"Did they die?" she asked, horrified.

"One died. The other girl lived. Lived and worked for me for a few months."

"Sam?"

"She told me what happened to her at that camp. I spoke to some others who'd gone to his camps. They confirmed everything she said. There's a thirty-two-year-old man in Queens who still has the burn scars from the electrodes on his testicles."

Maggie winced. Once Kingsley had realized Sam had betrayed him, he'd begun doubting everything she'd told him. But when it came to the camps, she'd been telling the truth. The man with the burns hadn't wanted to talk to him at first, not until Kingsley promised him that he'd do everything he could to keep Fuller from opening a church in the city. Kingsley had found him through a lawsuit he'd filed against Fuller and the church seeking restitution for his massive therapy and medical bills. The man hadn't had sex in five years because he couldn't bear to let anyone see the burns on his genitals.

"He's not a man of God," Kingsley said. "I know a man of God, and that man of God makes me think God might be on our side. But Fuller, he's a demagogue. And he's dangerous. And I don't want him in my town."

"I get it," Maggie said. "I can't say I want him or his church in my town, either."

"What about Irina?"

"They've 'lost' her paperwork. INS is as bad as the health department. Someone deep in the works is throwing a wrench into everything I try to do."

"You got her out of jail. That was a good start."

"Getting the charges dropped again was easy. They don't have any evidence. Keeping her from being sent back to Russia will be the hard part. Especially since she'd been twice arrested. She doesn't make a very sympathetic case."

"Her husband bought her, abused her, and she put eye drops in his drink so he'd be too ill to rape her one night and that's not sympathetic?"

"He was never charged for anything. She was. You know how the world works, King."

"I know. I don't want to know, but I know." He made a decision then and there, and he spoke it aloud before he lost his courage. "I can't let Irina be deported. I'll call Fuller. I'll tell him I give up. He wins. I lose."

"Are you sure?" Maggie asked.

He wasn't, but he didn't know what else to do. He could survive without the Möbius. He would beat any charges brought against him for tax code violations. But he'd made Irina a promise to take care of her, and he would keep it.

"I'm sure," he said. He sat back and put his boot on the chair across from him.

Then he kicked the chair so hard it flew ten feet across the floor.

"Kingsley."

He raised his hand to silence her. Maggie looked at him with compassion but said nothing.

"The club, it would have been something special, Mags. You would have loved it there. The Renaissance, it was perfect for it. I've never wanted a place so much in my life. That club was my baby."

"You can still build it. We'll find somewhere else for you. I'll help you any way I can."

Kingsley gave her a tired smile. It was a relief in a way, letting his dream die. He had all the money he'd ever need, all the lovers any man could want... It was fine. Time to move on. Sam had turned on him and he'd been too hurt to even ask her why. Whatever her reasons, he wasn't going to start a fight with her over it. No more causalities. The war was over.

And yet...

"I'm sorry, King," Maggie said, squeezing his hands. "I know surrender isn't your forte."

"If it was only me, I'd fight to the bitter end."

"I know you would. And I think a few years ago you would have kept fighting anyway, collateral damage be damned. You're getting noble in your old age."

"I'm twenty-eight. Same age as your boy-toy."

"Daniel's not my toy. I'm his." Maggie flashed him a seductive grin as she gathered her things again.

"I'll never forgive you for getting married."

"I didn't ask for your forgiveness." She stood up, bent over and gave him the quickest of kisses on the lips. "I'll contact Fuller's attorney for you. You stay away from the man. No more antagonizing him."

"You're enjoying telling me what to do, aren't you?"

"Remember that night you made me suck your cock for two straight hours?"

"That was as much work for me as it was for you."

"Go home," Maggie said. "I'll call you when it's all taken care of."

"I don't want to go home," Kingsley said, leaning his head back and running his fingers through his hair in exhaustion.

"Last call," Maggie said at the door. She pointed to the closed sign. "You don't have to go home, but you can't stay here."

She gave him a wink and walked out. He hadn't been kidding. As much as he loved Chez Kingsley, he was far too restless and worried to go home and sit waiting for Maggie to call him. He didn't want to go home. And he didn't want to be alone. And he didn't want to be sober another second.

He reached behind the bar and grabbed a bottle of Jack Daniel's. He sat it on the counter in front of him. If he closed his eyes he could picture Sam standing behind the bar, the bottle in her hand, flipping and catching it. He didn't want to drink the Jack. He wanted to inhale it, every drop until his heart stopped beating and his brain stopped thinking. And yet in the back of his mind he could hear Søren's voice.

Drinking is for celebrating, not for suicide.

Too bad he didn't have anything to celebrate.

Maybe it was a Catholic feast day or something. He pushed the bottle aside, picked up the phone behind the bar and dialed a number.

"What day is this?" Kingsley asked.

"It's Sunday," Søren said, "which means it's still been eleven years."

"Is it a saint's day or a feast day?"

"It's always a saint's day. It's also Clergy Appreciation Day, according to Diane. Seems to be the only explanation for why my desk is covered in baked goods," Søren said, sounding utterly bewildered.

"Clergy Appreciation Day. That will work. On my way."

"On your way?"

"Yes. I need to get drunk. I'm depressed and miserable and angry. And you said I can't drink unless I'm celebrating something. You and I can celebrate Clergy Appreciation Day together. And you owe me. I destroyed First Presbyterian for you."

"I owe you?"

"*Oui.*"

Søren paused. Kingsley waited.

"The rectory at nine," Søren said.

"You want to celebrate, too?"

"I'm a priest in love with a sixteen-year-old girl. Bring a big bottle. We'll both crawl inside it."

36

KINGSLEY LAY ON THE FLOOR WITH AN ALMOST
empty bottle of pinot noir in his hand and a full glass in the
other. Søren sat at his piano playing a familiar song. He wore
jeans and a black T-shirt, and if Kingsley could ignore the
crosses on the wall and the Bible on the table, he could almost forget Søren was a priest. The lamp-lit room throbbed
in time with the music. The piece ended, and Søren turned
around on the piano bench.

"That's a good song," Kingsley said, raising his glass in a
salute.

"No idea what it is," Søren said. "I heard it while making
hospital visits. I've spent the last week trying to work out the
melody. You know it?"

"Is called 'Purple Rain.'" Sam had that CD. She had a huge
music collection, and he'd come home one day to Prince, the
next day to Nine Inch Nails. He'd caught her and Blaise dancing to something called *The Humpty Hump* one rainy Thursday. "I'll buy you a copy."

"'Purple Rain?' Who's the composer?"

"A man named Prince."

"Prince? Is he an actual prince?"

"I don't think so. But am I an actual king?" Kingsley asked with a disdainful shrug. *"Pfft."*

"Pfft?" Søren repeated. *"Pfft?* Is that French for something?"

"Is French for *pfft,*" Kingsley said. "Where did you get the piano? You are a priest with no money."

Søren picked up his wineglass. "I told my sister Elizabeth how our dear father tried to bribe me into quitting seminary with a Ducati. She said she'd buy me a Steinway if I *did* get ordained. I thought she was joking. The piano showed up in June."

"Ahh…Elizabeth. You still talk to her?"

"She's my sister, not my ex-girlfriend."

"That, *mon ami,* is debatable," Kingsley said, watching the burgundy liquid swirl in his glass. "You are good, you and she? You and her? Fuck, I hate English. *Tu et elle.*"

"We're…better. We try to avoid being in the same room together. Too many memories." He stared into his wine like a red looking glass. "But we speak on the phone once or twice a month."

"How drunk are you?" Kingsley asked, raising his head to look at Søren. The room swam underneath Kingsley, and he could have sworn he heard the ocean. "Am I on a boat?"

"Five."

"I'm on five boats?"

"No, I am five drunk. You are not on a boat."

"Five?"

"On a scale of one to five."

"Clergy Appreciation Day…" Kingsley said. "Why haven't I celebrated this day before?"

"It was only invented last year."

"That would explain it." Kingsley rolled up and crossed his legs. He sat next to a fireplace with no fire in it. There was some symbolism in that, some meaning. If he were sober he might have recognized it. As he was not, he merely considered starting a fire. "Do you have a lighter? I left mine at home."

"You're not allowed to start fires when you're so drunk you think you're on a boat."

Søren stood up and walked to Kingsley. At least Kingsley thought that was what was happening. Søren held out his hand, and Kingsley took it.

"I'm not holding your hand, Kingsley. I'm taking the wine bottle away from you."

"That's much more in character," Kingsley said, taking his hand out of Søren's grip and replacing it with the bottle. "You were never much of a hand-holder."

"I held your hand," Søren said. "Didn't I?"

"You held my wrist," Kingsley corrected him. "And almost broke it."

"The wrist is part of the hand," he said without any hint of remorse. Søren took the bottle into the kitchen.

"I wasn't complaining. I liked it. You can break my wrist whenever you want."

"You're speaking Russian now. Thought I would let you know in case you didn't realize that."

"You're speaking English," Kingsley said.

"So?"

"You're speaking it with a British accent."

"I am?"

"You sound like John Major."

"How much alcohol is in this wine?" Søren asked, examining the bottle.

Kingsley mentally flipped his brain back to English. He hoped.

"What am I speaking now?"

"English," Søren said. "More or less."

"*Bon.* And you can't do that. You can't put pinot in a glass with cabernet sauvignon. That's worse than incest."

Søren ignored him and finished pouring the remnants of his pinot into the glass of cabernet.

"Can I ask in which direction your moral compass points?" Søren asked as he came back into the living room and sat down in his armchair again. Kingsley gestured in the direction his moral compass pointed.

"I'd figured as much," Søren said.

"I like your house," Kingsley said, looking around. "It's like a little wizard's house."

"Thank you. I think?"

"It's little and pretty and you have trees. What's the word? *Cozy.*"

"*Hygge,*" Søren said.

"No Danish," Kingsley said. "Anything but Danish."

"*Ja*, Danish. The word you're looking for is *hygge*. Coziness, comfort and being surrounded by friends and family. *Hygge.*"

"I tried to learn Danish. It's an evil language."

"It's not an easy language to learn," Søren said. "Even other Scandinavians struggle with it. Did they want you to learn it for your job?"

Søren put suspicious emphasis on the word *job*. Kingsley didn't blame him for it.

"*Non.*"

"Why did you try to learn it, then?"

"Because you said something to me in Danish once, and I wanted to know what you said."

"You could have asked."

"Would you have told me if I did?"

"Probably not. I certainly wouldn't have told you the truth," Søren said with a grin over the top of his wineglass. The smile, the sadism and the wine hit Kingsley all at once. He rolled onto his back again and looked up at Søren from the floor.

"You have the most interesting eyes of any man I've ever known."

"Kingsley."

"I want my club, and I can't have it. Give me more alcohol."

"You can have your club. Find another building. And I'm cutting you off."

Kingsley tossed his empty glass into the cold fireplace and relished its shattering. Søren didn't say a word about it.

"This hotel, I love it—beautiful, abandoned, lost. She needs me."

"*She* needs you? Don't you mean *it* needs you?"

Kingsley ignored him. "It's safe, too. I looked at it. Two exits. Easy to watch, easy to guard, easy to protect the people inside."

"Who are you protecting?"

Kingsley paused before answering. In that pause he thought of all the people he'd failed. Mistress Felicia. Lachlan. Irina. Sam.

Himself.

"Mistress Irina. She's my Russian. Her husband fucked her every night, she told me. He said it was his right as her husband. Sick, tired, bleeding—he didn't care. Even if she said no. My Irina. Who works for me. Who I've played with. She's twenty-two years old and her husband..." Kingsley met Søren's eyes. "I was your slave. You remember that?"

"I remember."

"You owned me...body and soul. Do you know why you owned me?"

Søren gazed at him steadily. Kingsley was certain Søren already knew the answer, but still he said, "Tell me why."

"Because I wanted you to own me. And I wanted you to

hurt me. And I wanted you to treat me like your property. And that's what made it right. That's what made it beautiful. Irina's husband treated her like a slave. She didn't want that. She was his slave, and it wasn't right and it wasn't beautiful."

"It's good what you did for her. What you are doing for her."

"You know who introduced me to her, to Irina?"

"Who?" He stood up, took two steps forward, and then sat next to Kingsley on the floor.

"He's a cop. Beat cop. Cooper. Big man, big as a house. He's black, too. Grew up in Harlem. Submissive. Loves submitting to women."

"It's always the ones you least suspect."

"He's terrified his squad will find out what he is. The biggest man I know, scared of other men, of lesser men. It's not right."

"No, it isn't right."

Kingsley turned his head back to face Søren.

"They put electrodes on Sam because she likes girls. They gave her drugs to make her vomit while they strapped her to a chair and forced her to watch lesbian porn. She was sixteen. She still has the burn scars. You want to look me in the eye and say our kind doesn't need protecting?"

"I know we do," Søren said. "And more than that. Eleanor has scars on her arms from where she burned herself. Second-degree burns."

"Someone needs to teach her how to hurt herself the right way."

"Someone does, yes."

"I could teach her," Kingsley said. "I'm good at it. Didn't know I was until I started teaching Irina. I used to do all this dirty work for a living—spying, tracking, guarding important people… I have all these skills. I wanted to put them to good use. You know, for us. We need that in this city. Someone to watch over us. Someone who can protect us. Someone to stand between us and them. What's the word for that?"

"A king," Søren said.

"A king..." Kingsley laughed. "Nice dream."

"You sacrificed your kingdom for your subjects. There is no greater sign of worthiness to be king than the willingness to set aside the crown for the sake of your people."

"A lot of good it does me."

"It doesn't do you any good. That's the point. I would sleep well knowing you were king of us all."

Kingsley narrowed his eyes at him. "You would?"

"I trust you with my secrets, with my life. I'll even trust you with my Eleanor."

"The Virgin Queen?" Kingsley rolled up. "Here? Where?"

Søren put his hand on Kingsley's chest and pushed him on to his back again.

"Behave."

"She's so..." Kingsley began, sighing with exaggerated drunken bliss.

"She's so what?" Søren asked, increasing the pressure on Kingsley's chest.

"Vicious."

Kingsley felt the pressure of Søren's hand on his sternum and tried to ignore how good it felt to be held down so roughly.

"Don't," Søren warned.

"Don't what?"

"Don't enjoy this."

"Too late," Kingsley said. "It would help if you moved your hand off my chest."

"I can't," Søren said.

"Why not?"

"I'm enjoying this."

Kingsley looked at Søren, who took measured breaths through his parted lips.

The heat from Søren's hand permeated through Kingsley's shirt and into his skin. With so much pressure on his chest, Kingsley had trouble taking a full breath. Or was it his intense arousal that set him panting?

"I'm going to stop right now," Søren said. The buttons on Kingsley's shirt bit into his skin.

"You don't have to stop," Kingsley said.

"I have to."

The hand remained. The pressure increased.

"I fucked a blond teenager because he reminded me of you," Kingsley said. "That's my drunken confession for the night."

"I never let you fuck me," Søren said, and Kingsley shivered at hearing Søren swear—a rare and erotic occurrence.

"Which is why I fucked him. What's your drunken confession for the night?"

"If you'd begged hard enough, I might have let you."

Kingsley's eyes went huge. Søren laughed, and then the pressure was gone from Kingsley's chest.

"I said you didn't have to stop." Kingsley rolled into a sitting position again. This time Søren let him up.

"Yes, I did. I wouldn't want to accidentally kill you. If and when I kill you, it will be on purpose."

Kingsley met Søren's eyes.

"You want me, don't you?"

With a groan Søren rolled backward and stretched out on the floor. Kingsley rested his head on Søren's stomach and waited for him to object. He didn't. Without a time machine, without magic, they were teenagers again, hiding in the hermitage at their old school.

"I wanted this club for you," Kingsley confessed. "The truth is, I was building it for you. I wanted you to have somewhere safe you could go and be you. Because I love you," Kingsley said.

"Kingsley—"

"I don't mean I'm in love with you. I'm not," Kingsley said hastily. "But I mean…"

"I know." Søren lightly tugged on Kingsley's hair. "I know what you mean."

"That day in the Rolls when we went to visit your sister, I promised you I would build you a castle, and you said to build you a dungeon instead. Why not both in one? I'll keep the promise someday. Once all this bullshit with Fuller blows over."

"You don't—"

"I know I don't have to. I want to. And not only for you. I want to do this for me. And for all of us."

"'Not what I have, but what I do is my kingdom.' Thomas Carlyle. You are a king when you act like a king, not simply because you have a kingdom."

"I can't believe you quoted a Calvinist."

"Proof of how drunk I am."

"They're nice words, but it's all a dream. I'm not a king. I don't have a kingdom. I don't have subjects. I don't have—"

"I'll be your subject," Søren said.

Kingsley rolled his eyes.

"You're not subject to anyone," Kingsley said. "You only pretend to be for job security."

Søren took a deep breath, one that Kingsley could hear and feel.

"I, Father Marcus Lennox Stearns, priest of the Society of Jesus, son of Lord Marcus Augustus Stearns, sixth baron Stearns, do swear that I will be faithful and bear true allegiance to His Majesty Kingsley Theophilé Boissonneault, his heirs and successors, according to law. So help me God."

Kingsley sat up and turned around. He looked down at Søren still lying on the floor.

"That's the oath to the British monarch," Kingsley said.

"I'm American," Søren said. "I can make it to whomever I want. I made it to you. And since the kings of old were always anointed by the high priest…"

Søren sat up and took the corkscrew off the side table. Without flinching or blinking he pressed the end of it into his palm, breaking his own skin as easily as popping a cork. He let a few drops of blood fall into his glass. Kingsley held out his hand, palm up.

"You are in the mood to play with fire tonight, aren't you?" Søren asked.

"Felicia doesn't do blood-play. I miss it. So do you," Kingsley said.

Søren's eyes flashed at him, but he said nothing. He took Kingsley by the wrist, thrust his palm up and pushed the sharp tip of the corkscrew into his skin. As drunk as he was, Kingsley hardly felt a thing. But Søren clearly felt something. His pupils dilated and his breathing quickened. But he sat the corkscrew aside, flipped Kingsley's hand over and let a few drops of blood mingle with his in the wineglass. Søren then dipped his two fingers into the blood and wine. With two wet red fingertips, he anointed Kingsley's forehead with the wine, then touched his lips and the center of each palm.

Kingsley felt something strange as Søren touched him with his wine-red fingertips. Even drunk, wasted even, he felt power. Power and the weight of responsibility.

"I still don't have a kingdom."

"You will," Søren said. "Someday you will. I have faith in you. Do you?"

Kingsley looked at his hands, the red stains in the center of his palms.

"If you do, I do."

Søren took Kingsley's face in his hands and touched his lips to his forehead. It wasn't a kiss so much as a blessing. To be kissed by Søren was to be blessed. Søren rose up on steady feet.

"Where are you going?" Kingsley asked.

"To bed."

"Can I come with you?"

"Yes."

"Will it be like old times?"

"Yes."

It was indeed like old times. Søren took the bed and ordered Kingsley to take the floor. But better one night on Søren's floor than a thousand nights elsewhere.

"Can I at least have a—"

A pillow landed on Kingsley's face.

"Merci," Kingsley said from underneath the pillow.

"Velkommen."

"No Danish," Kingsley said. "Not unless you tell me what you said."

"I said 'you're welcome.'"

"Not now. I meant in the car."

"You seem to be getting more drunk and not less. What car?"

"The Rolls Royce we took to see your sister that day back at school. Do you remember?"

"Yes, I think I would remember the day I met Claire for the first time."

"Do you remember what you said to me in the car while we were—"

"I remember," Søren said, his voice so low it was barely audible. But Kingsley heard it.

"What did you say to me?"

"I said *'Jeg vil være din family. Jeg er din familie.'"*

"What does it mean?"

"It means," Søren said with a tired sigh. "I want to be your family. I will be your family."

"You married my sister three weeks later."

"I wonder why."

"Søren—"

"It's ancient history," Søren said. "Let it go."

"But—"

"Go to sleep, Kingsley. Please."

If Søren hadn't added the *please* at the end, Kingsley wouldn't have gone to sleep. But something in the way Søren said "please," the way another man might say "mercy," silenced Kingsley's need to keep talking. Ancient history. Let the dead bury the dead. Instead of digging up the past, Kingsley slept.

When Kingsley awoke it was five in the morning. He was sore all over, his whole body. Now he remembered why he'd cut back on the drinking. Next time he decided to pass out at Søren's, he'd do it on the couch, not the floor.

He called for his car, splashed water on his face and threw up on principle. Wouldn't be a good binge without a little purge to top it all off. After his self-induced sickness and drinking half a gallon of water, he felt human, more or less.

Kingsley found Søren still asleep, lying on his side, the white sheet pulled to his stomach. In his lifetime Kingsley had fucked a thousand people, and he'd yet to meet anyone—man or woman—who surpassed Søren in sheer physical beauty. Unable to stop himself, Kingsley crawled across the bed and brought his face to Søren's neck. He inhaled and in one breath smelled new snow in the midnight air, ice on pine tree branches, the world frozen still and silent.

Søren pinched Kingsley's nose.

"I thought you were asleep," Kingsley said in a pained and nasal voice.

"I was asleep until a Frenchman started sniffing my hair." Søren released his nose.

"You smell like snow."

"Snow has no scent."

"It's like the winter all over your skin."

"I do not trust the sensory perceptions of a man who, not five hours ago, thought he was on a boat."

"Has no one ever told you that you smell like that?"

"Elizabeth mentioned something about it a long time ago. And someone else. Recently."

"Who?"

"Eleanor."

Eleanor. The Virgin Queen. It comforted Kingsley to know Eleanor could smell the winter on Søren's skin. It seemed portentous somehow—Elizabeth, Kingsley, Eleanor—the three who'd loved Søren, the three who'd been or would be his lovers. Maybe Søren was right about this girl. Maybe she was the one they'd dreamed of all those years ago. Kingsley dipped his head and pressed a kiss on to Søren's right shoulder. He kissed Søren's shoulder blade, his neck, the back of his neck, tasting the snow on his skin. Kingsley kissed his way down the center of Søren's back as he trailed his fingers over his rib cage.

"What do you think you are doing?" Søren asked.

"I'm trying to find out what a priest sleeps in," Kingsley said as he slipped his hand under the sheet.

Søren caught his hand and held it in a vicious, viselike grip. "This priest sleeps in a bed."

"You're going to break my wrist," Kingsley said, not the least bothered by the prospect. The pain from Søren's grip sobered him up, cleared his thinking and aroused him.

Søren tightened his grip and Kingsley winced. Nice to

know Søren hadn't been lying—the wolf was still there. Søren wasn't less dangerous at all. Kingsley just wasn't afraid anymore.

"Break it," Kingsley said.

Søren's grip tightened even more. But only slightly and then he let go.

"You didn't have to stop," Kingsley said. "You can break me all you want."

"I might be tempted to play with you if you had any sense of self-preservation whatsoever."

"Self-preservation is for the weak. I loved getting destroyed by you."

"You remember high school much differently than I do," Søren said. "I'd killed someone at my last school and was terrified I'd do it again. And then you came along and practically asked me to kill you."

"I didn't ask you to kill me," Kingsley said. "I begged you."

"And you wonder why I prefer to play with people who have limits."

"You know you miss me," Kingsley said, running his hand down Søren's side from his shoulder blade to his waist. He felt every muscle in Søren's body tense, and Kingsley lifted his hand.

"Did that hurt?" Kingsley asked, confused by Søren's sudden recoil.

"No, do it again."

Warily Kingsley placed his hand flat on Søren's back again and ran it down his body.

"Again?" Kingsley asked.

"Yes."

Kingsley knelt at Søren's side and, with both hands, rubbed his back from neck to hip. Slowly the tension eased. Søren had a beautiful back—long, lean and with broad shoulders etched with taut muscle. With his eyes closed, Kingsley ran his fingers down the line of Søren's spine. Søren released a sigh of pleasure.

"You like this?" Kingsley asked.

"I do."

"Why did you never make me give you back rubs?"

"I didn't know I liked them until now." Søren stretched out on his stomach and turned his head on the pillow to face Kingsley. "I was always wary of being touched. Which is fine. Apart from handshakes, priests are never touched."

Kingsley's heart clenched in sympathy. He forgot sometimes how much damage Søren's childhood had done to him. One night in their hermitage back at school, Søren had confessed to him everything that had happened between him and his sister when he was eleven and she twelve. No wonder Søren had shied away from being touched when even simple pleasures were tainted with shame.

"But this...this doesn't bother you?"

"No," Søren said. "But stay above the waist."

Kingsley laughed. "Yes, sir."

With more force now and confidence, Kingsley massaged Søren's back. It was almost better than sex, knowing he was the first person to ever touch Søren like this. Almost.

"You know," Kingsley began, "when I went to see your friend Magdalena in Rome, she insisted on telling my fortune."

"She did that to me, too."

"You know what she said?"

"I'm afraid to ask," Søren said. "But I'm sure you'll tell me even if I don't."

"She said you and I would be lovers again."

"Well, fortune-tellers make their living telling us what we want to hear," Søren said in a pointed tone. "Thus creating the likelihood of the prophecy coming true because of its self-fulfilling nature. We want it be true, so we work to make it happen."

"Is that so? What did she tell you that you wanted to hear?"

Søren exhaled heavily, and Kingsley felt the breath moving through Søren's chest and back.

"Among many other things, she told me I would have a son someday. I had to remind Magdalena that the vow of celibacy made this an unlikely occurrence."

"What did she say to that?"

"She said it would happen by the grace of God. Whatever that means."

"I think it means you want a family, too."

Søren rolled over on to his back, and Kingsley kept his hands to himself, a show of self-restraint he felt he deserved a medal for. If given permission, Kingsley would have spent the entire day kissing and touching every inch of Søren's body, which was without flaw but for the small round crater on his upper arm where he'd gotten vaccinated for smallpox as a child. Such a little thing, but it reminded Kingsley that Søren was human. All too easy to forget sometimes.

"I have a family," Søren said, looking Kingsley in the eyes.

A horn honked discreetly outside the house.

"That's for me," Kingsley said, wishing he hadn't called the car. He wanted to stay with Søren and talk. Talk? Yes, even more than pain and sex, he wanted to talk. But they had plenty of time for that. The rest of their lives. Søren had pledged his fealty to Kingsley, and nothing would tear them apart ever again.

"Goodbye, Kingsley," Søren said. Kingsley pulled away. Reluctantly. Very reluctantly.

He left Søren's bed. But before Kingsley walked out of the room, he looked back.

"Did you mean it?" Kingsley asked. "The oath? That you would sleep well knowing I was a king?"

"Vive le roi," Søren said and rolled on to his stomach.

Long live the king.

"Did you mean the other thing you said?"

"Which was?"

"Your confession?"

Søren adjusted his pillow, straightened his sheet and settled down back into his bed.

"I suppose we'll never know, will we?" Søren asked.

Kingsley decided to take that as a "maybe."

"Did you find the gift I left you?" Søren asked.

"Gift? No. What gift?"

"You'll find it." Søren rolled over on to his stomach and pulled the sheets up to his neck—by far the most sadistic thing he'd ever done in Kingsley's estimation.

On the drive back to the city Kingsley heard Søren's words echoing in his mind. *Vive le roi.* If Søren, the one man on earth Kingsley respected and loved with all his heart and all his strength and all his soul…if that man could swear his allegiance and loyalty to Kingsley, then how could he doubt his worthiness to be a king to their kind? If Søren was for him, who could be against him?

By the time he arrived at his town house, Kingsley had made a decision. Fuller or not, Renaissance or not, Sam or not, he would build his kingdom. He would find a place, a different place, a place he and Søren and all their kind could go and be safe and be themselves, and the rest of the world would be locked outside in the cold.

He wouldn't waste another day. He would do it for Søren because Kingsley would do anything for Søren. And he would do it for himself because a king must have a kingdom.

He would have started right that second if it weren't for

the alcohol lingering in his system. He should sleep more, wake up with his head on straight. His kingdom deserved his best, and so he would give it his best. He wouldn't even drink again until the night the club opened. He still had the bottle of champagne he had bought from Sam. He and Søren would drink it. It wouldn't be right, drinking it without Sam. But he would do it anyway, no matter how much he missed her, no matter how much he wished she was back, no matter how much he wanted to hear her voice.

Kingsley stepped inside his bedroom, turned on his lamp and pulled the covers down on his bed.

From behind him he heard a voice.

"Look what the pussy dragged in."

He spun around, suddenly sober.

"Sam?"

37

"DON'T KICK ME OUT," SHE SAID, HOLDING UP HER hands in surrender. "Please."

Kingsley couldn't quite believe his eyes. He gazed at her in shock, more curious than furious.

"Kicking you out was the last thing on my list of an infinite number of things to do right now. Asking you what you're doing here was the first."

"I stopped by the Möbius," she said, her words halting and nervous. "I wanted to say hi to Holly and the other girls. It was shut down. I called Holly, and she told me what happened."

"You happened," Kingsley reminded her, torn between fury at seeing her in his house and relief at simply seeing her again.

"I know," Sam said. "But, please, hear me out."

"I'm listening."

Sam took a breath. "I heard about Irina. They said she got arrested again, and they're going to deport her."

"My attorney's waving the white flag for me. I surrendered. But that should be enough to get Irina's paperwork un-lost."

"I can't believe you gave up."

"What choice did I have?"

"You could have not given up and let everyone suffer," she said, taking a step forward.

"What kind of king would I be if I let my people suffer for my mistakes?"

"You might not believe me, but you have to trust me." She ran her hands through her hair. She didn't have a suit on now. She wore jeans, a white shirt and black suspenders. She'd gotten her hair cut, and now she looked even more boyish than before. Boyish and beautiful as always. "I know what it's like to take the fall for someone else's sins."

"What's that supposed to mean?"

"It means you should get ready. Fuller's coming over here, and you and I are going to have a talk with him."

"Why? You have more information about me you want to sell him?"

"No. Because I want to destroy him as much as you. And we can."

"How?" Kingsley asked.

Sam reached into a bag at her feet and pulled something out.

"You were right, King." She held up a VHS videotape and smiled. "There's always something. And I found it."

38

SAM DIDN'T TELL KINGSLEY ANYTHING ELSE, AND IT was the greatest test of his faith not to press her into spilling all her secrets. Instead, she marched right to his office as if she owned it, turned on the television and put the tape in the VCR. She didn't hit Play.

"You're not going to talk to me?" Kingsley asked her. "You're not going to explain yourself?"

"The tape will explain it," Sam said. "And you have to trust me."

"I don't have to do anything but die and pay taxes, and I think I've found a way around the second one."

"Please, King. Let me do this for you. You did so much for me."

"You get one chance," he said. "One."

"One is all I need. I promise. I won't let you down again."

Before Kingsley could ask another question, Blaise opened the door and ushered Reverend Fuller inside. She shut the door behind him and made herself scarce. He didn't blame her.

"What's this about?" Fuller asked. He had on a suit and tie and looked as pastoral as Kingsley had ever seen him. "I was told you had something for me, Mr. Edge. Something I needed to see."

"Don't ask me," Kingsley said, knowing Fuller expected Kingsley to attempt to bribe him. Fuller likely had a wire on right now, recording everything. "I don't know anything. Ask her."

Reverend Fuller looked her up and down.

"You called me, didn't you?" Fuller asked. "Have we met?"

"Nope," she said. "But your wife and I have."

"You know my wife? How?" Fuller asked, warily.

Sam picked up the remote control.

"Close your eyes, King," Sam said.

Although he didn't want to, Kingsley did as ordered. And as soon as his eyes were closed, Sam must have hit the Play button because the next sound he heard was a woman—not Sam—having an orgasm.

Kingsley burst into laughter. He should have known.

"Turn that filth off," Fuller demanded.

"Filth?" Sam repeated. "That's your wife. And me. We aren't filthy. We'd just gotten out of the shower. She loves showering with me."

"Turn it off."

Sam hit the stop button. Kingsley opened his eyes. He would have kissed the girl, but he decided to save that for later.

"You seduced my wife and videotaped it?" Fuller asked, his hands curling into angry fists.

"Someone sent a goon to my apartment offering me money to rat on Kingsley. I asked to meet who Mr. Goon was working for. Turns out it was your wife. We had a nice long talk about you and her."

"You fucked Lucy Fuller," Kingsley said, still laughing. "You and your fetish for straight girls."

"Straight girls? Not this time," Sam said. "Lucy Fuller's a lesbian."

"My wife is not a lesbian."

"And yet you two haven't had sex in ten years," Sam said.

"She told you that?" Fuller asked, horror-stricken.

"Ten years?" Kingsley said. "I barely made it ten days. How do you do it?"

"Lucy says he masturbates all the time. She showed me his porn collection. He confiscated dirty mags from the kids at his church and keeps them for himself."

"You bitch, how dare you—"

Kingsley took a threatening step forward. Fuller's face was red, his jaw clenched. He looked like a man on the verge of a meltdown. Kingsley loved it.

"Watch your language," Kingsley said. "There are ladies present." He turned around and looked at Sam. "How did you know?"

"That night in your bed when I told you about me and Faith at camp...I hadn't thought about that in ten years. I didn't want to think about it. But Faith had said something I hadn't forgotten. She said she'd been sleeping with her youth pastor's wife, and the husband had caught them in bed together. Wife gets to stay in the ministry. Faith got sent off to camp, to die. WTL runs the camps. I had a hunch—turns out I was right. Faith Spencer went to WTL's first church. She was in your youth group," Sam said to Fuller. "Your wife killed my friend."

"Your friend killed herself."

"It was the only way out for us. But not for your wife. She gets to live in luxury, raking in millions of dollars by telling women how to live their lives. She stands in your pulpit and calls us all demon-possessed sinners. And meanwhile, she's sleeping with every little queer girl that crosses her path."

"Lucy is a very ill woman." Fuller lifted his chin. "I'm trying to get her help. But she is not a lesbian."

"Want to watch the rest of the tape? She seems to think she's a lesbian."

"You burn that tape and you burn it right now." Fuller marched over to the television.

"Go for it," Sam said. "I made copies. Dozens of them."

"Can I have one?" Kingsley asked.

Sam glared at him.

Fuller ripped the tape from the VCR and broke it into two pieces.

"Do whatever you want to it," Sam said. "There's more where that came from. Your lovely wife and I have been in bed together quite a few times by now. I've got a tape from my apartment, one from your bedroom in your house, one from a hotel... I like the hotels. Easier to hide the camera."

Fuller dropped the tape to the floor and stomped on it.

"Are you done with your temper tantrum?" Kingsley asked.

Fuller looked at him with a murderous gleam in his eyes.

"What do you want?" Fuller asked.

"I want The Renaissance," Kingsley asked. "We'll make it a fair deal, and I'll pay you half what you paid to the city."

"Done."

"And I want all your camps to close," Kingsley said. "All of them. Every last one of them. You are out of the conversion business."

"Those camps make us a lot of money," Fuller said. His every word sounded pained and restrained. If he dropped dead of a heart attack on this floor right now, Kingsley wouldn't have been surprised.

"I know," Sam said. "Lucy admits to that, too. She's quite a talker when you get some booze into her and give her a few orgasms. She loves being fisted. Want to see? I can go get another copy of the tape."

"That won't be necessary." Fuller took a deep breath. "Fine.

You have a deal. I close the camps and you buy The Renaissance. If a word of this gets out, it's over. For both of you."

"Are you threatening me? A man whose wife hasn't let him fuck her in ten years, and I'm supposed to be scared of you?" Kingsley asked.

"You piece of shit." Fuller raised his arm to throw a punch, but Kingsley caught him easily by the wrist.

"Let me go," Fuller said, struggling against him.

"A Catholic priest taught me this trick," Kingsley said, squeezing Fuller's wrist until he felt bone. "I'm more Christian than you'd think."

"Catholics aren't real Christians," Fuller spat back.

"Oh, no," Sam said. "You really shouldn't have said that."

Kingsley twisted his hand and broke Fuller's wrist. The snapping sound was music to his ears.

Fuller screamed like a demon was clawing its way out of his soul.

"I am so hard right now," Kingsley said with the biggest smile on his face he could ever remember wearing. "This must be how that blond monster feels all the time."

Sam stepped in front of Fuller and stared down at him as he cradled his broken wrist against his stomach.

"You're vile," Sam said. "You tell lies to children and make them think they're evil. And this whole time you're the evil one living with someone evil who is doing evil every day. Faith Spencer was in love with your wife, and your wife sent her to hell for it."

"I told you. She's a sick woman. She needs help and prayer and—"

"She is sick," Sam said. "But not because she's gay. She's a sexual predator who preyed on a confused teenage girl at your church. You both make me sick. Now get out of here. You don't deserve to be in Kingsley's house, to breathe Kingsley's air. Or mine. You call your lawyer, you draw up the papers, you close the camps—and you sell us The Renaissance, and you do it all in one week or every television news station, every newspaper, every Christian radio show will get a copy of that tape. Even the motherfucking *700 Club.*"

"Go to hell," Fuller said to Sam.

"I've already been to hell," Sam said. "That's where I met your wife."

39

WITHOUT ANOTHER WORD, FULLER STORMED OUT OF Kingsley's office, still cradling his limp arm.

Kingsley exhaled. Then he laughed. Then he turned to Sam.

Sam bent over a trash can by his desk. He could tell Sam was close to throwing up. Kingsley brought her a glass of water and waited.

"Sorry," she said, taking the water from him. "Fucking someone you don't want to fuck and pretending to enjoy is…"

"Hell," Kingsley said. "I've done it, too."

"It's okay. I closed my eyes and thought of Blaise."

Kingsley cupped the back of her neck. "Sam, are you…"

She waved her hand. "I'll be fine. I am fine."

"What did you come back here for?" Kingsley asked. Sam stood up and faced him. "Why did you do this for me? I fired you."

"I ignored that," she said, and made a valiant attempt at a smile. "I was always working for you, even when I was taking money from Lucy Fuller. I didn't plan on you catching me in the act, but it worked out for the best. After you fired me, that convinced Lucy I was on her side. I was never on her side. Never."

She met Kingsley's eyes.

"I can't believe you did this for me," Kingsley said.

"And me. And Faith. And every kid at those camps."

"It worked. You shut them down. Not me, you."

"Wish I could have done it years ago," Sam said. "Maybe Faith would still be alive."

Kingsley took her gently by the arm and pulled her to him. She cried in his arms, and he let her cry. She'd earned her tears and his trust. Her small body shook against his, and he kissed her hair. Soon she'd cried it out and was calm again.

"I would never have asked you to sleep with her," Kingsley said. "I would never have let you."

"I know," Sam said. "That's why I didn't tell you I was doing it. You would have ordered me not to."

"I wouldn't have let her near you."

"It's okay, I promise. It wasn't fun," she said. "But what's done is done. And now...I guess we win."

"We win," Kingsley said. "And we should celebrate."

Sam shook her head. "No celebrating. We have to work. The club is opening in November, and we've done nothing for it."

"Not nothing. We have an entire staff ready," Kingsley said.

"Do we have our two dominatrixes?"

"Felicia and Irina. Check."

"Male submissive?"

"Justin. Check."

"Female submissive?"

"Luka. Check."

"Bouncer and bodyguard?"

"Lachlan. Check."

"I guess we have everything. Wait. No. Male dominant?"

"Check."

"Who?"

"Me." Kingsley pointed at himself.

"You?"

"Why not?" he asked.

"I think it's the best idea I've heard all day."

He reached into his desk drawer and pulled out Sam's clipboard. He presented it to her like a king awarding a sword to his knight-errant.

With a smile and still shaking hands, she took it from him. With a flourish she made a check mark on the page.

"Check." She grinned up at him. "Now we just need a name. Any ideas?"

"I'm too tired to think of a name right now. I slept on the priest's floor last night. We got very drunk."

"You and the padre got smashed? What was the occasion?"

"Clergy Appreciation Day."

"That's a thing?"

"Apparently so. Got drunk with a priest last night. Broke a televangelist's wrist this morning. My new favorite holiday."

"I think you did more than break his wrist. Did he get blood on you?"

"Blood? Where?"

Sam pointed at Kingsley's stomach. A bloodstain the size of a quarter marred his otherwise pristine white shirt.

"That's not Fuller's blood," Kingsley said, lifting up his shirt. "It's mine."

"What the hell is that?" Sam dropped to her knees in front of him. "Jesus, you have something carved on your stomach."

"I do?"

"It looks like an eight inside a circle. Did Mistress Felicia do that?"

Kingsley looked down and saw a small curved line carved into his skin a few inches above his groin.

Kingsley laughed. "That priest—I'll kill him."

"What is it?"

"He signed me," Kingsley said. "I told Søren last night that Felicia doesn't do blood-play. He must have cut me while I was asleep. How much did I drink that I slept through that?"

A lot. He'd drunk a lot last night.

"Signed you?"

"This is how he signs his name," Kingsley said, pointing at the shallow cut. "It's the first two letters of his name. An *S* with an *O* around it and a slash through it."

"Well, it looks like an eight inside a circle."

An eight and a circle... The image stirred a memory. A rare good one.

"Have you ever read *The Divine Comedy*?" Kingsley asked. "The poem by Dante?"

"No," Sam said, coming to her feet. "Any good?"

"We were assigned to read it in school. One night in bed, Søren read to me from the *Inferno* in the original Italian." Kingsley had used Søren's stomach as a pillow while Søren read out loud to him in mellifluous musical Italian. "One of the rare better-than-sex moments of my life."

"Sounds like it."

"The eighth circle was where those who abused their power were punished. Simonists specifically."

"Who were they?"

"Corrupt priests."

Sam grinned mischievously at him.

She flipped the sheet of paper on her clipboard over, drew a curvy *S*, put an *O* around the *S,* and drew a slash threw it. It looked like an elegant slanted eight inside a circle.

"Wouldn't this look good on a house collar tag?" Sam asked.

"If we call the club The 8th Circle as a joke on the priest..."

"What?"

"I don't know," Kingsley said, happier than he'd been in a

long time. Happy to have his dream coming true but far happier to have Sam back with him where she belonged. "But I can't wait to find out."

40

November

THE RENOVATIONS TOOK THIRTY-SIX DAYS AND COST one-point-two million dollars. Kingsley handed over the credit card to Sam with his eyes closed and said, "Do what you have to do to make it perfect. Don't show me the bills." On opening night, Kingsley took Sam by the hand and kissed the center of her palm. She'd let him outshine her tonight. While she wore a basic three-piece pin-striped suit, Kingsley was dressed in Sam's favorite of all his new suits—an Edwardian-style formal tuxedo—vest, tails and an open collar. And of course, the boots she'd given him.

"It's perfect," he said as they stood at the ledge of the balcony overlooking the empty play pit below. "*Parfait.* And you did all of it."

"You paid for it."

"You made my dream come true," he said. "Worth every penny. It's everything I wanted and more."

"I have to show you the best part." Sam took him by the hand and led him past the bar to a door at the back. They walked through a large storage room that led to a hallway that led to another hallway that led downstairs and to the hall of the masters.

"What is this?" Kingsley asked as she stopped at a door—second to last one on the right.

"Your playroom." She pulled out a key chain and unlocked the door. She left Kingsley standing on the threshold while she stepped in and lit a lamp. "What do you think?"

Kingsley's eyes widened as he stepped into the room and looked around. Sheer white fabric hung over the walls and divided the bed from a side room full of kink accoutrements. Silk-covered sofas and pillows lay about in artful arrangements.

"It looks like..." Kingsley began.

"I told the decorator to think Lawrence of Arabia, Omar Sharif or a desert king. He did good."

More than good, the room was magnificent. No one could walk into this room and not immediately want to lie atop the bed with its blue, red and gold pillows and offer up their body and soul to the master of the house.

"Sam, I can't..." Kingsley's voice trailed off. "How did you know I loved Lawrence of Arabia?"

"I called the padre and asked him for ideas. He said something about T. E. Lawrence being kinky?"

"He did love a good flogging, I hear."

"I have one more little tiny gift for you." She pulled it from her pocket and put it in his hand.

"A key chain?" he asked, holding up the silver fleur-de-lis.

"You need a key chain for your keys to the kingdom. I had this one made for you. But not only the key chain. There's a key on it which goes to a lock."

"What's the lock?" he asked, finding the tiny key.

"This one." Sam grinned as she pointed to the little silver lock that hung over the top button on her suit trousers. "I told you I put a lock on my pants. I wasn't kidding."

"And you gave me the key?" Gone was all his cynicism, all his sarcasm.

"If you still want me, I'm willing to try. I also wasn't kidding when I said if I had to be with any man, it would be you."

"Sam…" He wrapped his fingers tight around the key chain. "Of course I want you."

"We have an hour before the club opens. I can't promise I'm going to be any good at it." Her voice shook, but she never lost her smile. "But I know a lot of queer girls who fuck guys. They say it's fun. A fun change of pace. And it's you, and I love being with you, so why not?"

Kingsley opened his hand again and traced the edges of the fleur-de-lis key chain.

"Why not?" he repeated. "I can give you one reason why not. Because you're perfect the way you are, Sam. And I love you the way you are. And you never have to change for me. And I hate to admit it and never tell him I said this, but Søren is right. I have all the lovers I need. What I could use is a partner and a friend and a second-in-command."

"I am your partner and your friend and your second-in-command already."

"Then I have all I need." Kingsley pressed the keys to his chest over his heart. "But don't think I'm not tempted. But I also know you're a little relieved, aren't you? Hmm?" He tapped her under the chin.

Sam winced. "A little," she admitted. "But also sad. Sort of. I wanted to do something special for you."

"You gave me my kingdom. You gave me all of this." He swept his hand around the room, the perfect room she'd created for him.

Sam took two steps forward and wrapped her arms around him. He held her close and tight and tears escaped her eyes.

"Can I tell you something crazy and inappropriate while standing in the middle of your new kink playroom?" she asked.

"Please," he said.

"I think you'll make an amazing father someday."

"I think that is the best thing to say in the middle of this room," Kingsley said. "If I'm going to be a father someday, the child will likely be conceived in here."

He gazed once more around the room. It was everything he could ever ask for. Almost everything.

"There is one thing I'd like to do in this room before we open. With you. I think I need to get it out of my system."

"Anything," she said. "I'm your girl."

Kingsley put the keys in his suit pants pockets and took a deep breath. He reached out and wrapped one arm around her shoulders, the other arm around her waist. He dipped her back as if they were in an old Hollywood movie and kissed her. And Sam, God bless her—Sam kissed him back as if her life depended on it. He kissed her mouth, she kissed his tongue. He bit her bottom lip. She bit his top. She ravished his mouth and he ravished her in return. He raided her, plundered her and sundered her. The world turned to light and heat, and if he opened his eyes and found himself standing in the middle of the desert with the sun blazing down on to them, he wouldn't be surprised, the kiss was that shockingly, knee-knockingly, world-rockingly hot.

And then it was over.

Kingsley stood her up on her feet and took a step back.

"Bon," he said, and straightened his jacket. "I needed that. *Merci.*"

Sam blinked a few times.

"You are very welcome." She smoothed down her vest, feigned a faint and Kingsley hauled her back to her feet. "Thank you, Captain." She gave him a jaunty salute.

"No fainting."

"That was a helluva kiss. Maybe I'll just go lie down until it's time to open the club. Maybe over here on the bed with my hand down my pants." She started for his bed, but Kingsley grabbed her by the arm.

"Later," he said. "I have a gift for you, too."

"A gift? For me?"

"Pour toi, oui."

"What is it?" Sam asked as Kingsley led her out into the hallway.

"Nothing much," Kingsley said. "A small token of my affection. You went above and beyond the call of duty. I thought you should be rewarded."

"You already pay me to do the best job in the world. I don't need anything else from you."

"You need this."

"If it's big I'm going to feel shitty," Sam said. "I only gave you a key chain. I didn't even give you one of those World's Greatest Boss coffee mugs. I should do that. I'm going to get you a World's Greatest Boss coffee mug."

Kingsley unlocked a door—an all-white door with an all-white doorknob.

"Your gift," Kingsley said and opened the door.

Sitting on the white bed in the middle of the room was Blaise in a gold satin cocktail dress in all her Gilda-esque glory.

"Kingsley asked me if I'd spend a little time with you tonight," Blaise said, giving Sam a seductive red-lipped grin. "I can't ever tell that man no, can I, monsieur?"

"Oh, Kingsley..." Sam rested her head on his chest for a moment and sighed. "There aren't enough coffee mugs in the world."

41

KINGSLEY STROLLED THROUGH THE CLUB, THE 8TH Circle. He looked in every room, inspected every corner. His club. His kingdom. His home. He stood alone in the hallway behind the balcony bar and listened. The doors had been opened, the people had arrived, the party had only begun. Everywhere he heard voices, laughter, erotic whispers and murmurs and secrets. Alone with no one to see him, he smiled. He'd done it. They'd done it, he and Sam. Only took nine months, two breakups and one physical assault on a televangelist, but they'd done it.

He heard footsteps behind him and smelled something cold, clean and pure in the air.

"How's the Virgin Queen?" Kingsley asked, turning around to face Søren. "Did you have your talk with her and tell her to knock before coming into my house next time?"

Kingsley had thrown a pre-opening night party at his town house a few nights ago and a certain sixteen-year-old girl had wandered into the middle of it.

"In her defense," Søren said, "Eleanor was stranded in the city and came to your house for help. I'm afraid she saw a few things that can't be unseen."

"She saw me."

"That's what I was referring to," Søren said. "Did she say anything to you?"

"No, but I think she wanted to claw my eyes out," Kingsley said, recalling how he'd come face-to-face with the black-haired, fire-eyed sixteen-year-old minx on his staircase a few days earlier.

"She wants to claw my eyes out now," Søren said. "I'm not her favorite person at the moment."

"Did you punish her for crashing my party?"

"She's being punished, yes."

"You beat her?"

"Worse. I grounded her."

Kingsley laughed, but Søren, he only smiled. A pained smile.

"She'll fit in here someday," Kingsley said. He wondered if he'd made a mistake all those months ago when Søren made his offer, his offer that the three of them could be together, lovers, if Kingsley could promise to be faithful to them. He'd said no for two reasons—he hadn't believed the offer was real. And he hadn't seen Eleanor yet. Ah, *c'est la vie.* He'd still have Eleanor someday—Søren had promised. And he had the rest of the city to seduce until then.

"She will," Søren said. "I look forward to bringing her here."

"We could always use an extra dominatrix."

Søren glared at him.

"Don't look at me like that," Kingsley said. "If that girl is a submissive, I'm a virgin."

"She'll submit to me."

"You're going to regret you ever met that girl. She's a tiger in a kitten's body."

Søren smiled enigmatically. "I always liked cats."

Kingsley only laughed. Time would tell what sort of beast

Søren's little kitten would grow into. Whatever she turned into, Kingsley could already feel her claws in him.

"Do you like it? The club?" Kingsley asked, glancing around.

"Does it matter if I do or not?" Søren asked, amusement in his eyes.

"No," Kingsley said. "I love it."

"So do I."

"Thank God," Kingsley said, sagging against the wall with relief. "I built it for you. This is your playground. You'll be safe here. I'll make sure of it."

"I know you will. I trust you."

Kingsley stood up straighter and took a breath.

"I have much sinning to do tonight. No time to dally," he said, and headed for the door.

"Kingsley?"

He turned around.

"I'm proud of you," Søren said.

Kingsley looked at him and asked the question that had been plaguing him for nine months.

"Why didn't you come to me sooner?" Kingsley asked. "You knew where I lived, where I was."

"I wanted to," Søren said. "I knew you could find me as easily as I could find you. When you didn't, I assumed you didn't want to find me."

"I thought the same thing," Kingsley said, "that you didn't want to find me. It's good then that your Virgin Queen got herself arrested."

"The Lord works in mysterious ways."

"You won't leave me again, will you?" Kingsley asked.

Søren sighed.

"You keep forgetting..."

"Right. I left you."

"Will you leave me again?" Søren asked. "Even if we never…"

"No," Kingsley said. "You're right. I have all the lovers I could want. It's friends I need."

"What about family?"

"I need that even more."

Søren walked to him, put his arm around him and embraced him like an equal, like a friend. It wasn't what he wanted from Søren, but he knew it was what he needed.

"I'm still going to try to get you into bed," Kingsley said as he pulled back and straightened his black tailcoat.

"Do your worst," Søren said with all his old, cold arrogance, and Kingsley decided then and there he would get Søren back into bed with him even if it killed him.

And considering it was Søren, it might.

Kingsley and Søren walked through the door and found Sam behind the bar.

"Check this out, King," Sam said. She lined up three champagne flutes. She poured the champagne into the flutes. Once empty she tossed the bottle in a spin and caught it by the neck.

"Tom Cruise can kiss my ass," she said in triumph.

"Very good," Søren said. When he reached for his champagne glass, Sam dipped her head and sniffed his arm.

"Sam?" Søren asked.

"Just a second." Sam pulled back Søren's sleeve and pressed her nose to his wrist. She inhaled deeply. Kingsley watched in curiosity and amusement.

"Why are you smelling me, Sam?" Søren asked.

"Weird. I don't smell anything," Sam said to Kingsley.

"C'est la vie," Kingsley said over the top of his champagne flute. "Maybe I imagined it."

"Let's toast," Sam said.

"What should we toast to?" Kingsley asked.

"To you," Sam said.

"Agreed," Søren said. "To Kingsley. *Vive le roi.*"

Kingsley swallowed hard and raised his glass.

"To me," he said. "And my three dearest friends in the world."

"Three?" Sam asked.

"The bartender, the blond and the booze."

"And to The Eighth Circle," Søren said, lifting his glass. "I will beat you for naming it that, one of these days."

"Counting on it, *mon ami.*"

They clinked their glasses and drank their champagne. It was the first alcohol Kingsley had tasted in weeks. He'd been drunk on hard work and happiness since Sam had come back to him; he'd needed no other intoxicant.

"Your subjects await," Sam said. Kingsley downed his champagne and set the flute on the bar. He tugged his vest into place and ran a hand through his hair.

He took a step forward.

"Kingsley?"

Kingsley looked back at Søren.

"Jeg elsker dig," Søren said.

"I hate it when you speak Danish," Kingsley said.

"I know you do."

"Will you tell me what it means?" Kingsley asked, too happy to be more than playfully annoyed.

"It means good luck."

Kingsley smiled back at Søren, gave a wink to Sam and knew then exactly what to say.

He stepped right up on to the ledge that overlooked the pit below. They'd expected a hundred, maybe two hundred people. Easily five-hundred packed the pit below. He saw financiers, CEOs, artists, entertainers, poets, politicians and plebeians. He saw somebodies and nobodies, and they were all his people. He would guard them with his life. Nine months ago he'd wanted nothing more than to crawl into the bottom of a bottle and drown in the dregs. Now he had before him five hundred reasons to live. And behind him, standing at either side of him, his two most important reasons to live.

The assembled crowd slowly quieted as his presence asserted itself. When at last silence reigned, he smiled down at them and in a loud clear voice spoke one and only one sentence to them all.

"Welcome to the Kingdom."

42

A SOFT SIGH CAME OVER THE BABY MONITOR AS Kingsley finished his story. Grace looked at Kingsley and smiled.

She stood up, crooked her finger at Kingsley, and he followed her up a short flight of stairs and down a darkened hallway. A light was already on in the room—a painted glass hot-air balloon in miniature. The toy lamp cast hues of red, blue, green and gold on to the walls, painting a rainbow of light around Fionn.

"What are you doing up?" Grace asked as she reached over the side of the crib and laid her hand gently on her son's small back. "Did you know we had company? Someone wants to meet you."

Kingsley gazed down on the boy in the crib in his pale blue-and-white footie pajamas. He had a swath of pale blond hair on his small head, his mother's bright blue eyes and a solemn expression on his face. Such a serious look on such a little boy. Kingsley almost laughed at him.

"May I?" Kingsley asked, not looking at Grace. He couldn't take his eyes off Fionn.

"Of course," Grace said. "He likes being held."

Kingsley gently lifted the boy out of his crib and cradled him against his chest. Grace gave him a soft blue blanket that Kingsley draped over Fionn's head and back.

"You're good at this," Grace said. "But you have more practice than I do."

Kingsley smiled but didn't answer. He couldn't answer. He couldn't speak. Not a word.

Kingsley laughed, and Grace, without a moment's hesitation, raised her hand to his face and wiped the tears off his cheeks.

"Merci," he whispered and pressed a kiss on to the top of Fionn's head. He smelled like a baby, like his own Céleste. The clean scent of lavender soap and innocence. "Fionn and I have something in common."

"And what is that?" Grace asked.

"We're both alive because of Søren."

"Yes. I suppose you both are." Grace touched his face again, wiped off another tear. Kingsley laughed at himself. "You're doing better than Nora did the first time she held him. She made it about three seconds before handing him back to me and bursting into tears in Zachary's arms. He teased her mercilessly about it."

"He's beautiful. No wonder she cried."

"She and Zachary talked a long time about Fionn," Grace continued. "The two of them can talk for hours."

"What did they talk about?" Kingsley asked, patting Fionn on the back.

"Nora being Fionn's godmother."

"I thought she was already."

"She is. But Zachary and I talked and considering everything…"

"You mean you want her to be his legal guardian?"

"Yes. If something happens to me and Zachary, we want
her to have Fionn. She hasn't said yes to that yet."

"She wouldn't say yes to it."

"Zachary's wearing her down."

"I thought he had a brother?"

"He does, and I have siblings, too, parents… But God for-
bid, I want him to go to Nora and so does Zachary. I want
him to be with someone who knows the truth about him,
someone who knows where he came from, and will love him
because of it, not in spite of it."

And Fionn would be close to Søren, which Grace didn't
say. But she didn't have to.

"She doesn't trust herself enough. But I can't think of anyone better to raise him if something happened," Kingsley said,
and meant the words.

"Neither can we."

"I'll talk to her about it," Kingsley said.

"Would you? Please?" Grace asked. "Tomorrow's his first
birthday. I can't believe my baby is already a year old."

"I still can't believe he's even here," Kingsley said, holding Fionn a little tighter. The boy didn't seem to mind. He'd
fallen back asleep and was quietly drooling on Kingsley's shirt.
Nothing he wasn't used to by now. "I never imagined… But
who would? He's a priest."

Grace smiled, and a soft blush appeared on her face.

"I don't know what came over me when I asked him,"
Grace said.

"You don't have to tell me what happened," Kingsley said.
"It's between you and him."

"But I need to tell someone. I didn't cheat on my husband.

He gave me permission to go have fun, as he said. No rules. Anything I wanted or needed. I'd been depressed and he knew it. Nora helped him. He thought she could help me."

"Nora has unusual methods for helping people in need. But they do work."

"They do. In that moment…" Grace began again, "I felt the rightness of it. And I knew if I didn't say something, if I didn't ask, I'd regret it the rest of my life. Now? I have a son. We have a son."

"We're all…" Kingsley paused and swallowed hard. In a low voice he said, "We were all very happy."

It was an embarrassing failure of words—*we were all very happy*. Shell-shocked by elation would have been a better description of how they'd all felt when they heard Søren had a son. The news was like a bomb going off, and the blast of joy had felled them all.

Kingsley bent his head and whispered to Fionn.

"I know your father," Kingsley said in French, a private message between him and Fionn. "He's everything to me. You are blessed to be a part of him. If the day ever comes you don't feel blessed to be his, you come see me, and I'll tell you why you are."

Kingsley kissed the top of Fionn's head. His heart clenched so tightly, his chest hurt. No wonder he'd sought after pain all his life. It felt just like love.

"Did he really tell you that? That his friend Magdalena had said he'd have a child by the grace of God?"

"He did. And she did tell me he and I would be lovers again. Real prophecy? Or self-fulfilling? It happened. That's what matters."

"That morning…" Grace began and paused. "Can I talk about it?"

"Please," Kingsley said. "You can tell me anything."

"The morning I walked with him to his sister's house, the morning he thought he would die," Grace said, picking up a blanket and folding it neatly. "He and I talked. He told me about Magdalena and something she'd said to him. Something about Nora and how it had come true."

"It all came true," Kingsley said. "Even Fionn."

"I wonder if he was thinking of it then, what Magdalena had said about him having a son. I wonder if it gave him hope that morning. I want to believe it did."

"You gave us hope that morning," Kingsley said. "If you hadn't gotten to me in time… I can't think about it. Destiny or not, you earned your son."

"As soon as I came home to Zachary I told him what had happened, what I'd done. And when I found I was pregnant, I had a feeling. A few months after he was born, I looked at him, and I knew and so did Zachary."

Kingsley looked at a photograph sitting on a side table— one of Zachary holding Fionn in his arms and looking utterly contented.

"Zachary loves Fionn. Fionn is his son in every way that matters," Grace said.

"My son, Nico, had a good father. It hurts to say, and I'll only say it to you—but as much as it hurts, I'm glad I didn't know about him until he was grown. Nico's perfect. I couldn't have done a better job raising him than his father did."

"Do you regret it? Not being a father to Nico when he was growing up?"

"Sometimes," Kingsley confessed. "But I don't regret it for him. I don't think I was ready to be a father until recently. I had too much unfinished business. Nico deserved better than I could have given him. His father was a good man and loved him. Now…it's hard for Nico to love me. But he's trying. He told me he was trying. And that's all I can ask."

Grace took a ragged breath and swallowed.

"It's hard," she said. "I don't want to hurt my husband, but I want Fionn to know his father."

Kingsley shook his head. "He knows his father. Zachary's his father."

"He is. But still…"

"I understand. I have a twenty-five-year-old son I didn't meet until this year. If anyone understands, it's me."

When Nora had told him about Nico, about the son he'd never dreamed he had, he'd been rent in two by the opposite emotions of joy and regret. Joy that he had a son. Regret that he only found out now, twenty-five years after the fact.

"That must have been hard for you," Grace said. "All those years lost."

"They were only lost to me," Kingsley said. "Nico lost nothing. Nico had a father in his life who loved him, adored him, raised him into a good man. The comfort to me in all this. Nico. Fionn. That's who matters in this."

"You matter, too," Grace said. "You do matter. And I'm certain if we asked your son he would say he would have wanted to know you."

Kingsley smiled at her. He wasn't sure he agreed with her, but it was kind of her to say.

With Fionn in his arms, Kingsley walked around the nursery. He ached to hold his own daughter. He'd left Céleste and Juliette this morning and already he missed them so much it felt like a physical ache. But some things needed to be done in person. Some things couldn't be said over the phone.

"He's a good boy," Kingsley said, straightening Fionn's blanket so it covered his little feet. "I can already tell."

"Thank you." Grace spoke in a hoarse whisper. "He must take after his father, then."

"And his mother."

"You know he's already walking and talking," Grace said. "A few words of English, a few words of Welsh. And Zachary can teach him some Hebrew. And French, of course. He spent a year in France in his twenties."

Fionn stirred in his sleep and opened his eyes for a few seconds.

"*Tu parles français?*" Kingsley asked, looking down at Fionn. Fionn released a heavy sigh, closed his eyes and fell back asleep. "I'll take that as a no. What was his first word?"

"*Ta,*" she said. "*Tad* is Welsh for *father* or *dad*. What was Céleste's first word?"

"*Non.*"

Grace laughed.

"I'm not joking," Kingsley said. "She gets it from her mother. If Fionn takes after his father, he'll learn languages easily."

"When he starts school we'll make sure he takes his foreign languages. And music, too. Piano lessons if we can afford them. But it's too early to think about that now."

"About that," Kingsley said. "I brought him a birthday gift."

"You didn't have to do that."

"I did. And if I didn't I still would have."

With reluctance Kingsley placed Fionn back in his crib and covered him with his blanket. He looked at Grace and pulled the envelope from his pocket.

"What is it?" Grace asked, her brow furrowing. She seemed reluctant to open it. Perhaps she sensed its contents.

"Like I said, a birthday gift."

Grace peeled back the seal on the envelope and pulled out a tri-folded sheaf of papers.

"When Søren joined the Jesuits," Kingsley began, "he took a vow of poverty. The money he had from his trust fund, he gave it all to me. Since I can't repay the father for the gift, I can repay the son."

Grace's eyes went wide.

"Kingsley, this is a trust fund."

"Yes," Kingsley said. "And it's worth roughly eighteen million pounds."

Grace covered her mouth with her hand in shock. Although it wasn't easy, Kingsley managed not to laugh at her.

"He's to go to the best schools," Kingsley said. "No expense is to be spared."

"We could buy a school for this much money."

"Buy one, then. You can teach in it," Kingsley said.

"We can't accept this." Grace started to fold the pages.

"I told you the story of my club for a reason, Grace. I needed you to know how much I owe him. That club I built for him has made me wealthy beyond your wildest imagining. The club wouldn't exist if it weren't for him. I wouldn't exist, either. I owe him everything—my life, my fortune and my family. I promise, Grace, this is the least I can do. I owe him a debt, and this is how I pay it back."

"But Kingsley…"

"You'll receive part of it now for living and education expenses. Everything else stays in a trust until he's eighteen. Then it's all his."

"This is all too much," she said, shaking her head in disbelief.

"There is one more thing."

"More?"

Kingsley reached into his pocket once more and pulled out a deed. "What I gave you is the exact amount of the trust fund Søren gave me. But this is the interest."

Grace took the deed with a shaking hand.

"Søren's father was a baron," Kingsley said.

"Yes, he told me that."

"The ancestral home is in the north. It's a beautiful crumbling estate called Edenfell. It was sold twenty years ago to developers who did nothing with it. It's been sitting empty for years. It belongs in his family. So now it's Fionn's."

Grace slowly sat down in a chair.

"Edenfell," Grace repeated, reading over the deed.

"It's in Fionn's name," Kingsley said. "It's his, not yours or Zachary's. When he's old enough, he can keep it or sell it or burn it to the ground. I don't care. But that's for him to decide."

"I'm going to be sick," Grace said, looking paler than usual. And then Kingsley did laugh at her.

"My sincerest apologies for playing God with your lives," Kingsley said. "I trust you and Zachary will do the right thing by your son."

"We'll try, of course. But—"

"No buts," he said. "Say *merci*, and love your son. That's all there is to do or say."

Grace took a deep breath, gave a long exhale. She looked up at Kingsley with eyes edged by tears.

"Merci," she said in a small voice.

"I should go. I have another flight to catch."

"Leaving already? But—"

"I'll visit again," Kingsley said. "If you'll have me."

Grace stood up and walked to him. She threw her arms around him, and he held her close.

"Your son is blessed to have had two wonderful fathers," she said. "And so is mine."

He kissed her cheek and let her go.

"Make sure Zachary doesn't neglect the French lessons," Kingsley said, nodding toward Fionn sleeping in his crib.

"I will. I promise. I've already started with Danish, too."

"You have?"

"Søren and I spoke on the phone after we told him about Fionn. He taught me *'Jeg elsker dig, min søn, og Gud elsker dig også.'* He asked me to say it to Fionn every night."

"What does it mean?"

"It means 'I love you, my son, and God loves you, too.' It's the last thing I tell him every night before I put him in his crib. He said…" Grace stopped and smiled. She looked on the verge of tears, but whatever tears there were she kept to herself. "He said that's how his mother told him good-night when he was a little boy."

"Jeg elskar dig. He told me that was Danish for good luck."

"It's Danish for 'I love you.'"

"He's a bastard, that blond monster."

"You know you love him."

"Entirely against my will," Kingsley said, "and with all my heart."

Grace kissed her fingertips and pressed them lightly to Fionn's head. She straightened his blanket and whispered her Danish prayer to her son.

They stepped out of the nursery, and Grace noiselessly closed the door behind her.

"You'll call me if you need me," Kingsley said, an order, not a request. "If anything happens, anything at all, you'll come to me first."

"Of course," Grace said as they stood by her front door.

"You don't have to work any more if you don't wish to. You or Zachary. You can work from home, buy a new house in the country, travel. I don't care. The money is yours and your son's. I know you'll put it to good use."

"We will, yes. I can't… Give me a few days to wrap my mind around all this."

"You have plenty of time."

"If Zachary has a heart attack tomorrow morning, I'm blaming you."

"Have an ambulance on standby."

"My God, Kingsley. I can't believe it."

"Believe it," Kingsley said. "After all that's happened, we should be able to believe anything by now."

Grace laughed, and he embraced her again.

"You'll tell him Fionn's well?" she asked.

"I will."

"Do you think he'll come visit his son?"

"When he's ready. Give him time. He doesn't want to interfere."

"It wouldn't be interfering. Tell him that."

"I will," Kingsley said. "He'll be jealous I held him."

"Kiss your beautiful girl for me," Grace said.

"With pleasure. Both of them."

"Where are you going now?"

"Paying a visit to an old friend," Kingsley said. "That's all."

"Speaking of old friends, what happened to your Sam?"

"What happened to Sam? Four years after she came to work for me the worst thing possible happened. She fell in love."

"That's terrible," Grace said. "Happens to the best of us, though."

"She moved out to California with her girlfriend. They got married a few years ago."

"Did you go to the wedding?"

"I was her best man. We wore matching tuxedos."

"Sexy penguins?"

"That was us." Kingsley threw his bag over his shoulder, crossed his arms over his chest. "I haven't thought about that year in a long time. Blaise and Lachlan are married now."

"You're kidding."

"He stole her from me. Not that I blame him or her. She

always had a weakness for accents. Australian beat French, apparently. They live in Sydney. Felicia moved back to London a few years after the club opened. Justin runs a home for gay runaways."

"Quite a crew you assembled."

"I was always a good talent scout," Kingsley said. "I knew what Nora would be the moment I saw her."

"You did. You were right."

"Twenty years ago... It feels like yesterday. Yesterday and a lifetime."

"I imagine it does."

"Twenty years," Kingsley said again. "All that time, Søren's been the constant. Him and her."

"Nora?"

"Twenty years ago she got arrested and that brought Søren back to me. Twenty years later she gets kidnapped and that brought my son back to me. I'm almost looking forward to the next time she gets herself into trouble. I always benefit."

"Nora get herself into trouble? I doubt you'll be waiting for very long."

Kingsley gave Grace a kiss on both cheeks and pressed his forehead to hers a moment.

"We're family," Kingsley said. "Søren is my family, and that means Fionn is, too. You understand?"

"Yes," she whispered. "If Nora's his godmother, you can be his godfather. Then he'll have four wonderful fathers who love him."

"Four?"

Grace glanced skyward. Four. Of course.

He let her go and walked from her home with a light step, buoyed by a deep contentment that left him feeling half his forty-eight years. It was good to finally tell someone the story of what Søren had done for him and why. He felt unburdened now by the telling of his tale, like a man walking from confession with his soul lighter and cleaner. But his confession hadn't been to a priest but about a priest, the priest he loved not despite all the sins they'd committed against each other but because of them, because the sins were what bound them together.

And the love. Of course the love. Always the love.

At dawn Kingsley boarded his plane. A short flight but the hour of sleep he caught was enough to refresh him. And when he emerged from the airport, he closed his eyes and for the first time in two decades, breathed in French air.

France, yes, but not home. Home was Juliette. Home was Céleste. Home was Søren. But even if it wasn't home, it was part of him. His parents were buried in French soil. His life had begun here, and when the time came, he, too, would be buried in the same Paris cemetery where they had laid his parents to rest. He'd already told Juliette those were his wishes. And because she loved him and knew how to obey an order and give one at the same time, she'd answered, "*Oui, mon roi.* But you're never allowed to die."

And he'd promised her he'd do his best to never let something like that happen.

He was tempting fate by coming back to France. He'd made enemies here, important ones. And certain people he'd known once had likely not forgotten his name. But he wasn't afraid. Twenty years had passed. He was a low priority now. He didn't plan to stay long anyway. Just long enough to do what had to be done.

He hired a car in Paris and drove into the countryside. The country had changed in twenty years, but not the beauty. The beauty remained. The rolling hills, the ancient churches, the crumbling castles on the roadsides, the farms, the cottages, old Europe, old magic… He would bring Céleste here someday.

By late afternoon he arrived as his destination. He parked the car at the end of a long dirt road and walked barefoot on the French soil all the way to the door.

He knocked and waited. A few moments later he heard footsteps.

The door opened.

Nora looked at him across the threshold of his son Nico's house.

She didn't look shocked to see him. She didn't look surprised. In fact, she looked as if she'd been expecting him. Maybe she had.

"Before you say anything else," Nora said without any trace of remorse on her lovely face. "Just answer one question for me. How much trouble am I in right now?"

Kingsley smiled.

"All of it."

★ ★ ★ ★ ★

ACKNOWLEDGMENTS

WRITING IS A SOLITARY PROFESSION, BUT EDITING takes a village. Thank you, Karen Stivali, Alyssa Palmer, Miranda Baker, Robin Becht, Melanie Fletcher, Cyndy Aleo and Andrew Shaffer who help me beat *The King* into shape. Thank you, Gitte Doherty for your help with Søren's Danish. Thank you to Susan Swinwood, editor extraordinaire, who has claimed Søren as her book boyfriend (sorry, ladies, I can't fight my own editor for him). And thank you to Sara Megibow, my dream agent who is a dream agent because she's helped me make all my dreams come true. Thank you, Andrew Shaffer, my fiancé, for being my best friend and toughest critic. Special kisses and pets to Buckley Cat and sad little Honeytoast Kitteh for keeping me entertained during long writing hours. Thank you to the good people at the Jesuit Spiritual Retreat Center in Milford, Ohio, for giving me an internet-free sanctuary in which to write *The King*. Apologies if I gave any Jesuits a heart attack when I honestly answered the question, "So what do you do for a living?"